RELEASED

HIGHGATE PREPARATORY ACADEMY
BOOK THREE

ROSA LEE

Rosa Lee x

DIRTY LITTLE PUBLISHERS LTD

Cover design provided by Jodilock Designs

BLURB

What if in order to defeat the monsters that plague us, we have to forget our morals, embrace the darkness that surrounds us and become the most deadly monsters of all?

Life is certainly not what I'd imagined it to be growing up. There are no white picket fences, no dream job, no handsome as f*ck husband...

Well, that last part isn't strictly true. I just didn't realise that his best friends would be my lovers too, one of whom is responsible for the new life growing inside me.

I guess this all started with rivers of blood, and that's how it needs to end. One drop at a time our demons will be exorcised.

I just hope we don't lose too much in the process.

***Warning: 18+ This book is a fast burn #whychoose romance so our leading lady won't have to choose and will end up with more than one lover. Please be aware that this is a dark contemporary romance with graphic scenes that some readers may find upsetting or triggering, so please read the author's note at the beginning. You will need to read Captured, Highgate Preparatory Academy Book 1 and Bound, Highgate Preparatory Academy Book 2 first. ***
Disclaimer: please note. Rosa Lee cannot be held responsible for the destruction of any panties, knickers, or underwear of any kind. She recommends that you take adequate precautions before reading Released to avoid any sticky situations.

I dedicate this book to all the squirters out there. We should totally start a club! And to all you men who take the time to learn how to make the flow explosive, kudos my friends.

Rosa Lee
Xxx

"You wrong me, and the world shall know it: though you have put me into darkness."

— WILLIAM SHAKESPEARE

I love books with playlists and I listen to my compiled playlist as I'm writing. I've even based some scenes solely around one track, let me know if you guess which ones! And you'll see a lot of the music mentioned in the book itself.

Listen to the full playlist on Spotify HERE

Gone - Blake Rose
Ride of the Valkyries - Richard Wagner
American Boy - Estelle, Kanye West
Bodies - Bryce Fox
Way down We Go - KALEO
Serial Killer - Moncrieff, JUDGE
Straight Jacket - Bohnes
Here with Me - Susie Suh, Robot Koch
Panic Attack - Liza Anne
Astronomical - SVRCINA
All Mine - PLAZA
Wasting My Young Years - London Grammer
Silence - Marshmello, Khalid
Wicked - Miki Ratsula
Maybe, I - Des Rocs
Tidal Wave - Chase Atlantic
Far From Home (The Raven) - Sam Tinnesz

It's A Man's Man's Man's World - Jurnee Smollett-Bell, Black Cherry
Right Here - Chase Atlantic
I Will Always Love You - Whitney Houston
You're Special - NF
Ain't No Sunshine When She's Gone - Black Label Society
Dancer in the Dark - Chase Atlantic
Drip - Asiahn
Collide - Justine Skye, Tyga
Lifts - Lia Marie Johnson
Call Out My Name - Mother's Daughter, Beck Pete
Lost Without You - Freya Ridings
Love Me Like You Do - Boyce Avenue
99 - Elliot Moss
Can You Hear Me Now - The Score
Rest in Peace - Dorothy
7 Years - Piano Fruits Music, Arthur White
Thinking Out Loud - Boyce Avenue
Dusk Till Dawn - ZAYN, Sia
Lost My Mind - Alice Kristiansen
Infinity - Piano Version - James Young
Dancing in the Moonlight - Jubël, NEIMY
365 - Mother's Daughter, Beck Pete

FOREWORD

Dear Reader,

Firstly, thank you so much for taking a chance on me and reading *Released*. I hope you enjoy it!

Also, as you may already know that I am British and so *Captured* is written in a mix of British and American English. This has been done on purpose, to reflect the different characters and their cultures, so some words will be spelled differently throughout depending on who's speaking or thinking! If you see some unfamiliar words, know that they are there intentionally and I hope you enjoy discovering new phrases!

As mentioned in the blurb, *Released* is a dark romance. There are many subjects explored that some readers may find disturbing.

For a full list of triggers please visit www.rosaleeauthor.com/trigger-warnings

Also a small word of caution. My books have a lot of BDSM vibes in them, and if they inspire you to dive into that kinky world, please do your research and educate yourself before trying out anything new for the first time. Take care my little smut bunnies!

CHAPTER ONE

LILLY

"*Enjoy your honeymoon.*"

A pained moan escapes my dry, cracked lips as I stir, my whole body feeling like it's been hit by a double-decker bus. The dull ache in my head turns into a sharp stab, sending another deep, pain-filled groan echoing around me.

Blinking gritty eyes open, a screaming wave of panic rushes in when all I see is darkness. My heart thumps in my chest when I close and open my lids again, but I'm still surrounded by the endless black of my nightmares.

"H–hello?" I croak out, my voice a broken thing, rasping among the shadows. Clearing my throat and winching at the dryness, I try again. "I–is anyone there?"

My breathing stutters as I'm met by silence, a full body shiver skittering over me at the cold that surrounds my body. Pushing up onto my elbows, I have to pause as my head swims and throbs all at the same time. Bile burns the back of my already sore throat, but I manage to breathe through it, waiting for the nauseating dizziness to subside. Clenching my hands into the soft bed underneath me, I focus on the cool linen sheets until I can sit up fully with only a slight waver.

Pausing once again, I'm able to concentrate a little more and see that the room is not as pitch black as I first thought. Soft moonlight filters through the cracks of what looks like wooden shutters across the room. *There must be a window over there.* The hair on the back of my neck lifts at the eerie sight of undefined shapes around the room, the lighting casting everything in a sickly yellow glow.

Gingerly turning my still pulsing head, I can see the dark outlines of various bits of furniture; a large wardrobe and a dressing table with a mirror that reflects a ghostly image of a pale, frightened girl back at me. I quickly move on from the sight to see that I'm in a lavish, chunky wood, four-poster bed with heavy drapes.

A sudden kick in my lower abdomen causes my hand to fly over my bump, a whooshing breath of relief rushing out of me when I feel another movement. I've no idea what has happened to me, but the thought that something may have harmed my unborn child brings forth a wave of anger so fierce that spots blur my vision and I have to go back to breathing deeply to calm down.

Taking one final inhale, I steel my spine and slowly shift across the linen, the whisper of the fabric against my bare thighs a comforting noise in the silence.

Wait! Shit, I should be in my wedding dress...shouldn't I?

Panic flares hotly inside me again, my pulse racing as I vaguely remember that I was wearing my wedding dress before...before everything went dark. Looking down, I touch the silk nightdress that kisses my thighs and furrows my brows as I try in vain to remember when I got changed. My hand clenches into a fist, wrinkling the fabric as useless tears fill my eyes, the memory eluding me.

Suddenly, a noise makes my head snap upwards, and I see the dark shape of a door across from me.

"H–hello?" I rasp, my chin trembling and hands shaking as I grasp onto the post and pull myself to standing. "Who's there?"

Silence.

A hatch in the bottom of the door springs open, and I almost lose my grip on the wood as my muscles violently jolt, soft light flooding the room for a moment as a tray is pushed through before the hatch closes again. I curse myself for being a coward, even as my heart pounds in my chest. *I should have fucking gone over there when it was open!*

Taking a step away from the bed, testing how steady I am, I notice a set of drawers next to the bed with an ornate lamp sitting on top of them. Walking over to it using the side of the bed for support, I switch it on, flinching and close my eyes briefly against the light as a sharp pain lashes through my head. I wait for the throb to subside before slowly blinking my eyes open and taking in the room properly.

It's decadent, with a beautiful, hand-painted bird wallpaper covering the walls, light walnut furniture, and cream and gold silk furnishings. The whole space reminds me of something out of a Jane Austen film, and only adds to the confusion.

Remembering the tray, I glance back over to the door and stare at the covered plate as if there's a severed head underneath the silver dome. *Fuck, for all I know, there might be.* My body shudders at the thought, and I debate whether I can just leave it there, that is until hunger makes its presence felt in my empty stomach.

Giving a firm nod of my head—though no one can see my act of bravery—I straighten up and make my way shakily over to the tray. Stooping down, I take an immense breath, grasping the cool metal handle in my only slightly trembling hand.

"Don't be such a fucking ballsack, Lilly," I hiss, because we all know pussies are the stronger of the two appendages.

Decision made, I pull the lid off with a small, very lady-like screech, a self-deprecating laugh escaping my lips when I see that it's only a plate of Welsh Rarebit—aka cheese on toast—with slices of cucumber and a bunch of red grapes. My mouth waters at the smell of melted cheese goodness, and I wonder how whoever made it knew that it was a favourite of mine. I'm not sure whether to be creeped the fuck out or comforted. I should probably be the latter.

Setting the lid on the plush, cream and gold Persian rug, I lift the tray and take it back to the bed, placing it on the top of the blankets and sit down next to it. Taking a piece of warm toast between my fingers, a pleasure-filled moan leaves my lips when the first taste of salty, melted cheddar hits my taste buds, and before I know it, the plate is clean and I'm licking my fingers.

I look around the room again and see that I'd missed a jug of water and a glass sitting on the table alongside the lamp. Taking the tray and placing it on the floor, I get up and pour a glass, glugging the cool liquid until that, too, is empty. Giving an almighty belch, the urge to pee hits me like a truck, and I desperately look round. Seeing a door next to the one with the hatch, I waddle-rush over there, trying to move quickly but not piss myself, as I hope with fanny flaps crossed that it's a bathroom.

Opening the door, I thank all the gods that exist when I spot a toilet and make a beeline for it, doing a hop jig as I pull my knickers down and sit. As I relieve myself, I look down to see that the knickers I'm wearing are at least the ones that Ash gave me on our wedding day.

Trying not to think about my fucked up situation too much and my pounding head, I wash up, my jaw cracking with a huge yawn. Making my way back towards the bed, another yawn that would make a lion proud takes over me, my body feeling heavy and sluggish as I drop down onto the soft mattress.

My vision goes hazy, and when my eyes blink open again, there's a dark figure framed in the now open doorway. My lids shut again, and I feel someone moving me tenderly on the bed, pulling the covers over my body, and smoothing my hair back before placing a kiss on my temple.

"Ash?" I ask weakly, but that can't be right. There's no spicy ginger smell. In fact, I can't smell any of my guys, just a sharp, almost overpowering, cloying cologne.

"Hush now, Violet. Time to get some more rest. We must take care of the baby," a deep voice whispers, and instead of being soothing, it sounds like nightmares and monsters in the dark, but also familiar somehow.

Before I can try and work out who it is, another wave of exhaustion crashes over me, drowning me in darkness once more.

ASH

"It's been three fucking weeks! What do you mean there's no fucking sign of her?"

Rage unlike I've ever known fills me as I launch my phone across the room with a yell, the sound of it shattering against the fireplace filling our dorm moments later.

My chest heaves as I stare at the glittering shards lying in pieces on the carpet, my fists clenching at my sides when the thought enters my mind that it's my heart, my soul, lying there as well as my phone.

"What the fuck is wrong with you, Ash?!" Loki shouts as he rushes down the stairs. The wrath that I thought couldn't get any worse increases tenfold when I look at him, red mist coating my vision. My pulse pounds in my ears, and my ability to see my surroundings tunnels, until all I can see is his failure to protect Lilly.

With an almighty roar, I launch myself at him, meeting him as he steps off the stairs with a brutal punch to his jaw that has his head snapping to the side. Not giving him time to recover, I hit him again, this time in the stomach, satisfaction filling my veins as all the breath whooshes out of his lungs, his hand clutching around himself. He straightens up a moment later, and a twinge of guilt runs through me at the sight of blood trickling down from his now split lip. Lowering his arms down to his sides, he looks at me with broken eyes, making the red mist begin to dissipate.

"Fight back, you asshole," I snarl at him, panting, but my raised fists begin to droop as he just stands there, looking lost. "Fucking hit me!"

"No," he states, squaring his shoulders. "It's my fault she's gone."

I raise my fists once more, nostrils flaring at his words. It *is* his fucking fault. *He* was meant to be watching her when she disappeared. When she was clearly taken from us.

But it wasn't just his fault. We were all meant to be watching her, and we weren't there when she needed us. With that thought, all the strength leaves my body, my arms falling back down to my sides, and my chest rising and falling with my heavy breaths. The crippling guilt leaves my chest feeling painfully tight.

"It's not just your fault, Loki," I tell him, my voice like sandpaper; all rough and grating.

Moisture fills his eyes, and my broken heart cracks more when he swallows hard, ready to argue. I know that he's taken this harder than the rest of us because he was meant to be with her at the time, watching over her at the reception party. But then he got caught by his dad, and we all got distracted, which we now suspect was purposeful. I have to tamp down the fresh rush of anger at that thought. That somehow, this stinks of Julian, my *father*. Especially as he doesn't seem as upset as a father-in-law should be at the kidnapping of his pregnant daughter-in-law. He's made next to no effort, bar speaking to the press, to find her. He's carrying on, as usual, declaring that 'it's out of our hands.' He knows something, I fucking know he does. Nothing is beyond the reach of Black Knight. Especially not a missing family member.

Reaching up, I clasp one of Loki's shoulders in my hand, pulling him towards me and wrapping my arms around him. My own eyes moisten as he takes a great heaving breath and clutches me back tightly.

"I'm so fucking sorry, Ash," he whispers, his voice thick and rasping.

"I know, brother. I know," I reply, my own voice hitching slightly with the pain that we both feel like a knife in the gut that can't be removed.

I release him just as the door opens and look towards it to see Jax walking in, swollen and split knuckles wrapped around his gym bag. We're all a mess without our Lilly to keep us in line. He kicks the door shut behind him, looking up at us with red-rimmed eyes.

"Anything?" he asks, and it's the only word that leaves his lips now since Lilly vanished. I can't blame him, the urge to cut myself has been so strong, I've had to get the guys to hide all the fucking knives and anything sharp. Kai keeps the kitchen ones under lock and key, and the others have hidden their razors from my reach. I shake my head, and he just grunts, dropping his bag and heading to the bathroom.

Loki and I watch him in silence, and just as he gets to the door, the front door bursts open again, crashing into the wall and making all three of us spin around, fists raised. My heartbeat settles a little seeing that it's Kai, glasses askew and hair an absolute fucking mess. He's clutching what looks like an open yearbook in his hands, looking down at it, and there's a flush on his cheeks.

"Guys!" he shouts, then winces when he sees we're all there in front of him. "Sorry, but I think I found something."

We all step forward, my stomach doing an uncomfortable flip as my heart races again at his words.

"Well?" Loki asks from next to me, not even giving Kai a chance to say another word. Kai just looks at him, his gaze softening briefly.

"I was looking through all the old yearbooks, trying to see if the 'Ace' you told us about after your father's strange phone call ever attended Highgate," he tells us, looking at me. "And I fucking found him!" he cries out, voice full of weary triumph.

Before we can answer, he turns the book around, and the world falls down around me as I look at the image on the page, unable to make sense of it at first. It's a photograph of a couple, a darkly handsome man who looks vaguely familiar, but it's the woman that he's got his arm wrapped around that sends chills down my spine.

"Is that..." Jax begins, his rough voice startling me from my own thoughts, though years of training mean that I don't show it outwardly.

"Lilly's mom, I believe," Kai tells us, his voice low. My gaze takes in the thick, wavy brown hair that tumbles over her slim shoulders, slightly darker in colour than Lilly's, and the hazel eyes, the pixie shaped face. There's a thud in my chest, a longing for my own pixie princess, that has become a constant companion these past few weeks.

"Not just Lilly's mom," I say, finally tearing my eyes away from the picture to read the description below.

"Fuck," Loki breathes out on my other side.

Couple destined for great things: Adrian 'Ace' Ramsey with his fiancée, Violet Rochester, pictured here at a gala celebrating the announcement of their engagement.

Fuck is right, and the fact that it's not the name which we knew of her explains why we couldn't find out much about her to start with.

"Does this mean that her uncle is actually...her dad?" Loki asks, and I tear my gaze away from the page to look at him, his tired eyes brighter than they've been in weeks, his brow furrowed with confusion.

"I think so," Kai responds, and I turn to look at him.

"And if Ace is Adrian..." I start, the pieces slotting into place, though I still can't believe that we may have a lead. I don't trust it. How can I if it turns out to be another dead end. Another split in my soul. Another rupture of my heart.

"Then he has Lilly," Jax growls out next to me, and the beast inside me purrs at the violence in his tone.

"Well, what the fuck are we waiting for?!" Loki shouts, looking like he's ready to swim to England right the fuck now if he needs to.

"Wait, we can't just go rushing in." I throw my hand out, my palm landing against his chest to stop him from leaving.

"Why the hell not?" Jax rumbles from my other side, and I can feel him practically vibrating with anger.

"Because there is a good chance that my shitstain of a father is involved, and we don't want him to do anything rash," I grit out, a headache beginning to form behind my eyes. I reach a hand up and pinch the bridge of my nose as I try to think of a way forward. "Plus, we have no idea if Ace–Adrian even has her. Yes, it's sketchy as fuck, but we can't just storm in and torture him if he's innocent." I shiver as Jax looks at me with dead eyes, like his humanity has fled and all that's left is the monster within. "She wouldn't want you to, Jax."

He blinks, and just like that he joins the rest of us with our gray moral compasses.

"We need eyes on her first, to confirm that she is there to begin with," I continue, my mind racing.

I snap my head up and lock eyes with Kai, knowing that he just had the same idea I did if the twinkle in his amber orbs is anything to go by.

"Willow," he murmurs, and I nod.

"The Shadows," I reply, starting to think aloud. "We'll owe them a favor."

"I'll give them anything bar Lilly and my firstborn," Loki states, voice clear, and my stare leaves Kai's to look at my redheaded brother. There's a rod of steel in his green eyes that I've not seen before, a pledge that tells me he's not messing around. My hand alights back on his shoulder, giving it a squeeze.

"We're all in agreement then? We contact Hunter and The Shadows?" I ask, looking from Loki, to Kai, and finally Jax. The latter hesitates for a few seconds, and I can see the need to burn down the world to save our girl in the blazing cold fire in his blue eyes.

"But if they can't find anything by Friday, I'll go to England and get the information myself," he tells me, his lips twitching with an evil smirk that makes me glad I'm not at the receiving end of his information-gathering.

"Deal. We'll all go," I assure him, copying his nod of agreement.

"Right," Loki interrupts the serious moment, and I know that whatever will leave his lips next would have our girl glaring at him. My dick twitches at the thought. "Let's go get our girl back so we can spank her ass for being such a naughty girl and leaving us with blue balls for this long."

A bark of laughter leaves me at how indignant she'd be to hear that the worst part of her kidnap was its effect on our balls. I know that Loki is just deflecting, using humor to cover his worry at what our girl is going through without us at her side.

As we turn to go, Kai and I in front, I hear a sharp slap and Loki's protest behind me. My lips split into a grin at the sound.

"What the fuck was that for?" he asks Jax in a disgruntled voice.

"Disrespecting Baby Girl," Jax replies, and although Loki grumbles, he doesn't argue with the big guy.

"Don't worry, Jax," Kai says as we leave the dorm, walking down the hall towards Willow's. "By the time we finish telling Lilly about what Loki said, his balls will be frozen solid before she'll touch them again."

Jax, Kai, and I laugh then, and even Loki gives a little chuckle. The sound lightens something in my heart, perhaps healing a small fracture too. We may not have much to go on, but it's more than we had this morning. It's a start, and for now, it'll have to be enough.

Just hold on, Princess. We'll find you.

CHAPTER TWO

LILLY

After a night plagued with visions of shadow men and swirling lights, I prise open my eyes, which are stuck together with sleep dust, to soft daylight that filters through the gaps in the wooden shutters. Groaning, my head thumping again, I look around and jump when I see a middle-aged woman waiting a little way away, a soft smile on her face.

"Sorry to startle you, dear, especially in your condition," she says, her voice gentle, and although I've never met her before, she puts me at ease instantly with her calming vibe. "I'm Jacky, and I'm going to be your nurse and midwife from now on."

I can't help the way my jaw suddenly gets tight at the fact that my autonomy has just been taken from me, but it's like I can't grasp my anger enough to throw it back at her creepy, smiling face. Gingerly sitting up, trying to ignore the dizziness and throbbing headache, I have to swallow a couple of times before I can answer.

"Um, sure, uh, do you know where I am?" I ask, my voice raspy. "Where is Ash?" She immediately goes over to the side table and fills a glass with water before handing it to me. I eye it for a minute, but I just can't grasp what my mind is trying to tell me, so I bring it to my lips and glug the cool water down in one go. "Thanks," I say, handing the glass back to her. Her brow is lowered, which makes my own dip down.

"You're in Wiltshire, dear, at your uncle's house. He's looking after you, and the baby," she tells me brightly, her arm coming round my upper back to help support me as I try to get up and out of the bed.

"Wiltshire?" I pause, feeling unsteady and wobbling slightly as I get to my feet. I'm not sure if it's the thumping headache or the news that I'm back in England, with my uncle, that leaves me stumbling. "Adrian's house?"

"That's right, dear," she replies, keeping her arm around me, and helping to guide me to the bathroom door, somehow knowing that I need a piss, like yesterday. "Right, let's get you washed and dressed, shall we? You'll feel right as rain then, and I can do some checks on the baby to make sure all is as it should be."

I should feel embarrassed that a complete stranger is helping me sit on the toilet, then helping me into the shower and to wash, and a small part of me is mortified, but it's like it's buried deep inside me, drowning and unable to make it to the surface. I can't seem to get my feet and legs to function normally. I'm like a newborn lamb, unable to get my feet underneath me enough to walk on my own. My head feels full of cotton wool, and all the colours of the room are dulled and lifeless like an old T-shirt washed too many times, so I'm mostly glad for the extra help.

After dressing me in a soft, cotton nightgown that she found in the chest of drawers, which, although clearly new and unworn, smells musty. Jacky supports me as I lie back on the bed then takes mine and the baby's vitals. She listens to the heartbeat which makes tears sting my eyes, the steady rhythm grounding me as it always does, calming my fluttering nerves at this new reality that I've woken up in. She also takes blood samples and all the other things that Lisa, my midwife back in Colorado, used to do. The tears threaten to spill at the homesickness which fills me up at the thought of Highgate and my guys. My Knights.

"Where's my husband?" I ask once she's finished up.

"Husband, dear?" she questions, her eyebrows dipped as she helps me up again and leads me to a small table near the window that has a covered tray similar to last night's on it. "I bet you're hungry, dear," she tells me, taking the lid off to reveal a large salad with fragrant marinated grilled chicken and buttered bread that looks and smells freshly baked. My stomach takes that moment to growl loudly, and she chuckles. "I'll open the shutters, shall I? It's a lovely day out."

I nod, sitting down, and immediately shove a forkful of the salad with chicken into my mouth, thinking that I'm sure I just asked her something, but now I can't remember what it was. The room is flooded with light seconds later as the shutters are flung open with a clatter, and once my eyes adjust, I see that she's right, the sun is shining and the sky is a beautiful light blue, not a cloud in sight.

My fork pauses on its way back down to my plate as I notice something that sits at odds with the beautiful day outside.

Bars.

There are metal bars outside my window, and as soon as I see them, a wave of claustrophobia washes over me, leaving my skin tight and itchy and my breathing shallow. My wide eyes look up into Jacky's brown ones, which are full of a gentle sympathy.

"Why are there bars?" I ask, my voice soft and small as I try to make sense of what is happening here, but my mind is too foggy, and I'm unable to grab hold of a thought for too long before it flies away like a petal on the breeze.

"Oh, dear girl," she says with a sigh, coming to crouch next to me as my gaze goes back to those lines of metal that are trapping me in this room. "Your uncle is just trying to take care of you and the baby. He doesn't want anything to happen to either of you, dear."

I look back down at her. "Where is Ash? Loki? Kai and Jax?" I question, my voice trembling, suddenly overwhelmed with the need to be held in familiar arms that chase all the nightmares away. Again, there's a flash of softness in her eyes that I can't work out the meaning of, the corners crinkling as she reaches out and takes my cold, shaking hand in hers.

"Why don't you finish your meal, and then I can take you back to bed? To rest. You look so tired, dear."

My eyes fill with tears. I don't want to rest, I feel like I've lost so much time already. Letting go of Jacky's hands, I, once again, pick up my fork and spear a piece of chicken, bringing it up to my mouth.

But as I continue to eat, washing it down with a glass of fresh fruit juice, I do start to feel so bone-weary that my fork clatters onto the plate as if I can't hold it up anymore.

"Come on then, dear. Let's get you back to bed," Jacky tells me, helping me out of the chair and back into bed, tucking me in like a child. I'm sure I hear her whisper something that sounds suspiciously like, "poor delusional girl," under her breath.

All too soon, I'm dragged under into blackness once more, unable to fight the crashing wave of exhaustion any longer or the nightmares that await me.

The next few weeks follow the same routine. Jacky is always there when I wake up, ready to aid me in getting up and dressed before taking me over to the window to look out at the manicured grounds and the woods in the distance of my uncle's estate. I can see quite far into the distance, being on an upper floor, and it's a mixed blessing as it taunts me as well as gives me something to gaze upon. Like a bird in a cage, placed next to an open window and being able to see freedom but not taste it.

I give up asking about Ash, my husband, or any of the guys as each time she expertly distracts me and avoids answering until I feel as though perhaps it was all a wonderful dream. Perhaps I dreamt of going to America, meeting the guys, and falling in love.

Maybe I've been here all along?

My mind clearly likes to torment me as I am plagued with nightmares of arms banded tightly around me which do not belong to any of my Knights. Of sweet words whispered in my ear, of being called Violet. The worst are the nights where I dream that I'm back in the library with cunt-face Robert, his hands in places that they have no right to be, and his breathing heavy in my ear.

After those nights, I wake up covered in sweat and feel sick to my stomach, my pillow damp and dried tears on my cheeks. I notice small bruises on my waist, hips, and breasts, yet I have no knowledge of how they got there.

My mind struggles to focus on even menial tasks. It's getting worse and increasingly muddled the more time passes until I can barely remember what my life once was.

Before this room.

Before the bars on the window.

The silence that surrounds me. The night terrors that haunt me.

One day I wake up, and after assisting me with washing, Jacky gets me dressed not in another nightgown but in a soft, blue pantsuit that looks like it's from the early two-thousands.

"Why am I getting dressed? In proper clothes I mean?" I ask, giving her a quizzical look.

"Well, your uncle and I agreed that you needed some fresh air and to stretch your legs," she tells me, her face split into a big smile as she takes me over to the small table, and I sit down, a bowl of creamy porridge in front of me. "So, after breakfast, I'm to take you out for a walk." She beams at me like this is her life's biggest achievement thus far. Shit, maybe it is for all I know. I hear a familiar masculine chortle that makes my head swivel, expecting to see Ash next to me. But then I remember that he might not even be real, just a figment of my imagination, otherwise he'd be here, right? Jacky would know about him, right?

Shaking my head at my apparent craziness, I feel excited flutters in my stomach at the prospect of leaving my gilded cell, and I rush to finish my food. I do pause as the depressing thought that this is what my life has been reduced to hits me.

Helping me to stand, as I'm still so fucking unsteady on my feet, we make our way towards the door, and I can feel my pulse becoming faster the closer we get to it.

Taking a small, silver key out of her pocket, she unlocks the door, opening it into the room. It's funny how an object so tiny can exert such control over my life. In front of me sits a wheelchair, and I baulk at the sight, halting our movements.

"It's just to help you get outside. You're very weak, dear," she tells me kindly, her face sincere.

Taking a deep sighing breath and nodding, we move forward once more, and she supports my arm whilst I sit in the chair, tucking a fluffy wool blanket around my thin legs. Even with all the food that I've been given, my muscles have started to waste away with inactivity, so I'm determined to at least try and walk a little today, in the hope that I'll build my strength back up.

Jacky begins to wheel me along the corridor, and I realise that I do recognise the light blue colour of the walls and the various old portraits and landscape paintings lining them. We go past the carved wooden staircase, stopping in front of a light-coloured panelled door that looks the same as all the others that we've just passed. Stepping away from me, Jacky presses a brass button, and a second later the door slides into the wall revealing a lift.

"That's new," I mutter, not remembering it from before as she pushes me in, pressing the down button. The doors close with a soft swish, and I feel a jolt as we descend. For a moment, the wild thought that I'm descending into Hell flashes across my mind. Then I remember I'm already there; too weak to walk, in love with dark Knights that may not exist.

"Your uncle put it in specially, thinking that you might need it, especially once the baby arrives," she tells me, her voice soft, interrupting my pity party.

"Huh," I reply quietly.

Chewing my lip, I think on her words. On the surface, they show my uncle as someone who's thinking of the comfort and ease of others, a selfless person who'd spend a small fortune ensuring that a relative has all that they might need. On the other hand, I can't help wondering why he'd think that, as a normal, healthy, young woman, I wouldn't be able to manage the stairs. Regardless if I'm pregnant or not.

We come to a stop, and the doors open with another quiet swish, disrupting my swirling thoughts. I realise with a start as we exit the lift, that today my mind feels clearer than it has in weeks. I'm able to hold onto thoughts, they don't slip through my fingers like sand as they did just yesterday or the days before.

As we approach the double front doors with their clear glass panels, the sunlight floods in, shining all around the large entrance hall, making it feel light and airy. Very un-Hell-like. The tight knot in my chest lightens the closer I get to freedom. I can practically taste the fresh, English countryside, like newly mown grass and daffodils. A wide smile takes over my face when the doors are opened by my uncle's butler, Smith, and I can take a deep lungful of the sweetest air I've ever tasted.

We pause at the top of the entrance steps, and my eyelids flutter closed, the sun warming my face and heating my blood as though I'm a cold-blooded creature that needs light to survive, or I'll waste away.

"Allow me, Miss, ma'am." An unfamiliar deep voice startles my lids open, and I'm staring into laughing, brown eyes the colour of fallen autumn leaves. I study him as he bends down to grab the front of the chair. He reminds me of a slightly older Jax—*if Jax is real of course and not a figment of my fucked up imagination*—with his dirty blond hair tied in a messy man bun, and his facial hair that's more than stubble but less than a beard. He's less stacked than my Viking, though still muscular. "Rowan, give me a hand, will ya?" he calls in a pure west London drawl, and I look to the side to see the same man walking towards us.

Doing a double take, I hear Mr laughing brown eyes chuckle.

"Are you..." I begin, looking back at him.

"Twins? Yes," he tells me as I feel the chair shift when they lift it and start to carry me down the steps.

"But I'm the better looking one," a smoky voice says behind me —Rowan—and a surprised bark of laughter slips from between my lips, my hand flying to cover my mouth. The guy in front just smirks, and I must admit, if I wasn't in love four times over with possibly imaginary guys, I'd be tempted to fall because of that smile alone.

"Thank you, boys, that was very gallant," Jacky flutters, coming up next to me with a blush on her cheeks as they set the chair down at the base of the steps.

"You're welcome, ma'am, Miss," the first twin says, straightening back up as Rowan comes to stand next to him. They look at me intently with an unreadable expression, as though they're studying me. "Anything else we can help you with?"

I interrupt before Jacky can say anything. "What's your name? And why are you here?" I ask, my eyes narrowing, noticing their all black clothing, and the radios attached to the belts at their hips.

"Apologies, m'lady," the first twin replies, hand on his heart, a boyish grin on his face that has my lips twitching, followed by a crippling twinge of pain that lances through my heart at the memory of another cheeky boy I know—*maybe know*—but with red hair instead of dirty blond. "My name is Roman Kent, this is Rowan Kent, and we are part of the security your uncle has hired to help keep you safe."

My brows drop at his words.

"Safe from what?" I ask, but before they can answer, Jacky clears her throat.

"Well, thank you once again, boys, I'll be sure to call if I need your assistance," she says, her tone not unkind but a little brusque. "Right, dear, let's take a turn around the house, shall we?" She starts pushing me in the damn chair, turning me away from the intriguing Kent brothers.

Feeling a prickling in my skin, a shiver that's completely at odds with the warm sunshine, I turn around, leaning past Jacky, only to find both guys where we left them, one of them with a phone to his ear, staring after us.

"Oh, just look at those lovely daffodils!" Jacky suddenly exclaims.

My head turns to face forward again, and though my eyes see what looks like a lawn of yellow flower heads cheerfully bobbing in the slight breeze, my mind is still wondering who Roman and Rowan Kent are.

And what could my uncle possibly need to protect me from?

CHAPTER THREE

LOKI

HUNTER 'SHADOWMAN' ANDERSON:

Found her.

"Guys!" I shout, my heart pounding in my chest like it's trying to get to my girl right the fuck now, the sounds of *Gone* by Blake Rose playing in the background. Leaping up and ignoring the slight wobble due to the heavy night of drink and drugs I've still not recovered from, I rush out of my room, almost colliding into Jax in the hall. "Did you see?" I ask him, almost breathless in my excitement. *Of course he fucking knows, dumb-ass, it was on the group chat we have with the leader of the Shadows Crew.*

"Yes," is all our quiet, giant of a brother says as we pound down the stairs to find Ash and Kai already standing in the main room waiting, heads snapping up as we approach. Ash strides towards us, hands slightly raised in an almost placating gesture, and I just know that what he's about to say will piss me the hell off.

"I need you to remain calm and hear me out. Both of you," he tells us, his voice hard but not unkind. My eyes narrow, and I stop in front of him, arms crossed over my chest, which rises and falls with my heavy breathing. I can barely contain the swirling storm of emotion running through me, like there's a sandstorm inside of me, waiting to burst free and suffocate anyone who gets in my way.

Jax comes up beside me, mirroring my pose, and a flash of respect and admiration runs through me at Ash, our leader, not flinching under our heavy scrutiny. Many grown-ass men would be cowering by now. Many have, but not him. His monster recognises its kin.

"Fine," I grumble out through clenched teeth. Jax just grunts.

"I've just spoken to Hunter, and the Kent twins have seen her," he starts, and a breath rushes out of me, my whole body tingling at his words. I was so fucking worried that she was gone for good, like a beautiful ghost, never to be seen again. "They say she's weak, likely drugged up, and seems confused, but looks like she's being fed and has a nurse with her."

My vision clouds, the red mist of my anger obscuring the room until everything else fades away, and the pounding in my ears is so loud it feels like the drums of war are sounding all around us in time with my racing heart. Jax's growling snarl brings me back to the present; Ash is still standing in front of us, spine ramrod straight, facing down the demons that have surfaced within his brothers.

"That dickhead cunt is drugging her?" I question, my voice cold and measured as I plot all the ways I'm going to remove his body parts while keeping him alive. No one hurts my Pretty Girl and gets away unscathed.

"They think so, but don't know for sure." He grimaces, and I feel my face twitch, knowing that there's more that will enrage my beast. "The point is, we can't rush in and rescue her."

As soon as the words leave his lips, Jax's fist connects with his jaw, and Ash stumbles back but manages to stay upright. My arms lower, hands clenching tightly, itching to do the same, even though I know that he'll have a good reason behind his orders. Kai comes over, standing between the two men, though Ash shows no sign of retaliation, just rubs his jaw as a line of blood trickles down his chin from a busted lip.

"If we rush in, it could get Lilly killed!" Kai snaps, his outstretched hand trembling, as if that would keep Jax back. He lowers it when Jax just stands there, chest heaving, but makes no move to hit our leader again.

"Explain," I bite out, arms folded once more to try and curb the desire to destroy everything and everyone in my path.

"There is no way my *father* is not involved, and if we suddenly ride off on a rescue mission, he'll know what we're up to. All it would take is one phone call, and she's gone...permanently," Ash informs us, and I know that he hates this just as much as we do. His controlling nature won't allow anything less than everyone he cares about being within arm's reach, safe and protected by him. But more than that, our fearless leader loves our girl with all his dark and wicked soul. He needs her light, just as we all do. We can no longer survive without it.

I've slipped back into drinking and taking drugs every night, seeking oblivion, chasing her spectre. Jax is working out harder than ever, and I suspect he's been taking part in the more illegal fighting circuits if his own bruises are any indicator. Kai looks as though he hasn't slept in weeks, working all the hours he can trying to find a lead. Fuck, even his schoolwork has dropped off, and he's not been on us to keep our grades up either. And Ash, he got us to hide all the knives and shit, but I've seen bloody tissues and bandages in the trash can in his room.

We're falling apart without her, and I don't know how much longer we can go on.

"What do you suggest?" I ask, my very soul feeling bone tired. I just want my–our girl back.

"Kai's birthday is in three weeks. We will book flights to Amsterdam, it is his nineteenth after all, but once we get there, we fly back to England and meet up with the Shadows. We'll need their help.

Meanwhile, we replace her current nurse with one of our own. Hunter knows someone, so we can keep a closer eye on her and try to help where we can and stop the drugging," Ash tells us, his penetrating gaze swapping from mine to Jax's, trying to gauge our reactions. It's what makes him not only a good leader but a great one. He takes our opinions seriously. It's the one reason why our monsters heel to him.

"Three weeks?" Jax murmurs, voice laced with the sweet taste of promised violence and bloodshed.

"Three weeks," Ash replies, a sharp nod in Jax's direction. The big guy's nostrils flare, taking in a huge inhale.

"Okay," he responds before turning around, grabbing his gym bag which has taken up permanent residence by the door, and leaving. Ash turns to me.

"Three weeks and not a day more," I state, nausea swirling in my stomach. How will she forgive us for leaving her there, knowing that we might have been able to get her out sooner? How can we forgive ourselves?

"Not a day more," Ash vows.

"Not an hour more," Kai adds, and the promise settles on our shoulders, a weight that I know we will all bear until we're holding our soul safely back in our arms.

Hold on, my love, we're coming for you. Just a little longer now.

LILLY

The next few days establish my new routine. I wake up, and with Jacky's help, get washed and dressed. Then she takes me outside in the chair, and I practise walking, again with her help, getting a little steadier and stronger every day. It's fucking crazy, my new life, but maybe this is the way it's always been? And everything I think happened before was just a beautiful, wonderful dream?

My stomach frequently gives an almighty heave, my unborn child making its presence felt and making me think that it all couldn't possibly have been imagined. Otherwise, how did this one come into existence?

I often see the Kent twins and they always make me smile, reminding me of each of my potentially imaginary lovers in various ways. Their playful banter, their sense of brotherhood, and the darkness that lurks within them, waiting for an outlet.

One morning, about a week after my first trip out of my room, I'm outside, walking around the rose garden with Jacky and admiring the buds that are just waiting to burst into fragrant bloom. One of the boys—Roman, I think, as his face is a little fuller than Rowan's—rushes over.

"Thank fuck–I mean thank goodness I found you, Jacky," he says, his voice a little breathless, although the lack of colour in his cheeks gives lie to the picture that he ran all the way here. Or maybe he's just that fit. "Your mum is on the phone, something about your father having a fall and in hospital."

A pained gasp leaves her lips, and I stagger as she shifts forward, loosening her grip on me slightly.

"Oh goodness!" she exclaims, looking round trying to spot the chair to help me back to it. But it's nowhere in sight, I was trying to push myself today and managed to go further, meaning that we're inside an arched walkway, out of sight of the house and patio where the wheelchair sits.

"I can help Lilly if you want to go now. She sounded pretty upset," Roman adds, and although he looks sincere, I've had some experience—*I think*—with trickster boys, and there's something a little off about his expression. Almost triumphant. My eyes narrow at the same time as my skin prickles while looking at him, sure that he's up to something.

"I–I don't know. I'm not meant to leave her alone..." Jacky frets, and I'm sure she'd be wringing her hands if she weren't supporting me.

"I'll be fine," I assure her, feeling a pang at the thought of her dad in trouble and her mum all alone. "I won't be alone. You should go."

She takes another millisecond, chewing her lip, but worry obviously wins as she gives me a small nod, her gaze already back towards the house.

"I'll take good care of her," Roman persuades her, wrapping his arm underneath mine. He's taller than Jacky, around the same height as Ash I think, so he has to stoop a little, but seems to be okay. Then I shake my head. *Ash might not even be fucking real, Lilly.*

We watch as Jacky rushes off, and he doesn't speak until she's rounded the corner and is no longer in sight.

"They said you were like a pixie," he tells me, and my heart stutters in my chest, the world dropping away at his seemingly innocent sentence.

"W—what?" I reply, my voice a breathy, trembling whisper as I crane my neck and look up into his usually laughing brown eyes. Today they're full of seriousness, and a touch of melancholy.

He doesn't respond, and I catch movement in the corner of my vision. I look down to see that he's reaching into his pocket, my chest tightening painfully at the move, then flinch my head back slightly when he pulls out a white earbud headphone. Before I can utter another word and give voice to this fluttering in my stomach, he pops it in my ear with a kind, sad sort of smile.

"*Princess?*"

My limbs go weak, and Roman grunts quietly as he takes more of my weight, my fingers digging into his arm. I know that voice, dark as a moonless night, but the kind of dark that hides you from the monsters seeking to steal you away.

"*Princess, tell me you're there,*" the voice begs, a catch that I've not heard from my darkest Knight before.

"A—Ash?"

"*Fuck, Princess...Fuck, it's so good to hear your voice,*" he replies, a sort of hiccupping laugh sounding in my ear as tears rush to my eyes.

"You're...you're real," I state, not a question, more a breath of relief, the yearning in my soul increasing tenfold at just the sound of his voice.

"*Yeah, Baby Girl, we're real,*" another deeper voice tells me, a similar stutter to Ash's marring his usually gravelly tone.

"Jax," I rush out with a sob, my free hand flying to cover my mouth, the other wrapped around Roman's waist. The salt of tears drops onto my lips, letting me taste my relief, my sadness, my heartbreak at being apart from the other parts of my soul.

"*Don't cry, Pretty Girl,*" yet another voice pleads, one that's usually full of mirth and mischief.

"Loki!" I cry out, my palm moving to my rounded stomach, and our baby gives a kick, as if it knows that its fathers are on the other end of the line, and is desperate to meet them.

"*We don't have much time, darling,*" the final of my Knights says, the melody of his voice dulled slightly.

"Kai," I whisper, closing my eyes as a smile tugs the corners of my lips up, the shadows cast by the plants around us feeling like the caress of my men. My Knights.

"*I told you that we were bound for all eternity, my darling. We were always going to find you. You're our beating heart,*" Kai tells me, the strength of his conviction flowing into me until I can stand a little taller. I open my eyes, my mind clearing a little more with each word, each syllable they make.

"What happened? Why am I here?" I ask, desperate to know the truth.

"*Your...uncle...took you,*" Ash replies, seeming a little unsure of his words. "*And we think my father is involved too.*"

"Adrian?" I question, my head giving a slight shake. "Took me?"

"*Yes, and we think that he might be drugging you to keep you compliant,*" Loki interrupts, a sound of pain followed after. "*What? She needs to know,*" he hisses, but I can barely hear him, my mind replaying all of the times that I ate, then felt so exhausted I had to sleep for hours. All of my confusion, all of my weakness suddenly made more sense.

My fingertips trace the fading bruising on my hips, the ones in the shape of fingertips. The nightmares, the visions of shadowed men, and dreams of Robert, the guy who tried to rape me. *Were they imagined too? And what about my baby?*

"*Princess?*" Ash asks, his voice laced with concern. "*You still there?*"

"Yeah," I reply softly, clearing my throat and blinking. *One thing at a time, Lilly.* " I think it's in my food. The drug, I mean."

Silence.

"*Shit,*" Ash curses, followed by the muffled sound of something smashing that makes me wince. "*Keep it together!*" Ash barks, but clearly, the comment is not aimed at me. "*I'll sort it, Princess. Don't stop eating.*"

A fissure of pleasure rolls through me like a feline stretching at his commanding words.

"So, what's the plan?" I question, getting back to business, though the wonderful warming haze of knowing that they exist, that I didn't dream up our time together, settles over me in a comforting blanket. Roman's head is turned the other way, giving us as much privacy as he can, though I've got the feeling whatever happens next will involve the twins.

"*That's our girl,*" Loki praises, and I can hear his smile, lighting up the sunny day even though I'm hundreds of miles away from him as I stand in the rose garden.

"*My birthday is in two weeks,*" Kai interjects, and I can just picture him pushing his glasses up his nose as he speaks, my breath hitching at the thought of the gesture. "*We plan to fly to Amsterdam to celebrate.*"

"Okay..." I say, trying to figure out what the next step is, but my fucking head is still so clouded.

"*Once we get there, we'll catch a plane to England, and with the help of our Shadow Crew friends, we'll come and get you,*" Ash adds, taking up where Kai finished.

"Oh." I look back up at Roman, seeing a smirk on his admittedly pretty face. "Oh!" I gasp when it finally clicks. "The Shadows, Willow's brother's crew!"

Roman winks, then looks over his shoulder, his brow dipping.

"Gotta hang up now, pixie girl," he tells me, his voice softening when he sees what must be my face falling.

"I love you, wife," Ash murmurs in my ear, and if I close my eyes, I can pretend that he's the one holding me up instead of a stranger.

"I love you, husband," I whisper back, trying and failing to keep the tremor out of my voice.

"I love you, Pretty Girl. Give our baby a rub from me," Loki tells me, his voice thick, and my lip trembles, tears freely dripping down my cheeks.

"I will. Love you too," I respond, my heart aching so fiercely that I rub at it, trying in vain to ease the hurt.

"I love you, darling," Kai whispers, his voice etched with sorrow.

"I love you too, my soul," I tell him, feeling as though no truer words have ever been spoken. They are my soul as it no longer resides in me, and the pain of being parted is almost unbearable.

"I swear to you on my blackened heart and all that is left of my soul that we will come for you, and fucking dance in the blood of those that have harmed you, my love," Jax vows, and his declaration is full of love and vengeance in equal measure, making my heart thrill.

"I love you with all that I am, Jax. All that I will ever be," I say in return.

"Good girl," he commends, his deep voice a rumbling growl that sends a shiver to my core, lighting me up from the inside out.

Before I can say another word, I hear footsteps on the grass behind us, and Roman plucks the earbud out, pocketing it and turning us around as I wipe my tears off my face with my sleeve.

I see Jacky hurrying over, her face damp and eyes puffy, and the thought that maybe her father's accident wasn't so accidental suddenly occurs to me. I freeze for a moment, but then realise that although I feel sorry for her, it doesn't horrify me, nor the idea that my guys may have had a hand in the misfortune of an innocent bystander. I'm clearly not as lily-white as I used to be, and somehow, I'm not ashamed of that.

"My father has had a nasty fall, and I'll have to take over his care," she informs me, fussing as if she plans to take over from Roman, but he doesn't let go, instead, he helps to lead me down the walkway and back to that fucking chair. "So the agency is sending a replacement this afternoon. I'm sorry, dear."

"Tha–that's fine," I respond, trying to work out what this means. Roman gives my waist a little squeeze, and I think he means to assure me that this, too, is linked back to my guys.

We make it back to the chair, which waits innocently in a patch of sunlight, unknowing that it now represents everything that is wrong with my situation. *I wouldn't fucking need it if my uncle wasn't drugging me!*

Roman supports me as I get settled into it, and I grudgingly admit to myself that I'm feeling drained, both emotionally and physically, so it's a welcome relief to finally sit down. Jacky takes hold of the handles and starts pushing me back towards the house, unaware of the maelstrom of my thoughts and the swirling storm of my emotions.

Two weeks.

Fourteen days and I'll be in their arms again.

I just need to hold on.

CHAPTER FOUR

LILLY

I'm left alone in my room for a couple of hours after that, the new agency nurse is not able to arrive for a little while. It's the first time I've spent in my own company for almost a month, and it's nice not having eyes on me the whole time, watching my every move. Although the feeling of being observed doesn't disappear completely and I glance around the room warily, wondering if there are hidden cameras in here. I wouldn't put anything past Adrian at the moment, and just because I haven't seen him yet, doesn't mean that he's not keeping tabs on me.

The plate of food that I arrived back to sits on the small table in front of the window, uneaten. I know it's going against what Ash commanded; that I keep eating. But I just can't force myself to, knowing that it's more than likely drugged by my wankstain of an uncle, and may be harmful to my unborn child. I'm not sure how soon Ash will be able to make good on his promise and ensure that it's not drugged, so for now, I'll hold off as long as I can. My stomach grumbles, reminding me that I've not eaten since breakfast, so I take

a sip of water from the glass that I'd filled up from the bathroom tap
—I can't trust the water given to me either.

What I can't seem to work out is why he would go to such
lengths to keep me placid, unaware, and compliant. It's not as if I can
escape from here anyway, being in the middle of bumfuck nowhere,
and with my shit sense of direction I'd get lost or picked up even if I
did try to run. And I don't have any way to contact the guys. Well, I
didn't up until this point. Especially as I thought them to be a
figment of my imagination.

The warmth that covered me when I was talking to my Knights
fills me again, my entire being aching to be with them once more, to
be ensconced in their arms, surrounded by their loving embrace. I
burrow into the feeling, wrapping my blanket tighter around myself
as I watch the rain of a sudden shower hit the window panes with a
tinkling sound. The rain and birdsong are the only music I get to
listen to now.

The sun begins to lower in the sky when I hear the lock of my
door turning with a click, and I twist in my chair to see the door
opening and a woman younger than Jacky but older than me steps
into the room, the door closing softly behind her. Her wheat blonde
hair is in a neat ponytail, and her slight frame is covered by pastel
pink scrubs uniform. It's her laughing brown eyes that give me
pause, plus the tray that she's holding in her hands.

"Hi, Lilly. I'm Mai and I've bought you something to eat," she
tells me, carefully stepping towards me, and placing the tray on the
table while making sure not to knock the plate already there off. "I
made it myself, and no one else has touched it," she divulges, looking
me straight in the eye with a frank and open look on her face. *She
knows about the drugs, right?*

"T–thanks," I reply, looking down to see a bowl of steaming
soup. It looks like chicken and vegetable, and my stomach growls
loud enough to be heard over the drizzle outside. *Yum!*

I hesitate for just a moment, unsure if she is someone my guys have sent or another of one of my uncle's minions. She leans in closer, her light, floral perfume fresh rather than cloying.

"Ash told me to tell you 'rubber duck' if you had any concerns," she whispers in my ear, my eyes widening at the phrase. Only Ash and I know about it, no one else. My pulse spikes thinking about when he was meant to use it, if he was feeling the urge to cut, and worry floods my veins at the thought that he may have self-harmed and I've not been there to help.

Worry about that later, Lilly. Just get through this first.

Not taking my eyes off the bowl—just in case someone *is* watching us—I take the spoon, dip it in, and bring it to my mouth. The soup is delicious, clearly homemade, and full of warm comforting flavour. There's a bread roll to go with it, and before I realise it, the bowl is empty and I'm feeling full but clearheaded. A contrast to how I've felt after most meals I've had here.

"Thanks, that was amazing," I say with a sigh, seeing the corner of her eyes crinkle with a wide smile. "Have we met? Your eyes remind me of someone."

"The twins are my cousins, bloody reprobates," she answers, laughing as she hands me a bottle of water, then sits in the chair opposite me. That makes sense; she has Roman's eyes. "So, what do you usually do around here?" she asks me, another sigh leaving my lips as I play with the tassels on the blanket.

"Nothing really, mostly I sleep after eating," I confess, seeing the laughter leave her eyes as her jaw clenches, and a flush stains her cheeks.

"Well, how about a game of Go Fish?" she finally questions, pulling out a pack of cards from her pocket, along with a chocolate bar which makes my mouth water. "Winner gets this," she tells me, eyes alight with challenge.

"You're on!" I tell her, beaming as she moves the trays to the floor next to us, then deals the cards. "But fair warning, I was a champion back in primary school. I even won Sally Weston's favourite, pink sparkly headband, which pissed her off no end."

She lets out a peal of laughter, and suddenly the room feels brighter, the grey day less dismal as we begin to play.

I lie down, the sweet taste of victory still on my tongue as I savour the last cube of chocolate melting on my tongue. Mai left after dinner, telling me she'll be back tomorrow at breakfast, and it feels so nice to finally have an ally here. Three if you count the twins, which I think that I can, considering Willow and the guys know them.

I shut my eyes, waiting for the familiar blackness of sleep to descend, but it eludes me tonight. Maybe it was the conversation with my guys earlier, their voices echoing inside my head like a shout in a cave. Even now I can hear them, and for the first time in weeks, it feels as though I'm close to them once more.

It's the middle of the night, and the room is in complete darkness before I start to drift off, only to be startled awake when I hear the soft click of what sounds like the lock on my door. A shadow fills the doorway briefly before it's closed again, the lock sounding once more. My heart thuds painfully in my chest, my body freezing up as the figure approaches the bed. It pauses briefly in front of me before moving towards the bottom of the bed, out of my line of sight.

My breathing becomes shallow when cool air hits my back as the duvet is lifted, the mattress dipping as the figure gets in behind me. Nausea swirls in my stomach when the heat of a body hits my spine through my nightgown, fingers digging into my hips painfully as a hardness is ground against my arse.

"Violet..." a deep, male voice groans, his painful grip loosening, then his palm glides down my thigh, fingers searching for my hem and leaving a sickening tingling in their wake. All whilst his hot, alcohol-scented breath washes over the back of my head, making me want to throw up.

Remember, Baby Girl, go in hard and fast, like you want to push through your attackers' body.

Jax's voice sounds in my head, as if he's right in front of me, and before my brain has time to catch up, I'm throwing my head back with a yell. The satisfying sound of cartilage breaking sounds in the room, and warm liquid hits the back of my head, coating my hair.

"FUCK!" the male voice shouts, the heat of his body moving away from mine.

My head throbs, the dark room spinning as I struggle to sit up, my breaths laboured and sawing out of my chest.

"Lilly?! Everything okay?" a loud voice sounds from outside the door, the handle rattling.

"Rowan?" I croak, turning just as the dark shadow of a man flies across the room, pausing at the wall opposite the bed before disappearing through it. *What the fuck?*

"We're coming in, Lilly," Roman's voice calls this time just as I hear the lock click, and the door swings open, hitting the wall with a crash. The room suddenly fills with light, and I squint at the harsh brightness, my hand flying up to shade my eyes as I manage to sit upright. "Fuck, why are you covered in blood?"

Both boys rush over to me, Rowan kneeling on the bed next to me to inspect the back of my head.

"Ow!" I hiss when he touches a particularly tender spot.

"Sorry, pixie girl," he soothes, his fingers becoming a little more gentle. "It doesn't look like you're bleeding. What in the ever-loving fuck happened?"

"There was someone in my bed..." I shiver, tears filling my eyes and my cheeks reddening with shame at what I have to say next. "H— he was—he was touching me, so I headbutted him with the back of my head," I tell them, feeling a drop of liquid hit my hands which are resting in my lap. "He called me Violet."

"Motherfucker!" Roman curses, running his fingers through his shoulder-length hair. His all black outfit looks a little rumpled, but I guess it would be if he's been on duty all day and into the night.

"Where is he now?" he questions, looking around as if he'll find him hiding under the bed.

"He disappeared through that wall," I tell them, lifting my trembling hand and pointing to the spot opposite me. I can see a very faint outline in the wall, the right size for a door. Roman walks over to it, running his hands along the tiny gap.

"Servants' door, all the old manors have them. Can't have the help cluttering up the hallways. Fucking elitist pricks," he mumbles as a small click sounds in the room, and a second later the door opens to reveal a dark passageway. "He definitely went this way," he tells us, stepping to one side and shining the torch on his phone onto the floor, highlighting spots of red.

"Check it out, I'll wait here," Rowan says, getting off the bed and holding out a hand. "I'll help get you sorted, Lilly."

"Just because you're four minutes older, doesn't make you the fucking boss," Roman grumbles, but does what Rowan says and heads into the gaping darkness, shutting the secret door behind him.

"Has anything like this happened before?" Rowan asks me, his voice laced with gentle concern as he helps me out of the bed, tucking my trembling hand into the crook of his elbow. My other hand strokes over the fading bruises on my hip.

"I–I think maybe, but I've been too out of it to know if it was just a dream or not," I confess quietly, pausing when his steps stop. I look up to see that his jaw is clenched, his face hard. I swallow thickly, trying to find the courage to ask a question in return. "D–do you know who it was?"

His eyes close, a deep exhale leaving his mouth before he turns, facing me, his hand coming over mine and tucking it further into the crook of his arm.

"We're not sure, but I wouldn't be surprised if your uncle has a broken nose and two black eyes tomorrow." His eyes soften, his hand squeezing mine gently.

"Adrian?" I whisper, but don't hear if he replies as I tear from his grip, making it just in time to throw up in the toilet. I heave until there's nothing left, stomach acid burning the back of my throat.

I hear the sound of Rowan talking to someone, but my mind is too full of what he just implied. My uncle has been stealing into my bedroom at night, touching me, sexually abusing me, whilst I was too drugged up by him to defend myself.

All of a sudden the walls feel like they're closing in, my breaths coming in short, sharp pants as the weight of that knowledge sinks in.

"Hey, Princess," a deep voice I vaguely recognise sounds as if from far away. *"Look at me, Lilly,"* the voice commands, and I turn my head, finding familiar grey eyes full of worry looking back at me. *"That's it, my love, good girl. Now breathe with me, in and out,"* Ash orders, and it takes me a second to realise that he's on a phone screen and not actually in the room. A wave of almost crippling sorrow hits me, but I do as he orders and follow his deep breathing until the edges of the room go back to their usual place.

"Ash?" I rasp, my throat raw and tears dripping down my cheeks as I wrap my arms around myself, still sitting on the bathroom floor in front of the toilet full of my own vomit. "H–he touched me, Ash."

"I know, Princess, I know. And I will personally chop off each and every one of his fingers for daring to lay a hand on you," he growls out as a deadly fire burns in his eyes, a fire that warms me enough to sit up straighter. *"I wish we could come and get you right the fuck now but we can't, Princess."* Frustration is clear in the way he says the last part through clenched teeth. *"If my father even suspects...shit, he may order Adrian to kill you, and I just can't live in a world that you are not a part of. That's not an option, Princess."* His eyes beg me for my understanding, for my forgiveness.

"I–I know, Ash," I reply softly, lowering my gaze as my throat constricts at the thought of spending one more second with the fucking pervert that is my uncle.

"Look at me, Princess," Ash directs once more, voice hard, so I do

as he says. *"You will not have to face him again. One of the boys will be with you, day and night."*

"How can you make that happen?" I ask, mind swirling with the game that we're playing, the tightrope that we're walking.

"We'll tell him that Julian has given us orders to," Roman tells me, and I look away from Ash into his laughing brown eyes, which currently are full of evil humour. It also confirms my suspicions that Julian has something to do with this.

"He won't question it if it's my father's orders," Ash interjects, and I look back at him. *"Because then he'll have to admit what he's been doing, and Julian won't like that one bit."* His lip curls, and I shiver at his words. Not for the first time, I curse being a woman, curse the fact that these old men all want something from me that I am not willing to give them, so they will try and take it by force. *"We won't let Julian near you either, Princess. I swear."*

I gaze into his eyes, full of a fierce fire and love, and I nod, scrubbing my own eyes with my hand. "Okay," I say, my voice a little scratchy but stronger than before.

"That's my girl," Ash tells me, pride making his eyes shine. *"Now, Mai is on her way to help you get sorted, and the boys will be with you until she gets there."*

"I love you, Asher Vanderbilt," I confess, beyond grateful for everything that he is doing for me.

"I love you, Lilly Vanderbilt," he replies, voice soft. *"I'll see you soon, okay, Princess?"*

"See you soon," I respond, my heart dropping as he ends the call.

Somewhere, a clock chimes one in the morning.

Thirteen days. I'll see him and the others in thirteen days.

All I need to do is survive until then.

CHAPTER FIVE

JAX

Pain explodes across my knuckles when my fist meets its target, wet droplets of ruby red hitting my face as my opponent's lip splits. A heady sense of euphoria rushes over me when he goes down, lightness suffusing my limbs at the sight of his crumpled, defeated form. It's followed by a sharp, edgy feeling, my nostrils flaring at the fact that he stays on the ground, forcing me to leash the demon inside that's desperate to break free. That needs to wreak havoc and cause bloodshed.

The sounds of the crowd filter back into my ears, a mixture of hollers and jeers as some win the bets they placed earlier in the night while others lose.

"The Black Knight remains undefeated tonight!" the ref shouts, my still clenched fist pulled into the air, blood dripping down my arm, much to the crowd's screaming delight. They don't call it bare knuckle fighting for nothing, and I relish the sting that throbs along the limb almost as much as the agony I forced upon the guy lying prone on the dirt floor. "Is anyone else brave enough to face this Goliath?"

Silence greets his call, the clear night's sky surrounding us, stars twinkling in the inky depths above. My lip curls at the thought of taking a second's enjoyment when my Baby Girl is trapped in a hell not of her making. My jaw tightens like it does every time I think about her, and how fucking useless we are at the moment, leaving her there. It feels too close to abandonment for my liking.

"I'll fight him," a familiar, deep voice states into the quiet, and the crowd parts like the red motherfucking sea to let Asher Vanderbilt saunter through, his signature smirk plastered on his lips.

"Think you can win, rich boy?" I snarl, baiting him, letting my gaze travel up and down his body. He's fit, and pretty stacked, but not a match for me and my bulk.

"Pot and kettle, *Black Knight*," he teases back, stripping off his white tee and exposing all that inked-up flesh. He's been wearing suits less since Lilly went missing, opting for sweats and T-shirts like the rest of us. My lip tilts at the thought of calling him out on it. That'll rile him up for sure.

"Well, don't complain when that pretty face of yours gets all bloodied up, *Vanderbilt*," I volley back, rolling my neck as he steps right up to me, his bare chest brushing my own sweat and blood-covered torso.

A fissure of guilt runs through me at the knowledge that either Lilly would hate this—us fighting—or really fucking love it. Kai and Loki told us all about how much she enjoyed their company. Fuck, I can't wait for her to be back with us. I'd even touch this asshole's dick if she asked me to, just to see that fire in her eyes again.

"You think I'm pretty, Griffiths? I'm afraid you're not my type, too much between your legs for me," Ash retorts, and I can't help the dark chuckle that falls from my lips at the comment.

"We both know that your wife certainly enjoys what's between my legs," I reply, grinning smugly when a dark flush creeps up his neck. "What does she call it again...oh yes, my monster cock. But I'm sure that you're...adequate, pretty boy."

It's a testament to our years of training that the only reaction he gives me is a clenching of his fists and flared nostrils. He's as unflappable as a statue, which is just one of the reasons that he's our leader.

"You two done flirting, or do you need a moment alone to jerk each other off?" the ref interrupts loudly, the crowd laughing and whooping in the background.

I spit blood at Ash's feet, a wave of probably unwarranted anger washing over me. He's part of the reason why I'm not holding my girl right the fuck now. Well, his cunt of a sperm donor is, and it's far easier than I like to admit to transfer that purple-tinged rage to the son instead of the father.

I can see his face shift, eyes burning molten with wrath as he gears himself up for the fight, and I know he's just as pissed at himself as I am at my own inadequacies with this situation. I have a moment of hesitation, knowing that I surpassed him a few years back in terms of sheer strength.

"Don't you dare fucking hold back on me, Griffiths," he grits out, still issuing orders.

"Don't worry," I assure him, a rare smile tugging my lips up. It must not be a nice one as I see him flinch ever so slightly. "I won't."

Wasting no more time, I throw a punch that lands a solid hit to his jaw, snapping his head to the side as the sound of his teeth clacking together fills my ears like the finest symphony. He recovers quickly, not like the other shitbags I've fought tonight, whipping his head around and landing a closed-fisted strike to my gut that almost has me doubling over. Almost, but not quite, as my own training kicks in.

"You've gotten better," I rasp out, and he gives me a feral grin, his teeth covered in blood.

The next several moments blur into a violent dance, both of us exchanging blows, landing an almost equal number of hits. Blood paints our skin, streaking it with red until we look like demons that have stepped out of hell, covered in our sins. Panting hard, Ash has put up more of a fight than I expected, I'm a little tired from my previous three fights and pause for a millisecond to take a breather. But, unfortunately for him, it looks like I'm still stronger than he is as in the next second I land a solid punch to the side of his temple and he goes down like a sack of shit.

"The Black Knight wins again!" the ref calls, but I sidestep him, going to my fallen leader, kneeling down in the dirt, and giving him a shake. He groans as his long, black eyelashes flutter—*no wonder Baby Girl fell for him so hard, fucking pretty boy indeed*—and he rolls onto his back.

"Fuck you, Jax," he rasps, coughing and spitting blood next to my knee.

"Yeah, fuck you too, Ash," I reply, grabbing his hand and hauling him to his feet.

"Urgh, careful, you fucking neanderthal," he complains as I settle his arm across my shoulders, wrapping my own around his torso a little more tightly than necessary, eliciting a hiss of pain from his swollen lips. "You were the one that beat the shit out of me, what do you have to be salty about?" I look down into his grey eyes, one almost swollen shut, and just give him a look. "You're still sore about me marrying Lilly, aren't you?" he questions, a stupid fucking smile on his face. "I just did what I had to do."

Another sharp grunt of pain leaves his throat as I poke what I suspect is a very bruised rib.

"Sure you did," I reply, huffing as his smile remains fixed. People give us a wide berth as we exit, probably on account of the grinning idiot next to me who can barely walk but seems ecstatic about it. Luckily we rode together, as I doubt he'd be able to drive himself, stupid fuck.

Goosebumps pebble my skin as the high of my fights leaves my system, and Ash sighs next to me when we get to my truck. I open the door for him, and before he gets in, he turns to me, his bruised face weary.

"There's been a development," he tells me, eyes shrewd once more. My heart gives a painful thud in my chest

"What kind of development?" I question, knowing that it relates back to Baby Girl.

"I'll tell you when we get back to the dorm," he replies, and the metal of the car creaks when my fingers tighten on the edge of the door.

"I should have fucking hit you harder," I grumble, stepping away and making my way around the front to the driver's side.

"Yeah, you should have," I hear him mumble, before he steps in and closes the door behind him.

Hand clenching the door handle hard enough that my bloody knuckles turn white, I look to the star-freckled sky and send up a prayer to whatever motherfucker might be out there.

Keep her safe for me.

KAI

I flinch as Jax throws the coffee table across the room, the tinkle of shattering glass at odds with the violence swirling in the room. Loki isn't faring much better, his fists clenched, breathing hard as he tries to remain in control of himself and his wrath. But I see it, clear as day, swirling in the depths of his emerald eyes. A fire that rages and burns, threatening to consume us all.

I can feel my own pulse spiking, Ash's revelation about his phone call with Lilly in the early hours calling to my own inner demon. Her situation is so similar to my own, her uncle is as much of a pervert as mine. More so if he is actually her father. Sick fuck. The blackness of my own rage threatens to consume me, eating at the corners of my vision, but I keep my head. Pushing it back until it simmers in the corner, waiting for its target; Adrian Ramsey.

"We have to get her now, Ash," Loki bites out through clenched teeth. "We can't leave her there, you must know that?" My heart thuds at his pleading tone, my spirit breaking that much more at the knowledge of what she's up against.

"We don't have any other fucking choice!" Ash shouts, throwing his hands out wide, an ice pack clutched in one. I wince at the bruises already marking his face, the purples and blues of them already visible. "If Julian even catches the slightest whiff of what we're planning..."

He doesn't need to finish his sentence, we all know what Julian Vanderbilt is capable of. The depths he will go to in order to gain more control over the company. Although...

"Are we sure that he'd order her death?" I question, Ash's head snapping to look at me. "I mean, he knows that we care for her and that if any lasting harm came to her, we'd rebel big time."

"But as far as he's aware, we believe that she's missing," Ash answers, rubbing his face then hissing when he hits a sore spot. "She could stay missing, he could move her or just cut his losses. Unless we confront him about it, which just feels too risky with her still there, I can't see any other way forward but to wait until it's too late for him to do anything about it."

I nod, hating his words but knowing them to be the truth. We can't give Julian any reason to hurt her, to kill her. And I've no doubt that he would if he felt so inclined. He may find her...appealing, but if she were to die, all her assets go to Ash and thus stay under Julian's control. For now anyway.

"So we just fucking wait?" Jax snarls, and at least he's calmed down enough to speak. "And leave her with that pervert?"

"I know, I fucking hate it as much as you do," Ash confesses, voice fractured and pain-filled. "But I'd rather that than not have her at all. We can help her get over this. We can't bring her back from the dead."

We all flinch at his last words, feeling them to the pit of our very tortured souls.

"Fuck!" Loki exhales, though with a sad resignation and not the anger of a few moments before. "How will she ever forgive us for this? We're leaving her in the hands of a monster."

"She'll have the Shadow twins," Ash assures us, as much as himself I think. "One of them will be with her twenty-four seven. Plus she's got Mai now, to make sure she's no longer drugged."

I clear my throat. "I've been able to hack into his security system," I tell them, narrowed eyes swinging my way. "We can watch her using the CCTV cameras and see for ourselves that she's okay." It's the only reason that I'm able to keep my beast in check right now.

"And you didn't think to tell us this before?" Ash questions, one brow arched, his voice cold.

"Not my fault you don't check your phones. The app has been on there all evening." I shrug, a small tilt lifting my lips when they all rush to take their cells out of their pockets, Ash cursing as his sore fingers fumble with the screen of his brand new iPhone. I walk over and snatch the device out of his grip, earning a feral growl. "Let me."

A couple of swipes later, the image of our beautiful girl pops up on the screen. She's sitting at a small table, eating a bowl of something with the sun filtering through the window, while who I assume is Mai talks to her from another seat across from her. My heart swells when Lilly laughs, the musical, joyous sound fills the room even though there's no sound on the feed. I can hear it clearly in my mind.

We watch, enraptured, as she finishes her meal, breakfast most likely given that it's early morning in England, and with Mai's help stands, her rounded stomach obvious in her thin nightgown.

"She's gotten so big," Loki whispers, and I look up to see his eyes glued to the screen, tracing every line, every curve of our girl. I look back down to see her go through what I assume is her bathroom door, which closes behind her. Mai waits outside, giving Lilly her privacy which I am grateful for knowing just how much her life has been monitored by that fucking scumbag these past few weeks.

"I've sent the twins a burner phone, so soon we will be able to communicate with her too," I tell them all, my voice soft as I watch the closed bathroom door on the screen, desperate for another glimpse.

No one replies, though I feel the tension leak out of Ash next to me as we continue watching, waiting for our next fix.

We stay that way for a long time, drinking in the sight of the girl who stole our hearts, our souls, before we'd even realised what she was doing.

CHAPTER SIX

LILLY

The next couple of days are like a breath of fresh air, like I can finally breathe fully again for the first time in weeks. Each day that Mai brings me freshly prepared food that only she handles, my head clears until I no longer suffer the effects of being drugged after each meal, and so my strength returns. I still use the wheelchair when she takes me out, something telling me not to let my uncle know how much stronger I am now. Truth be told, I'm not quite at full strength yet anyway, having been so inactive for the past few weeks.

I'm getting bigger too, most noticeably my growing stomach now that I'm six months gone. My tits are bigger, and randomly my nipples too, which Mai says is all normal. Baby seems to be getting along well, though not having access to an ultrasound means that we can't check everything. But all the checks that Mai does are fine, and my blood levels are okay.

One of the twins is with me at all times, even at night. The day after 'the incident'—as I'm now calling it because I just can't process what happened right now—the boys moved the massive, wooden wardrobe in front of the secret door, blocking it completely. They could only just about manage it, so I doubt that my uncle could move it alone. And although I haven't seen my uncle, Roman told me that he left to go into Harley Street to see about a nose job after apparently being kicked in the face by one of his horses. *Like that's fucking believable!*

Several days after 'the incident,' Mai and I are walking in the rose garden, once again under the archway. Mai helps me in order to keep up the pretence of my drug-induced state. Can't have my uncle thinking that I'm not weakened by the drugs. Some of the roses are in full bloom now, their heady scent wrapping around me in a floral perfume. There's a soft breeze that plays with the tassels on my light shawl, the loose trousers I'm wearing fluttering around my ankles as we stroll along. It's the weirdest thing. The wardrobe and chest are full of brand new maternity clothes, some with tags still on, but they're all just a little out of date and slightly musty smelling. Like they've been shut away for a while. They're mostly comfy if a little upper-class-rich-woman-who-goes-to-lunch for me, so I can't complain.

As we walk towards the end of the arch, intending to head out towards the man-made lake today, someone calls my name. I turn and smile to see Rowan jogging towards me. Both boys have become like the brothers I never had, teasing me to keep my spirits up and fiercely protective when it comes to my safety.

"Good morning, pixie girl, sis," he greets when he reaches us, not even a little puffed out. Bloody bastard. "I've a present for you, Lilly," he tells me, a mischievous glint in his brown eyes.

Raising an eyebrow at him, he just gives me what I am coming to realise is one of the twins' signature naughty smirks, then he reaches into his pocket and pulls out what looks like a brand new iPhone.

"What's this?" I question, my heart rate picking up as I take the device from him and tap my thumb on the screen. Immediately, I see a message waiting for me.

KAI EVIL GENIUS MATTHEWS:

So we can keep in touch, darling xxx

I quickly open it, rereading the message again as a smile tugs at my lips. I startle when another message pops up.

LOKI YOUR FAVOURITE BOYFRIEND THORN:

winking face emoji

Fucking cuntmuffin!
Followed by another.

ASH OUR ALMIGHTY LEADER:

Who the fuck gave us these stupid-ass nicknames? Hello, Princess xxx

A laugh tinkles out of my mouth at seeing his words, and I can just imagine his grumbling tone of voice as he says them. Another message comes in, and I can't help a bark of laughter that rings around the spring morning.

JAX WEAPON OF MASS DESTRUCTION GRIFFITHS:

I'm betting Loki, fucker. Baby Girl, you there?

LILLY SEXY AF BABY MAMA:

I'm here. And I like the nicknames *kissing face emoji*

LILLY SEXY AF BABY MAMA:

Are you sure this is okay? It's not going to be tracked? Xxx

I nibble my bottom lip as I wait for a reply, knowing that Mai and

Rowan act as a lookout whilst I stare at the screen like the lifeline that it is. A reply soon appears.

KAI EVIL GENIUS MATTHEWS:

> It's a burner, my darling. Untraceable, so just keep it hidden xxx

Loki Your Favourite Boyfriend Thorn changed the group name to Lilly's Not Gangbang Boyfriends.

My hand slaps over my mouth as a shout of laughter leaves my lips.

ASH OUR ALMIGHTY LEADER:

> I'm her husband, dickhead *middle finger emoji*

I feel a small tap on my shoulder, and I tear my eyes away from the screen to look up at a beaming Mai.

"We probably should be heading back, it looks like it might rain," she tells me kindly, and I look up to see dark clouds beginning to cover the blue sky. I did not miss the changeable British weather when I was in Colorado.

LILLY SEXY AF BABY MAMA:

> Got to go, I'll text later. Love you all xxx

I pocket the phone before they can reply, otherwise, I'll never put it down, and with Mai on one side and Rowan on the other, we make our way back to the chair on the patio.

My pocket buzzes—I must turn the vibrate feature off just in case —and a warm glow fills my being at the lifeline that I've been given, the connection to my guys the best kind of feeling.

L ater that night, after a delicious dinner of creamy pasta that Mai cooked and brought up, I snuggle into bed with my new phone in my hands under the duvet, the screen's brightness turned low as it will go. I still suspect that my uncle has a camera in here somewhere, watching me, and although he's not visited me since that awful night, I'd rather not give him any reason to. Or lead to the discovery of my new phone.

The screen lights up with a message from Kai outside of the group chat.

KAI:

Having trouble sleeping, darling?

LILLY:

How did you know?

I narrow my eyes at the screen while those little bubbles tell me he's writing.

KAI:

There's a camera in your room…

I fucking knew it! My heart races as I poke my head up, looking again to see if I can spot it. The screen flares just before it was about to black out.

KAI:

Don't worry, darling. I've looped the feed so that it only shows your uncle you sleeping at night, and then doing your usual routine during the day.

A breath of relief whooshes out of me, my fingers tingling as I type my reply, not bothering to hide my phone.

LILLY:

> What can you see?

Those damn bubbles are back, and for reasons unknown I hold my breath, waiting for his response.

KAI:

> You...in bed...

KAI:

> Wearing too many clothes...

I slowly release my breath as tingles race over my skin.

LILLY:

> I can't exactly sleep naked, especially with Roman in the corner...

A moment later I hear shuffling, then my door opening as I look up to see Roman leaving the room, closing the door softly behind him. One of the brothers has been taking the night shift in here with me, and I've been sleeping better knowing that I'm watched over. I feel better now knowing that Kai has his eyes on me too.

KAI:

> Problem solved, Pet...

A shiver runs down my spine at the nickname. Laying down the phone on the pillow beside my head, I slowly, teasingly, push the thick duvet down my body, kicking it to the end of the bed with my bare feet.

KAI:

> Good girl, now that nightgown.

Sitting up, I gather the garment up and pull it over the top of my head, dropping it to the bed beside me. My nipples harden in the cool air, my breath leaving my body in a shaky exhale. The phone lights up, the group chat flashing up this time.

ASH OUR ALMIGHTY LEADER:

> What are you up to, Princess?

Both nicknames bring a smile to my lips. Another message from Kai pops up outside of the group chat.

KAI:

> Prop yourself up on your pillows, Pet, legs open.

A sense of breathlessness overcomes me as I get into position, my pulse becoming fast.

LOKI YOUR FAVOURITE BOYFRIEND THORN:

> Naughty, Pretty Girl, giving us a show like such a good little slut.

I lick my dry lips, waiting for Kai's next instruction, my eyes glued to the screen.

KAI:

> Such a clever, beautiful girl. Now, suck your fingers, two should be enough.

I do as he commands, bringing my slightly trembling pointer and middle fingers of my right hand to my mouth, pushing them slowly in. There's something so exciting about knowing that I'm being watched by my guys, but not where the camera is or being able to watch them in return.

KAI:

That's it, Pet, make them all nice and wet.

My muscles relax as a smile pulls my lips upwards, my fingers popping out of my mouth, glistening with my saliva.

JAX WEAPON OF MASS DESTRUCTION
GRIFFITHS:

Baby Girl...fuck you're killing me here...

I can't resist one long lick up the side of my finger, swirling my tongue around the top just as I've done countless times to their hard cocks, hoping that they remember the move too.

KAI:

Take them to that beautiful wet cunt of yours, Pet. Rub your clit nice and slow for me.

I do as instructed, trailing my fingers down the centre of my body, coming round the side of my swollen stomach, using touch to locate my pussy. At this stage, I can no longer see it if I look down, but my fingers find it easily enough, and just as Kai described, it's already slick with my excitement.

A heady moan leaves my lips at the first touch, pleasure zinging over my body when my fingers make contact with my engorged bud. The phone lights up beside me, and I turn hooded eyes to read the message.

ASH OUR ALMIGHTY LEADER:

You are a fucking goddess, wife. I'm as hard as stone for you right now, Princess.

Using my other hand, a little awkwardly, I type out a reply.

LILLY SEXY AF BABY MAMA:

> Grip your dicks hard for me, pretend it's my hand wrapped around them.

JAX WEAPON OF MASS DESTRUCTION GRIFFITHS:

> Shit, baby…that feels so fucking good.

My fingers move faster on my nub, imagining my Knights tugging and pulling at their hard cocks, and trying to pretend it's one of them playing with my body.

KAI:

> Dirty Pet, getting so worked up over their filthy words. I'll have to get Ash to spank you again when you're home.

The ache that's permanently in my chest flares at the mention of home, but I shove it down, focusing back on the electric pulses that are starting to shoot from my core.

KAI:

> I would do such dirty, terrible things to your body, Pet. Indulge all of your darkest fantasies, and play with all of your fears until you don't know whether to beg me to stop or keep going.

Heat flushes over my entire body as I read his words, my other hand reaching down to my aching breast and squeezing it. A gasp falls from my lips, my teeth sinking into the bottom one as I bring my fingers down to my opening and thrust them inside myself, fucking my hand hard and fast.

The phone lights up on the pillow next to me, and I have to open my cracked eyes wider to read the message.

LOKI YOUR FAVOURITE BOYFRIEND THORN:

> That's it, baby. Fuck your hand like you would my cock. I wanna see you come all over yourself.

I feel myself getting higher and higher, the pleasure almost too unbearable after so long without it. I've been craving a release, needing to rid myself of this pent-up energy and frustration that being incarcerated has left me with.

Adding a third finger and closing my eyes, I call to mind four pairs of hands on me, gliding over and inside my body as I grind down on my fingers. I give into the intense feelings racing over my skin, uncaring as cries leave my lips with abandon.

Feeling myself reach the cliff's edge, I pull my fingers out, hitting my G-spot on the way as an orgasm rips through me and sends me into the stratosphere. Wetness coats my hand and the bed beneath me as I writhe, letting the stars fill my eyes and waves of exquisite torture run through and over me, leaving me gasping.

Lying back, relaxing completely into the mound of pillows behind me, I let my breathing slow, languidly looking over at the phone to see several messages in the group chat.

ASH OUR ALMIGHTY LEADER:

> That was perfection. You are perfection, Princess x

KAI EVIL GENIUS MATTHEWS:

> Such a good little Pet x

JAX WEAPON OF MASS DESTRUCTION GRIFFITHS:

> Fuck, Baby Girl. you are so fucking beautiful when you cum x

LOKI YOUR FAVOURITE BOYFRIEND THORN:

> *eggplant emoji**three drops emoji*

I chuckle at Kai, messaging the group as if he didn't orchestrate the whole thing like a conductor.

LILLY SEXY AF BABY MAMA:

> Show me. I wanna see what I do to you all.

An influx of picture messages arrives a moment later. Toned abs glistening with cum and still hard dicks that make my mouth water.

LILLY SEXY AF BABY MAMA:

> Soon, I'll lick it all off. Every. Last. Fucking. Drop.

It takes a couple of moments, but a reply lights up the screen moments later.

LOKI YOUR FAVOURITE BOYFRIEND THORN:

> Fuck, Pretty Girl! I'll hold you to that *purple devil emoji*

I get up on only slightly shaking legs, smirking at the power that I'd forgotten I wield when it comes to these guys. It goes some ways to soothing my feeling of entrapment, of vulnerability, and being completely out of control at the moment.

Gathering the now wet sheets, I leave them in a pile, rooting through the drawers until I find fresh ones. I put them on the bed, and then head to the bathroom to get cleaned up.

Eight days left.

Just over a week until it will be their fingers inside me, their cocks I come all over.

My unborn child gives a strong kick, my hand flying to rest over the spot and feel the push of a foot or elbow.

Soon, love. We'll be with them soon, I swear.

CHAPTER SEVEN

LILLY

The next week passes by in excruciating torture, the days growing warmer now that we're nearing the height of the English summer. Sure, we still get a couple of dull, rainy days—this is Britain after all—but on the whole, we are blessed with blue, cloudless skies, a complete juxtaposition to the twisting storm that's spiralling inside me.

This nauseating mix of hope and despair swirls in my stomach like curdled milk; knowing that my time being held captive here is coming to an end, but that it won't be without bloodshed. I'm hoping that it'll be just my uncle's life-force staining the walls, but there's always the chance that someone I care about will be caught in the crossfire.

I manage to message the guys every day, and even a few whispered FaceTime calls late at night, Roman and Rowan leaving the room to allow us to talk in privacy. I find seeing my guys heartbreaking and comforting in equal measure. Feeling so close, yet so far away, leaves my soul keening when we hang up and I'm returned to my isolation.

The day of reckoning arrives, another beautiful, clear morning with the dawn chorus serenading the sparkling dew on the clipped lawns surrounding the house. I was ready before Mai even got here, my mind restless and unable to settle into a deep sleep last night, regardless of how tired my body was.

"Can we go outside?" I beg, and she laughs at my widened, pleading eyes.

"Sure, I mean, it's like seven in the morning, but what the hell!"

I grab her arm, almost causing her to drop my tray of granola and fresh juice.

"You must eat first," she orders, her voice stern yet a smile teasing her mouth. "Then we can go."

"Fiiine!" I pout, letting her arm go and rushing over to the table in front of the window where I take all my meals.

After a rushed shovelling of cereal in my gob, I'm practically hopping on my feet as I drag her to the doorway, a chuckle escaping her whilst she opens the door. Unlike Jacky, she's never locked it. The freedom the unlocked door offered was an illusion and one that I just couldn't force myself to fall for. My uncle could be around every corner, every turn, and I can't let him know that Mai is on my side. Plus, I don't want to face that jizzcheese wanker anytime soon, even with one of the twins by my side.

I questioned her about the other midwife, desperate to know if she was party to my uncle's plot, but as far as Mai knows, Jacky was told that I was a danger to myself and my unborn child due to 'mental instability,' hence the need for sedation and monitoring. Mai knows this because she was told the same, my uncle not realising that she was connected to The Shadows and put into place by my Knights.

Mai also told me that the drug I'd been given is a type of strong antihistamine, and it's basically an antihistamine that, if given in high enough doses, can cause nightmares, dizzy spells, plus feeling tired all the time and unsteady on your feet. It's used for insomnia, hence my tendency to knock out after I've eaten the drugged food. Luckily, it's perfectly fine for pregnancy. The overwhelming relief I felt that my baby hadn't been harmed was staggering, my whole body sagging with the weight that was lifted from my shoulders.

The damned wheelchair waits by the door, parked up against the wall like a silent spectator, waiting for my downfall. With a cursory glance, I stride past it, deciding that today I will remain on my feet. After all, I no longer need to keep up any kind of pretence that I'm weak. I want to be ready for when my guys come, to show them how strong I am.

Especially as when I suggested that I could try and escape sooner without them, they wouldn't hear of it, Ash ordering me to remain where I was or face dire consequences. *Arsegobbler.*

I was tempted to disobey, but when Loki mentioned the pregnancy and the possible harm the baby could come under were I to be caught, not to mention the stress involved, I relented. I can't jeopardise the life and health of our unborn child, not for my own pride.

"Are we..." Mai starts, indicating the wheelchair behind us with her hand as I head towards the stairs.

"We don't need it today," I calmly inform her, pausing at the top step and gazing into her kind eyes. "I won't need it ever again after today."

Her eyes widen a fraction, realising what I'm saying, then she pulls me into a tight hug.

"I'll stay with you the whole time, and afterwards. Make sure you and baby are okay and well," she whispers into my ear.

I cling back just as tight, tears pricking my eyes, soaking in her support and letting it shore me up for the trial ahead. It means so much to have her with me, beside me. I know that she can handle it, she's told me a little of growing up in The Shadows before Hunter paid for her to go to med school and train to be a midwife several years ago. She said that she owes him a debt, and not just in terms of money, but he refuses to let her pay a penny back, stating that knowing that she's 'out of the life' is more than enough. And this is the only time he's ever asked anything of her in return, and even then he gave her a choice.

Even though we spend a good portion of the day outside, having a picnic lunch on the lawn that Mai prepares, the day drags unbearably slowly, time mocking me with each tick of the clock in the main hall. Taunting me from afar. Eventually, after I've bitten my nails down to the quick, Mai suggests that we head inside and that I try to rest.

It's so frustrating not knowing exactly what's going to happen. Or even when they're going to get here, and I feel like a child waiting for their parents to return home after a trip spent apart, desperate to see them again, full of barely contained excitement. The guys refused to tell me the whole plan just in case something had to change, and I think because they didn't want me to worry about anything. But what they don't realise is that not knowing worries me more, and fills me with edgy anxiety until I'm ready to burst.

Once we're in my room, I find it almost impossible to settle, sitting at the chair then getting up almost immediately to pace over to the bed and back again.

"Lilly…" Mai scolds from her seat in one of the chairs by the window, and I pause, wringing my hands and drawing my bottom lip under my teeth. "This won't make them come any faster, you know."

I hear Loki's snort in my head at her word—*bloody, filthy-minded bastard!*—and I know that she's right, but the tension coiled up inside me refuses to be quietened.

Standing there, I look out of the window at the beautiful landscape that surrounds us; the trees swaying gently in a soft summer breeze, the sound of birds chirping as we move closer towards evening even though the sun is still pretty high in the sky. Taking deep, even breaths, I allow myself to soak in the beauty, the majesty of nature. The world keeps turning, regardless of what happens today, and we must accept that nothing will stop that. Life will go on.

My baby gives a small movement, my warm palm coming to my stomach over the floral maxi dress that I'm wearing today. Perhaps not the most practical attire for escape, but it makes me feel good and is really comfy, so I refuse to change out of it and my flip-flops.

Just as the sun sets below the horizon, I hear the opening strains of *'Ride of the Valkyries'* by Wagner fill the room, the entire mansion seeming to vibrate with the sounds of the violin strings.

"What the fuck…" I trail off as the wardrobe starts to rock violently, my heart beating faster with each tilt. Mai rushes to my side, pushing me slightly behind her as the piece of furniture comes crashing down with an almighty boom, the floor trembling and a couple of pictures falling off the wall, landing with a smash of glass.

Two black-clad figures emerge from the darkness as the music builds to a crescendo, and my heart stills in my chest as they look straight at me. A fallen angel with hair of fire and a Viking with piercing, blue eyes.

"Hey, Pretty Girl," Loki whispers, and I'm not even sure if I hear him over the music or if his voice sounds in my head, but the low sensual sound of it races across my skin, setting me alight and leaving me breathless.

"Baby," Jax rumbles, his deep timbre stroking my soul and wrapping me up in smoky notes, cutting through the music.

"You could have just used the door, fucking heathens," a familiar drawl sounds from across the room, and my head snaps in that direction as two more black-clad figures enter the room.

Grey eyes lock on mine, and before I can say a word, think a single thought, Ash leaps onto and over the bed in a feline move, gently pushes Mai to one side, grabs my face in both his palms and slams his lips onto mine.

His kiss is devastating, full of pent-up longing and desperate sorrow. Each stroke of his skilled tongue is begging for my forgiveness, every caress of his lips a declaration to never let me out of his sight again. I return his embrace, trying to breathe him in, absorb every part of him into my own being.

My fingers clench into his T-shirt, my cuticles ripping with a sharp sting against the webbing that seems to cover parts of him, no doubt holding weapons. But I don't care. It's been so long, too fucking long since I've been in my husband's arms.

He pulls back, albeit reluctantly, his grip on my face still firm as his eyes trace over my features, drinking me in like a dying man.

"Hello, wife," he murmurs, his voice thick with emotion. He swallows hard, his Adam's apple bobbing. "Fuck, I missed you, Princess," he confesses reverently, dipping his head once more to rub my nose with his in a gesture so heartbreakingly sweet that tears fall down my cheeks.

"Hello, husband," I choke out, holding him to me for another moment, knowing that it won't be enough. It'll never be enough.

But my soul needs to feel the others with my own hands and lips to know that they're real. As if sensing the direction of my thoughts, Ash lets me go, his hands slipping down my face when he steps aside to reveal Kai.

"Darling. God, you are a sight for sore eyes," he says, his gaze devouring me as he steps into Ash's space and engulfs me in his fresh, woodsy scent. His fingertips brush my cheek, coming away glistening with my tears, and he pops the digits into his mouth, tasting my overwhelming happiness leaving tracks down my face.

"Kai," I can't think of a single thing to say, my entire being thrumming with his nearness after being away from them all for so long.

"It's okay, love, we're here now, and it'll all be okay," he assures me, eliminating any space between us, his hand tangling in my hair and angling my face as he kisses my trembling lips.

Like Ash's kiss, there is sorrow and regret in Kai's, but also a deep possession and assurance that lends credence to his words of moments ago. His lips and tongue tell me that he, they, will keep me safe, and never again will I have to endure this horror. My tongue matches his, our movements in perfect synchronicity as we relearn what each other tastes like.

The embrace ends with a bittersweet final peck of lips, and Kai steps away with a deep breath, letting Jax take his place.

My protective Viking wastes no time on sweet words or gestures, his huge hand wrapping round my throat and pulling me to him, crushing his lips to mine with the same force that he undoubtedly pushed the wardrobe over. He decimates me with tongue, teeth, and lips, punishing me for my absence, then soothing me a second later as his other hand gently strokes the side of my rounded stomach.

As if in reproach of his barbaric behaviour, the baby gives his palm a vicious kick, and Jax's mouth abruptly leaves mine, a dark, pride-filled smirk on his lips.

"I will fucking chain you to my bed if I have to, Baby Girl, but you are never to leave us again. Got it?" he growls at me, and I can't stop the visceral reaction I have at the sound of his voice and his words. It's fucked up, but my cunt clenches at the raw dominance coming off him in waves, and he fucking knows it as his smile gets wider, flashing me his pearly whites in what might be considered a snarl. "Good girl."

He too steps to the side, releasing my throat, and my eyes land on the perfect beauty of my trickster. But unlike the others, Loki stays back a few steps, avoiding my seeking gaze.

"Loki?" I question, advancing towards him on unsure steps, coldness suffusing my limbs as I worry about what might be causing this strange behaviour. Stepping right up to him, I can feel the tension vibrating in his body, his muscles twitching. "Hey, what's wrong?" I reach out, cupping his strong jaw in my palm and turning him to face me. I startle when I see his eyes swimming, his face a mask of tortured pain that cracks my fragile heart clean in two. "Talk to me, my love. Tell me what's wrong, please?"

His head drops, then slowly rises as the breath rushes out of his chest. His emerald eyes study me, cataloguing all that has changed over the past five weeks. His jaw tightens as he undoubtedly notes the slight gauntness that I still have from all the meals I missed when I was in a drug-induced sleep, the purple bruises under my eyes from the sleepless nights, all those times that my nightmares consumed me, nightmares that may have been more real than I knew.

"Fuck, baby, I'm so fucking sorry...I—" he cuts himself off, his voice cracking, full of rage and self-loathing, his upper lip curling upwards. "I shouldn't have left you that night."

My own chest empties as the breath leaves me at his confession.

"Loki, no, none of this is your fault. None of it," I tell him firmly, my eyebrows dipped as I will him to accept my words for the simple truth that they are.

Before he can argue further, and I see the reply about to leave those lush lips of his, I brace my other hand on his firm chest, lifting myself up onto tiptoes, and press my own mouth to his. My eyes close as the sweetness that is Loki Thorn rushes over me. He freezes for a millisecond, then with a panty-destroying groan, he wraps his arms around me, pulling me tight into his hard body as he kisses me back. His tongue seeks forgiveness that I readily give, and I willingly drown in his vanilla scent, needing him with a desperation that rivals my need to breathe.

Our kiss is interrupted by the crackling of a radio, Roman's voice sounding in the now silent room, their epic entrance song having finished at some point during our reunion.

"The dirty rat has been trapped in the library, Conrad. I repeat, the dirty rat has been trapped in the library. Over and out."

"I'm destined to spend my days surrounded by fucking imbeciles," I hear Ash grumble, and a giggle escapes my lips.

"Come on, Pretty Girl," Loki tells me, turning and slinging an arm over my shoulders. There's still a look of haunting guilt in his eyes, and I've the feeling that it'll take a while for that to vanish completely. "Time to skin ourselves a rodent. I made a playlist especially for the occasion."

"Of course you did," I respond with a chuckle, and a fissure of adrenaline rushes through my body at the fact that I'm being included in what they have planned. There's no hesitation in him, no protest from any of them as Loki guides me down the small gap between the fallen wardrobe at the end of my bed towards the door.

I look behind me as we exit the room, the others and Mai following us as we head towards the stairs. Catching Ash's eye, he gives me a small nod, an affirmation that he believes in me and my ability to cope with what lies ahead. I also like to think that he recognises my thirst for vengeance.

I stride down the stairs, one Knight beside me with three others following behind, my steps sure and steady. I look inside myself and realise that I, too, don't falter, don't pause at what is undoubtedly about to be a very bloody end for my uncle.

A smile that is most likely quite terrifying in its peaceful serenity tugs up my lips as I reach the bottom step, knowing that my only living relative will not see another sunrise. The thought fills me not with horror, but with grim satisfaction, and with a sense that justice will be served in my name once more to a monster, doled out by monsters much bigger and more frightening than he is.

Not for the first time, I know that I am one of them.

And damn proud of it too.

CHAPTER EIGHT

LILLY

We enter the library as a group, Mai heading off after the guys told her that she needed to leave and there was someone from The Shadows waiting to escort her home. She was pissed and didn't want to leave me, but once the boys assured her that I would be looked after and no harm would come to me, she reluctantly left saying that I'd hear from her tomorrow.

The soft glow of the lit wall sconces is the only light in the vast space, the heavy curtains drawn over the huge windows so the rest of the room is in shadow, and there's a solitary, high-backed wooden chair in the centre of the room. In the chair is my uncle, bound with cable ties cutting into his wrists and ankles, tying him to the arms and legs of the piece of furniture. It's a beautiful piece, all carved wood and looks antique, the triangular back reaching above his head and making it look more like a throne than an ordinary seat. A throne of death perhaps.

His eyes widen when he sees our group, and he thrashes around, his cries muffled by the piece of gaffer tape that covers his mouth.

Two shadows push off from the wall, making my heart thrash a little in my chest until the Kent twins' faces are revealed, dressed in their usual black and with matching, maniacal grins across their faces. A third shadow disentangles itself from the corner, the hulking figure making his way towards us.

He, too, is dressed fully in black, tactical gear, his body stacked, giving even Jax a run for his money in terms of bulk. His dark blond hair is cut short to his head, his jaw square like a Disney prince. But the darkness that swirls in his green eyes leaves me sinking further into Loki's embrace, his arm tightening around me as the man comes closer. And he really is a man, older than the twins by maybe a couple of years if the lines etched around his dark eyes are any indicator.

"Hunter," Ash's deep voice sounds in the room, Jax and Kai coming to stand on either side of Loki and I, framing us. Ash moves just a little in front of me, giving his protection too.

"Asher," Hunter replies, his own voice as cavernous as the endless caves that can be found in nature. The ones that people disappear into and are never seen again.

The boys clasp hands and exchange a firm handshake, clearly testing each other's mettle. Hunter gives Ash a half smile and nods, slapping him on the back as if he'd passed some sort of test. He then leans to the side, letting go of Ash's hand and ensnaring me in his piercing gaze.

"This is the pixie that's caused so much trouble, huh?" he teases, and I realise that he has Willow's smile. This must be *the* Hunter, Willow's brother. The boys tense round me, Jax issuing a growl that does inappropriate things to Her Vagisty given the current situation. "Calm yourselves, boys, I'm only teasing," he tells them, his tone light and unafraid. "My sister speaks very highly of you, Lilly Vanderbilt. Tells me you helped her out over there, over some cunt called Amber."

"That's right, Willow is my best bitch, and we look out for each other," I tell him, deadly serious and hoping he sees how much his sister means to me too. He gives me a nod.

"You have The Shadows' protection for life," he tells me, voice full of a heavy gravity, and by the way the guys take an inhale around me, I know that this is a big deal.

"Thank you," I whisper back, realising that I have more chosen family around me than I ever realised.

"Family takes care of itself, pixie girl," Roman tells me, giving a sly wink that makes Loki bristle.

"Speaking of..." Hunter interrupts with a roll of his eyes at the mischievous twin, turning to gesture with an outstretched arm at my uncle. I swear the room gets colder by several degrees as my guys swing their gazes towards him, tied up and helpless.

Anger burns in my veins at how helpless I was when I first came here, when he was drugging me and sneaking into my room at night. I can feel my expression tightening, my body tensing as I look at the man before us, usually so put together and suave. He's wearing silk pyjamas, his hair a mess, and his face red as he tries in vain to free himself from his bindings. I smirk when I see his still puffy nose, a strip of tape over the bridge of it and bruising along each side and under his eyes.

"Nice work, Baby Girl," Jax praises from beside me, and I preen at the attention.

Rowan strolls up to him, casually grabbing an edge of the tape and ripping it off with a sound that reverberates around the huge room.

"I should have known it was you fucking boys, especially Julian's spawn, behind all this!" he spits out, still tugging at his bindings. "Julian won't stand for this, you little shits! He'll have your balls for hurting me!"

"What Julian will, or will not stand for is not your concern," Ash tells him, tilting his head to the side and studying the man as one might an insect you are about to dissect. "What is your concern, however, is how you might be of use to us so that we don't end your miserable existence in the most painful of ways right now."

"Fuck you, Vanderbilt! I don't fucking answer to you! Or your father!" Adrian screams, spitting at Ash. The globule doesn't even come close, yet Ash's lip still curls in disgust. Ash heaves a great sigh, as if this is all just so tiresome, and I watch with bated breath as he lazily strolls towards Adrian.

"This can go one of two ways, you know," he tells my uncle, voice bored as he inspects his nails. "You can answer our questions in full, thus helping yourself. Or you can resist."

"I hope he resists, don't you, Pretty Girl?" Loki asks me, loud enough for Adrian to hear and squirm more. Loki's body thrums next to mine, full of pent-up energy. "It's always so much more fun when they do."

I look up into his shining, green eyes, twinkling like jewels in the lamp light, and see an evil smile sitting on his face as he gazes hungrily at my uncle. And I'm not afraid like I might have been once upon a time. I look at each of my Knights in turn, all of them with a matching hunger in their eyes, a need to dish out vengeance on this man who has wronged me.

"I'm not going to tell you shit, boy," Adrian snarls, his confident smile wavering slightly at what he must see on Ash's face. I can't see, as my darkest Knight's back is to me, but I can imagine that it must be terrifying if my uncle's expression is anything to go by.

"I was hoping you might say that," Ash's voice sends chills across my skin, his words a promise of pain, and I shiver with how much I enjoy the sound. "Jax."

My Viking steps forward, sparing me a quick glance and a devastating smile that leaves my stomach full of butterflies. Without any preamble, he draws his fist back and punches Adrian square in the face, snapping his head to the side and drops of red spraying across the floor. I wince when I hear the crack of bone as presumably, his nose breaks again.

"That was for being a fucked up pervert and for sexually

assaulting your own daughter!" Jax screams in a guttural roar, his whole body shaking, his huge neck corded.

"Wait, what?" I stumble out, my mouth falling open. All the boys freeze, turning towards me with looks of regret on their faces. Kai steps in front of me, cupping my face in his warm palms, and I can't help leaning into his touch.

"Adrian isn't your uncle, darling. He's your father. We believe that your mother wasn't called Laura Darling, but Violet Rochester, and that she was carrying Adrian's child when she ran from him," he tells me softly, trying to soften the blow with the caress of his thumbs.

"Fucking worthless whore that she was!" my un-father-Adrian scoffs, his voice thick and a little muffled. "Couldn't even get knocked up properly, not for lack of trying on my part." I look past Kai to see Adrian's deceptively handsome face, the monster underneath finally showing in the swelling on one side with blood dripping down his chin. "You boys think you know everything! Well, I'll tell you one thing. That good-for-nothing slut got herself knocked up with some other cunt's baby. Lilly is no more my daughter than she's my niece. The paternity test last year proved that."

He looks at me, his lip curled in a sneer as my world tilts on its axis, and I try to process the information that I've just been given.

"Why take me in then?" I question, Loki's grip tightening round my shoulders as Kai keeps his hands on my face even when he steps aside slightly, both lending me their strength. "If we're not related, why pretend that we are?"

"That's the billion dollar question now, isn't it, little whore?" He smirks, his head whipping to the side again as Jax delivers another punishing blow.

"Don't you even look at her, you fucking piece of shit!" Jax barks, grabbing a fistful of Adrian's dark hair and pulling his head back, snarling right in his face.

"Shit!" Loki exclaims next to me, dropping his arm from around me and fumbling in his pocket. My heart hammers in panic, my head whipping round to face him, Kai's grip dropping from me as well.

"What?" I ask, voice breathy and high, my pulse pounding. He brandishes his phone triumphantly.

"Almost forgot the playlist! That really would have been a disaster," he responds, the sound of another fist hitting flesh loud in the room. It's so utterly ridiculous that a giggle escapes my lips, my hand flying to cover them as the tension feels like it drains from the room. "That's the spirit, Pretty Girl!" Loki beams, scrolling, and in the next second *American Boy* by Estelle and Kanye West starts blaring from speakers hidden somewhere in the room, drowning out the sounds of the beating that Jax is currently issuing. "Dance with me!" Loki shouts, grabbing my hand, twirling me so that my back is to his front, and pulling me to him.

He moves us as I outright laugh, his hips gyrating with the beat and letting me know how happy he's feeling right now.

"Loki, you are incorrigible!" I gasp out, his hands bringing my own up and draping them over his neck behind me. I glance over to see Jax hit my–Adrian again, and what looks like a tooth flies from his mouth, skittering along the polished wooden floor.

"Talk dirty like that again, baby, and I'll show you the meaning of the word," Loki whispers in my ear, shivers making my nipples harden which is so many shades of inappropriate it's unreal. "Kai, join us!"

I look up to see Kai step back in front of me, a sexy smile fixed on his face as he moves in as close as my bump will allow. His palms trace the roundness, his hips moving to the beat as we dance while Ash watches on with a softness in his eyes. Jax pauses in his beating to look over, a rare smile lifting his lips when he sees us dancing. The twins and Hunter are standing in the shadows, the latter stoic as he watches us, the former bobbing their heads to the beat. I knew they were our kind of people.

"You are all fucking insane!" Adrian shouts, his voice clear during a lull in the song. Loki doesn't pause or falter, spinning me so that my back is to Kai, who presses his own hips snugly into my arse, his arousal grinding up against me.

"All the best people are!" I call back, laughing as the boys spin me between them until the song ends.

"Ready to answer some questions?" Ash inquires, bending over slightly as Jax uses his grip on the top of Adrian's head to lift his drooping head up to face Ash. The older man's face is a bloody mess, his eyes almost swollen shut, and ruby red liquid drips from his nose and lips.

"Fuck you, Vanderbilt," Adrian rasps out in a pained mumble, spitting blood into Ash's face. My husband doesn't react, and from my position, I see a terrifying grin spread across his face before he straightens up and turns to face me.

"I made you a promise, wife," he tells me, accepting something from Rowan. He holds them up for us all to see, the blades of the secateurs glinting, and Adrian gives a pained groan, but clearly no longer has the strength to fight his bindings anymore. Ash turns to him. "I promised my wife here that I would cut each and every one of your fingers off for daring to touch her."

Adrian finds some strength to begin his struggle, but it's futile, the cable ties too tight and numerous to allow him much movement. His first scream is cut off by a new song blaring over the speakers, *Bodies* by Bryce Fox filling the room with the strains of a guitar and the beat.

I watch as Loki engulfs me from behind, his vanilla musk mixing with Kai's fresh, woodsy scent as the latter wraps an arm around my waist from the side. I expect to feel sick, to feel something apart from a detached sense of numbness whilst watching Ash cut off all the fingers on one hand with the bolt cutters, each one landing at his feet.

But I watch Adrian's vain struggles with a sick satisfaction running through my veins, enjoying the fact that his screams become more strained and gurgling as each digit falls. Ash pauses, and Jax holds something under Adrian's nose to wake him up after he loses consciousness. Ash makes a gesture, and Loki lowers the volume so that we can all hear the conversation about to take place.

"P–p–please..." Adrian whimpers, his voice so full of pain that I should feel remorse, but I don't. I feel nothing as I watch him twitch and shiver in front of us, knowing that he drugged me and touched me without my consent.

"You ready to confess your sins, Adrian Ramsey?" Ash interrogates, the secateurs dripping blood from their now red blades.

"Anything, yes, I'll answer your questions," Adrian murmurs, voice laced with agony.

"Why did you take Lilly?" Ash asks, tone hard and unforgiving. I step closer, Loki and Kai letting me go, then following along behind me. I move until I can see the dull light in Adrian's eyes as he answers.

"Julian wanted to punish her, and I offered to remove her for a time to teach her a lesson. But I was under strict orders not to harm the baby, in case it really is Julian's grandchild," he tells us, his chest heaving, his voice grating and raw.

"Why offer?" Kai interjects from beside me. "Why did you want to take her?"

Adrian traces his cracked lips with a bloody tongue just as the song changes to *Way Down We Go* by Kaleo.

"Because her mother stole something from me, and I was angry. Initially, I planned to just kill the girl, taking what was owed to me as her next of kin. But your fucking father had other ideas and married her off so that I could never get my hands on what belonged to me by rights!" His anger gives him strength, and he levels a venomous gaze at Ash, then moves to me. "It was too late to ever get my shares in the company back, especially after she cashed in the bonds and bought more shares, but I wanted to see you suffer for the sins of your whore mother."

Before I know what I'm doing, my hand snaps out and slaps him so hard across the face that my palm stings.

"Watch your mouth, or Ash will start on the other hand," I snarl, dark rage filling my veins at this man and all his revenge plans.

"Not quite like her then, too feisty," he comments dryly, teeth missing and blood running down his chin, and Loki holds me back from slapping him again as I step forward.

"Why drug me?" I ask, my voice cutting with my disgust at his actions. "How many nights did you climb into my bed, you fucking waste of oxygen?" I can feel my heart racing, my palms sweating at how angry I am that all this really had nothing to do with me.

"You look so much like her," he replies, his eyes softening, and bile rises to my throat, a sickening thought occurring to me.

"The outdated clothes...you tried to dress me like her?" The room spins, Loki and Kai's touch the only thing centering me and bringing me back to the library, and the disgusting creature in front of me.

"I loved her, in my own way, and she betrayed me, stealing from me and letting another man touch what was mine," he seethes, the anger towards my mother still fresh.

"How did Violet escape from you?" Ash interjects, and the question takes me somewhat by surprise, the name Violet still somehow not seeming to belong to Mum.

"I have no fucking idea. She had outside help. She drugged me, fucking bitch." I don't get time to step forward as Jax punches him in the chest, Adrian doubling over as much as his bindings will allow.

"Watch your mouth," my Viking tells him, my chest swelling at his defence of my mum even though he never knew her. Coughing and spitting out more blood, Adrian continues.

"For years I fucking searched for her, without even a whiff. And then, almost eighteen years after she disappeared, a contact saw an article in a London newspaper of a girl who he said looked eerily similar to my Violet." He stares right into my eyes, and though his own are mere slits as the skin around them is so puffy he can barely see, I feel the horrible truth sink in like a terminal disease.

A rushing noise like a fast-flowing river sounds in my ears as I'm transported to that fateful day, my mum clutching that very article that I tried to keep hidden, knowing that she'd be pissed. It all makes sense now, not being allowed any social media accounts, not even being allowed to be on anyone else's. My mum was hiding from this vile monster, and I led him right to our door.

"Pretty Girl?" Loki's voice penetrates the spiral that I'm tumbling down, dragging me back up and into the present again. "Talk to me, Lilly."

His arms band tight round me, and I blink to see Kai has once again blocked my view of Adrian, my face once again cupped in his palms.

"Whatever it is, it's not your fault, darling," he tells me, his serious tone willing me to believe his words.

"B–but it was me in that article, Kai. Even though I knew Mum would be mad, I agreed to do it anyway as I was so damn proud to have won that stupid writing competition. I—" My voice cracks as tears stream down my face, tasting like despair.

"Kai's right, baby," Loki whispers in my ear, nuzzling the side of my face. "It wasn't your fault this fucking freak couldn't let go."

I try to draw comfort from them, I really do. But I know that this sickening guilt will stay with me for many years to come.

"What happened next?" I ask as a thought occurs to me, not taking my eyes off Kai's comforting, amber ones, his thumbs brushing the tears from my face. "When you found Mum."

Adrian laughs, and the sound chills me to the bone. I just know that something awful is about to leave his mouth, but like a train crash, I am powerless to stop it.

"I found her in the kitchen. She thought that I was you, and started to apologise for your argument earlier. That must hurt, knowing that your last words to your own mother were in anger." I would stagger under the blow of his words if my two Knights weren't holding me up. Another muffled grunt sounds out, followed by another sound of flesh hitting flesh.

"Let him finish, Jax," I say, cold dread filling my body up until I'm numb. Kai holds my gaze, lending me what strength he can.

"She refused to tell me where the bonds were, told me that I'd never get my hands on them and that they belonged to you. I laughed at her. The pathetic, useless woman thought that she'd bested me. And then I took a kitchen knife and drove it into her body over and over again, watching the life drain out of her eyes."

My knees give way, the room changing once more to my old kitchen, covered in my mum's blood. A low keening noise sounds around me, and it takes me a moment to realise that it's coming from my lips as Loki holds me in a crumpled heap in his lap, Kai stroking my hair.

A scream cuts through my mourning, and I look through bleary eyes to see Ash cutting off all the fingers on Adrian's other hand, blood pumping from the severed digits. Jax blocks my view of the tortured man, the sound of ripping fabric loud over the broken, pained whimpers. Ash hands him the secateurs, and a second later a garbled animal shriek reverberates round the room, a lump of flesh hitting the floor at Jax's feet.

I watch with a sense of numbness as Jax steps back, revealing a gaping wound in Adrian's crotch. I should feel sick, but I feel nothing for this man, this monster who stole my mum's life long before he killed her. Ash hands Jax a small blowtorch next, and Jax lights it just as Ash wakes Adrian up with smelling salts.

Adrian's eyes widen, incoherent wails falling from his lips as Jax lowers the torch, the wails becoming more anguished as the sweet smell of cooking meat and burning fat fills the room. Bile rushes into my throat, threatening to spill over, but somehow I manage to hold onto the contents of my stomach, forcing myself to watch as justice is served.

What feels like an age later, Jax steps away, dropping the now unlit blowtorch and wiping his forehead with the back of his hand, leaving a bloody trail. He glances over to me still on the floor, his piercing gaze pained, refusing to meet mine.

"Jax?" I question, his stare finally meeting mine, but he doesn't move, doesn't come closer. "Help me up?" He takes a deep inhale, his nose wrinkling at the smell as if he's only just noticing it now. He still hesitates. "Please?"

Heaving a great sigh, he steps towards me, holding out a bloody hand for me to take once he reaches me. I grasp it, knowing that his hand is covered in the blood of my enemy. He added another black mark to his soul for me, and I love him for it, even as my soul hurts for him.

"Thank you, my love," I whisper once he's pulled me up to standing, and I place my other hand on his chest, his T-shirt damp with sweat and blood underneath my palm. Leaning in, I kiss him, worshipping my Knight in tarnished, bloody armour with tongue and lips. My protector and saviour deserves nothing less.

"I would do all this and more for you, Baby Girl. I'd burn the whole motherfucking world to the ground if you asked me to," he confesses against my tingling lips as we part, his free hand coming up to cup my face, the blood staining my skin.

"And I will always love you for it, no matter what you do," I whisper back, pulling away slightly so that he can see the truth in my eyes. "You belong to me, Jax Griffiths, and I belong to you."

The song changes and *Serial Killer* by Moncrieff & JUDGE breaks the heavy tension in the room.

"Fucking Loki," Jax mumbles, his lips tilted in a half smile at his friend's choice of music.

"What?" the man in question asks, bouncing up to us and throwing his arms round our shoulders. "It's the perfect song!"

We laugh, Kai and Ash joining in, and some of the heady tension in the room easing.

"You're all fucking crazy!" an inhuman-sounding rasp cuts through our mirth, and we all look over to see the mess that is Adrian Ramsey.

"All the best people are," I tell him once again, smiling at my collection of dark Knights, my monsters.

CHAPTER NINE

ASH

I glance over at Lilly, taking her in in all her majesty. She's a fucking goddess walking this Earth, looking over at that cunt with all the disgust a lady would look at the shit that dared to get on her shoe.

Her statement rings true down to my very soul. All the best people I know are in this room, including the Shadows lingering in the corner. And we're all as mad as hatters, psychos that delight in bloodshed, that thrive when the light leaves our victims' eyes.

I gesture for everyone to form a semicircle around the waste of space.

"Adrian Ramsey, you have been found guilty of being a murderer, a pervert, and a general waste of oxygen," I tell him, my voice grave with the edge of a sneer. I look up at the people surrounding me. "What punishment shall we give this monster?"

"Punishment?!" Adrian gasps, his voice that of a broken man, and my blood sings to hear it. It's been too long since I let my own inner demon out to play. "Haven't I suffered enough? You said there were two ways this could go! I told you what you wanted to hear," he babbles as snot, blood, and tears leak down his face. I'm actually kind of impressed that he's still with us. I guess shock is a great masker of pain.

I turn back to look at him, my face a blank mask of indifference.

"I lied."

"If I may make a suggestion?" one of the twins—Roman, I think —asks. I nod for him to continue, folding my arms to hear him out. "During the Troubles, in Ireland," he continues, eyes alight with fevered excitement, "traitors to The Cause were given a six pack. Six shots, one in each ankle, knee, and elbow."

My lips tilt upwards at the idea, liking the sound of it. Turning to the guys, I raise my brows in silent question.

"Sounds good to me," Loki answers, hand clasped in Lilly's.

"Me too," Kai adds from Loki's other side, turning back to look at Adrian with dark eyes. Adrian doesn't know how lucky he really is; if we'd let Kai loose on him, he'd be in much worse shape than he is now.

Jax grunts his approval, his big hand wrapped around Lilly's, Adrian's blood coating their hands.

"Princess?" I ask, looking directly at her and seeing that Jax has left a bloodied handprint on her cheek. It makes her look like an angel of death, and my dick stirs in my combat pants just seeing it there.

She gives a sharp nod, her beautiful, hazel eyes boring into mine with her own monster front and center, gazing out with approval.

Hunter steps forward, clicking the safety off of a handgun just as *Straitjacket* by Bohnes starts to play.

"Y–you can't do this, you fucking bastards!" Adrian seethes, his voice barely above a whisper and his movements slow and sluggish. "Julian won't stand for this!"

Hunter hands the gun to me, its weight a comforting familiarity in my hand.

"Ah, I'm afraid that's where you're wrong," I tell him, stepping up close and taking aim at his left elbow. "Julian will never know."

The sound of the shot is loud, no need for silencers when we're the only ones here. The twins made sure of that. A garbled cry leaves the older man's ravaged throat as he slumps in his seat. Jax immediately steps up and revives him with ammonia. I pass the gun to Hunter, who's stepped up on Adrian's other side. He knows the drill, we all have to have something at stake here. All have to be involved.

Another shot rings out when he shoots the right elbow, Adrian groaning and whining with the pain. Hunter passes the gun to Jax, who steps around and points it at Adrian's knee. I watch without flinching as another shot rings out, Kai taking Jax's place and shooting his other knee out. Loki is up next, coming to stand beside me and shooting out the now, almost unconscious man's ankle.

He goes to pass the gun back to me to finish the job, but a small, dainty hand reaches for it instead.

"Princess? You don't need to—" I start, but she cuts me off with a fierce look in her eyes.

"He took my mum's life long before he drove the knife into her body, Ash," she tells me, staring down at the gun as if it's an inevitability. "So yes, I do need to. Show me?"

The last is said with a thread of uncertainty, her eyes wide and pupils blown with the adrenaline no doubt coursing through her veins. I cannot deny her, now or ever. She owns me, body and pitch-black soul.

Stepping up behind her, I pull her in close until our bodies are flush. I can't help but nuzzle her hair with my nose, my fingers tightening on her hips.

"Focus, husband," she chastises, but I can hear the smile, and a small growl sounds in my throat at the term. I fucking love it when she calls me that.

I push my semi into her, thriving on the gasp that leaves her own lips when she feels me growing. Deciding to play with her a little more, I remove one hand from her hips, gliding it down her arm, goosebumps following in my wake. Wrapping her hand more firmly round the gun, I place my own on top of hers and use it to take aim at his other ankle.

"Such a good girl knowing not to put your finger on the trigger until you're absolutely ready," I praise, my breath tickling her ear, and I delight in the shudder that rocks her body. "Now place your finger on the trigger. Yes, that's it. Take a deep breath, let it slowly out, and pull when you're ready," I instruct, holding her aim straight so that it doesn't waver.

"P–please...Lilly..." the bastard whispers, and I look to see his eyes pleading with her, but my wife shows no mercy, ignoring him completely as she exhales and then pulls the trigger, just like I told her to. His ankle shatters, blood and bone flying from it. She doesn't flinch, just lowers her arm, taking her finger carefully off the trigger and letting me take the gun. I hand it back to Hunter, an unspoken trust passing between us. We are brothers in bloodshed now.

"Done like a pro, my love," I whisper, placing a soft kiss on her neck before letting her spin round and face me.

"What happens next? How will Julian not find out what happened here?" she questions, a cute as fuck frown marring her forehead.

"Now, we burn this shit to the motherfucking ground!" Loki crows, whooping like the fucking pyro that he is. A grin takes over my face before I can stop it, and I cast my glance down at Lilly to see how she's dealing with this.

"Where are the matches?" she asks, giving me the sexiest smile known to man that has my dick rock-hard in an instant.

Unable to hold back, I grab her face with my free hand and give her a bruising kiss, telling her how much I love her with my lips and every caress of my tongue. We break apart panting, the stinging smell of expensive brandy burning our nostrils as the guys smash bottles around the room, pouring it liberally on Adrian's prone form. He splutters awake, eyes unfocused as he tries to make sense of what's happening around him.

"Brandy?" Lilly questions as her nose twitches, and she turns to look around the room.

"The finest we could find in this dickhead's cellars," I tell her, slinging my arm across her shoulders and pulling her close. "And it's less suspicious than petrol."

She makes an impressed sound, her head bobbing, and my lips twitch to see her act surprised that we know what we're doing.

"Not our first arson, Pretty Girl," Loki tells her as he comes to stand with us, Kai, Hunter, and the twins following.

We all watch in silence as Jax picks up the blowtorch once more and lights it, flames racing across the books and curtains where the alcohol has seeped into them.

"I can't believe that you're burning all these innocent books," Lilly admonishes as we watch Jax make his way round the room setting the books and curtains alight, Adrian's futile attempts to escape boring by now. "Fucking heathens."

"Can't make an omelette without breaking a few eggs, pixie girl," one of the twins says with a grin, and I flash him a glower, which only makes him smile wider. *Fucker.*

We stand sentinel as Jax approaches the man in the chair, watching as the flames catch on the alcohol that was poured over him. His mouth opens in a soundless scream as he's engulfed in fire, and I feel nothing other than a swelling sense of satisfaction that he will no longer be alive to torment Lilly. That revenge has been enacted on behalf of her mother.

"Let's go," my wife says, my arm dropping as she turns around and walks towards the door.

We all follow her out, her Knights, her lovers, her soulmates.

CHAPTER TEN

LILLY

Wearily, we pile into two cars, me and the guys in one and the Shadows in another. I'm so tired, so strung out and bone weary that even the excitement of finally being reunited with my guys isn't enough to keep my eyes open. I fall asleep sandwiched between Ash and Loki, each one of my hands tangled with one of theirs.

I wake up a couple of hours later as we arrive outside a ware-house-type building next to the river Thames, the late night sounds of London filtering into my consciousness when a blast of cool air hits my face from an open door.

"Where are we?" I croak out, rubbing my gritty eyes then grimacing when dried blood flakes off my fingers.

"A safe place that no one else knows about," Ash tells me, pushing some of my hair back, his fingers trailing down my cheek and sending tingles racing across my skin.

I look around to see that it's quiet, although it appears that the other warehouses have been converted into apartments, much like the one before me. Ash helps me out of the car, and I lean on him as Kai leads us up the steps to the large, solid, wooden door.

"Who else lives here?" I question as he opens it, the door making no sound.

"Just us, Pretty Girl," Loki grins, taking my hand and pulling me away from Ash just as the place floods with soft light when Jax hits a touch panel on the wall.

The place is breathtaking, all exposed brick and wood and industrial metal, a mezzanine level creating an upstairs, with the downstairs completely open-plan. It feels light and airy, yet homely and cosy all at once, and huge windows look out over the Thames, lights twinkling on the opposite bank. I can spy a pool in a large courtyard on the other side of some glass doors. There's even a lawn and what looks like raised flower beds made from railway sleepers.

"I love it," I breathe out, feeling like this could be a place I settled. A home for us all. Although, I would miss the mountains of Colorado.

"We hoped that you would, darling," Kai tells me with a smile. "That's why we bought it." I beam back, a yawn quickly overtaking my smile. "Let's get you cleaned up and to bed. Would you like something to eat?"

My stomach chooses that moment to grumble loudly, and he huffs a laugh, kissing my hand and passing me over to Ash, who guides me towards the stairs. Suddenly, Ash sweeps me up into his arms, carrying me bridal style.

"Ash!" I yell, laughing as he proceeds to carry me up the metal and oak staircase.

"It's not quite a threshold, but it's better than nothing, right?" he queries with a tilt to his lips that leaves the butterflies in my stomach all aflutter.

We walk down the open corridor, and he takes me through a huge bedroom with an enormous bed up against one wall. I don't get to see much of it as we quickly enter the en suite, where Jax already has the shower running and is beautifully naked, washing off the blood from earlier. The water is tinged pink as it runs off him, but I feel no revulsion knowing where it came from and how it came to be splattered all over my Viking Knight. Loki is dressed only in sweats, placing a towel on the heated rail and he gives me a cheeky smile and wink when he notices me staring at Jax. My mind goes back to the first time that I met him back in the bathroom at Highgate and he helped me dry off. Fuck, that feels like forever ago, but it's been less than a year. Jesus, my life is crazy.

Here with Me by Susie Suh plays softly in the background as Ash sets me down, his hands going to my waist, well, what was my waist before I was pregnant. It seems to be disappearing somewhat. With gentle, worshipping hands that are covered in dried blood, he starts to strip me of my maxi dress, the stretchy fabric sliding down my shoulders and pooling on the ground around me. Knowing that these were clothes which Adrian bought for my pregnant mother sends a shiver across my skin, and I feel the tension release from my body as they fall off me.

Next goes my maternity bra, a cute, navy blue one with lace, and matching knickers until I'm standing naked, looking out of the huge window that takes up a whole wall and shows me the river. His fingers skate down my side, goosebumps following in their wake as he caresses my skin.

"I missed you so fucking much, Princess," he whispers in my ear, his breath tickling me and making my nipples harden. I let the sensations wash over me, pushing aside what happened at my uncle's house, just focusing on the here and now.

"Time for that later," Loki chuckles when I gasp as he takes my hand once more and pulls me away from Ash yet again. A growl sounds behind me, which makes Loki grin wider, but Ash lets me go, and I hear the sounds of him undressing too.

I step into the massive, glass shower, Jax turning round and giving me one of his half smiles as he takes my hand and pulls me under the blissfully hot spray. He steps in close, the heat from his body warming my back as a huge arm moves past me to grab the bottle of shower gel from the built-in shelf. Squeezing a generous amount into his hand, I am surrounded by his sweet lemon scent as he lathers up and proceeds to run his large palms all over my body, washing me from top to toe.

I groan and squirm when he bypasses where I really want him to go yet again, as he gets up from washing my feet from behind, not letting me turn round once.

"Jax..." I groan, my core desperate for touch, my skin alight and pulsing.

"Yes, Baby Girl?" he questions with what I can feel is a smirk against my shoulder. I hear another shower start and look beyond Jax to see Ash start to wash under another shower head on the opposite side of us. "You were saying?" Jax reminds me, and I push back into his front, his hard length pressing into my lower back.

"I need you, Jax. Please," I beg, not above pleading, the band of his arms not allowing me to turn fully and give him puppy dog eyes.

"I'm here, baby, I'll always be what you need," Jax whispers in my ear, his rinsed hand sliding around the swell of my stomach, his whole frame leaning over me as his fingers play with my damp, lower curls.

I grasp his forearms, and he glides a single thick digit between my slicked folds, finding my clit instantly and circling it teasingly. A deep moan falls from my lips at the heady pleasure as he plays with the nub, the feeling of his long-awaited touch almost bringing me to climax then and there.

"Jax...fuck, Jax..." I murmur, my eyes closing and his finger strumming a tune that I never want him to stop playing.

The swipe of a tongue on my pussy has my lids snapping open again, and I look down but my bloody baby bump stops me from seeing whose head it is. His fully tattooed back is clear, however, and I know that it's my husband, my dark Knight on his knees in front of me. Looking to the side, I see Loki watching us with heat in his emerald eyes, his image wavering in the droplets that drip down the glass. He's got his dick gripped in a tight fist, and I swallow hard at the sight of him pumping his hand up and down, the metal of his Prince Albert piercing glinting.

Ash opens my legs wider, and I lean on Jax as Ash's tongue dives inside my cunt, shooting stars flashing in front of my eyes as pleasure overtakes me with every stroke. Jax growls his appreciation as his finger moves faster on my nub, my breaths panting out of me as the tingles from their combined attention race all over my body.

It doesn't take long for my climax to detonate, and they hold me as I shatter into a thousand particles, crying out incoherently when the pleasure consumes me. I stay in Jax's arms, Ash's tongue making me twitch as he gives a final few licks before getting up. He looks at me with a fire turning the grey of his eyes molten, and a second later his lips are on mine, his tongue delving into my mouth.

The taste of my own release on his lips and tongue has me mewling and squirming once more, my fingers tangling in his wet locks and pulling him closer, trying to inhale his very essence.

We break apart slowly and reluctantly, his forehead pressing to mine as his solid member presses into my stomach. The baby gives an almighty kick, causing him to jerk back with a laugh.

"All right, I'll leave your mother alone," Ash murmurs, his hand coming to rest over the place where the kick was. "For now, anyway," he tells me, looking up with a wink, and I damn near swoon.

He turns around, shutting the shower off, and Jax unwinds himself from my back, helping me out of the shower where Loki waits with the biggest, fluffiest towel that's toasty and warm.

"Thanks, love," I tell him, my eyes darting down to see that his dick is back in his grey sweatpants and no longer looks hard.

"Don't worry, Pretty Girl," he assures me, "he'll be back later."

I laugh as he leads me out of the bathroom still wrapped in the towel, feeling a lightness inside myself that I've not felt in weeks.

LOKI

A piercing scream wakes me a few hours later, my heart racing as I bolt upright in bed.

Lilly struggles next to me, sheets tangled around her legs as she thrashes and whimpers, her head moving from side to side.

"Hey, Princess, shhhh," Ash whispers from her other side, his hand reaching out and stroking her face gently.

Another cry leaves her lips as she sits upright, her eyes wide like moons in the darkness. I can see her pulse beating a fast rhythm in her neck, her cheeks wet with tears that continue to fall down her face. She swallows, blinking, her eyes focusing on mine, and my heart shatters at the lost look in them.

"Loki?" she rasps, voice hoarse, and she coughs to clear her throat.

"I'm here, baby," I assure her softly, reaching out my own hand to brush the tears away. She flinches, and my hand stops, a lump forming in my throat. "You okay, Pretty Girl?" I ask, begging with my eyes for her to let me in.

"I–I'm fine, just a bit hot," she mumbles, awkwardly getting to her knees and crawling to the end of the bed.

"Lilly?" Kai questions from beside me, and I turn to see his forehead creased, his tired eyes dull with worry.

"I just need some air," she replies, getting out of bed and putting on one of Jax's shirts, the huge, black garment covering her completely, though her rounded stomach is starting to push the fabric out.

"Want some company, Baby Girl?" Jax asks from the other side of Ash, his voice thick with sleep and an undercurrent of concern.

"I'll be fine," she says, racing out of the door, not even turning to look back at us.

We all watch her leave the room, and there's a tightness in my chest, an uncomfortable feeling slithering over my skin. The feeling increases as *Panic Attack* by Liza Anne filters up from the speakers downstairs.

"Ash?" I inquire, biting my lip as my throat constricts.

"She just needs some time," Kai interrupts, ever the peacemaker, his hand stroking soothingly down my arm.

"She needs us," Jax growls out, and I glance at him in time to see him run a jerky hand through his long hair.

"Ash?" I repeat, looking to our leader to see what he thinks, needing his calm control as I can feel the edge of my world spinning out of control at the thought of losing her again.

He looks up at me, the grey swirling in his eyes, his brows pinched and neck tight.

"Let's do as Kai suggests and give her time. She needs to know we're here for her, but have the space to process what she's just been through." He sounds more confident by the end of his speech, though the way he swallows and looks down tells me that he's not a hundred-percent certain.

We all settle back down, my arm going to the gap that should be filled by our girl, the bed cool and no longer as inviting as it was when we all lay down together several hours ago.

CHAPTER ELEVEN

LILLY

The guys come down the next morning, looking clean yet anything but refreshed. My own eyes feel gritty and dry, my throat tight when I remember last night.

I woke up feeling suffocated, unsure where I was or who was in bed with me. I couldn't stand the heat from their bodies, something I've always found comforting but ever since that night when I awoke to my uncle getting into bed with me, knowing that he'd been doing it the whole time...

I look up, catching grey orbs full of concern. Ash's image wavers as moisture fills my own eyes.

"I—I'm so s–s–sorry, Ash," I whisper brokenly before burying my face in my hands. The sofa I'm lying on dips next to me as I'm gathered up, the achingly familiar scent of ginger filling my senses.

"Hey, there's no need to apologize, my love," he murmurs, his lips brushing against my tangled hair. "It's okay."

"It's not okay!" I wail, lowering my palms and catching piercing blue eyes as Jax crouches in front of me. "How is any of this okay?"

"It's not," he tells me, his deep voice a soothing balm to my hurting soul. "But we're here to look after you now, baby." He grasps my hands in his large ones, rubbing his thumbs over mine. My lip trembles as I try to contain my emotions.

"What happened last night, Pretty Girl?" Loki questions, the sofa on the other side of me dipping as he takes a seat, his hand rubbing my back.

I sigh, giving Kai a watery smile as he holds out a cup of pepper-mint tea, Jax releasing my hands so that I can take it. It's the perfect temperature, allowing me to wrap my fingers around the mug and absorb some of the comforting warmth.

"I had a bad dream I guess," I tell them, looking down at the surface of the tea, wishing that it held all the answers to the mael-strom that is my current mental health. "I woke up thinking...think-ing..." My voice chokes, the surface of the drink rippling as a tear drops into it.

"Thinking you were back there?" Ash questions, the vibrations of his voice calming my pounding heart.

"Yes," I answer quietly, brokenly. I take a deep breath and look up to meet kind, amber eyes full of warmth and love. "And that he was the one in the bed," I say, my eyelids falling shut with shame.

A soft brush of fingertips has them fluttering open again, Kai's face wavering as more tears spring to my eyes.

"I understand," he says softly, a haunted look entering his stare, and my throat tightens at this hateful thing we now have in common.

Carefully thrusting my mug at Jax, I launch myself at Kai and wrap my arms around his neck, sobs wracking my body as I cling to him. His own arms band around me, pulling me as tight as my preg-nancy will allow, and I feel wetness on my neck where his face is buried.

We cry together, the pain of the evil that exists in the world less-ening now that we have another to share it with, to understand how much it hurts, how dirty and tarnished you feel.

W e decide to stay in the apartment, snuggled together on the sofas until Mai arrives later in the afternoon to check on me and baby. She declares that everything is fine, but recommends an ultrasound scan as I missed my twenty-week one. Ash gets straight on the phone and books one for the following day on Harley Street, using his name to get the best paedi-atrician in the country to fit us into his busy schedule.

I feel a slight chill at the thought of having to deal with Julian, who no doubt will hear of my return soon enough. But for now, I decide to set it aside, enjoying this reprieve before we have to face reality again.

After Mai's visit, and with it being such a beautiful summer's day —*a rarity in England I can assure you!*—I feel the overwhelming urge to see what the pool is like and float in the water for a time.

Getting up from the sofa where we were all lounging, none of the guys follow me as I head to the glass doors, which are open, letting in the slight breeze and city noises that I find I've missed a little.

"Where you off to, Pretty Girl?" Loki asks lazily, and I spin round giving him a lopsided smile before whipping Jax's T-shirt over my head and shimming out of my yoga pants. The guys had bought me some of my clothes, placing them in the closet in our room.

"For a swim," I tell him, pulling my soft maternity bra off, and beaming as all four guys sit up straighter, heat brightening their eyes. This effect I have on them, their desire for me, is addictive and always sends tingles racing up my spine. "Coming?" I lift a single brow, smirking as I step out of my knickers, leaving them in a pile as I turn and walk out into the garden.

Looking around, I'm glad to confirm that we're completely enclosed by our building, the garden being in the middle and no windows overlooking us, telling me just how much this place cost given the price of real estate in London.

I smile as *Astronomical* by SVRCINA starts playing on the outside speakers, the pleasure of having music back in my life making my skin quiver. It pebbles for an entirely different reason as a hot, naked body presses up against my back, arms dusted with auburn hair and littered with tattoos wrapping around me, a hard length poking me in the back.

"I fucking missed you so much," Loki whispers in my ear, placing teasing kisses along the column of my neck that leaves fire pooling in my core.

"Loki..." I moan, my whole body feeling heavy and aching with need. His palms glide down my sides, over my stomach, and find my pussy already wet for him.

"Did you miss me, baby? Did you miss my fingers inside you? My cock inside your dripping cunt?"

Fuck me, this boy and his filthy mouth. Another deep groan of need sounds in my throat as I try moving my hips to direct his touch. Luckily, he doesn't seem to be in a teasing mood, his musician's fingers dipping inside my damp folds and finding my opening. He thrusts two inside me, and I swear I see stars, my knees almost buckling at the searing pleasure that threatens to cleave me in two.

"More, Loki," I beg, my voice deep and my nails raking down his forearms. "I need you to fuck me, please."

His masculine laugh rumbles through me, his nose nuzzling my neck.

"As you wish," he murmurs in a sexy as fuck, husky whisper that has my inner walls clenching around his fingers. He pulls them out and I whimper, frustration lancing through me like a lightning bolt.

Taking my hand, he leads me to a wooden table that's about waist height for him. Leaving me there, he walks over to a blanket box, giving me a magnificent view of his arse and back, and grabs out an armful of thick blankets and cushions. Stepping back up to me, my skin quivering at his nearness, he layers the blankets and cushions on the tabletop, creating a soft surface towards the side edge of the table with a cushion presumably for my lower back.

"Up you get, baby," he orders with a devastating smile that melts me that much more. With his help I climb up onto the table, my legs dangling off the edge. "Lie back," he commands, his voice dropping an octave as he gives me a searing look. I do as commanded, lying back under the shade of the umbrella, the gentle, warm breeze tickling my skin. I raise my hands up over my head, taking a slight stretch and loving the way my muscles pull.

Loki disappears from view, then one of my legs is lifted, quickly followed by the other as he places them over each of his shoulders. Anticipation lights me up, making my breathing quicken until the swipe of a warm tongue has my eyes rolling and a keen falling from my lips. My fingers curl into the blankets underneath me with the bliss that rolls across my body.

"Fuck, I missed the taste of this pussy, Pretty Girl," he growls out, thrusting his head harder between my legs, pinning them open as he proceeds to take me to heaven with his tongue, making my legs quake and tremble as I come over and over again.

A shadow falls over my closed lids, so I open my eyes and see a pierced cock surrounded by black ink in front of my face.

"Open up, Princess," Ash demands, a shining bead of precum dotting the head of his shaft.

I do as ordered, and the sound that leaves his lush lips as he pushes his way in as far as this angle will allow sets me alight again. I groan as the salty, masculine taste of him fills my mouth, my hand grasping his base and pumping what won't fit. Another deep moan vibrates around his cock as Loki pushes inside my dripping cunt, his own piercing hitting all the right nerves.

"Shit, you feel so fucking good," Loki hisses, filling me completely at the same time that Ash pushes in as far as he will go, a deep sound echoing in his chest.

I lose myself to the rhythm of their thrusts, my eyes closing as pleasure rolls over me in spine-tingling waves. My nerve endings fire like fuses, lighting me up over and over again until nothing exists apart from our bodies and the carnal dance we are performing.

"Fuck, Princess, I'm gonna come," Ash growls out, his cock

growing impossibly hard in my mouth and hand. I open my eyes to stare up at him through watering eyes, watching his climax colour his face in pained ecstasy before his seed fills my mouth. I swallow every drop greedily, my tongue swirling and licking until I've captured his release fully.

Clearly not liking my attention straying from him, Loki starts pounding into me hard and fast, his hands gripping my thighs in a bruising hold, his pace relentless.

I quickly let Ash pull out of my mouth, my back arching as much as my bump will allow as Loki builds me up again. Stars begin to dance in front of my eyes, my muscles tightening as my climax crashes over me, my own pleasure coating Loki as I come hard. I'm barely over the peak when I feel Loki stiffen above me, a deep groan of satisfaction leaving his lips as he, too, finds release.

We stay locked together, panting, letting the summer breeze caress our sweat-covered bodies as we come down from our high. Fingertips trace my cheek, and I turn into the touch, looking up into calm, grey eyes.

"You are exquisite, my love," Ash praises, leaning down and placing a kiss on my swollen lips. "Jax and Kai missed you too." He looks at me, a question in the furrow of his brow, and I know what he's asking.

"I missed them, all of you, so much," I reply, my hand coming up to stroke his damp cheek.

He pulls back with a smile, and I look past him to see my two other Knights lying on wide sun loungers, their underwear-clad bodies tense, but dicks hard, waiting with an air of uncertainty.

Grumbling, Loki pulls out and there's a rush of wetness that seeps out after him, our combined releases dripping down my inner thigh. He places a kiss on my thigh, stepping away as Ash takes my hand and helps me to stand on wobbling legs, leading me over to where Kai is lying on the cast-iron lounger.

All Mine, by PLAZA comes over the speakers, the beat washing over me, my hips swaying automatically. Kai gives me a beatific smile as I gaze down at him, drinking in all his glorious ridges and dips.

"Lube up, Kai," Ash orders, and Kai raises a brow, but leans over and grabs a bottle of lube off the small table between him and Jax, because of fucking course there's lube there. "Princess, Kai's going to fuck that pretty, little ass of yours while Jax fucks your beautiful pussy," he tells me, his eyes shining with excitement and I notice his dick starting to stiffen at the thought.

"I–I'm not sure how that's going to work..." I reply, trying to work it out in my pleasure befuddled brain and coming up empty.

"Don't worry, I'll help get you in the right position," Ash assures me with a devilish smile that renders any protestations I may have null and void. "Hop up, reverse cowgirl style."

I give him a raised brow, telling him with my look that women who are six months fucking pregnant don't hop anywhere. He just smirks, keeping hold of my hand as I climb up on the lounger, thankful that it seems pretty fucking solid and doesn't shake under our combined weight.

Once I'm hovering over Kai's crotch, his shaft so hard that it's lying flat on his stomach, the piercings lining the underside glinting in the sunshine.

"Lube her up, Kai," Ash commands, taking my other hand and pulling me slightly forward to give Kai better access.

I'm about to tell him that I may look like a fucking whale but I object to being spoken about like one, but the words come out as a garbled moan as Kai spreads the lube around my puckered hole then inserting his thumb and sending sparks racing across my skin.

My heart races, my breaths coming fast as he pumps it in and out, his fingers reaching between my legs to toy with my clit.

"Shiiiit..." I breathe out, the sensations his thumb creates peaking my nipples.

"Up on your feet, Princess, knees bent," Ash directs next, taking hold of my other hand and helping me to get into a low squat, my feet on either side of Kai's hips.

Kai pulls out his thumb, using the new angle to guide the tip of his slicked-up cock to my puckered hole, gently breaching the ring of tight muscle and making me see fucking stars as his piercings rub along my walls. Ash lets go of one hand, leaning down to rub at my clit as Kai keeps thrusting forward, the pleasure from Ash's touch making me relax more into Kai's intrusion.

"Kai...oh my god, fuck," I rasp, uncaring that I'm not making any sense.

"That feels so fucking good, darling," Kai grits out, pushing the last inch inside me with a grunt. His swearing lets me know just how much this is driving him crazy, and I relish in the power that I wield over him.

Kai's other hand grips my hip, his fingers digging in as he starts to pulse his hips in shallow movements, both of us making low, desperate noises. Kai pauses, and lightning zings across my skin as I open bleary eyes.

"Lean back on your hands, Princess," Ash tells me, letting go of my other hand. Kai supports my waist as I do as directed, placing my hands behind me on the lounger so that I'm leaning back. Ash steps away and to the side near my head, Jax taking his place with one of his rare, delicious grins.

"Hey, baby," he rumbles, his huge shaft gripped in his hand as he kneels between Kai's legs. "Room for one more?"

I chuckle, hearing Kai groan under me as my inner walls clamp around him. "Always," I tell Jax, ripples of excitement flooding adrenaline through my veins as well as a shot of fear at whether his huge cock will fit.

He gives me another pussy decimating smile, then brings his leg up and over ours on one side so that he's propped on one knee and one foot. I can't see what he does next, but I fucking feel the stretch as he starts to push his way inside my slick cunt, Loki's cum helping to ease his way.

"Fuuuuck..." I murmur, my head tilting back as Jax impales me on his monster cock. "I'd forgotten how fucking big you were, Jax."

He gives a manly snort, which morphs to a deep growl as he bottoms out.

"A lesser man would get a complex, darling," Kai teases beneath me, enacting his revenge as he drags almost all the way out and then thrusts hard back into my arse.

A sharp gasp leaves both mine and Jax's lips at the move, Jax holding still to let Kai do it again. And again. And again, until I'm quivering and shaking, crying out his name. He pauses, panting hard, and lets Jax take control whilst he holds me still.

Jax doesn't hold back, reminding me of just how large and powerful he is with every hard, snapping thrust into my dripping pussy. I let them use me, giving myself over to them completely as they work in symbiosis, wrecking me in the best possible way.

I'm soon unravelling between them, my limbs shaking with the force of my orgasm. Yet they don't let up, fighting my body's tightness to keep pounding into me with devastating precision, knowing exactly the right spots to hit to keep me coming over and over again.

"Loki, let's show our girl what she does to us," I hear Ash say, voice strained and husky.

Opening my eyes, I see him still standing on one side, dick hard and gripped in his fist as he pumps it with furious speed. I turn my head to the other side to see Loki doing the same, and the thought that they will be covering me with their cum whilst Jax and Kai fill me up with theirs has me whimpering with need.

Fuck, I am literally going to die from too many orgasms.

There are worse ways to go, I suppose.

Kai and Jax speed up, the noise of our bodies slapping together loud in the quiet of the summer afternoon, the sound of the river and music a backdrop to our love-making. Moments later, Jax slaps the side of my arse before going rigid in front of me, the mixture of pleasure and pain forcing me to follow him into oblivion with a scream that accompanies his own roar.

Kai follows soon after, thrusting hard and deep as he pours his release inside me, a pained groan sounding in his throat. First Ash then Loki groan, the hot splash of their climaxes coating my breasts and stomach, triggering another rush of liquid to coat Jax's dick as I come again.

Utterly spent, I practically fall on top of Kai, Jax slipping out of me with a rush of warm liquid between my thighs. Panting, my heart beats a strong rhythm as I lie back, unapologetic that I could be crushing Kai beneath me. I don't have to worry for too long as he turns us on our sides, spooning me, his own now soft member slipping from my arse. He holds me to him, uncaring that I'm covered in his friends' cum, and hugs me close, whispering praise in my ear, melting me completely.

I close my eyes, snuggling into his embrace and letting his love wash over me in a comforting wave. This is where I'm meant to be, in the arms of one of my lovers, my soulmates. Being loved, protected, and cherished by them all.

A dark kernel tries to make its presence felt, trying to drag me back into the nightmare that I've only just escaped from. I push it aside, trying to claw back the happy, contented feeling of moments before, but it feels tarnished now, and I can't help but shiver in the afternoon sun, its warmth not reaching the place where I need it most.

CHAPTER TWELVE

LILLY

The next morning we go to the clinic, and I'm filled with a dizzy relief when the image of my baby appears on the screen, wriggling and moving around like a loon. The doctor declares all to be well, and with a clean bill of health, we go back to the apartment.

The next couple of days go by, the guys showering me with affection and making love to me at every opportunity. I love it, truly, but a part of me yearns for the freedom that I've been denied for weeks. To be able to just leave the house and walk around the city, go shopping, or just live unconfined.

The boys try; Loki taking me shopping to all my favourite stores, including Irregular Choice on Carnaby Street, Kai taking me to some amazing restaurants, Jax coming on some walks through the city's parks, and Ash and I visit the big museums.

It's wonderful to be back with them, but I can't help feeling a little smothered as it becomes apparent that I'm not allowed to go anywhere by myself. I understand, hell, I'm worried about being taken again too. However, I feel like I can't even broach the subject, Ash quickly shutting down any ideas I might have of independence, citing my safety as a cause for concern.

The nights are awful.

I can no longer sleep with them in the bed, waking up covered in sweat and panting, their hands morphing into those of another, unwelcome touch. I take to sleeping in one of the other bedrooms, or on the sofa when sleep just won't come.

I know they're worried, the pinched brows and frowns telling me how much. But I can't find it in me to talk about it, any of it. I can barely think about it without my pulse rocketing and the black tendrils of panic clawing at the edges of my vision, and it gets worse knowing that soon, we have to go back to America. My time here is running out, and the thought of leaving fills me with equal parts relief and dread.

The night before we're due to return is particularly bad, sleep refusing to come no matter how many sheep I count. Eventually giving up, I head downstairs, the cool quiet of the night feeling oppressive and choking. Unable to stand it a moment longer, I grab my phone, bringing up Roman's contact and dialling before I can think twice.

"Lilly?" he answers, voice slightly croaky from sleep. *"Everything okay?"*

I open my mouth to say yes, as I have done for the past few days whenever one of the guys asked, but when tears spring to my eyes, I find that I can't lie. Not anymore and not to someone who was there.

"Lilly?" he asks again, voice laced with worry.

"I need to get out, Roman," I tell him, closing my lids as a single drop of sadness trails down my cheek. I hate myself right now, for not wanting them and wanting to escape. "Know any clubs open or parties happening?" He's silent for a beat.

"Sure, you know Depravity? In Shoreditch?"

I'm nodding before he's even finished, spying the bags of clothes that I hadn't yet taken upstairs and run through my outfit choices.

"Yep, I'll grab a black, taxicab. Gimmie, say, twenty, and I'll meet you there?" I reply, jamming the phone between my ear and shoulder as I rifle through the bags, spotting a floral mini dress that'll work for a club.

"Alone?" he questions, his tone guarded.

"I'll see you there, Roman," I respond, not answering his question then hanging up.

Grabbing the dress, I ignore the nausea floating around my stomach, the guilt trying to tighten my chest. *I'll leave a note, and I'll be with Roman, maybe even Rowan so it's not like I'm all alone,* I reason to myself as I strip out of my PJs, grabbing a new bra out of the bag and getting ready. *I'm a grown arse young woman, why the fuck shouldn't I go out?*

LOKI

Gone out with the twins, back later
Lilly

I read the note, my stomach dropping. Ash is going to lose his shit when he sees this. Letting out a deep breath, I run my hand through my hair trying to decide on the best course of action.

"Lilly's fucking gone," Ash rasps out, his voice tight and panicked as he comes clattering down the stairs, the circles under his eyes prominent in the dark. *Aw, shit.*

With a resigned sigh, I hand over the note, watching his forehead crease and the paper crumple in his hand. I wince at the punishment Lilly will receive for this.

"She just needs—" I start, stopping mid-sentence when he looks at me with flared nostrils and swirling eyes. Beneath the rage is a desperate worry, his hand coming up to twist and pull at his hair.

"We're losing her, Loki," he murmurs, his shoulders slumping as his arms fall down by his sides. "I don't know how to bring her back and let her have her freedom."

"I know," I assure him, reaching out and clasping his shoulder. I have no words of comfort to offer, nothing that will fucking help us. We can't make her talk about what she went through.

Jax and Kai stomp down the stairs, the sound loud in the quiet of our misery.

"Lilly's at Depravity," Kai states before he's even reached us, and I notice that they've both hastily gotten dressed. "One of the Shadows' clubs."

"How do you know?" Ash interrogates, and even I grimace at his harsh tone.

"Roman sent a text to us all," Jax interjects, holding up his phone for us to see. Ash snatches it out of his grip, his eyes tracing across the screen.

"Maybe we should..." I suggest, and three sets of eyes land on me. "You know, leave her tonight?"

"No," Ash states, voice hard and jaw clenched so I know that I've already lost. "She can't just disappear, not again."

"Okay," I say gently, catching his eye and begging him to calm the fuck down. "Just let me talk to her first."

He doesn't respond straight away, his ink-covered chest rising and falling with deep breaths. Then he gives me a single, sharp nod, a slight dip of his head, and the breath leaves me in a quiet whoosh.

Pretty Girl, I hope you're ready for the wrath of your Knights.

———————

LILLY

I let the haunting voice of Hannah Reid from London Grammar wash over me as I sway my body to the beat of *Wasting My Young Years*.

The vibe is chilled tonight, indie pop being the music of choice currently by the very talented DJ up on stage.

I left the twins at the bar to weave my way through the crowd and lose myself to the music, to the press of hot, sweaty bodies, and the anonymity of being lost in a sea of people.

Suddenly, a hard, hot body presses to my back, strong hands grasping my hips and pulling me tightly against what is undoubtedly a man. I'm about to step away when aching familiarity washes over me with his vanilla and cocoa scent.

Not wanting to break the illusion of dancing with a stranger, I don't say a word, bringing my hands up to tangle in his soft hair and pull him closer. If his feel and smell didn't tell me who he is, the way his figure moulds to mine as we dance is enough to assure me that my trickster Knight is at my back, pressing his torso and pelvis flush with my back as we dance.

We move together, not saying a word, even when the song slows and we're barely more than swaying side to side. Although with Loki, it's never just a simple dance, his body is undulating like some kind of erotic dancer until I'm all kinds of flushed and panting from more than just the heat in the room.

The song changes into *Silence* by Marshmello & Khalid, and another body presses against my front, sweet lemon filling my senses and forcing my closed lids open. I see my gorgeous, Viking Knight reaching out for me and pulling me closer to him.

He looks devastating in a tight black tee that clings to every muscle and makes my mouth water, and I forget why I wanted to be alone whilst we dance together, our bodies moving like water over rocks. The song is perfect for us, the lyrics resonating in my soul. We've found peace in each other, and I love all my Knights fiercely, their violence calling to me and surrounding me in comforting protection.

Letting go of Loki's hair, I reach up and grab Jax by his luscious locks, messing his man bun up as I pull his face to mine and kiss him with all the desperation I feel in my soul. I tell him with every stroke that I'm sorry I ran, that I'm tired of staying silent about what happened, and beg him to show me the way out of this darkness that I've fallen into.

We break apart gasping, the lights from the club painting his face in changing shades of blue and purple. Before I can utter a word, Loki spins me around, planting his plump lips on my still tingling ones, my eyes closing on instinct. His kiss brings tears to my eyes, it's crushing softness gut-wrenching. He shatters me with his forgiveness, with his understanding as his palms reverently cup my face, and he pulls back, pressing his forehead to mine, my eyes still closed.

"Ash is pissed, beautiful," he murmurs, his breath tickling my face.

I heave a dejected sigh.

"Take me to your leader then," I reply, a wobbly giggle leaving my lips when Loki chuffs out a laugh at my terrible joke.

With a final kiss pressed to my lips, he takes my hand, Jax grasping my other as we thread through the still dancing crowd, Jax making sure I have enough room, to the bar where Ash, Kai, and the twins stand. I flinch under Ash's intense scrutiny, unable to hold his stare, so I find Kai's, feeling that sticky guilt when I see that his brow is furrowed deeply.

As soon as we get there, Ash grabs my wrist and drags me away towards the front doors, ignoring my protests like the jizzmuffin that he is.

"Ash! You're fucking hurting me!" I shout as we leave the club, the relative quiet of the night outside jarring after the pounding music of the club. He lets go, and I rub my wrist which aches with the remnants of his tight grip. He spins around, his eyes wild, and I brace myself, my legs widening in a defensive stance, ready for the verbal lashing that I know is coming.

"What the fuck were you thinking?!" he shouts, stepping close to me, using his height to try and intimidate me. "You can't just fucking disappear like that! We had no idea where you were, Lilly!"

"I left you a note," I reply petulantly, craning my neck to look up at him with a glare, not showing him that my heart is racing a mile a minute.

"A note!" He throws his hands up, a cruel look taking over his features. "Forgive me for worrying, *Princess*," he sneers, and the barb cuts deeply, his use of my nickname spoken like a curse. "After all, you left a note with no fucking information on it, so I must be some kind of cunt for not getting that you couldn't stand being with us. That you wanted to run after we'd only just got you back."

His voice cracks with the last of his words, and tears rush to my eyes at the unwitting hurt I caused him, caused them all, by pushing them away, emotionally at least. I lick my suddenly dry lips.

"I would wake up with bruises on my hips, my breasts, and have no fucking idea how they got there," I confess, the wetness spilling over and tracking down my cheeks as my voice grows thick. "He hurt me in ways that I'll never know, never remember, and every time I close my fucking eyes, I can feel him getting into bed with me that night, and I'm frozen under his grasping hands. I feel his breath on my neck, and his–his dick pressed up against me. I'm drowning, Ash, and I don't know how to swim to the surface."

"Shit, Lilly," he rasps, his own eyes filling as he stares into mine. He pulls me to him, enveloping me in his strength, in his familiar, ginger scent that helps to calm my racing heart. "I'll bring you to the surface, my love. Or drown with you. But you are not alone. You don't need to fight this by yourself."

I break down, letting all the dark rage and anger out as I sob into his chest, my fingers fisting his shirt until they tingle. Under the London night sky, I shed every tear that I've been holding in, every drop of misery that I've kept bottled up inside me ever since I woke up in that room all those weeks ago.

Ash holds me tightly to him the entire time, lending me his unwavering strength and wordless comfort as I shatter into pieces in his arms.

CHAPTER THIRTEEN

LILLY

I make my way downstairs the next morning, after having slept in the bed with Ash and Loki, sleeping the rest of the night away in blissful slumber for the first time since they rescued me. I've no doubt that nightmares will still plague me, but I feel so much lighter confessing my struggles to the guys.

"Good morning, darling," Kai greets me as I approach the kitchen area. I can see, and smell, that he's in the middle of cooking something delicious for breakfast, a spatula in his hands as he turns to face me, wearing sexy as fuck navy sweats and a tight, white T-shirt. *Wicked* by Miki Ratsula plays in the background as Kai moves his hips to the sultry beat.

Without skipping a beat, I throw myself into his arms, the utensil clattering to the floor as his own come around me in a crushing hug.

"Kai, I—" I begin, my voice cracking as I remember the hurt in his eyes at the club.

"It's okay, darling," he shushes me, pulling me even closer as he places a kiss on the top of my head.

"No, Kai, it's not okay," I tell him, my voice firm as I pull back so that I can stare up into his eyes, my face reflected slightly in his glasses. "I'm so fucking sorry, my love. I was a first-class arsehole last night and should have just talked to you guys instead of running away."

He stares into my eyes, his face soft and his own full of so much love and understanding that they're practically shining.

"Apology accepted," he says, then his lips tilt up into a very Loki-like grin. "And yes, it was an *asshole* thing to do." He emphasises the word, pointing out that we say it differently, with a waggle of his eyebrows.

"Cockwomble," I grumble with no heat behind it, leaning in to press a kiss to his soft lips.

He groans in the back of his throat, one of his hands coming up to angle my face so that he can kiss me deeper, his tongue plundering my mouth. I whimper, letting him ravish me and feeling exactly like one of those fucking fairytale princesses, my foot wanting to pop just like in *Princess Diaries*. An acrid, burning smell tickles my nostrils, and I pull back, Kai chasing my lips before his nose twitches.

"Shit!" he exclaims, letting me go as he turns to the hob and pulls the pan off the heat, the remains of a charred, black pancake smoking inside it.

"Oops," I say with a giggle, my breath catching when he turns around, a look of hunger in his amber depths and his sweats tented.

I swallow hard as he stalks towards me, forcing me to back up until I hit the kitchen island behind me. His fingers caress my hips, a shiver cascading down from his touch, and then hooking into my sleep shorts he pulls them down, letting the garment pool at my feet. My breathing picks up when he grabs the hem of my vest top and yanks that off over my head when I lift my arms. He lets that fall too, his piercing stare setting my body alight as it roams over my naked body.

In a move that surprises me, he lifts me up under my thighs, placing me on the cool marble, a hiss leaving my lips at the frigid temperature against my heated skin. Before I know what he's doing, he sinks down onto his knees, placing one of my feet, then the other onto his shoulders so that I'm spread open for him.

"So wet for me already, Pet," he coos, swiping a finger down my exposed folds which are indeed already slick. "Your distraction made me ruin my breakfast, and while I can make more, I've decided I want something else to eat."

Fuck. Me.

Kai dirty talking does things to Her Vagisty which should be illegal.

"Lie down, Pet," he orders, and although I wince at the cold as it hits my back, I obey his command, fluttering anticipation filling my stomach as I wait for his next move.

He doesn't make me wait long, and without further ado, a warm tongue swipes across my lower lips, a deep groan leaving my chest as he does the move again.

"So fucking delicious," he purrs, his breath caressing over my sex and making me even wetter.

He sets to his task with a determination that I'd be astounded by if I wasn't writhing around losing my fucking mind as a tsunami of tingles race up from my cunt.

"Kai..." I moan, my fingers clawing uselessly at the smooth surface of the worktop.

He doesn't relent, doesn't even pause as he keeps eating me like I'm the most delicious thing he's ever tasted. I can feel my inner muscles clenching, the world around me shifting as I come with a scream, my body bucking off the marble. My whole being is alight, the pleasure almost painful in its intensity.

It takes several moments for me to even be able to open my eyes, and when they do, they immediately lock onto stunning, emerald ones filled with fire.

"Good morning, Pretty Girl," Loki rasps out, leaning over to kiss me deeply, then pulling away, turning to Kai. "Are we having Lilly for breakfast?"

Kai stands up, walking round to stand in front of Loki, his lips and chin glistening with my release.

"I was," he tells him, then grabs the back of Loki's neck and pulls him in for a blistering kiss. I gasp with the ferocity of it, my pussy pulsing in time with their tongues as Loki licks my juices from Kai's mouth. Kai pulls back, glances at me then turns back to Loki. "On your knees, Pet."

Maybe, I by Des Rocs starts to play and my mouth pops open when Loki does as ordered, looking up at Kai with wide eyes of expectation. I swallow, my pussy fluttering when Kai pulls his hard length out of his sweats, the tip glistening with precum. He paints Loki's lips with it before Loki's tongue darts out to taste it and a whine leaves my lips that I barely recognise.

Loki starts kissing and nibbling Kai's pelvis like he just can't help himself. A moan sounds in my throat, this is really fucking happening and my eyes are glued to the scene before me, to Loki on his fucking knees about to give Kai a blow job.

Holy shitballs.

"Have you ever given a blow job before, Pet?" Kai asks in a deep voice as he stares down at my trickster, pulling Loki away by his hair. Loki's gaze flicks up.

"No."

"I'll let you take it slow this time then," Kai offers, his hand reaching down to trace his fingertips over Loki's jaw. "Open up, Pet."

I watch, enthralled, as Loki opens his mouth and takes Kai's rigid shaft inside, a deep groan sounding in Kai's chest at the move.

"Fuck," I whisper, my stare not wavering as Loki reaches up to grab hold of the base of Kai's dick, holding it steady as he bobs back up. He pulls off, licking the tip a few times before taking it in his mouth again and gliding back down.

"That's it, Pet. Right fucking there," Kai mumbles huskily, one hand fisting in Loki's auburn mane. His other comes up and runs through his own hair, an almost pained look on his face.

I rub my thighs together, the ache at watching the show they're giving building in my core until I'm filled with pulsing desperation.

"Need some help there, Princess?" a deep drawl sounds at my feet, and my gaze swings to look down my body and I find a smirking Ash and Jax near my dangling feet.

"Yes," I say with a gasp, need roaring through me. The two share a look, then Jax steps around the side of the island, making sure not to block my view of Loki and Kai.

His large hands travel over my body, reaching for my sensitive breasts and tugging at my nipples, sending jolts of lightning through me. He's distracting enough that I don't notice Ash until he's pressing inside me, that delicious, magic cross piercing of his rubbing my inner walls maddeningly.

"Yes, fuck yes," I groan out, my back arching when he bottoms out.

"You feel fucking exquisite, wife," Ash growls the words, pausing before slowly pulling out and then thrusting back inside me, hard, sending my whole body jerking on the smooth, stone top, only his firm grip of my hips keeping me in place.

That's the only pause he gives me before pounding hard into me over and over again, making me see double as I desperately try to keep my eyes open to watch the others. I grit my teeth, all my nerve endings tingling like electricity is passing over my skin.

"Swap," Jax grits out, and Ash stills, panting hard, his fingers digging into my soft flesh. He does as Jax demands, pulling out as I whimper at the loss.

Jax is there in a hot second, pushing inside me as I squirm at the burn of his massive cock, watching his brow furrow as he tries to take it slow and let my body accommodate him.

"Hand, Princess," Ash orders, and I look at him, extending my arm out. He grasps my hand in his, wrapping it around his shaft that's slick with my juices. He wraps his own hand over mine, and moves us up and down his length, his head tipping back in pleasure.

"Oh shit, Pet," I hear Kai rasp, and I look back in their direction, my panting breath stilling as I watch Kai basically fucking Loki's face. "Make yourself come when I do, Pet."

"Holy shit," I breathe out, watching enraptured as Loki brings out his own dick in his spare hand and starts pumping furiously.

Jax chooses that moment to give up the pretence of patience and thrusts all the way in, his hands grabbing my hips in a punishing hold as he fucks me hard and fast. My body moves on the worktop with the force of his thrusts, sounds that I barely recognise as my own falling from my lips at his violent love-making. Ash, too, picks up speed, and I glance at him to see sweat beading his brow as he watches my face whilst our hands wank him off.

Pleasure zings and sparks over my body like a high voltage wire is being passed over me. I can barely breathe, any sound I make becoming strangled and incoherent as I try to watch them all, all the while being fucked good and proper.

Kai is the first to erupt, snapping his hips forward as he comes down Loki's throat. Loki gags slightly but takes it like a champ as he, too, comes all over the floor, his eyes rolling as he spills his seed.

The sight sets me off, my cunt clamping down on Jax as I follow the boys into oblivion with a silent scream. He thrusts hard a few times then stills as he follows me, coming deep inside me with a growl. Ash is the last to achieve his release, his free hand landing on the marble with a slap as he spurts cum all over my stomach and breasts.

We stay that way for several moments, panting hard as we try to remember what our bodies feel like. My eyelids close as I lie there, completely spent and drowsy from the bliss I'm experiencing. Moaning when Jax pulls out, Ash lets go of my hand as they step away. I crack my lids to see Kai helping Loki up, planting a soft kiss on his lips and wiping away the tears that leaked down his cheeks during that epic BJ.

"Good boy," Kai whispers, then steps away with a lingering touch.

Loki looks over at me, his naked chest glistening with sweat and still heaving. He walks towards me on shaking legs, coming to stand in between my legs and pulls me up to sitting. Lowering his mouth to mine, he kisses me gently, his tongue seeking entrance. I moan when I taste Kai's essence on his tongue, my fingers landing on his pecs and digging in.

The kiss ends, and I look at him with heavy-lidded eyes.

"You okay?" I check, looking into his eyes for any sign that what happened with Kai was too much for him.

"Fucking amazing," he tells me with a smirk, his voice rough, his hand cupping my cheek. I beam back at him, nuzzling into his touch.

"That was hot as fuck, Loki," I tell him, and he gives a deep chuckle.

"Let's get you cleaned up, baby," he says, helping me to hop off the counter and catching me when I wobble.

"I love you, Loki Thorn," I confess, wrapping my arms around him and pressing close as I lean into him.

"I love you too, Lilly Vanderbilt." He says my new surname with a tilt of his lips, then gives me a peck. Without missing a beat, he picks me up under my thighs and carries me up the stairs to the bathroom, murmuring sweet nothings in my ear the entire way.

CHAPTER FOURTEEN

LILLY

We clean up, eat a yummy breakfast of pancakes with all the trimmings, and pack all our bags, ready for our flights later tonight back to Colorado. I plonk myself down on the sofa next to Jax, snuggling into his huge frame and loving it when he wraps one of his big arms around me, pulling me closer.

"So, what's the plan for the rest of the day?" I ask, looking around at the others who all seem to be staring anywhere but at me causing a slight chill to slither up my spine. "What? What aren't you telling me?" I go to sit up straighter, but Jax keeps a firm grip around me so that I can't fucking budge. Stupid man muscles being used against me.

"Princess, Lilly," Ash starts, leaning forward in his own chair and resting his elbows on his thighs. He looks directly into my eyes now, his own grey and as unreadable as a cloudy sky. "When we discovered who your mother was, what her real name was, Kai looked into her family."

"Yeah?" I ask, glancing quickly over to Kai who's also now looking my way with a sympathetic softness to his face as he holds his iPad.

"Yes, and she has living relatives, Lilly. Well, lots of relatives, but her parents are still alive. Harold and Petunia Rochester, aged eighty-seven and eighty-four respectively," Kai tells me, and there's a slight whooshing in my ears at his news.

"I have grandparents?" I question softly, my fingers tightening into Jax's T-shirt for support, glad that he pulled me so close to him.

"Yes, you do, Princess," Ash interjects, and I swing my wide eyes back towards him. "And they live in London, Kensington to be exact."

"Kensington?" I repeat, my mind spinning with how close they are, how close they may have always been.

"Would you like to meet them, Pretty Girl?" Loki asks me as he comes to crouch in front of me, taking my suddenly cold and tingling hands in his.

"B–But the flight?" I enquire, my mind going straight to practicalities.

"Can be delayed," Jax rumbles underneath me, and I feel the vibrations against the side of my face that's resting on his chest. "If you want it to."

I momentarily flashback to when I first met Jax and how quiet he was, only speaking when necessary. He talks more now, and I love the sound of his gravelly voice.

"Do you?" Loki repeats, and I blink, trying to remember the question.

Ah, yes, my grandparents. *Shit, do I want to meet them?* My pulse increases as I chew my lip, thinking about the answer to what feels like a loaded question. My baby gives a small movement, reminding me that it's not just me anymore.

"Yes," I reply, looking into Loki's emerald eyes, then up at Kai's, and finally Ash's. "I would like to meet them. Today if we can."

"We've already made contact and told them that if you wanted contact or to meet we would take you there. They're waiting for you, as long as you're sure?" Ash questions, and although I'm slightly taken aback at how fast this is moving, I appreciate the way they've put things into place. Also, my grandparents are in their eighties, and I'm guessing if I just turned up, they may have a bloody heart attack given how similar I look to Mum.

"I'm sure," I tell him, finally sitting up straight, Jax letting me go. I take a deep breath. "Let's go now."

Ash gives me a blinding smile as Loki stands up and offers me his hand, pulling me to my feet. He uses his grip to pull me to him, nuzzling my neck until his lips are close to mine.

"You are so fucking incredible, Lilly," he murmurs, placing a kiss on my cheek. I feel tears prick my eyes—fucking hormones—at the compliment. He pulls back, a twinkle in his own eyes. "Let's go meet your grandparents, older ladies fucking love me!"

I cringe, thinking back to Clarissa, and raise a brow in a *did you really just go there?* look. It takes a second, but his face drops, his mouth opening and closing in a grimace.

"Fuck— Shit...I didn't mean— Shit," he stutters, and I can't help but laugh, covering my mouth with a hand.

"Come on, Casanova." Ash chuckles, grabbing Loki's shoulder and pulling him towards the door.

"Coming?" Kai asks softly, pausing in his own walk towards the door, his hand extended. I take a deep breath, square my shoulders, and put my best foot forward, as Mum used to say.

"Yes," I tell him, grasping his warm hand in mine and letting him lead me to a family that I had no idea existed until today.

We park outside what can only be described as a Chelsea mansion in Upper Phillimore Gardens in Kensington. I look up at the imposing, white building, the sun making it sparkle and shine like it's touched by heaven. It's an old building, Victorian I guess, with five stories, four bay windows, and white marble steps that lead to a double, painted front door, columns on either side holding up a substantial porch. Window boxes filled with colourful flowers sit on every windowsill, making the whole place feel homely and inviting.

The sounds of traffic are dulled here, birdsong ringing in the air but doing nothing to soothe the butterflies in my stomach or my racing heart.

"Are you doing okay, Princess?" Ash inquires, his hand resting on my waist. I have to swallow a couple of times before answering.

"What if they don't like me?" I ask in reply, wringing my hands in front of me and not taking my eyes off the currently closed, front door. Ash lets go of my waist, stepping in front of me as the others crowd round, circling me.

"They will love you," he tells me, looking deep into my eyes as his fingertips stroke my cheek. "Just like we do."

"You're fucking awesome, Pretty Girl!" Loki practically shouts, making a choked laugh escape my dry lips when I turn my head to look at him. "And sexy as hell," he adds with a waggle of his auburn brows.

"Lilly, what is there not to like, my darling?" Kai questions me, drawing my gaze to his, the sun hitting the side of his glasses and reflecting my image back at me. "You're smart, beautiful, funny, and a wonderful person who isn't afraid to take on four broken boys and make them into men."

A tear trickles down my cheek at his words, my lips forming a wobbly smile as I take a shaky breath. My eyes close of their own accord when a lemon-scented warmth coats my back, and strong, large hands grip my hips.

"And the bravest fucking person I've ever met, Baby Girl," Jax declares, his deep rumble invading my very soul and making my nipples pebble as it always does. "So get that beautiful *arse* up those steps and show them how fucking amazing you are," he orders, making me chuckle at his faux British accent.

I take another deep inhale, dropping my shoulders, and reopen my eyes, giving Ash a curt nod. He smiles a devilish grin at me, my knees going a little weak at the sight of it.

"Good girl," he praises, holding out a hand as he steps back.

I take it in a firm grasp, allowing him to lead me up the stone steps. Before we can knock or ring the bell, the door opens to reveal an elderly gentleman in a butler uniform, face full of the wrinkles of a life well lived.

"Good morning, madam, sirs. If you'd care to follow me?" he asks in a well-to-do British accent, stepping back and holding a steady arm out to indicate that we come in.

I step inside the brightly lit entrance hall, loving the bright and airy feel, the old Victorian, black and white tiles shining, and the pale, lemon-coloured walls covered in mirrors and some landscape paintings.

"This way, please, Mrs Vanderbilt," the butler says, and I startle at the name. I mean, I know that it's my surname now, but, I guess I'm just not used to it yet from anyone other than my Knights.

"Sure," I reply, following next to him, Ash holding my hand on the other side and the others following behind us. "What's your name?" I ask, needing to fill the silence with chatter as my heart rate picks up with every step that we take.

"Jefferies, ma'am," he says, dipping his head in respect which feels all kinds of weird. "I've been with the Rochesters since your mother was a baby." He drops that small bombshell with a wistful smile, a faraway look in his eyes. He pauses when he realises that I've stopped walking. "Ma'am?"

"Oh, um, sorry," I rush out, Ash squeezing my hand and giving me a small reassuring smile as I start walking again. "I'd, um, love to hear any stories you have one day, Jefferies," I tell the old man, who beams back at me.

"I'd be honoured to share them with you, ma'am," he tells me, stepping towards a door on the right and reaching to open it. I place my hand on his arm, his head coming up to look at me with a quizzical, fuzzy, grey brow raised.

"It's Lilly," I tell him. "Please call me, Lilly."

His chin wobbles slightly like this is some great honour too.

"Your grandparents are waiting for you in here, Lilly," he tells me softly, and I release his arm as he starts to open the door. "They are so excited to meet you. All of you," he adds with what I would describe as a mischievous smile at the guys. *Huh.*

I'm momentarily blinded by the sunlight that streams from the room that we step into, and it takes several blinks for my eyes to get used to it. When I can finally see again, I see an elderly couple standing in the middle of the room, her hands clasped in a firm grip in front of her, his hand on her shoulder. I take them in, from their kind, lined faces, to her twinset, and perfectly set hair, and then to his dapper, fitted suit and moustache.

"Lilly, darling?" she says in a thick voice, stepping towards me. Her movements are like a little bird, she looks so small and fragile standing in the streaming sunlight, dust motes surrounding her like a halo. "You look so much like her," she adds, reaching me and stretching out a hand as if to cup my face, but then pauses, looking a little unsure.

"Grandma?" I whisper, seeing a familiarity in the shape of her face, and the thickness of her grey hair.

"Oh, darling girl," she murmurs back, her eyes glistening, and without thought, I let go of Ash's hand and step into her embrace, the scent of violets engulfing me as I wrap my trembling arms around her and hug her tight. Her thin arms go around me, encasing me in her loving embrace, and it reminds me so much of my mum that I burst into tears, sobs wracking my body as she holds me tighter to her. "My darling, darling girl," she whispers, stroking my hair and planting kisses on the top of my head. "You're back now, that's all that matters."

I feel another set of arms envelop us, and I look up with tears still running down my face to see my grandfather's cheeks wet as he holds us both. He leans down to kiss my cheek, mumbling in my ear, "Welcome home, Lilly."

Clearly not wanting to miss out on the reunion, my baby gives a mighty kick, causing my grandma to let out an oomph sound. She pulls back, looking down at my rounded stomach.

"Harold, oh, Harold, look!" she exclaims, more tears dripping down her cheeks as she laughs and places a hand over my baby. "We're going to be great grandparents! Oh, you clever, clever girl!"

I laugh as my grandfather loosens his arms and steps back to have a look, his face wreathed in smiles too. "And who's the lucky father?" he asks, looking behind me, and I can't help the slight cringe at the question. I'm not ashamed about our unconventional relationship, just the thought of trying to explain it to my newly-found grandparents...*eek*.

"I am, Mr. Rochester," Loki steps forward, hand out to shake my grandfather's.

"Congratulations, son," Harold says, pumping Loki's hand enthusiastically. "Pleasure to meet you, Mr Vanderbilt."

"I'm Mr Vanderbilt, Lilly's husband," Ash says, holding out his hand, and I bite my lips together at the confusion on the old man's face. Harold drops Loki's hand and automatically takes Ash's, shaking it with a befuddled frown on his face.

"Ash is my husband, Loki, Jax, and Kai are my..." I pause, trying to think of what to call them. Boyfriends doesn't feel like it adequately describes our relationship. "Soulmates. They're all my soulmates."

My grandfather's grey eyebrows go almost into his receding hairline, his eyes wide.

"Oh, don't look like that, Harold," my grandmother scolds, finally letting me go and stepping towards the guys. "Have you forgotten the Woodstock of sixty-eight?"

"Petunia!" my grandfather exclaims, a blush tinting his cheeks as he looks at his wife. She just gives him an innocent yet calculating look, one perfect, silver brow raised. Loki looks on amused, while I can't help wondering what she might be referring to. The nineteen-sixties were wild according to all the stories, a time of sexual freedom.

"Let he who is without sin, my love," she tells my grandfather, placing a gentle kiss on his lined cheek, grasping his arm in her hands. He looks down at her with such love that my heart swells, feeling like it'll break free from the confines of my chest.

He looks back up, taking in each of the guys in turn with a serious look.

"You take care of her? All of you?" he asks, tone firm and unwavering. I'm suddenly hit with the thought that he's asking out of concern for my well-being, that he would take them all on if their answer isn't satisfactory. Warmth suffuses my limbs at having more people in my corner.

"With our lives," Ash tells him solemnly, not breaking his gaze until my grandfather looks at Loki.

"And our hearts," Loki declares, and there goes my own heart again, trying to escape once more.

"She's our souls," Kai adds, glancing my way briefly before looking back at my grandfather, who nods, then looks towards Jax.

"And we're hers," Jax states in that gruff voice of his, and I'm nodding, my cheeks wet again. Fucking hell, I'm surprised there's any water left in my body at this rate.

"Well, all right then," Harold confirms, his head bobbing. "I would have hated to have had a chat with my friends down in Vauxhall," he adds, still looking at the guys. Ash gives a respectful nod, although fuck knows what the old man is waffling about.

"Harold!" my grandmother chastises, whacking him in the chest. "Don't threaten Lilly's beaus with MI6!"

Oh shit. My grandfather has connections with the British Secret Intelligence Service. Good to know, and possibly, dare I say it, may come in handy too?

"Well, now we all know where we stand, Petunia," my grandfather reasons, patting her hand, my grandmother rolling her eyes at him as they walk back to me. "Let's have some tea, shall we?" he asks, holding out his spare arm, and I slide my hand into it, a sense of lightness filling up my entire being at being here with them, my blood family.

CHAPTER FIFTEEN

LILLY

Although I desperately wanted to stay a few more days to get to know my grandparents better, they insisted that I head back to Colorado and back to school, stating that education is the key to success. So reluctantly, I get back into the car after hugs and promises of meeting up again soon.

I clutch my rolling stomach as we get off the plane some hours later, nerves leaving a sour taste in my mouth and tiredness making my eyes feel gritty and my limbs heavy. I've no idea what to expect from school come Monday, luckily it's only Friday—actually Saturday—morning, so I have the weekend as a reprieve.

"Daughter," a snake's voice sounds as we approach the waiting cars, the balmy, Colorado night air teasing my damp hair. My head snaps up, my feet freezing on the tarmac, and adrenaline waking me up in an instant as I'm transported to the night of my wedding.

"Enjoy your honeymoon."

I start to pant, blackness edging my vision as I stare into the hard, grey eyes of Julian Vanderbilt, his devil's smile firmly in place, his arms opened wide and a calculated look of concern all over his lying fucking face. He was the one to whisper that to me before everything went black that night. He played an active role in my kidnap.

Spicy ginger washes over me as Ash pulls me to him, his long, beautiful, inked fingers grasping my chin and turning it so that I face him, breaking his father's curse.

"It was him, Ash. He was there when I was taken," I tell him in a broken whisper, nausea whirling in my stomach. His jaw clenches.

"You don't have to talk to him, Princess," he assures me, his own grey eyes just as hard as Julian's, but full of a raging fire that I know is aimed at the older man. "Or look at him, or even let him fucking breathe near you."

My lip trembles as his words leave the air rushing out of my lungs, my skin tingling with relief.

"Take me home, please," I beg my husband, my Knight. He gives a sharp nod, flicking his gaze behind me briefly. "Take her to the car."

Vanilla and lemon surround me as Ash steps away, and Loki and Jax sandwich me between their hot bodies, Jax wrapping a huge arm around my shoulders and pulling me close into his warmth. Loki grasps my hand, and they lead me to the car awaiting us, Jax's huge form blocking Julian from my sight as I hear Ash murmur to him in a tight voice.

"How did you know she was going to be with us?" Ash asks, his voice clipped and completely emotionless. Julian's dark chuckle scrapes across my skin like an unwanted caress, and a revolted shiver takes over my body. Both boys gather me closer, and their mingled scents are a comfort and help combat the way my skin itches around Julian.

"Oh, son, you really should learn that I know everything that concerns me. Especially when it concerns my missing daughter-in-law. It was lucky you boys were there to help, fated some might say. And poor Adrian, dying in that horrible fire. They still have yet to find the body, apparently, it burned so hot that only dust remains. I did warn him that old English manor houses always had faulty electrics. Does Lilly know?"

My heart thumps in my chest, and I'm straining to hear Ash's reply as Loki opens the car door, releasing my hand to get in, then waiting for me to follow.

"Yes, Lilly is aware and has been through enough, don't you think?" Ash bites out, clearly aware of the insinuations of Julian's tone and little speech. Jax releases me and places a hand on my back, leaning in to whisper in my ear.

"Ash will tell you everything later, Baby Girl. Let's get out of here."

Deciding that he's right and that I just want to be as far away as possible from that fucking cunt, I step into the car, scooting next to Loki as Jax gets in behind me.

"Good evening, Mrs. Vanderbilt," I hear from the front, and I look up to see Tom smiling warmly at me in the rearview mirror. "Welcome back."

His kind words and the genuine look of concern on his face make tears spring to my eyes, and I have to swallow hard to be able to reply.

"Thank you, Tom."

He gives me a nod and another warm smile, the divider screen moving up into place as the car starts to pull away. My breath catches, my stomach suddenly dropping.

"Wait!" I yell. "What about Ash and Kai?" I ask, looking frantically behind me to see Ash still talking to his father and Kai waiting off to one side.

"Hey, baby, it's okay," Loki soothes, grabbing my hand and rubbing my arm. "They'll make their way back when they're ready. We've other cars they can call."

"Oh," I mumble, my cheeks heating as I chew my lower lip. "You sure they'll be okay?" I ask, turning my head to be captured by his beautiful, emerald eyes. Shit, I missed them and will never grow tired of looking into their variegated depths. His lips tilt upwards, his hand coming up to cup the side of my face.

"Ash is the big, bad wolf, Pretty Girl, and Kai can more than handle himself. Don't worry about them." I nod, still chewing my lip, and he tuts. "You know what you need, baby?" he asks me, a decidedly wicked gleam entering the green globes as his lips tilt up in that panty-melting smile of his.

"If you say a distraction, I'll…" I reply sternly, fighting the pull of my own lips as his go up in a Cheshire cat-like grin.

"You'll come all over my face while you ride Jax reverse cowboy style? Okay, baby, as you wish," he tells me, and I lose the fight, my body heating as the grin splits my lips at his *Princess Bride* reference. I made them all watch it when we were holed up at the warehouse apartment, confessing my undying love for Westley which Loki takes every opportunity to tease me about.

Loki lets go of my face, taking his phone out of his back pocket and hooking it up to the car's sound system. *Tidal Wave* by Chase Atlantic starts to play.

"Loki," I chastise when he slips into the footwell, which luckily is deep because this isn't just your usual SUV, it's a Knight car with seats that face each other in the back and plenty of room.

"Don't worry, I made sure poor Tom can't hear your cries this time," he teases, grabbing my loose, harem pants and tugging them and my knickers down my hips.

I could fight, but fuck, I need the release, my body wound tighter than a spring. Lifting my hips, I let him take them off until I'm naked below the waist, only a tank top covering my torso. I shiver, but as it's warm in the car so I know it's not from the cold.

Heated lips caress my neck with a growl that hardens my nipples to aching points as Jax kisses my sensitive spots, setting my skin alight. I gasp when a hot tongue licks up my slit, glancing down to see Loki's head between my spread legs.

Fuck, yes, please.

I give in, closing my eyes, and just let sensation take over, feeling in the moment. Hands and tongues caressing my skin and dripping pussy, Jax pulling out my breast and showering that with attention too. I drown in ecstasy, my fingers gripping Loki's soft hair and pulling his face closer with a sharp tug as I come nearer to my release.

"Shit, Loki, don't fucking stop," I beg in a strangled voice, so bloody close I can taste the orgasm, my whole body trembling with my impending release.

And like the fucking angel that he is, he goes harder, licking and sucking, grazing his teeth on my clit until I explode, seeing white as I come hard all over his face. Jax slams his lips onto my own and swallows my scream of pleasure as fire races across my nerve endings, lighting me up like a firework.

I go boneless, slumping in the seat as I relearn how to fucking breathe again.

"One," Loki says, his voice deep and so fucking husky that I almost come again just from the sound. I crack my closed lids to see his shit-eating grin, his lips and chin glistening in the passing street lights.

"One?" I question, my own voice raw, heat flooding through me when he bites his bottom lip. *Why is that so goddamn sexy?*

"We're gonna make you come at least twice more before we get back, aren't we, Jax?" he replies, and I swallow hard at the dark promise in his eyes.

"Sure are, Baby Girl," Jax rumbles, his own voice fifty shades of fuck me now, it's so deep and growling. "Now, come sit on my cock like a good girl."

I take a deep, shaky inhale at his words, my heart still racing but Her Vagisty begging for round two. *Who am I to deny royalty?* I think as I glance over to see Jax has his pussy clenching dick out, leaning back against the leather seat as he leisurely pumps it in his huge hand. I sit up, intending to swing my leg over and ride him like Seabiscuit when Loki places a hot hand on my bare thigh.

"Facing me, beautiful," he instructs, his eyes dark and nostrils flared as he licks that plush bottom lip. "I wanna see you impaled on that monster cock."

I'd laugh at his use of my nickname for Jax's dick if he didn't look all kinds of sinful and horny as he speaks.

"As you wish," I whisper back, that biteable mouth tilting up in a smirk as I repeat his words from earlier back at him.

Unable to help myself, I lean forward, sucking his bottom lip into my mouth, my pussy clenching at the sexy as fuck groan that sounds in his throat. He grasps the back of my hair, pulling me forward more as he kisses the shit out of me, the sweet and musky taste of my release coating our tongues.

Firm hands grab my hips, manoeuvring me so that my legs are on either side of Jax's massive thighs, my feet on the floor of the moving car. I go to pull back from Loki, but he fists his hand in my hair, holding on tightly as he uses his grip to push me back, not breaking our kiss.

A low, deep keen leaves my mouth, and Loki swallows it down as I feel Jax begin to push into my opening. It feels like all my synapses are firing, my pussy walls stretching to accommodate him, although Loki paved the way with my first orgasm so that I'm nice and wet.

"Fuuuuck," Jax groans in his rough as sandpaper voice, and my already hard nipples pebble further at the sound. I love that I can bring these boys to ruin with my body, just as much as they regularly destroy me with theirs.

My breath hitches and my eyes roll behind closed lids as Jax bottoms out, sheathed inside my wet heat and touching my fucking cervix. Loki finally releases my mouth, and I gasp with the intensity of Jax inside me. Sitting back on his heels, Loki looks at us with hooded, bedroom eyes.

"Now that's a fucking beautiful sight," he states, and my eyes dart down to watch him undo his fly, his rigid member springing free and making my mouth water at the drop of precum beading at the tip. "Time for that later, Pretty Girl." He smiles smugly, pushing himself up onto the seat opposite and mirroring Jax's pose.

I whimper as Jax begins to lift my hips, sliding me up his shaft until just the tip remains. He pauses, the sound of my racing pulse loud in my ears and vying with the sound of the music that cocoons us. The flexing of his fingers is the only warning I get as he slams me back down, and I cry out with how fucking good that feels. He repeats the move again and again until I'm a quivering, gibbering mess, the windows all steamed up.

"Jax, oh shit–fuck, Jax," I pant, my nails digging into the backs of his hands as he relentlessly fucks me, harder and harder until I'm seeing stars for the second time.

"Two," Jax growls out, stopping his thrusts and letting me ride out my climax while I twitch on top of him.

"Lean our girl forward, brother," Loki grits out, and I raise my gaze to see him scooting forward on his seat, holding his dick in a firm grip.

Hells to the fuck yes!

I eagerly lean forward until I can place my lips around the head of him and lick the precum that's shining there.

"Oh, goddamn, baby," Loki rasps, and the way his voice hitches as I swallow him whole does things to Her Vagisty that should be on some kind of danger list. Jax grunts behind me as I clench around him, then he resumes his thrusting, pushing Loki's cock further into my throat.

I relax, letting them take control and allowing them to use my body like it was made for their pleasure. The rolling waves of ecstasy that capture my body, binding me up in ribbons of exquisite sensation tell me that no truer statement exists. We were crafted for one another, moulded to be exactly what the other needs.

The boys build me up again, one of Jax's hands coming around to my front and toying with my aching, engorged clit until I'm squirming around both his and Loki's cocks.

"Come for us again, baby," he orders, electric pulses racing across my entire body and leaving me tingling.

My jaw starts to ache with Loki's treatment, but the way he fucks my throat just winds me up tighter, my third climax fluttering just out of reach.

"One more, beautiful," Loki grits out, just as his balls tighten up and he thrusts so hard that my lips touch his base, and his hard member cuts off my air supply as he pours his release down my throat.

It's the push I need, and I come hard, bucking wildly as I shatter into thousands of pieces, spots of black coating my vision with the force and the air deprivation.

I milk Jax, hearing him roar behind me as he snaps his hips up, pushing Loki's dick further down my throat. Just as the dots start to join up, Loki pulls out, and I take a huge gasp of sex-scented air into my burning lungs. Loki helps to push me back onto Jax, who is still sheathed inside me, as my whole body flops, my chest heaving and sweat covering my skin.

"Fucking hell, baby mama," Loki gasps, flinging down beside us, his softened cock still out as he drops his head back onto the headrest.

I see Jax raise a palm, and Loki slaps it like a fucking wanker, but I'm too fucked out—*yep that's a legit state of being*—to call them out on their bullshit. Twisting around as Jax slides out of me, I snuggle into his lap, uncaring that his cum is dribbling down my inner thighs.

The sound of his rapidly slowing heartbeat lulls me into a blissed-out coma, and I feel Loki cleaning up some of the mess between my legs before sleep claims me in a warm and fuzzy embrace.

CHAPTER SIXTEEN

LILLY

The next morning passes by in a blur, the guys cocooning me in their loving embrace that a week ago felt stifling, but now feels like a warm security blanket, protecting me from the harshness of life.

I'm snuggled on the sofa with Loki and Jax, the latter massaging my feet which feels like utter fucking bliss as he rubs the tension away, when a frantic knocking sounds at the door. My heart leaps, and I sit up, pulse pounding until I hear Willow's voice on the other side.

"Stop fucking those hotties and open up! I know you're back, Lilly!"

A small laugh barks out of me as Ash strides over to the door, opening it with a scowl. Willow, bloody awesome bitch that she is, just brushes past him without so much as a pause in her step and stops when she sees me, her eyes welling up.

"Hunter told me what happened, and—shit. I'm so glad you're back, babe," she hiccups before bursting into tears, and I rush to get up and get my arse over to her, wrapping her now sobbing, fairy form up in a tight hug.

"I missed your crazy, lovely," I tell her, my own voice thick with tears.

We hold each other for a few beats, and it dawns on me how much I needed her these past few weeks, my new bestie. And also how much I might owe her and her brother. Pulling away, I look into her crystal eyes, the tears on her lashes making them shine like diamonds.

"Willow, your brother. I owe you all so fucking much," I say, sincerity in my tone. I definitely would have gone mad without the twins and Mai. She scoffs at my words.

"You don't owe anyone shit, babe," she tells me, her blonde curls bouncing as she shakes her head. "You're family, Lilly, and family helps each other, no questions asked or debts owed."

It's Ash's turn to snort at that, and we both look over to him, a question in my expression, but Willow beats me to it.

"Something to say, Vanderbilt?" she sasses him, and I love her for it. I think even Ash approves as I see a hint of a smile on his gorgeous lips.

"We are clearly not family as the Knights owe the Shadows a favour, according to your brother," he states, crossing his arms and levelling her with his stern, grey eyes. I can't say that I'm all that surprised, isn't this how gangs work after all?

"Please," Willow says, rolling her eyes and turning back to me. "It won't be something that you're not willing to do. The Shadows aren't those kinds of monsters."

There's a darkness in her eyes at the end, like clouds that sweep over the sun, leaving you shivering, and I'm reminded that Willow has her own past, her own tale of woe that she's yet to share. I won't push her though. She'll tell me when she's good and ready.

"How about a movie?" I suggest, grabbing her hand and leading her to the sofa, making scooting motions with my other hand at Loki and Jax so they give us some space.

"I'll make some popcorn," Kai offers, putting down his iPad and getting up to go over to the kitchen.

"Sweet and salty?" I ask, giving him pleading eyes, and he chuckles, placing a kiss on my lips as he passes.

"Of course, darling," he replies softly, and I beam at him.

"Urgh, you're all so in love it's almost sickening," Willow mock-scoffs, and I stick out my tongue, knowing that she doesn't mean it.

"So, tell me all the gossip that I've missed out on," I command her, and she wrinkles her nose as she thinks for a moment.

"Honestly? Not much happened," she says, and then her eyebrows lift as she clearly thinks of something. "Oh! There was one thing now that I think about it." She leans closer. "The ex-Governor's daughter has gone missing, presumed kidnapped but no one knows for sure. Apparently, his son, R-something, used to go here but left shortly after Halloween last year, no one knows why."

"Robert?" I ask, my heart beating fast at the mention of my would-be rapist.

"Yes! That's the one! His sister went missing as it's been all over the local news. She's just vanished without a trace, kinda like you." She winces as she says the last part. "Soz, babe."

"It's okay," I reply absently, looking up at Ash whose jaw is clenched. "Did you know?"

"Of course," he answers, arching one perfect brow in that way of his. "It wasn't important, given the circumstances."

Oh yeah, given my abduction he means. Fair point.

"Well, I hope that they find her soon," I say to the room.

"I hope that they don't," Kai murmurs as he walks back, carrying drinks while the popcorn begins to ping in the pan. I look at him.

"Why?"

"The shit that we planted on the Governor's laptop was nothing compared to the rumours of what he'd planned to do to his daughter. Word was that he'd put her virginity up for sale to the highest bidder, so long as they had good connections," he sneers, and suddenly I feel sick, taking my iced tea from him but not wanting to take a sip after that.

"What?! But he went to prison, didn't he?" I ask him, a coldness spreading across my limbs.

"Twelve-month suspended sentence provided he undertook psychiatric treatment," Kai practically spits out, his nostrils flared. "He argued that he wasn't well and needed help."

"Plus, the Benjamins helped," Loki adds, his upper lip curled in a sneer.

"Why is it always the rich ones? Why does their money make them untouchable?" I ask, my eyes stinging as I think about the things that I—and my mother—have had to suffer at the hands of these corrupt, despicable men.

No one can give me an answer, and we sit in silence for a few moments, each lost in our own morbid thoughts.

"So, how's the baby?" Willow finally asks, and I give her a grateful smile.

We spend the rest of the afternoon catching up a little—though Willow is careful not to ask about my time in England and mostly regales me with all the latest Highgate gossip—and watching terrible rom-coms on the massive TV. It's so normal that my skin begins to itch, and I fake exhaustion to go upstairs to Loki's room, well, my room too, as I don't want Luc's old room now even though Ash did offer it to me. I need some time alone, still not used to so much contact with different people. I get jittery seeing the tightness in Willow's and the guys' eyes as they glance at me. We all know something is up, I'm not the same girl as I was before, and I hate that they might think it's them that's the issue. It's not, it's me. I'm... broken.

And that pisses me off. The fact that cuntbag, Adrian, has made me feel uncomfortable with the people that I love. Has changed me irrevocably that I feel like I no longer know myself.

Isn't the princess meant to live happily ever after once the bad guy has been slain by her Knights?

Yet, he isn't—wasn't—the only villain of my story, was he? I only have to think of Julian cuntish Vanderbilt's wicked smile and lingering touch, Rafe Griffith's lecherous gaze, and Stephen Matthews'—*fucking paedo prick*—cruel words.

No, Adrian Ramsey was not the only evil that needed to be eradicated. There are still yet more waiting for their karma.

Sunday night rolls around and I can't sleep, slipping out from between Ash and Kai who did their best to exhaust my body with so many orgasms I lost count. But my mind won't settle, the sticky dread of what tomorrow morning will bring occupying my jumbled thoughts. It's the first day back in class, and I don't know how I'm meant to function, how I'm meant to be after all this time of being away.

I quietly pad downstairs and hook my phone up to the speakers, turning the volume down but needing the noise after the silence of my confinement. I pause as I realise with a start that I am now more like the guys than I was before. We can't stand the silence, needing music to drown out the demons that threaten to take over and pull us under. How fucked up is it that it's our trauma that binds us? That the people who were meant to take care of us scarred us instead so badly that we had to take refuge in each other, our broken pieces fitting together far better than our whole selves ever could.

Far From Home by Sam Tinnesz begins to play, the song expressing how I felt for all those weeks, trapped and unable to escape my beautiful prison.

"Can't sleep?" I hear from behind me, and I turn to see Kai standing there limned in the silvery moonlight that's filtering in from the window. I asked them not to draw the curtains, needing to see the glittering night sky of Colorado to remind myself that I wasn't in Wiltshire at my, I mean, Adrian's house.

"No, my mind is racing," I confess in a whisper, wrapping my arms around myself even though the air is warm. I've a feeling that this isn't the kind of cold that a warm jumper will be able to fix.

"A wise and beautiful, young woman once convinced me that

keeping things bottled up would only allow them to fester," Kai says, his lips tipped up in a soft smile, and he steps towards me until his fresh woods after the rain scent caresses my nostrils. "Talk to me, darling." The end of his words lilts up so that it's almost a question, as if he doesn't want to push me but knows that I need to spill out my troubles. I sigh, closing my eyes briefly. It makes the words easier to say somehow.

"I'm so fucking angry, Kai," I grit out, my jaw tight and fists curled. I feel the flood of rage flow through my blood, making my heart pound like the sound of war drums. My eyes snap open, looking up into his eyes. "I'm spitting mad that all these men think that they can just do as they damn well please, taking and taking and never thinking about their own fucking evil. That what they are doing is wrong on so many bloody levels it's obscene."

My chest heaves, the frustration at everything and feeling so fucking powerless spilling over, sitting like oil on water coating everything in its path and suffocating all that is pure and good.

"My whole life has been dominated by men controlling it, and I'm just a fucking pawn being placed where they want me to be. Shit, even before I was born, I was running from a man!"

I move away, pacing as my hands run through my hair, but I can't stop the flow of words that blurt out of me.

"M–my mum was killed because of a man. A man forced me to marry Ash. A man fucking kidnapped me. All because of what, Kai? Why do they think they can just take and take, never bothering to let me make my own choices?" I know I'm practically shouting now, tears streaming down my cheeks as I throw my hands wide, then drop them down at my sides, defeated. "I just want to be able to make my own decisions, choose my own destiny. Is that too much to ask?"

I turn to him, my shoulders slumped as I sob quietly, feeling so beaten.

"And the worst part?" I ask, looking up at him through blurry eyes. He just stands there, jaw working as if it's taking a gargantuan effort not to rush over and hold me as I break. "It's not over. They're still out there. What fresh hell will be next, Kai?"

"Lilly—" he starts, losing the battle within himself and striding over to me, wrapping me up in his embrace and pulling me so close I can feel his pounding heart matching the rhythm of my own. "We are all fucking pawns to them, my darling," he tells me, his own voice growling with frustration. He pulls back a little, placing a finger under my chin and raising it to meet his gaze. "But I swear to you on everything that I am, you will get your pound of flesh. You will be free, we all will."

I stare up into his face, his eyes a savage amber flame with his vow.

"I liked hurting him, Kai," I confess in a whisper, saying aloud what I've barely even admitted to myself. "I liked taking that gun and making him bleed."

I watch his reaction intently, my heart racing for an entirely different reason now. What if, after all this time, this admission is too much? I'm not the same Lilly who walked into this dormitory less than a year ago, hurting but with clean hands. Yet if anyone can understand this craving for violence, it's my dark Knights.

His beautiful mouth curves up into a smile that may give some men nightmares, but I relish in its depravity.

"That's because you are a warrior queen, made to shed the blood of our enemies," he tells me, a fierce pride in his tone as one hand comes up to stroke down the side of my face. "And you are perfect, Lilly Vanderbilt. Just right for us."

A shiver runs down my spine at his words, my inner demon preening at his praise and acceptance.

After all, what better way to defeat the monsters that plague us than by becoming monstrous ourselves?

"Wait here," Kai orders, placing a soft kiss on my cheek, his fingers trailing down my arm and leaving goosebumps in their wake. Anticipation swirls in my lower stomach as I watch him walk across the room and up the spiral staircase.

I hear quiet murmurs from upstairs, my breath speeding up when multiple footsteps start to descend the stairs. All four of my Knights alight at the bottom, Jax, Ash, and Loki looking deliciously sleep rumpled as they surround me in a wide circle.

It's A Man's World by Jurnee Smollett-Bell and Black Canary begins to play over the speakers, and I take in a deep inhale as one by one they all sink to their knees.

"Use us, Princess," Ash says, his voice deep and husky, his tattooed chest bathed in moonlight.

"Take back control, Pretty Girl," Loki adds, his eyes twinkling in the dark.

I swallow hard, my breath leaving my lungs in a shudder as I fill with love for these men, men who are all naturally alpha but are willing to set that aside to give me what I need right now. Reaching down, I pull my tank over my head, my nipples hardening underneath their heated gazes. Next, I shimmy out of my panties, and I relish in the sharp inhales that sound around me as I stand naked before them.

"She's going to kill us," Loki rasps under his breath, and a bark of delighted laughter leaves my lips.

"Nah, I like your cocks too much for that, Pretty Boy," I sass him, and his lips tip up into a grin that turns salacious as I step towards him, running my fingers through his hair before grabbing a fistful and tugging his head back. "Lie back,"

Releasing my grip, he obeys, lying on his back with his head in the centre of the circle the others have created.

"Good boy," I praise.

"Sexiest fucking thing ever," he groans, adjusting his tented sweatpants.

"Glad that you think so," I reply, arching a brow at him and loving the sense of power I feel at bossing Loki around. I can only imagine what it'll be like to boss all of them. "Now, you're going to lick me out like you're starving, and the rest of you will watch but no touching yourselves." A thrill runs through me as I look at each of them.

"Yes, ma'am." Loki salutes, and I can't stop the grin that tugs my lips upwards.

"Anything you say, Princess," Ash drawls in a low voice, and my eyes dart down to see his sweats straining at the crotch.

I look at Kai, who gives me a disarming smile. "As you wish, darling."

"Yes, my Queen." Finally, I look at Jax as he answers, and a full-body shiver cascades over my skin at the term. I like that coming from his lips, a lot if the wetness seeping down my thighs is any indication.

"Good," I state, turning my attention back to Loki, lying there patiently waiting for me. I walk over to him, placing my feet just under his armpits and making my way to my knees, facing the others. It's not as graceful as it used to be, but with the noise of manly desire that he makes low in his throat, I don't care. He wants me, regardless if I'm becoming more whale-like with each day.

"Jesus, Pretty Girl, you smell fucking divine," he moans, his hands grasping the globes of my arsecheeks and pulling me closer to his waiting mouth.

I gasp as his tongue makes a slow pass from my opening to my clit and back again, delving inside my channel and swirling around.

"I can taste them inside you, baby," he rasps, his voice muffled.

"It's rude to talk with your mouth full," I say back, my voice low and husky with the pleasure that he's already giving me.

His chuckle vibrates across my core and a deep moan leaves my lips at the feel of him between my thighs. Without saying anything else, he dives in so to speak, licking and sucking like I really am his last meal on earth, and it's all I can do to hold on, my head thrown back in ecstasy. My knees dig into the rug beneath us, but I hardly feel the ache as I hurtle towards a climax that I know will shake my very being.

"Loki..." I whine, my eyelids fluttering closed as I lose myself to the please that his naughty tongue is giving me.

More quickly than I'd like to admit, he builds me up until I'm shaking above him, my hands curled into fists and stars begin to burst behind my closed lids. He doubles his efforts, and soon I'm hurtling down the rabbit hole, crying out and soaking his face with the force of my orgasm.

He stills underneath me whilst I pant and sweat drips down my spine. Moving back a little to give him some breathing space, I glance down to see his mouth and chin glistening in the moonlight.

"Good boy," I breathe out again, and he chuckles deeply once more, his hands flexing on my arse.

"I aim to please, my Queen."

His smile grows wider as he feels my thighs clench. I really do like that term.

I tear my gaze away from him, my eyes finding Jax's, his stare intense and making my already hard nipples tighten. An idea springs into my head, and suddenly I'm desperate to feel him inside me whilst I ride that monster cock.

"Your turn to watch, Pretty Boy," I tell Loki, crawling off him and over to Jax. "Lose the pants," I order, kneeling in front of him. One of his blond eyebrows raises at my command.

Without a word spoken, he does as I request, his huge dick springing free and my mouth waters at the sight of the bead of precum glistening at the tip. Unable to resist, I lean down and lick it off, the hiss of breath that leaves his lips making my insides flutter. Straightening up, I look him in the eye, the desire in his stare almost burning me with its intensity.

"Your turn to lie down, big boy. Same position as Loki so the others can see my face."

The song changes to *Right Here* by Chase Atlantic as Jax does my bidding, again remaining silent as he gets into position. I wet my lips as I watch him, marvelling that this powerful man, these powerful men, are so quick to obey me. It's a heady aphrodisiac.

On my hands and knees again, I crawl over his body, my knees settling on either side of his hips, my legs spread wide to accommodate his size. Taking his shaft in my hand, I give it a few pumps just because I can and I love the way his hips jerk when I do. Then I place him at my opening, using touch to feel my way as my stomach now prevents me from seeing what I'm doing.

His hands come up to rest on my thighs, his fingers digging in as I slowly sink down, a deep, keening moan leaving my lips as I take him all the way to the hilt.

"Fuck, baby," he hisses out, his eyes leaving the place that we're joined and rolling to the back of his head.

"I intend to," I quip, wasting no time and moving my hips in a way that has him massaging my inner walls.

"You look so fucking beautiful like that, Queen," Ash tells me, and I look up to catch his scorching stare as he watches us, his hand drifting to his clearly rigid member. My core tightens around Jax at the nickname, making him groan deeply.

"Same rules as before Vanderbilt, no touching," I tell him and I pick up the pace, Jax helping me to move up and down more on him.

Turning my attention back down to the big man beneath me, I catch his gaze, my lips tilting up in what I know is an evil smirk.

"No coming for you yet, big guy," I tell him, and he arches a brow at me again, but then just gives me a nod to let me know that he's agreeing to my request.

I start to move faster, the tingling tell of a second orgasm starting up in my core. My breath pants out of my chest, my breasts swinging as I begin to slam my hips down, the bite of pain as he hits me deeply, sending me closer to that edge. But there's something I want to try before jumping off.

Leaning down, I stretch my arms out until my hands can wrap around his thick throat. His eyes widen a fraction as he holds my stare, and a part of me can't believe that the idea of choking Jax as I fuck him has a rush of liquid pooling between us.

"Oh shit." I hear Loki whisper as I press tighter, feeling Jax's pulse beat wildly underneath my fingertips.

Jax's hands grab my waist, and he uses his grip to start pulling me up and down hard and fast so that I don't lose the rhythm.

Fuck.

It feels so fucking good, his dick pounding into my dripping cunt, my hands around his throat, choking him. My inner walls start to tighten, and I'm gasping and whimpering as my orgasm threatens to overwhelm me. Just before I fall off the edge, Jax pulls me off him and fuck me, he hits something on the way out that has a literal fountain squirting out of me, coating his abs and lower stomach. I scream, my nails digging into the side of his neck as I convulse over him, wave after wave of pleasure crashing over me with the intensity of a stormy sea.

He lowers me down and I slump, panting and everything practically glowing as I tingle from one of the strongest orgasms I've ever had. His large palms smooth down my thighs, his deep whispers of how fucking beautiful I am settling deep into my soul and soothing the anger inside me that's been present since my capture.

After a few moments, I lift my head to look around at the others and see the look of adoration and lust present on all of their faces. I feel sated, and I know exactly how I want this to end.

Pushing up to sitting, Jax's hard length trapped under my swollen pussy lips, I look down at him and then back up at the others.

"I want to taste you," I say to them. "All of you."

Some people believe that being on your knees for a man, his dick in your mouth is a place of submission, but I don't. It's a place of power, a place where you can be in control of how much pleasure, or pain, you give him, and I want to watch as they all come undone on my tongue, coating my mouth and upper body with their seed.

"Are you sure, baby?" Jax asks as he curls upwards, his arms banding around me and pulling me flush to his body.

"Yes."

Ash is suddenly there next to us, holding out a hand to help me up on shaky legs. He, too, pulls me close, placing a kiss on my lips. He steps back, keeping hold of my hand and leading me to the centre of the space, where Kai has placed a large throw pillow to cushion my knees.

Still holding Ash's hand, I lower once more to my knees, my head level with his bulging crotch. Letting go of his grasp, I pull his sweats down, freeing his rigid shaft, and watching as it bounces slightly then, begging to be touched. I grab the base, rolling my eyes upwards and watching as I open my mouth and take in his head, playing with his magic cross piercing before pushing forward until he's hitting the back of my throat.

"Fucking hell—" he groans, his hands coming to tangle in my hair and hold me as I sink deeper, breathing through my gag reflex until my lips meet the base of him. I pull back, my eyes on his almost pained expression as I bob my head up and down, coating him in my saliva and tasting the precum that's leaking from his tip.

Pulling back with a gasp, I turn to find Kai's cock ready and weeping precum. I take him in my slick hand, pumping slowly as I take him in my mouth but only playing with the tip, swirling it around my tongue, sucking and grazing it with my teeth until I feel him shake.

"Jesus...Lilly..." He gasps as I'm relentless in my pursuit of his pleasure, my other hand stroking Ash.

I let go of both of them, taking their hands and wrapping them around their own shafts, with a silent instruction to keep pumping. Shuffling around, I find Jax's cock in front of me next, glistening with my release and I waste no time in taking him into my mouth, my lips stretching wide to accommodate his girth.

"That's it, Baby Girl," he murmurs, his hand coming up to the back of my head and gripping my hair. "Right. Fucking. There."

His hand pushes down, forcing me to swallow more of him, my throat working around his shaft as I breathe through my gag reflex.

Tears stream from my eyes as I gaze up at him, my hand fondling his balls and massaging the space behind them.

Someone takes my free hand, wrapping it around a hard member and guiding the stroking. My thumb finds the tip and I realise from the piercing that it's Loki, my hand working him in a steady massaging motion that I know makes his knees weak.

I keep fucking Jax's dick with my mouth and throat, his thighs beginning to tremble and his shaft goes rock-hard moments before a roar escapes his lips and hot, salty cum fills my mouth. I swallow some down, pulling away as he's still squirting so that the rest dribbles down my chin and breasts.

As soon as he's finished, a hand tangles in my hair, and Loki pulls me to him, thrusting his dick inside my mouth, Jax's release acting as lube as Loki face fucks me. I relax, letting him take his pleasure as both of my hands are wrapped around Kai and Ash who have stepped up close next to Loki. I look to the side as much as I'm able to, watching the pleasure on their faces and then Loki's, and I feel my own body begin to react at the power that comes from bringing these men to the brink of insanity.

"Fuck!" Loki yells, pulling out and coating my lips, chin, and chest with his climax, hot spurts of cum hitting me and coating me.

I'm panting as he steps back, letting Ash and Kai close ranks. I smile up at them, my chest heaving as our hands continue to move on their hard lengths.

"You look so fucking beautiful like that, Queen," Ash grits out between clenched teeth, his fingers coming under my chin and angling my head towards him. "Open up for me, tongue out."

I decide to obey him this time as that's exactly what I wanted to do, and so I hold his stare as I open my mouth, sticking my tongue out and waiting for him to finish on me.

It doesn't take long, his jaw ticking as a deep groan escapes his lush lips seconds before his warm release hits my tongue, dripping down onto my chin and chest.

As soon as he's finished, he pulls me off and turns my head to face Kai who weaves his fingers in my sweaty hair.

"I want to pour my release down that beautiful throat of yours," Kai tells me, his hand wrapped over mine, our grip punishing. "May I, my Queen?"

My thighs clench at that name again, wetness seeping down them.

"Yes, please," I whimper, gasping when I feel something wriggling between my slick thighs. I look away from Kai to see Jax with his face underneath me, his hands pulling me down until his hot breath fans over my lower lips.

Kai feeds me his dick, the piercing on the underside clacking against my teeth, at the same moment that Jax thrusts his tongue inside me. I cry out at the spark of lightning that shoots up from my inner channel, Kai taking the opportunity to push the rest of the way in until I'm choking on his dick.

A deep animalistic sound leaves his throat as he pulls out a little, only to snap his hips forwards and thrust back inside, my eyes streaming as I gag.

"So fucking precious," he coos, and I whine deep in my throat when hands grasp my breasts, pinching my nipples and smearing the cum all over them.

"Such a beautiful Queen," Ash praises, his hand coming up to the front of my throat and wrapping around it, making Kai hiss as Ash tightens his grip.

"And all ours," Loki adds, his scalding tongue flicking my cum covered nipple in time to Jax tongue fucking my cunt.

Fucking hellballs.

I'm consumed by them all, another orgasm building in my core as they build me up to a raging inferno. I become a shaking, quivering mess, and my hands grasp Kai's thighs, my nails digging in until I feel wetness seep from the wounds as I race towards the explosive finish that I know is waiting for me.

"Fuck! Lilly!" Kai shouts, thrusting deep as he does exactly what he asked and pours his hot seed down my throat.

It triggers my own climax, and I cry and tremble as electricity makes my limbs go rigid, more wetness shooting out of me as I come, and come, and come. I swear I black out for a while there, as the next thing I know I'm being lifted into strong arms, Jax's, I realise as I crack my eyes open.

"Thank you," I croak out, my voice raspy as only a good face fuck will leave it.

"You don't need to thank us, Baby Girl," Jax replies, walking us into the bathroom, the soft lighting around the mirror coming on.

"It's what we're here for, Pretty Girl," Loki adds, placing a kiss on my cheek as he strolls past and opens the shower. The sound of water falling fills the room, alongside steam.

"We will never take your control, my love," Ash tells me, his palm cupping my cheek as he presses our foreheads together, uncaring that I'm covered in his friend's cum, and held in the arms of one of those friends.

"And we will always love you, no matter what," Kai finishes from my other side, and I twist my head to see him standing next to us, his own fingers grazing my damp cheek.

"And I will always love you," I reply, pressing a kiss to his fingers.

The tender moment is interrupted, as usual, by Loki singing *I will Always Love You* by Whitney Houston, using the shampoo bottle as a mic, and I turn to see his hair sticking up and covered in bubbles. He obviously changes the words so it's not about leaving someone, and his terrible rendition, sung in key, has me laughing so hard I think I might pee myself.

Fucking bellend.

CHAPTER SEVENTEEN

LILLY

It's my first day back, and I feel sick to my stomach, chewing my lip nervously as I walk down the wide, sweeping staircase with my guys around me. As we reach the bottom, Jax tugs my lip from between my teeth with a small rumble.

"You don't need to be afraid, Baby Girl," he tells me, pausing and turning me to face him, his clear, blue eyes piercing into my very soul. "You are the strongest fucking person I know, these cunts are nothing."

Tears sting my eyes, and I swallow hard as his words sink in, coating my insides like a life-giving elixir. I hear the others murmur their agreement as I'm enclosed in their circle, the mixed scents of ginger, vanilla, lemon, and fresh woods soothing my fractious nerves. I take a deep breath, inhaling their strength into myself until my heartbeat calms and the black claws of panic recede.

"Okay," I tell them, turning my head so that I can look at each of them in turn. "I'm ready."

"That's our girl," Jax praises, leaning down to place a soft kiss on my lips that sends tingles all the way to Her Vagisty. He catches my slight gasp, and the sexiest smirk graces his lips as he pulls away. I clear my throat, trying to tell Her Vagisty that we can't just spend the rest of our lives with their dicks balls deep. She doesn't believe me and fuck if my knickers don't look like the bottom of a bird cage most days.

"I need to freshen up," I inform them, Jax's smirk blooming into a full-blown smile that does nothing to help my underwear situation. I'm a lost fucking cause by this point. "Fuck off," I grouch at him, stomping—*okay, there's a bit of a waddle going on*—to the girl's bathroom.

I feel them all at my back, not leaving me alone for a second, though thankfully none of them follow me into the lav. Part of me wishes they had when I look up as the door closes to see Amber and her two Cuntmuffins applying lipstick to already perfectly made-up faces.

She spots me in the mirror, her gaze narrowing, and her lip curling as she takes me in. I go to make a snarky comment about the fact that her make-up clearly isn't vegan and I'm pretty sure the brand that she's using was involved in an animal testing scandal a couple of years ago.

But then I just stop. I'm so fucking tired of all the drama.

"Why are you so afraid of me?"

"What the fuck?!" Amber scoffs, spinning to glare at me, crossing her arms and curling her upper lip. "Why would I be afraid of orphan trash like you?"

"I have four amazing men who will love me no matter what. I'll never be alone, never be lonely. I'm married to Ash Vanderbilt, heir to a billion-dollar empire. I have majority shares in that billion-dollar company. My future is secure and full of love."

A thought occurs to me then and gives me pause. Maybe Amber and I have more in common than I first thought. We are both pawns in a game of chess played by greedy men.

"You don't have to do as he says, you know," I tell her, looking her directly in the eyes, even as she raises her chin. "You don't have to be a pawn in your father's game. You are a strong woman, Amber. Don't become what he wants you to be."

Her facade cracks a little, like the fine lines of a porcelain cup that's been left out in the frost. Her lip wobbles ever so slightly, and her crossed arms appear more like they are hugging her and protecting her from this cruel world. Then I watch as she straightens her spine, adopting that mean girl persona once more like armour.

"Fuck you, Lilly," she spits out, turning on her Birkenstock heel and sweeping out of the bathroom, her clones giving me a confused look before following after her.

Well, that could have gone worse I suppose.

CHAPTER EIGHTEEN

LOKI

I watch from the couch as Lilly comes down the stairs with heavy-lidded eyes. But the fact that she's here and not asleep in the middle of the night tells me that she, too, is having trouble sleeping. I know that she's been this way since we got her back. Restless, unable to relax.

And who can fucking blame her after what she went through. I want to bring that cunt back to life just to torture him all over again for hurting our girl, and don't get me fucking started on Julian.

She spots me sitting in a shaft of moonlight, her lips tilting upwards, and my heart pitter-patters in my fucking chest at her smile.

"Can't sleep either?" she asks in that beautiful voice of hers. It's like music to my love-struck ears, and I never want to stop hearing it.

She comes over to me, sitting next to me on the couch and snuggling under my arm. Shit, I still can't believe that we got her back and she's now here. Prickly guilt stabs into my chest, the blame of her being taken still raw for me, no matter how many times she tells me that it wasn't my fault.

Shaking my head, I wrap my arm around her and breathe the sweet scent of her hair in. Well, Ash's ginger scent as she's still using his shampoo, which the asshole lords over the rest of us at every opportunity. I'm waiting to point out to him that she may use his shampoo and be his wife, but I was the one to put a baby in her. Not sure I'll be able to run fast enough when I do remind him of that little fact.

"Did I ever tell you about the fallen angel tattoo?" I ask her, wanting to distract her from the worries that are creasing her brow as I look down at her.

"No," she replies, eyes alight with curiosity.

"Well," I begin, pulling her closer to me so that I don't have to look into those stunning eyes of hers. It's funny how I can torture and kill a man without a shred of fear, but talking to this goddess about my past fills me with fucking dread. "I got the piece done after Luc…" I swallow, the wound of his suicide still a sharp pain, though it is duller than it used to be. "After Luc killed himself. I felt like I'd let him down. Fuck, we were close, and I didn't see it coming at all. At the time, I blamed myself for not seeing the signs of how badly he was hurting, thinking that I could have stopped it somehow."

"It's not your fault, Loki, love," she interrupts, and I smile into the darkness at just how fucking good this woman is. She's always trying to help us, assure us, and I fucking love it. I squeeze her tighter.

"I know that now, Pretty Girl. But then, I was fucked up. Turning to drugs and pussy to try and forget. I think that the fact that my parents didn't give a shit about me also contributed to feeling like I wasn't enough," I confess, feeling a lessening in the tightness that I always carry around in my chest. She doesn't interrupt this time, other than to snuggle into my chest. "I wanted to mark my skin, to see the wound I was carrying inside on the outside. I looked up fallen angels. They have been thrown out of heaven. Lost the battle and are a symbol of pain, suffering, and sadness. Of shame," I whisper the last part into the darkness, taking another deep inhale of her scent. I love how it's often a mixture of all of ours, plus her own fresh spring smell. It calms my raging emotions.

"They are also a symbol of rebellion against society's rules," she tells me, pulling out of my grip and swinging her leg over mine until she straddles my hips, her hot, panty-clad core right over my rapidly hardening shaft. Fuck.

She reaches a hand on either side of my face and tips it up until I am staring right into her beautiful eyes.

"So, maybe your ink is about your future as well as your past?" she asks, and my hands tighten on her hips, my throat thick with emotion for this girl. She has this ability to make me find the light when I'm drowning in fucking darkness.

"I fucking love you, Lilly," I tell her, speaking around the lump in my throat. She leans in, her breath, sweet and minty, fanning over my lips as she replies.

"I fucking love you too, Loki."

With a deep groan, I close the minuscule distance between us, pressing my lips to her soft, pillowy ones and devouring her with my kiss. Fuck, I would go all Hannibal on her if cannibalism didn't mean that she'd be dead.

She kisses me back just as hotly, her hips moving and grinding down on my now rock-solid cock.

"Loki," she pleads, breaking the kiss and rewarding me with a gasping moan as my lips travel down her neck, biting and sucking, and fuck loving the marks that I leave there.

"Yes, beautiful?"

She answers me by pulling off her tank top, and it's my turn to groan as her full, heavy tits are revealed, her pert nipples calling me like a fucking siren song in the moonlight. I lean into her, ducking my head to close my lips around one of the buds and suck, her hips bucking in time to the movements of my tongue.

"Shit, Loki," she says with a moan, grabbing fistfulls of my hair and pulling me forward. Her confidence in demanding what she wants sends a bolt of lightning straight to my dick, and I reward her by biting down on her flesh, making her cry out.

Moving one hand down the swell of her stomach—shit, there's something about knowing that the baby growing inside her is mine that makes me fucking crazy—I dip into the top of her panties, hissing when I feel just how fucking wet she is.

"Such a good fucking girl for me, baby. Wet and aching already."

She whimpers, and the sound does things to me that the devil would blush at. Grabbing the crotch of her panties, I give a quick tug, smirking at her gasp and the ripping sound as I tear the fabric to grant me the access that I need.

"Fucker," she scolds, but I can hear the smile on her lips.

I soon make her forget all about the damn things as I insert two fingers into her wet heat, not fucking around and rubbing at that spot just inside that drives her fucking crazy.

"Shit, Loki, fuck, I'm coming!" she gasps, moments before a rush of liquid leaves her cunt and soaks my hand and sweats underneath.

As she pants and shivers, I remove my hand, using it to pull my hard length out and slicking it with her release, groaning at the feel of her juices already coating me. Taking both of her hips in my hands, I lift her, hovering her over my dick as I let go with one hand and guide my cock to her opening.

"Loki," she moans in a deep, husky voice that has me almost coming as her still pulsing cunt grips my dick as I push inside her.

Fumbling for my phone on the cushion beside me, I hit play on *You're Special* by NF, the song filling the quiet and I sing along, knowing by the way her breath catches and her fingernails dig into my chest that she loves it when I do this. Moving my hips to the beat, I fuck her slowly, savouring the feel of her inner walls gripping me like she never wants me to leave.

It feels so fucking good that I lose the words of the song, my movements speeding up even as I want to prolong this pleasure for as long as humanly possible.

"Fuck, Lilly, baby. Your pussy feels so fucking good gripping my cock," I grit out, and her inner walls flutter around me, her hips matching my thrusts with movements of her own as she rides me hard and fast. "That's it, Pretty Girl. Ride my dick like it will never be enough."

And I know that my words are fucking true; it will never be enough. I will always want more. More of her, more of this.

Tingling begins at the base of my dick, and I feel my balls drawing up as I get as solid as fucking marble. Reaching between us, I start to pinch and rub her clit, a husky cry leaving her throat as her head falls back and she moves even faster. Just as I feel cum surge up my shaft with the force of a fucking rocket, her pussy clamps down around me like a vise, and she climaxes with a scream, her nails raking bloody furrows down my chest.

But I'm beyond caring as stars fill my eyes, an animalistic groan ripping from my chest when I thrust hard to the hilt inside her, growling like a goddamn wolf as I come inside her, filling her up with my seed.

"Loki, you are more than enough, my love. You brought me back to life," she whispers in my ear, her body draped over mine and my cock still buried deep inside her.

I pull her closer, marvelling that she came into our lives just a few months ago, and now none of us can live without her. She's our harbour, our refuge, and these past weeks, when she was gone, were legit the hardest of my fucking life.

"I can't breathe without you, Pretty Girl. I no longer exist when you are not there," I confess, peppering her neck with kisses and smiling when I feel her pussy walls spasming around my rapidly hardening cock. "You brought us all back from the dead, baby." I punctuate my words with the movements of my hips, holding her close to me as I shallowly thrust into her. Fuck, this will never get old, having her wrapped around me.

I spend the rest of the night showing her the truth of my words, worshipping her body until we fall into bliss over and over again and eventually pass out, still connected in every way.

CHAPTER NINETEEN

LILLY

One week.

One week is all I have until finals and then graduation. That is if I've enough credits, which I'm not certain I do given the time that I've missed.

Shitballs. I'm royally fucked, and not in the good, four peens at once kind of way.

The week goes by in a whirlwind of revision classes and trying to catch up with almost two months of missed work. Luckily, Kai and the guys help me on that front, plus all the teachers seem suspiciously accommodating, giving me only a few extra projects even though I must have missed a fuck ton more.

I'm ready to leave campus when Saturday rolls around, desperate for some space from the silent judgement and curious stares of the student population that have made my skin prickle for the past five days. They don't dare say anything, but I know they all whisper about me, my disappearance, and my pregnancy. *Fuck them all to hell in a handcart.*

"Why don't we go paintballing?" I ask hopefully as we all finish up breakfast, remembering the Christmas presents I'd gotten the guys and suddenly thinking that we all just need a bit of fun.

Ash gives me what can only be described as a withering Ash-hole stare, and I want to slap him for it, my fists clenching around my cutlery.

"You can't go paintballing in your condition," he states with an eye roll as if that was the stupidest thing I could have said.

Suddenly my lower lip wobbles and before I know it, I burst into tears, throwing my knife and fork down with a clatter and shooting up to my feet. They're not delicate lady-like tears either, but great heaving sobs that rack my chest, and I'm sure snot slides out of my nose.

"Shit–Princess–fuck–I—" Ash stammers, his eyes wide and hands raised, and it would be funny if, you know, I wasn't crying so hard. Fucking hormones.

"You fucking asshole!" Loki hisses, shoving a still floundering Ash in his chair, and Kai gives him a chilling death glare across the table.

Jax whacks him upside the head, causing Ash to wince, getting up and then my Viking strides over to me and wraps me up in his huge, comforting embrace. Immediately, my sobs lessen as I inhale his warm, lemon scent. All the guys make me feel safe and secure, but Jax is like my refuge, my security blanket. He holds me, rubbing a huge palm up my spine until I quieten, my fists tight in his black tee.

He pulls back a fraction, just enough so that he can look deeply into my no doubt, puffy eyes.

"It's not safe for the baby for you to play paintball, Baby Girl," he tells me gently in that deep, husky voice of his, his thumb brushing the tears from my face. I heave a sigh, knowing he's right, but hating that there feels like so much I can't do, or eat because I'm growing a baby. "But," he adds, a mischievous twinkle in his ice blue eyes, "if you want to watch from the viewing platform, I'll shoot Ash in the dick just for you."

"I'd like to see you fucking try," I hear Ash grumble, and it pretty much seals his fate as I let a positively evil smirk tug my lips up.

"Deal."

Getting dressed, I decide on a cute as fuck denim, mini dress with a brightly-coloured, vintage scarf tied in a knot at my neck fifties style, and some brand new, red, sequin chuck-style high tops by my favourite shoe brand.

Apparently, after the guys discovered where I was, Loki went on a shopping spree and bought me a shit ton of maternity clothes in my style as well as several pairs of flats which he brought back with us from England. God, I love that boy.

I grab my sunglasses and phone, heading out of the room I share with Loki, bumping into Kai in the corridor.

"Jesus, Lilly, darling," he rasps, his eyes travelling down the expanse of my bare legs and his lips quirking at the glittering shoes. "You are so beautiful."

He steps into me, his fresh scent filling my nostrils as his hand snakes around my thickening waist and pulls me closer. My pulse speeds as he nuzzles my neck, kissing his way up to my ear and leaving me breathless and my knickers damp.

"Come with me, Pet."

I take in a sharp exhale at the name, my whole body feeling like a live fuse wire as he pulls me to his room, opening the door and then closing it behind us. He leads me to the bed, but instead of pushing me down onto it as I expect, he turns me around sharply so that my back is to his front. I groan as he grinds his hardness into my lower back, and I arch into him, telling him with my body what I want. He tuts, biting my earlobe hard.

"Naughty, impatient, Pet," he says, chuckling huskily as his hand slides down my side and his fingers hook under the hem of my short dress. "Hands on the bed, ass in the air."

I do as he commands, feeling him take a step back as I move, pulling the back of my dress up and over my arse. He laughs, no doubt at my choice of rainbow and unicorn patterned knickers. "Cute." He pulls them down to my knees, leaving them there and not taking them off.

I frown when a moment later my back is cold, and turning my head, I watch as he walks over to his cabinet of curiosities, aka toys to fuck you with. I can't see what he takes out, but he's soon turning back, stalking towards me with a wicked fucking smile on his lips. With his glasses, and hot nerd look, he's like a filthy Clark Kent, and I am fucking here for it.

He stops in front of my face, leaning down and opening his fist to show me a gleaming, metal butt plug in rainbow colours and with a pink jewel on the end. My breath catches, and I look to see a wide smile on his handsome face.

"I thought that you'd like this one, Pet. On account of your underwear choice," he tells me, running the plug up and down my bare arm. Goosebumps rise on my skin from the cool touch. "You'll wear this all day. Only I'm allowed to take it out, understand?"

"Yes, sir," I breathe, shivering slightly.

"Such a good Pet," he praises softly, straightening up and going around to my arse.

I hear the top of a lube bottle opening, then gasp as his fingers, coated in the cool lubricant, start to rub all around my back door, spreading it around. A groan leaves my lips as one finger enters me, then a second as he works the lube inside my hole.

"Kai," I moan, rubbing my forehead on the soft, cotton duvet cover as pleasure starts to build in my core, which flutters, desperate to be filled.

He withdraws his fingers, only to replace them with the cool metal of the plug, and I breathe in through my mouth as he pushes it inside me. There's a sharp pain as the wider part breaches my tight muscles, and he coos, stroking my arse as he coaxes me to take it all.

I'm a shaking, hot fucking mess, sweaty hair sticking to my forehead when he's finished, and I just lie with my cheek pressed to the covers of his bed as I get used to the delicious feeling of intrusion. Kai pulls my knickers back up and then my dress down before he encourages me to stand.

I quiver with the movement, the plug making its presence felt in the most distracting way.

"Good girl," he whispers, pushing my hair off my forehead and placing a kiss on my lips. "Let's go downstairs, the others are waiting."

Taking my hand in his, holding his other, slightly shining hand by his side, he leads us out of the room and down the stairs and I feel every. Damn. Step.

When we reach the bottom, he excuses himself to go wash up, and my cheeks burn as three sets of jewelled eyes lock onto me, assessing and narrowing.

"What's wrong?" Ash asks, striding over to me and taking my face in his palms, tipping it up to look into my eyes, worry creasing his forehead.

"N–nothing," I stammer out, feeling my cheeks heat up even more as the burn of the plug in my arsehole makes a lie of my words. I hear Kai chuckle and look over to see him casually sauntering over to us.

"Turn round, Lilly," he commands, and although he doesn't use his pet name for me, I feel my body wanting to do as he orders.

Ash lets go of me with a curious look in his eye, one jet-black brow raised, as I do what Kai says.

"Raise your dress and show them your new accessory," is Kai's next order. With my cheeks heating even more, I turn around, lift up the back of my dress, and pull my knickers back down before bending over.

"Fucking Christ," I hear Ash exclaim in a low voice, then a sharp sting hits my arse cheek as a cry of pleasure mixed with pain leaves my lips as he smacks me. It jostles the plug, and I feel the effects deep inside me, wetness slicking my thighs.

"Fuck me, that looks so pretty sparkling in your ass," Loki groans out, and Jax makes a growl of agreement.

"Right, time to go," Kai interrupts firmly. "Lilly, get dressed."

Swallowing, unsure how in the ever-loving fuck I'm going to get through this day with a butt plug inside me, I do as instructed. Taking a deep breath, I turn back around to find all of my Knights with hungry, almost desperate looks on their faces. It's then I realise that I'm not the only one who is affected by it.

"Ready," I announce unnecessarily. I stride past them, each step sending waves of sensation through me as I walk, my nipples hard and pussy aching by the time I reach the door. "You guys coming?" I ask, turning back to see them blinking, and I can't help the chuckle that falls from my lips.

They spring into action, grabbing various items before we all head out of the door and down to Jax's truck which sits idling by the front doors. A valet gets out, handing the keys to Jax with a nod, and disappears into the building behind us.

"Huh," I say aloud as we climb in and grit my teeth as that move sends sparks from my arsehole through me.

"What's up, beautiful?" Jax asks, turning in his seat to look back at me in the backseat. I'm sandwiched between Loki and Kai, both of whom have a hand on my exposed thighs.

"I've not seen Mr Smythe, that crow who showed me to the dorm my first night around for a while," I state, frowning. My gaze flits from one boy to another as they all look elsewhere. "You know some-thing!" I accuse, turning to Loki who is staring out of the window. I grab his face, physically turning him to face me. "Tell me."

He grimaces, his eyes flicking to Ash in the passenger seat before coming back to me.

"Well, when I told the guys how he'd treated you when you got here," he starts, his free hand coming up to rub the back of his neck, and I hear Jax growl from the front as he starts the engine.

"You didn't fucking kill him?!" I shout, looking away from Loki to Ash who is turned towards me with an evil fucking smirk on his pretty lips. If fairies come with Jax's voice, they die with that smile of Ash's. I mean, the butler was a complete cumbucket, but I'm not sure he deserved to die because of it.

"We're not amateurs, Princess. Give us some fucking credit," Ash tells me, rolling his eyes like I'm being overly dramatic and didn't watch them castrate a boy or torture then kill a man, both of whom had wronged me. "We just made him see the error of his ways and had him relocated."

"Relocated to where?" I ask, looking at the amused smiles on each of their faces.

"He's now a semen collector for the Tailors' racehorses," Loki tells me, his face split into a wide grin.

"What?!" I question, my hand flying to my mouth to stifle my chuckle.

"He holds an artificial vagina for the studs in order to collect the semen so that they can inseminate the female horses and ensure good crossbreeding and stronger stock," Kai informs me, his face completely straight and deadpan. A slight twitch of his lips tells me he is holding in a laugh too.

"He's a horse wanker?" I enquire, my lips trembling with the effort to hold in my laughs.

"We thought that it was a job suited to his talents, being a *wanker* anyway," Ash replies, turning back to face the front.

"And he always did have a *stable* hand," Loki adds, and I fucking lose it, a bark of laughter bursting out of me, and then a groan as the plug shifts around. After a few chuckles, I manage to calm down enough to ask another question that has just popped into my head.

"Aren't the Tailors one of the gangs caught up in that turf war in Whetstone?"

"Yep," Ash answers, looking back around at me. "And Aeron Taylor owed us a favor."

I'm about to ask more, wondering who this Aeron is and why I'm only now finding out about him, but Loki squeezes my thigh, and when I turn to look at him, he shakes his head. So I leave it, deciding that it's not worth the hassle of getting pissed when Ash refuses to tell me. He'll open up about it eventually if it's important.

CHAPTER TWENTY

LILLY

The rest of the drive to the paintballing site is spent quietly, listening to *Ain't No Sunshine* by Black Label Society as we drive through the summer morning. Soon after, we pull into a driveway carved into the woods, a warehouse-looking building nestled amongst the trees. Getting out, we head inside, Loki's hand wrapped around my own, the guys all carrying their bags of kit.

We're welcomed by a young-looking guy, maybe a few years older than us who, to be honest, looks like a bit of a stoner with his faded band tee and long hair. He seems to know what he's about though, shaking each of my Knight's hands professionally and telling them that they're up against a group of eight Navy Seals.

"Excuse me?" I interrupt, all eyes turning my way. "Did you say Navy Seals? Eight Navy Seals?" I question, thinking that I must have misheard him.

"Uh, yeah. Is that a problem?" stoner dude—*Mark, maybe*—answers, looking at the guys with a raised brow.

"It's no problem," Ash informs him, not looking away from me with a devilish smirk on his face. He steps closer to me until the front of our bodies are pressed together, and I shiver as he tucks some loose hair behind my ear. "Are you doubting our abilities, Princess?"

I swallow, my throat dry with the sexual tension that thrums in the air between us.

"N–no," I whisper, taking a sharp inhale as his fingers trace down the side of my neck and across the scoop neckline of my dress.

"Good," he mumbles back, placing a small kiss on my pulse point, and I feel him smile against my neck when he feels how much it's racing. *Fuckcrumpet.* "We're going to get changed. Wait here with Mark, and we'll see you in a minute."

He steps back, and they all head to some changing rooms on the far side of the entrance space. Mark gives me a friendly smile, opening his mouth to say something, then flicking his gaze behind me when we hear the door open. There's the sound of male cama-raderie, and I turn to see what must be the Navy Seals if their matching buzz cuts are anything to go by.

"Excuse me," Mark apologises, going over and greeting them, with a similar talk that he gave my guys.

I cast my eyes over the new arrivals, wincing when I see that they're all pretty stacked, although maybe not quite as big as Jax. They give me curious looks in return, clearly wondering what a preg-nant teenager is doing here. I see the disbelief on one of their faces, then the wide grins and laughs as all of their attention shifts behind me, so I turn back and my own laughter rings out as my Knights walk towards me.

I'd completely forgotten about the costumes that I'd bought them to go with their paintballing equipment, and I must admit they look fucking hilarious.

Ash and Jax frown as they spot the guys behind me, but Kai and Loki just grin widely at me. I devour them with my gaze, admitting to myself that they still look fucking hot enough to eat, regardless of the onesies each of them wears. Ash is in a skintight devil costume, complete with a forked tail. His ink peeks up his neck and wrists, and the costume just highlights the valleys of all his muscles.

Jax looks almost like he might burst out of his bright green, Hulk onesie, and he's left it open all the way to his belly button, making my mouth water at the delicious pecs and abs on display. He catches me licking my lips as my eyes dip below his waist and I notice how tight the costume really is over his crotch. Fucking hell, he's not even hard and I can practically see all the veins on his dick.

My gaze flicks over to Kai, his Stormtrooper onsie fitted and showing off his ripped physique, his glasses adding to this fuck me now geek vibe. He's left off the helmet and gives me a cheeky grin and wink as he catches me perving.

And of course, Loki steals the show and fucking knows it too. He's dressed in a bright pink, fluffy, bunny onesie, complete with hood and attached ears, and Jesus have mercy on my cunt because he looks fine as fuck. The zip is open to just above his crotch, his happy trail on full fucking display, and I've never wanted to fuck the Easter bunny so much.

"Keep looking at me like that, Pretty Girl, and I'll have to fuck that pretty mouth of yours," he tells me, and I snap my gaze back up to see the cocky as all get out grin splitting his lips wide.

Deciding that I need to gain the upper hand in this dickfest, I sashay up to him, running my hand down his exposed chest and pressing myself closer to his hot body. Running my hand back up, I grasp his furry ear as I lean in, placing my lips against his actual ear.

"Maybe I'll grab these whilst I ride *your* pretty mouth."

His hand comes up to my side, squeezing tightly, and he takes in a deep breath.

"Fuck, baby. Now I'm gonna go out there with a boner that'll be fucking easy to spot. Why don't you take that beautiful ass of yours over to Jax and give him a matching one? They'll see him a mile off with that monster standing to attention."

I shout a laugh as the man in question tells Loki to fuck off, then pulls me away from Loki's touch, wrapping a hand around the front of my throat and pulling me in for a searing kiss. I wrap my arms around his neck, pulling him close—or as close as my pregnancy will allow anyway—and give as good as I get, kissing him stupid until we break apart, panting. I lift a corner of my lips, my eyes flicking down between us.

"Done," I say, loud enough that Loki hears and chuckles. Jax's own lips lift in an almost smile at my comment.

"Give the others a good luck kiss, baby," he orders me, and I raise a brow in a semblance of protest, but we both know that I'm going to do it regardless.

Loki grabs me anyway, and I laugh into his kiss when I hear one of the Seals make a comment about 'that kid's smuggling an anaconda in his pants.' Loki swallows my amusement, pulling me closer with a hand on the back of my neck as he deepens the kiss and makes my knees go all weak.

"Good luck," I manage to breathe out, shivering when I feel someone at my back, pressing me into Loki. Kai's fresh scent washes over me as he kisses my neck, his hands on my waist turning me around.

Ever so gently, he places his lips on my now swollen ones, teasing me with his light kisses and swipes of his tongue in moves that I know he's used on my pussy before, leaving me begging for more. Like he has all the time in the world, he deepens the kiss, everything around me disappearing beneath his touch. He ends the kiss just as gently, pulling away, and I open my eyes to stare into his amber ones, full of warmth and heat as they flick down my body.

I shiver and have to bite my lip to stop the moan that wants to escape as the feeling of the plug rushes over me, my inner walls clenching around it. Kai gives me a rare smirk.

"Wife," Ash calls, disrupting our moment, and I hear the Navy guys behind us splutter and whisper. Rolling my eyes at Ash's blatant attempt to shock them, and his Daddy Dom need to claim me, I saunter over to where he stands a few steps away.

Tilting my head to look up at him, I see the mischief glinting in his grey eyes.

"Yes, husband?" I ask, my tone laced with fake sweetness as I give him a brilliant smile, batting my lashes up at him.

"Were you planning on wishing me good luck too?" he questions, standing there, arms folded across his broad chest.

"As you asked so nicely," I sass back, pulling his arms open as I lean into him as if I'm about to kiss his lips.

Coming within touching distance, I bypass his lush mouth and instead dip down to his neck, dropping my mouth to it and beginning to suck. A deep, surprised groan sounds above me as I keep sucking, and his hands alight on my hips, clenching tightly. I can feel a hardness growing between us, which leaves me grinning against his neck.

"Fuck, Princess," he breathes in a rasp. "I'm going to come in my pants if you keep that up."

Deciding that as funny as that may be, I want him to come inside me or all over me later so I release my grip, beaming when I see the large hickey on the side of his neck, visible for all to see even through the black ink that covers him to his jawline.

"Good luck," I tell him, my tongue darting out to trace my moist lower lip at the dark fire which burns in his steel eyes.

"Where's Willow?" he asks instead of responding to my challenge, and my phone vibrates at that exact moment.

"Why?" I question, lifting it out of my pocket and looking at the screen. It's a message from the girl in question, apologising about not being able to make it today due to horrible period cramps.

"She's unwell," I tell him, glancing back up, having worked out that he'd organised her to keep me company whilst they played. His mouth draws into a straight line. "I'll be fine, Ash. Go have fun, and I'll watch you get your arses kicked from the viewing platform."

I point to the stairs that lead to a large lounge-like area and bar where people can watch the game below in the woods.

Ash just smirks at my taunt, his eyes promising retribution for that little slight. I hope it's in the form of his hand on my arse, but I guess I'll have to wait and see.

We all turn and head in the direction of the large doors that lead outside to where the game will take place. The Seals head that way too, and we end up walking next to one who gives Ash and I a curious look.

"So she's your wife?" he asks, clearly letting his curiosity get the better of him.

"Yes," Ash replies, giving the man a cursory look, his fingers linked with mine as we walk across the warehouse.

"But you let her kiss your friends?" the Seal continues, and I have to give him some credit for having the balls to ask. There's no judgement in his tone, just curiosity. Before Ash can answer, I do.

"Didn't your mummy ever tell you that sharing is caring, soldier?" I ask with a grin, and his jaw drops as my guys snigger. After a moment, he roars with laughter, the others all following suit, clearly having heard our conversation.

"Touché," he replies, still grinning as they start to head out and my boys pause at the door.

"Go," I tell them, letting go of Ash's hand and giving them each a shove. With a final look and goodbye kisses from each of them, they do as I say, and a pang of disappointment hits me at not being able to join them.

CHAPTER TWENTY-ONE

LILLY

Giving myself a mental shake and pulling my big girl panties up, I walk towards the stairs and bar area, consoling myself with the thought of all the fried food that I plan to order and my latest read just waiting on my kindle app.

After ordering at the bar, impressed by the setup even though I'm the only one currently occupying the space aside from the guy behind the bar, I settle into a soft, worn, leather sofa that faces a wall of windows which overlook the battleground. Music fills the space, *Dancer in the Dark* by Chase Atlantic giving the room an eighties feel. I smile and give my Knights a small wave when they look up and spot me, then they turn back to each other and put their heads together, clearly planning their strategy.

The ground is wooded with many areas open but also plenty of obstacles as well as hiding places. From my vantage point, my view is unobstructed, and I look to the right, spotting the Seals in a similar position to my guys, heads bent and obviously planning their strategy as well.

A loud horn blares, making me jump and then chuckle to myself at being a scaredy-cat. I watch the game, my book forgotten as I trace Ash, Loki, Kai, and Jax as they split up and start stalking towards the area that the Seals were in. Their opponents stick together in teams of two, and my heart begins to race at the idea that it's two Seals to one Knight.

"Don't worry, daughter darling," a voice that haunts my nightmares whispers behind me as hands alight either side of my neck. "We trained them well."

I freeze as he strokes my pulse points, chuckling as he no doubt feels my frantic heartbeat, my body turning arctic cold. The black claws of panic scratch at the edges of my vision, and I can't move, can't fucking breathe, as Julian Vanderbilt continues to caress me from behind. Bile rises in my throat when I realise that his groin is level with my head, the rapidly increasing hardness of his erection pressing into the back of my skull.

I no longer see the bright sky outside, or my guys playing paintball below me as my vision swims, the badass bitch who shot my fake uncle gone as terror fills me. I don't know why Julian makes me feel this way, what sway he has over me, but I can't fight him, my head screaming at me to do something, anything, but my body just freezes further. It's like my subconscious recognises the predator within him, the danger that he possesses, and thinks that if I only stay still and quiet, he'll go away.

"Are you okay, miss?" a concerned voice asks, snapping me out of my panic enough to take in a deep breath, sweet air filling my empty lungs once more. Julian's hands tighten on my neck.

"Y–yes," I manage to stammer out. The young guy, the one I ordered from at the bar, flicks his gaze up to Julian, then back down to me.

"If you need anything else, I'll be right over there. Okay?" he questions, his eyes trying to give me a message that I appreciate but just can't respond to. Not verbally anyway. I dart a look behind him to my guys below, then look back at him, hoping that he may get the message to somehow get my guys up here.

"Thank you," I reply softly.

"That'll be all," Julian says over the top of me, his voice hard and cold. One of his hands leaves my neck, and I breathe slightly easier. His hand appears over the top of my head, a folded wad of notes held between his fingers. "My daughter and I would like some privacy."

The young man's eyes widen, looking at Julian's outstretched hand and then back down to me. He must see the sheer terror in mine because he hesitates a moment.

"Now," Julian snaps out, and the boy visibly flinches, his hand shooting out and grabbing the notes. He scurries away after that, and trembles take over my body when I hear the guy's steps echoing down the metal stairs. "Alone at last, *darling*."

I hear the slight creak of his leather shoes as he crouches behind me, seconds before his breath whispers against my ear, and I can't stop the shudder of revulsion that I feel with his nearness.

"Did you enjoy your little visit back home?" he murmurs in my ear, his fingers playing with the neckline of my dress. "I must say, you seemed to enjoy the nights when Adrian joined you, thrashing under his touch like the wanton whore your mother was."

My lips wobble, and a hot tear burns a path down my cheek at his words. It's all I can do not to vomit all over the floor, knowing that he witnessed my abuse and knows what happened more than I do. But I hold it in, not wanting to give him the satisfaction of a reaction. I bite my lower lip, tasting copper. He growls, his nails digging into the flesh just under my neckline, and I whimper, inwardly cursing the sound of weakness as it falls from my lips.

"It's a shame that he didn't have sound on the feed, but I still gripped my cock as I watched you shatter around his fingers, darling—"

"Father!"

Relief floods me as I turn at the sound of my husband's voice, his tone sharp and cutting as he strides across the room, his face full of rage. Julian gets up from his crouch unhurried, his fingers leaving one last caress that lingers on my skin like an acid burn.

"Son," he replies, with no hint of shame or anger in his tone at being interrupted accosting his son's wife. "I came to tell you about the board meeting next week."

"And you needed to tell me in person?" Ash replies, coming to a stop right in front of me and crouching down.

His steel-coloured eyes lock with mine, dismissing Julian completely as he takes in my trembling state. One hand still holds his paintball gun, and the other reaches out and grasps my cheek, his thumb brushing away the wetness there. His eyes narrow, the vein on his neck bulging, and he looks back up at Julian with murder in his eyes.

"Email me the details, and I'll make sure we are there," he states coldly, quickly looking back down to me and dismissing his father once again. That must really piss Julian off, and I almost smile at the thought, then remember what Julian said, and my head dips, heat burning my cheeks as tears fill my eyes. "Anything else?" I hear Ash ask.

"I've said all that needed to be said," Julian states back, and I know that his words are aimed at me, his words hitting their target as I want to curl into a little ball and break down. Vaguely, I hear Julian's footsteps as he walks away, the sound getting quieter when he gets further away from us.

More footsteps rush towards us moments later, and I tense up, only to relax when Loki speaks.

"Why the fuck was your father here?" he asks. "Lilly?"

"What happened, darling?" Kai questions, and I flinch, a sob tearing from my throat at that nickname. It's tainted now. I can only associate it with that vile man.

"Don't call me that," I mumble quietly, my voice thick and muffled. I lift my head and stare directly into amber eyes full of worry and concern. "Never call me that again."

"I–I'm sorry, love," he replies, hurt flashing in his eyes, his hand reaching out and stroking the cheek that Ash isn't still cupping.

"What. The. Fuck. Did. He. Do?" Jax snarls, each word bitten out like he's struggling to contain his rage, and my gaze finds his eyes flashing blue, his neck thickly corded, and his hands clenching and unclenching around his gun as if he's considering using it on Julian.

"Take me home, Jax," I plead, tears rushing to my eyes, and Jax doesn't hesitate, throwing his gun at Loki and pushing the others aside to pick me up. Wrapping my arms around his neck, I bury my face into it, shutting my eyes as sobs threaten to overwhelm me.

Jax holds me steady as he strides down the steps, his boots loud on the metal. I hear the others following behind us and then Ash's voice.

"Thank you for coming to get me," he says, and I look over Jax's shoulder to see the young guy from earlier looking after me with concern.

"She looked like she needed help," I catch him saying just before Jax walks out of the door and into the bright sunshine.

The warmth of its rays doesn't touch me, shivers wracking my body as we head towards Jax's truck. Without missing a beat, or letting me go, Jax gets the keys from somewhere and tosses them to Kai, the truck unlocking with a click.

Loki opens the door, and Jax doesn't even attempt to pry me off as he somehow manoeuvres us into the vehicle, keeping me on his lap as he settles into the seat. I nuzzle back into his neck, my shivers getting worse, and I try to take some of his warmth into me.

"She's in shock," I hear him rumble against me. "Grab a can of Nos from my bag, Loki," Jax continues, and I hear the rustle and slide of a zipper from next to me. The sound of a ring pull is next, followed by the hiss of a fizzy drink.

"Here you go, baby," Loki coos, and I lift my head enough to see him holding out an orange can, with the word 'NOS' on the side. "Drink some of this."

He holds it to my lips, which is a good thing as my hand is

shaking too much to even think of holding it without the drink spilling all over us. Tilting it ever so slightly, I part my lips as fizzy, sweet mango fills my mouth. Swallowing slowly, I drink, pulling away when I've had enough. I do feel better, and my shaking has quietened down to a slight tremble now.

"Good girl," Jax soothes, his hand stroking down my back as I snuggle back into him, letting his scent of warm lemon mixed with fresh sweat calm me further. My eyelids droop, the adrenaline leaving my body exhausted, and Jax's touch and the motion of the car soothing me to sleep as I give into the darkness, welcoming it like an old friend.

CHAPTER TWENTY-TWO

LILLY

I wake up as Jax carries me into our dorm, and for a moment, I just relish being held in his strong arms, his sweet, lemony scent washing over me in a comforting whisper. Ice fills my veins as the memory of what happened today at the paintballing centre rushes over me.

"I can walk, Jax," I tell him softly, placing my hand on his pec. His heart thuds underneath my touch, and there's tension in his muscles as his arms tighten around me. "Please."

He heaves a sigh but gently lets my legs down until I'm standing on my own two feet.

"What did he say to you, Princess?" Ash asks, standing in front of me, his tone gentle and not the demand that I expected to hear from him. Kai and Loki are on either side of him, all with matching looks of concern on their faces, eyebrows drawn and foreheads wrinkled.

Shame heats my cheeks. My skin feels too tight, and my hands are clammy as I wrap my arms around myself in a tight hug, stepping away from Jax, his hands falling from my waist where they had come to rest.

"I need a shower," I tell them, swallowing hard and unable to meet any of them in the eye.

"What did he tell you, Pretty Girl?" Loki asks, and he takes a step towards me.

Tears blur my vision, and a lump forms in my throat that's so big I don't know how to swallow past it. How can I tell them that I came, that I climaxed over Adrian's fingers? That my body enjoyed his intrusion, even if my mind was absent?

I shrink further into myself, my head dropping to my chest as the wetness overspills and traces down my cheeks.

"Adrian—" I begin, clearing my throat and feeling the vibrations as my body trembles. "Julian told me that I orgasmed for Adrian. That I came all over his fingers, a–and that he watched it all. M–masturbated over the footage."

There's a ringing in my ears, and lights dance in front of my eyes as the words leave my lips. Warmth is at my back suddenly, the lemon scent of Jax mixing with the spicy ginger of Ash at my front, followed by Kai's fresh, woodsy musk on one side and Loki's vanilla-cocoa perfume on the other. They surround me, grounding me and comforting me with their presence, lending me their strength.

A hand grasps my chin, bringing my teary gaze up to meet swirling, grey eyes.

"You have nothing to be ashamed of, my love," Ash tells me, his voice as fierce as I've ever heard it. "We do not blame you for your body's reactions."

A sob tears through my chest, more tears flowing at his words. He knew my deepest fear, that they would somehow reject me for this. Stupid, really, as I know our bond is stronger than that. I turn my head to the side as fingers trace over Ash's touch. Loki's emerald gaze is full of fire and conviction.

"You are not to blame, beautiful," he tells me, and another breath catches in my throat as I realise that he's talking from experience. His time with Clarissa and what she did evident in his assurance.

More fingers turn my face to the other side, Kai's kind, amber eyes full of pain and hurt for what I've been through.

"It was not your fault," he whispers, and another sob rips through me, this shared trauma we have cutting me to the quick.

Large hands wrap around my throat from behind, tilting my head a little so that I am looking, once again, at Ash as Jax murmurs in my ear.

"We will never stop loving you, Baby Girl," Jax tells me, his fingers grazing my pulse point. "That dead man cunt does not own any part of you. Julian does not own any part of you. We do. We own all of you, just like you own all of us, and that will never change, precious."

I shiver as one hand leaves my throat, tracing a path to the zip at the back of my dress.

"And you're going to give each of us an orgasm to prove that, aren't you, Baby Girl?" His voice is louder this time, and I see Ash raise a brow while feeling Kai and Loki stiffening either side of me.

A whimper passes my suddenly dry lips, my shame transferring to raging desire. Jax clearly realising that I need to get rid of this taint that Adrian and Julian have left behind.

"Yes," I whisper, my hands coming up to the zip in Ash's devil onesie and pulling it down as Jax pulls down my own zipper. Ash keeps one eyebrow arched, but he doesn't stop me, letting me push the garment off his muscled arms and revealing his inked-up torso. Gods, this man is too beautiful for words, all dark swirls of ink and hard lines.

My dress hits the floor, breaths hissing out of them as they see my teal, lace bralette. It doesn't match my knickers, which are the rainbow and unicorn patterned one they saw earlier, but I'm beyond caring right now as three sets of hands caress my sides, rounded stomach, and enlarged breasts.

"Have I told you how fucking hot I find you being pregnant is?"

Jax growls in my ear, hot palms stroking over my bump. I groan, my eyelids fluttering as Kai and Loki hook a finger each in my knickers and draw them down.

"Eyes on me, wife," Ash commands in a thick voice, and I obey, shivering as his heated gaze runs all over my body. "Good girl," he praises, taking a step closer and pressing our naked bodies together, he must have taken off the onesie and his boots whilst I was distracted. His hand comes up into my hair, and he angles my head upwards.

Another moan leaves my lips to tickle his as he slants a gentle kiss over them, feathering his lips teasingly over mine until I'm mewling like a fucking cat, desperate for more.

"Please..." I beg, my own hand clinging onto his inked arms, my nails digging into his skin.

"Please what, Princess?" he asks just as Kai places a kiss to one shoulder, Loki to the other, and Jax nibbles and sucks my neck.

"Please make me come," I ask, my voice a breathy moan. "Please bury yourselves so deep inside me that I forget my own name."

Four groans fill the air, my words making them as desperate as I am as they all step even closer, their hot bodies a fever against mine.

"Upstairs, my room," Ash orders, picking me up under my thighs and pulling me from the others, who all snarl and growl like animals.

"That fucking plug is still there," Loki says with a drawn-out moan.

My arse clenches as Ash carries me, and I feel it, having somehow forgotten its presence.

"She'll be more than ready for us then," I hear Kai respond as I look over Ash's shoulder to see them all stripping out of their own onesies, dicks hard and bobbing as they undress, and what a fucking sight it is.

My pulse skyrockets when Ash kicks his door open, striding over to his bed and dropping me down on my back with a bounce. Before I can utter a sound, he's covering my body with his and sliding inside me in one hard thrust. I scream, the burn delicious as he pulls out almost all the way and pounds back inside my tight channel, his piercing rubbing along my inner walls, jolting the plug and sending tingling waves of euphoria all over my body.

"Fuck, Ash."

"I want your first orgasm before they get up here, Princess," he grits out, thrusting hard and fast, barely pausing between. "And you will give it to me."

One palm holds my hip in place, the other encircling my throat and squeezing as he fucks me so hard the whole bed shakes. The feel of him inside me, the movement of his hips brutal and snapping against my body, and the plug still lodged in my arse has me screaming and clawing as stars blind me and I come so hard my legs shake uncontrollably.

I peel open my closed lids when his pace slows, but he's still fully erect inside me, letting me know that he didn't come. Not yet.

"Good girl," he purrs, nuzzling the side of my face and peppering my jawline with soft kisses.

"You gonna share now, Vanderbilt?" a drawl comes from near the door, and I peer around Ash to see the others waiting, Loki's arms crossed over his naked chest. *Drip* by Asiahn begins to play, courtesy of Loki's playlist obsession no doubt, the sensual sound making my inner walls clench around Ash.

A surprised squeak leaves me as Ash switches our position so that I'm on top, his cock still buried deep inside me.

"Have at it," he lazily replies to my trickster, his hands on my hips and guiding me to move, both of us groaning at the new angle.

I love this position with him, he hardly ever lets me go on top, his need for control in the bedroom is no less than in his life. I tell him with my eyes how grateful I am that he's given me dominance, knowing that he understands my current need is greater than his. His own expression softens, his palm cupping my face and bringing me down into a kiss that sets my soul alight. A kiss that tells me he will always give me what I need, without question, and without needing to be told or asked.

A body warms my back, a large hand skating down my skin in a tender caress. My eyes go wide as a lubed-up finger pushes inside my already filled pussy, alongside Ash's hard length.

"Shhhh, baby," Jax soothes when I whimper and squirm, pumping his finger and leaving me gasping.

Ash distracts me with his soft lips once more, and I lose myself in his kiss, gasping into his mouth when another finger enters me. Ash groans, his hips taking over my movements with shallow thrusts. One hand tangles in my hair, the other coming between us to rub and tease my clit, making my hips buck at the extra sensation.

"Such a good fucking girl," Jax praises, adding another of his thick digits, and I make a sound in my throat that would be embarrassing if I gave a shit. But right now, I have no more fucks to give as Jax finger fucks me and Ash cock fucks me from underneath, his finger dancing over my clit.

A sound of protest leaves my throat when Jax withdraws his finger, and my eyes almost bug out of my head as he replaces them with the head of his monster dick.

"You can take him," Ash assures me through clenched teeth, his fingers finding my clit and rubbing circles around it. "Just relax, Princess."

I try to do as he says, relaxing under his expert touch as he plays with my swollen bud, Jax slipping in another inch.

"So fucking tight," he groans, his hands gripping my hips tight enough to bruise.

"Fuuuck," Ash curses when Jax keeps pushing. I whimper as the burn of being stretched by them both threatens to overwhelm me.

"Lilly," Kai's soft voice calls from the side, and I look over, gasping when I see Loki on his knees, Kai's hard dick in his mouth as Kai guides him with a firm grip in his auburn tresses, their bodies turned to the side to give me the perfect view.

Wetness floods my core, letting Jax slip all the way in, and I cry out at having both men inside me whilst I watch my other lover give head to Kai.

"Shit, Baby Girl," Jax groans, Ash cursing again as they give me a minute to get used to them. "I can feel the plug inside you too."

My eyes threaten to roll at the reminder, and I gasp when Kai forces Loki to take him deeper, Loki's fingers digging into Kai's arse.

"Shit, I can feel her fluttering around us just watching you two," Ash grits out, his finger still rubbing and playing with my clit, driving me crazy.

"Please," I ask, my voice full of desperate need. "Please, fuck me," I beg them, needing to feel them move inside me, even though I'm not completely convinced that they won't tear me in two.

They don't question me, don't ask for clarification, and settle into a rhythm of thrusting inside me that soon has me mindless with pleasure. I can't think, can barely breathe, and just feel as they fucking destroy any intelligence I may possess with their hard cocks and gripping hands.

"You feel incredible stretched over both our dicks," Ash grits out, and I open heavy-lidded eyes to see sweat glistening all over his inked skin, dripping down the side of his face.

"So perfect, baby," Jax murmurs behind me, his hand snaking up the column of my throat to wrap around just under my chin. "And you're gonna come for me like a good little girl, aren't you?"

I whimper as his grip around my windpipe tightens, making it harder to breathe.

"Yes, sir," I croak out, my voice barely above a breathy whisper as his hand tightens further, and his hips move faster.

Ash puts more pressure on my clit, moving his finger in a way that has my eyes rolling.

"Now, baby," Jax commands in a strained tone. "Come all over our dicks right. Fucking. Now."

I'm helpless to disobey, my body following his order as I explode, a silent scream leaving my mouth as I bask and writhe between them both. Fire races across my body, my nerve endings tingling and fizzing like a live wire is brushing across my body as I keep coming. I drag them under with me with animalistic roars, both thrusting to the hilt as they pulse inside of me, filling me up with their seed and prolonging my own release until I'm crying for it to stop. Begging for a reprieve.

I droop over Ash's chest, my rounded stomach making me arch my back a little, both of us panting and groaning when Jax slides out and flops beside us, also breathing hard. The bed shifts behind me, hands stroking down my body, and I feel the tug of the plug being pulled out of my arse, leaving me hissing into Ash's neck.

Moments later, the tip of a hard, pierced cock pushes against my rosebud, and I moan long and low as it slides in with ease.

"God, I love this fucking ass, Pretty Girl," Loki moans as he pushes all the way in, his teeth nipping my shoulder.

Ash's arms are wrapped around my slick body, holding me for Loki who wastes no time in finding his rhythm and fucking my arse with firm strokes. Exquisite pleasure rolls across my skin from inside me, and it's all I can do not to pass the fuck out with how good it feels.

"Loki," I whimper, the tingles returning as Ash begins to harden inside my pussy. "Ash..."

"Do you like it when I fuck you over your husband, baby?" Loki asks in a husky voice, grunting when Ash begins to move his hips too, both of them filling me up with their hard members.

"Yes, God, yes, I fucking love having your cock buried inside me," I reply, my nails digging into Ash's large shoulders as the intensity of what they are doing to my body overwhelms me.

"I love it when you talk dirty, baby," Loki growls out, picking up the pace, the sound of his hips slapping my arse loud in the room.

I become lost to the sensations once more, the push and pull as they take me to the edge and demand that I jump, their movements becoming frenzied as they chase their own releases.

"Fuck, baby," Loki breathes against my ear, stilling deep inside me as he climaxes. Ash pauses, but I hardly notice as I fall into oblivion with Loki, my whole body trembling with the force of my orgasm. The world stops moving, the planets aligning as waves of pleasure roll over me, dragging me under a sea of bliss and drowning me in ecstasy.

I groan as Loki pulls out, only to be replaced by another solid shaft pressing against my used hole.

"I c–can't," I plead, my voice hoarse and stuttering as Kai ignores me and continues to invade my arsehole.

"You can and you will, Pet," Kai tells me firmly, thrusting all the way in with a hiss. "You still owe me an orgasm."

Ash cups the side of my face in a tender gesture, and I look into his beautiful, grey eyes which are full of love and lust, his cheeks flushed and his hair stuck to his sweat-slicked forehead.

"You can give us one more can't you, Princess?" he asks, and I find myself agreeing with a slow nod just as Kai starts to pull out. "Good girl, I knew you could. You're our perfect treasure."

Holy fucking hotness, Ash praising me does all the things to my body, and when he starts moving too, I relax into their possession and let myself go under once more. Ash continues to hold my face, demanding I keep my eyes on his as they fuck me.

"Ash–fuck–Kai—" I babble incoherently, the intensity in my dark Knight's gaze undoing me just as sure as the movements of his hips. His other hand is gripping my hip, yet I feel fingers wiggle between us to play with my clit, and I look away for a second to see Loki's arm disappearing between our bodies.

"Eyes back on me, wife," Ash demands, and I do as he says, holding his gaze as they work to build me up once more.

I feel a large palm wrap around my throat, and I don't need to look to see that Jax is the owner.

"Just once more, angel," he tells me, his thumb caressing my racing pulse. "Come all over Kai and Ash, Baby Girl. Show them who owns that pussy and ass."

At Jax's dirty words, I explode, tears springing to my eyes when my orgasm hits me like a fucking sledgehammer. I can feel myself clamping around the guys, demanding that they join me in the abyss as my body tries to milk them. Their growls and rumbles, combined with the sudden stillness, tells me that they indeed followed me over the edge.

I feel weightless, my whole body liquifying as I give myself over to the exhaustion that only incredible sex can bring. We lie together, tangled in a heap of limbs, and the last thought to float through my mind before sleep takes me under is that Jax was right.

My Knights own me, body and soul, and no one can take that away from me.

CHAPTER TWENTY-THREE

LILLY

The next week is finals week and passes by in a blur of frantic revision and nervous, frenetic energy. Apparently—and luckily for me—Highgate holds its exams later in the year than most, some shit to do with giving its bright, young students the best possible start in life. I guess it worked out for me as I didn't actually miss my finals, so at least I have a chance to pass.

I've no idea how well I'll do, or if I even stand a hope in hell of passing any of them. When I mention this to the guys one evening, Ash just gives me a mildly condescending look and calmly declares that I don't need to worry about failing, as I won't. When I jokingly state that he can't just buy me a high school diploma, his answer, without missing a beat is, "Why not?"

With the week finally over, we spend the weekend lazing around the dorm and just relaxing before the graduation ceremony the following week. It's Sunday evening now and we are watching Marvel on the huge TV, Ash on one side of me and Kai on the other as we snuggle while eating hot, buttered popcorn, homemade of course.

Ash's phone dings with a text, and I watch as he picks it up off the arm of the sofa before he frowns as he reads the message, his lips set in a grim line.

"What's up?" I ask, not able to see the screen but shifting so that I'm sitting up straighter and facing him. Someone pauses the film as Kai keeps a hand on one thigh, Ash still holding the other. His grey eyes lift up to me, and the set of his brow tells me that he's not happy with the content of the message.

"There's a Black Knight board meeting on Monday morning, first thing," he begins, still looking at me intently. I shake my head slightly, holding his gaze.

"And?"

"And my dad requires your presence, Princess. As the majority shareholder."

My jaw loosens, a hot flush creeping over my skin like ants crawling across my body.

"She's not fucking going anywhere near him!" Jax growls from across the room, and I look away from Ash to see Jax sat bolt upright, his lips flattened and his huge arm muscles flexing, which in any other situation would have me drooling.

"I know she can't go. I just don't know what his game is," Ash answers, and my gaze swings back to him as he grips my thigh tighter.

"He likely just wants to fuck with us," Loki adds, and I look over to see him sitting forward. "We can just say that she's sick or something."

My spine stiffens, eyes narrowing as they continue to discuss the subject as if I'm not in the room. Warmth coats my back as Kai leans closer to me, sensing my tension.

"Enough!" I yell, all conversation halting, and three sets of eyes swing my way. "For fuck sake, you talk about me as if I'm some weak and feeble female who needs coddling, and I'm fucking done!"

I get up—Kai and Ash letting me go—and begin to pace in front of them, the red of my ire colouring my vision. I pause in my steps, taking a deep breath and closing my eyes as I try to formulate in my mind what it is I want to say.

"I've been controlled my entire life, not trusted to make my own decisions, even though I wasn't given all the facts in order to make sensible ones," I tell them, my eyes still closed as I unburden my mind. "Even coming here was Adrian pushing me more than my own free choice. The first thing I truly ever decided for myself, was loving you all." I open my eyes then, looking at them, and my forehead creases as I look into each of their faces. Jax has his fists clenched, his gaze on the floor as his jaw works. Loki looks poised to leap up and wrap me in his warm embrace. Kai gives me a pained smile, an apology in his amber depths, even though he remained quiet before. I look at Ash last, his face an unreadable mask, his shoulders tense as I catch his eye. "Don't take my control from me too. I couldn't bear it."

"Shit, Princess," he grunts out, standing up and stepping up to me until I have to tilt my head to look at him. *Tall fuckwallop.* He lowers his head down, pressing his forehead to mine and tangling his fingers in my hair. My lids drift shut once more at his touch. "I'm an asshole, and I swear I will never leave you out like that again."

My throat goes thick, and I have to swallow hard.

"I know it came from a place of concern, Ash, but I need to be in charge of my own destiny," I tell him softly, my lips almost brushing his.

"What would you like to do, Lilly?" Kai asks, and I tilt my head to look over at him, giving him a grateful smile.

"I want to go," I reply in a firm voice, and I feel Ash heave a sigh against me.

"Fine, wife," he relents, straightening up, and I give him a wide grin as I glance up at him. His own lips twitch. "But you will not leave my fucking side, do you hear?"

"Yes, sir," I tease, and his fingers tighten in my hair as a low growl escapes him.

"I mean it. One of us is to be with you at all times," he insists, and I just can't help myself and roll my eyes. His grip on my tresses becomes punishing, and god if it doesn't make me wet between my thighs.

"I think my wife needs a lesson in obedience, boys," he states with a devilish grin that has my knickers dampening to soaking point and my thighs clenching.

JAX

I don't fucking like this, I think as we all pile into the elevator at Black Knight HQ, a modern glass building as cold and unfeeling as the fucking cunts who run the crooked company. I catch a glimpse of my reflection in the mirrored walls, large arms crossed, forming a barrier as I feel the walls that I have to erect whenever I have anything to do with these bastards slam into place.

I see Lilly move, reaching for my forearm as she goes on tiptoes clearly intending to whisper something in my ear. I lean down, not unfolding my arms so that she can reach, and the warmth of her palm on my bare skin lights a fire under it. God, she's so fucking tiny, even with the sexy swell of her belly.

"Just imagine how amazing it would be to fuck in this lift, seeing my naked body from all angles as you pound into me from behind," she whispers in that sweet voice of hers.

Fuck. Me.

Just like that the walls come crashing down under a wave of lust that threatens to buckle my knees. Blowing out a low, steady breath, I straighten back up, ignoring the massive semi-chub I'm now supporting in my slacks. We all have to dress smartly for these bastards. I watch with a single raised brow as she faces the front, holding my stern gaze and giving me a wink and a fucking devastating, secret smile.

Great. I'm now going to walk into that boardroom with a raging hard-on.

"You alright, man?" Loki asks from my other side, and I just nod, not trusting myself not to slam my palm on the emergency stop button if I repeat what our naughty, little pixie just whispered in my ear. Jesus, Loki is just as likely to push that button as I am if he knew.

All too soon, the elevator comes to a stop, the doors opening with a ding to reveal a white, impersonal foyer. God, I hate this fucking place. It's so cold and sterile, but worse than that, it's all a fucking lie. The pure, clean look is just a cover up for the dark and depraved nature of the demons that run this company. It's a veneer covering up all the rot, the sweet, sickly air freshener trying to disguise the stench of decay.

I step out with my brothers in arms, all of us slipping into a formation that surrounds and protects our woman.

"Ah, boys." A tall, leggy blonde stalks towards us on black stilettos, the look in her blue eyes predatory as she rakes her gaze over each of us before settling on Ash. "How wonderful to see you. It's been too long," she purrs, running a hand down Ash's arm.

"Do you make a habit of touching what doesn't belong to you?" I hear Lilly ask in a tone that would freeze your balls off, and see Michelle pause and her smile falter.

"Excuse me?" she asks, looking as Lilly steps between us and wraps her hands around Ash's other arm, tugging him away from the other woman's grip.

"I asked, do you always touch other women's husbands and lovers?" Lilly replies, her voice light but sharp, and my cock twitches in my slacks at the possessive note in her tone.

"I–um—" Michelle stutters, her cheeks flushing as she's called out.

"Sorry, Mrs Vanderbilt. I will never touch what belongs to you again," Lilly prompts, face expectant, and I have to cover a laugh with a cough, Loki copying me as we gaze upon our Queen.

"S–sorry, Mrs. Vanderbilt. It won't happen again," Michelle responds, dropping her head and sinking into herself.

"Good," Lilly states. "Oh, and just so we are crystal fucking clear, all these men belong to me."

Michelle's wide eyes fly up for a moment then drops back down.

"Of course," she says quietly, clearing her throat and nodding her head. "This way, please."

She takes off down a corridor, and we follow after her, Ash keeping a tight hold on Lilly's arm which is still wrapped around his.

"That was so fucking hot, wife," he murmurs, loud enough for us to catch what he says. "I'm so hard for you right now."

"Welcome to the fucking club," I grumble, and Loki gives a bark of laughter, coming up on Lilly's other side and linking arms with her.

"You can piss on me any time, Pretty Girl," he states, and I see Michelle stumble in front of us as she reaches a pair of grey double doors.

We pause, and Kai steps up behind Lilly, bending down to whisper in her ear, this time just us to hear.

"I like being claimed by you, Lilly Vanderbilt." I hear her gasp as he presses his hips into her lower back, clearly feeling his hardness too. At least I won't be the only one walking in there with a stiffy.

Michelle opens the doors, and we step into a light boardroom that has floor-to-ceiling windows on the wall opposite us, giving us a view of the town below and the mountains beyond.

I glance around the huge table, noting my cunt of a father, Julian Vanderbilt, Chad Thorn, and Stephen Matthews all seated and staring at us. It takes a huge effort not to curl my lip or let my fists fly at their smug fucking faces. I know they were the reason Lilly was taken, and have no doubt that they were all involved or at least aware.

Taking a deep inhale, I try to calm the rage that's threatening to overspill. It's then that I notice another figure, a man of similar age to our parents, his hair and eyes dark and his tailored suit clearly expensive.

"Boys," Julian greets, a lying smile on his lips. His grey eyes take us all in, pausing on Lilly, and his grin widens. A pounding starts in my ears, and I can feel my lips pulling back as I step closer to her. "Lilly, darling."

He doesn't get up, and it's a good fucking thing, as I don't doubt that I wouldn't be the only one to do him harm if he came near her again. Pictures of having him at my mercy while I take my blowtorch to his eyeballs for daring to even look at her like that flit through my mind, and I know that my snarl turns to a feral grin. He sees it too when he looks back at me, his face paling ever so slightly at the promise in my eyes.

Oh yeah, fucker, I'm coming for you.

Movement interrupts our stare off, and I see the dark stranger get up and move towards us. He stops in front of our group, in front of Lilly, and she lays a hand on my arm when I make a move to step in front of her.

"Mrs Vanderbilt," he says, and I'm surprised by his cultured British accent. "A pleasure to finally meet you. I knew your mother, and I must say you are the spitting image of her."

"You knew my mum?" Lilly asks, the hand that is still resting on my forearm frozen.

"Yes, I met her not long after she arrived in London and began working at Grey's. She was captivating when she danced, even more so when her pregnancy began to show." He looks down at Lilly's rounded stomach then, but not in a leering way. More like a fatherly way, his face soft and wistful.

"Mr Black?" Lilly asks with a gasp, and it suddenly clicks into place. This is the man who has the second biggest stakeholder claim in Black Knight Corporation. I look at the other guys to see matching looks of interest on their faces, though Ash still has a hard jaw and a possessive grip around Lilly's waist.

"Now that this little reunion is done with," Julian interrupts in an annoyed tone, and again images of committing violence against Ash's father pop into my head. "Shall we start the meeting?"

Glaring at him and the rest of the scum that sit at the oval table, we take our seats opposite them, Mr Black resuming his chair at what might be considered the head of the table.

"Right, let's get started, gentleman and lady," Julian begins, and I really don't like the way his eyes keep raking over Lilly. It makes my hackles rise, my shoulders vibrating with tension. "Shall we begin with our plans for our heirs to take on more responsibility?"

CHAPTER TWENTY-FOUR

LILLY

What a fucking waste of time!

That meeting wasn't about the boys taking on more responsibility. Julian and the others may have tried to present it in that way, but they were giving the guys crumbs, nothing more than what you might get a work placement student to do. *Fucking joke.*

And any suggestion I made was shot down straight away, and I was treated like the silly, little woman who didn't know how the big men ran things. *Fucking cockwombling knobheads.*

It was interesting the way Mr Black sat back and took it all in, then made a few suggestions that I could see Julian didn't want to consider but had to because they were the best thing for the business. Like expanding the software development arm of the company by looking at recent graduates from top Ivy League colleges.

He also put forward a proposal that Black Knight Corp start to use a company based in the city of London called Cavendish Brothers' Investments as our wealth managers, taking over how we invest our profits. It's run by two brothers, one of whom is the Marquis of Bath no less, and apparently, since they took it over from their parents several years ago, the company has made billions for its clients across the globe.

I could tell that Julian hated taking anyone else's suggestions on board, but the gleam in his eyes when Mr Black talked about the money to be made told me that he did take the recommendation seriously. When we all voted, it was a unanimous affirmative in favour of hiring the brothers.

The meeting dragged on after that, and most of what they were saying went completely over my head. I'm just not used to business speak, and I fucking hated feeling so stupid and lost. I had to keep suppressing yawns by the time it came to a close, and I barely managed to hold back a sigh of relief when all business was concluded and we were finally allowed to go.

Ash kept me close the whole way back to the car, Mr Black giving us a warm goodbye before stepping into his own waiting vehicle. I wondered about him, having a very vague recollection of Mum talking about her biggest fan. She never seemed to think he was a sleeze like some of the others could be. In fact, I do remember that he would scare off anyone who made her even the slightest bit uncomfortable when she was performing.

I'm too tired to ponder much more as we drive back, and soon am lulled to sleep, resting against Ash's chest with Loki on my other side as the guys talk quietly. I wake up when we arrive back at Highgate, the sun casting the old building in a beautiful, mid-afternoon glow.

"I need a shower," I declare, my muscles aching a little after the long drive and needing to wash off Julian's lecherous gaze. Leaving the boys to do whatever they feel like, I make my way to the bathroom and strip off the blouse and stretchy, cotton jersey, navy skirt I'd worn in a bid to look professional. I fucking hated it, the lack of colour and boring maternity clothes making me feel frumpy and unlike myself.

I leave them in a disgusted pile on the tiles, stepping into the shower, and groaning at the wonderful heat of the water cascading down my body. Looking down, I sigh as I find that my toes are completely obscured by my rounded stomach. My baby gives a little 'fuck you, bitch' kick, and I huff out a laugh.

"Sassy womb monster," I murmur, reaching for the shower gel and deciding to use Kai's fresh, woodsy-scented one today.

Collide by Justine Skye and Tyga starts to play over the bluetooth speakers, and my body begins to move to the sensual beat as I soap myself up, turning when I hear the snick of the bathroom door.

Giving my dark Knight a sultry smirk through the glass door of the shower and needing to feel sexy and see the heat in his grey eyes, I continue to rub my hands up and down my soap-slicked body as I move, revelling in the way his eyes stare at me hungrily.

I dance facing him before stepping back into the running water, and letting it cascade over my body and tease my peaked nipples. My smile grows wide as I watch him snap, striding up to the shower and stepping in fully clothed in sweats and a T-shirt.

"Do you know how fucking hard I was when I walked into that meeting earlier, Princess?" Ash drawls, voice low and like another sensation caressing my now sensitised skin.

"Oh really?" I reply, giving him wide, innocent eyes as I continue to move to the beat. He stares at me, water soaking through his shirt and letting me see all of his inked up muscles, my breath catching at his masculine beauty. He doesn't speak, just waits, staring at me with a ravenous hunger and building the tension until I feel like I might break this time.

With a movement that I should have seen coming but didn't, my back is hitting the shower wall and Ash is dropping to his knees in front of me, gazing up at me, his black hair plastered to his stunning face.

"I'm going to make you as hot as you made me," he whispers, moving his face closer to my aching pussy. His fingers skirt up my thighs, both hands grasping my hips, and he huffs a breath against my wet folds. "As desperate for my cock inside you as I was to fill up this delicious cunt when you claimed me as yours in front of that secretary." I groan at his dirty talk, knowing that he will make good on his promise and I'll be a wreck by the time he's through.

Using my hips, he guides me towards the other end of the cubicle, still on his knees as we move away from the spray.

"Turn around, hands on the bench," he orders, and I do as he says, placing my palms flat on the marble bench seat, excitement making my skin itch. "Fucking perfect."

Without another word, I feel his tongue lapping my slit from clit to opening, and I groan loud and low, my fingers flexing on the smooth surface of the marble.

"Ash," I breathe out, the expert movements of his tongue causing flutters in my lower belly and sparks to fly across my skin.

He destroys me with his tongue, and I go fucking wild when he starts to circle my puckered hole with it, pushing two fingers into my wet heat as he laps at my tight hole. He works me into a frenzy, his fingers and tongue obliterating me until my limbs shake and I can barely hold myself up.

"Come for me, Princess," he demands, reaching round and pinching my clit with his other hand so fucking hard I combust, screaming my release as I break apart. The noise of the shower becomes dull as I go blind and deaf all at once with the strength of my climax, my body convulsing around his still pumping fingers.

He gives me no break, and the next thing I know, he's pushing his hard pierced cock inside my still pulsing cunt, his fingers gripping my hips in a firm hold as he fights against my clamping inner walls.

"Fucking hell, Princess," he grits out, his voice tight and strained. I almost come again from the sound, knowing how much I affect him is the strongest aphrodisiac.

He starts bucking his hips hard and fast, just how I love it, and I'm soon tumbling towards a second orgasm, my pussy walls vice-like around him. Heat suffuses my limbs, and I have just enough brain cells left to squeeze my inner walls tighter.

"Come with me, husband," I demand, and he groans his sexy as fuck sound that shivers down my spine and pushes me closer towards bliss.

Thrusting hard once, twice, and a third and final time, he comes with a roar, his fingers digging into my hips hard enough to bruise, the bite of pain making me see sunshine and fucking rainbows as I scream for him. My whole body lights up like I'm the personification of electricity, my limbs twitching with the strength of my orgasm.

He pauses, buried deep inside me as we stay there and just breathe, the shower still running and steam filling the bathroom as we soak in each other.

Without pulling out, he bends over me and kisses my spine, wrapping his arms around me and standing us up so that my back is to his chest. I whimper when he slips out, and he chuckles in a self-satisfied, manly way.

"Don't worry, wife," he rumbles in my ear as he walks us backwards under the spray of the still hot shower. "After we wash, I'll get you all dirty again," he tells me, letting go with one hand as the other reaches for the soap, his this time, and brings it in front of us to squeeze a dollop into his other hand. "And again," he murmurs as he soaps up my breasts. "And again." My rounded stomach gets attention this time. "And again." His hand dips between my legs, and I can already feel the need burning in my core.

Jesus, sex addict much?

I mean, can you really blame a girl when she's surrounded by four, hot as fuck guys who all want to fill her up with their cocks?

CHAPTER TWENTY-FIVE

LILLY

We get two days to chill out after that shitshow and spend it wrapped up together, listening to music and enjoying each other's bodies, making up for lost time.

The night before graduation comes all too soon, and the guys are all called away for Black Knight business. It leaves my stomach in knots, as they don't know if they're being summoned to deal with a competitor or just some more training.

"It'll be alright, sweetheart," Kai assures me, pulling me close as the others head out the door after kissing me goodbye.

"I hate this," I whisper into his chest, gripping his T-shirt in my fingers. "I hate that you have to keep doing this."

"I know, my love," he murmurs into my hair. "But it won't be for long. The summer hunting trip is coming up, and after that things will be different."

His words don't reassure me though, knowing that the plan to deal with their parents and Kai's uncle will be bloody and potentially dangerous. I pull back, my forehead creased, and stare deeply into his warm, amber eyes.

"Just, stay safe tonight. Keep each other safe."

"Always, love," he replies, placing a soft, parting kiss on my lips before leaving and locking up behind him. I'm reminded of Ash's stern words to not open the door for anyone as I stare after them, feeling a little bereft.

Trying to shake off my trepidation for the guys, I head into the bathroom and start to run myself a bubble bath. I'll grab my kindle and continue reading about those poor souls who are trapped in an insane asylum, loving each other despite all of the fuckery going on around them.

Surprisingly, the evening passes by quickly, mostly due to getting absorbed by my current read. I get up from the sofa where I was snuggled in one of Jax's huge T-shirts, intending to head to bed when a knock at the door to the dorm sounds, and I freeze, my heart pounding as I glare at it. My phone dings with an incoming message at that moment, making me jump out of my fucking skin, and I look to see a message from Ryan, Mum's old boyfriend and the closest thing to a father I had growing up.

Ryan: Surprise!

I look to the door again, and then back at the message. Hesitantly, I step towards the front door, peeking through the peephole, and then squeal in delight at what awaits me on the other side.

Unlocking the bolts, I throw the door open, a wide grin on my face.

"Ryan!" I shriek, throwing my arms around him and eliciting an oomph sound from his chest.

"Hello, Little One," he chuckles, steering us back into the dorm and softly closing the door behind us. I pull back to look up into his smiling face, noting a slight tension in the lines around his eyes. He lets out a sigh, his smile faltering before saying, "Apparently, I've come to kill you."

ASH

Fucking bastards keeping us out all night and then making us attend a debrief so that we have to head straight to the graduation ceremony. I guess we should count ourselves lucky that it wasn't a mark this time, just some intel gathering and boring-ass surveillance.

I look at my phone again as we wait in our seats for the ceremony to start, biting my lip when I see that Lilly still hasn't replied to the message I'd sent this morning letting her know that we would meet her here.

"Still no reply?" Loki asks from my left, and I turn to see his tired eyes full of the same concern that I have, his cap and gown an artful mess. *Douche.*

"No," I reply curtly, glancing back down at the blank screen that's taunting me, like the empty space to my right where my wife should be sitting. I don't fucking like this, and my stomach churns with a feeling of unease.

The principal starts to speak, some shit about us being the best and brightest, but only half my attention is on him, my mind wondering where the fuck Lilly is and if something is wrong. He's halfway through his speech when my phone buzzes in my hand, and I look down with a small smile on my lips which freezes as I see it's a picture message from my cunt of a father. I glance back to find him in the rows reserved for parents behind us, and he looks at me with a cruel smirk on his lips that leaves me sick.

I look down at my phone, opening the message, and at first, my eyes don't make sense of the image before them, the color red causing me to blink a few times to try and focus. When I do, I wish that I hadn't, as my whole body goes ice-cold and a buzzing sounds in my ears.

It's Lilly, my beautiful Lilly, sprawled out on the floor and covered in so much crimson I can't tell where the wounds are. I can see her glassy eyes, sightless, her body in a pool of blood that surrounds her.

"No—" a strangled whisper escapes my lips before I can clamp them shut. My vision blurs, and for the first time, I understand why Luc found solace in the choice to no longer live. For there can be no life without her. Pain unlike any I've ever experienced wracks my body and threatens to double me over, only sheer determination and years of training hold me upright in my seat as I continue to stare at my worst nightmare come to life.

"Ash?" Loki whispers next to me, and I clutch my phone to my chest as I turn to face him, my movements sluggish as if my body is underwater. "Was that from Lilly?"

"N–no," I instantly reply, my mind racing as I try to work out how to tell him, how to tell them all that we've just lost our light. Lost our soul and reason for living. Before I can utter another word, our names are being called for us to go up and collect our diplomas.

Taking the reprieve, I practically leap to my feet, earning a curious look from Loki as I follow behind him to the stage. I have no recollection of what happens next, and I'm suddenly striding from the area outside where the ceremony is being held, rolled up diploma in one hand and my phone in the other as I round the corner of the building and lean against it, breathing hard.

Footsteps pound after me, and I look up through a haze of tears to see the concerned faces of my brothers by choice surrounding me.

"Ash, what's happened?" Kai demands, his voice unusually hard as his eyes take me in.

I open my mouth to speak, then close it, shaking my head as the tears fall from my eyes, scalding a path down my cheeks, and I close my eyes, willing the devil to strike me down so that I no longer have to breathe the air that she doesn't.

"Ash?" Loki asks, his voice trembling. "Ash, man, you're scaring us."

Opening my eyes, tears glistening on my lashes, I look at each of them and prepare to break their hearts and rip out their souls.

"Lilly's—" I start, my chin wobbling, and I have to pause to take a deep inhale, unable to look any of them in the eye when I voice the truth that is breaking me apart. "Lilly's dead."

Silence.

"That's not fucking funny!" I hear Loki yell, and I turn to watch him shaking as he clenches his fists.

"Fuck, I wish it was—" I start, feeling sick as I drop the diploma and bring up my phone, unlocking the screen to be faced with that fucking picture again. I don't say anything else, just turn the phone around and show them.

Silence.

Then I watch them all shatter, and I'm too broken myself to help them.

Loki drops to his knees, his face deathly white as tears stream down his cheeks and he shakes his head. "No, no, no, no," he whispers over and over again.

Kai shuts down, his whole face blank as he studies the image on the screen with an air of detachment that would piss me off if I didn't know that he's retreated inside himself.

Jax explodes, turning his back and walking over to a huge stone urn full of plants. With the pained roar of a wounded animal, he lifts it up and throws it onto the stones lining the path, the urn cracking and spilling soil and brightly-coloured blooms all over the path.

I watch them all, my brothers in arms, and I don't know how to fix this. Even the great Asher Vanderbilt can't fight death once the grim reaper has taken a soul, and I fucking hate myself for it.

My phone buzzes once more, and it's pure instinct that makes me turn the device so that I can see the screen. My eyes narrow as I see it's a message from Enzo this time, and I unlock the phone to read it properly.

Enzo: Need you all at the gym. Now.

I look up to see Kai has his phone out too, presumably reading the same message from Enzo as he sent it to us all. He glances up a moment later and catches my eye. A glint of something enters his gaze, pushing through the deadened look that has taken over his features.

Looking down at Loki, I see that he, too, has his phone out, and I flinch when he raises his head and his agony-filled eyes find mine.

"We need to go," I tell him, reaching out my free hand to help pull him to his feet. It's a testament to his loyalty to me that he places his hand in mine and lets me help him to stand. I give his hand a squeeze, then look up to see Jax panting and staring at us with dark eyes. "Enzo needs us," I tell him, and although his brow dips slightly, he knows like I do that Enzo wouldn't call us if it weren't an emergency. Doesn't mean that I'm not torn between answering his summons, or going over to my father and stabbing him in the fucking eye where he sits back at the ceremony.

We head to the parking lot, stripping out of our gowns and caps just as we hear cheers from where the rest of our class is celebrating graduation. We leave our caps and gowns on the path, graduation doesn't matter, nothing does anymore. Silently, we all climb into Jax's truck, Jax having wordlessly handed over his keys to me when I held out my hand. He's in even less of a position to drive than I am.

The drive to Enzo's gym is also silent, just the sound of Jax's heaving breaths and Loki's occasional sniffle accompanying us as we weave through the mountain road towards town. My mind races, and I can hear Kai tapping away at his tablet, likely trying to discover the origins of the photo, desperate for anything to tell us that it's fake. That it's not real. That she is still alive.

It should worry me that I don't remember how we got here as we pull up outside the gym, the inside unusually dark for the middle of the day, but I just can't find it in me to give a fuck, so we get out and make our way up the steps to the front doors. A memory of bringing Lilly here hits me with such force that I actually stagger, Kai reaching out to steady me as Jax goes to push the doors open.

They don't budge, but a moment later they open a sliver as Tom, our driver and Enzo's brother-in-law, peeks out, and upon seeing it's us, opens the door further.

"Hurry," he instructs in a low voice, shutting and locking the door as soon as we step inside. His strange behaviour breaks through the fog of my grief, and I step forward to ask him what the fuck is going on when someone throws themself at me.

My body starts to react before my mind has a chance to catch up, my fist lifting, but before I can do my attacker any harm, I catch a voice that forty-five minutes ago I thought I'd never hear again.

"I'm so fucking sorry, Ash," Lilly says through her sobs, her slender arms wrapped around me so tightly I can hardly breathe. "It was the only way, but, fuck... I'm so, so sorry."

I grab hold of her biceps and yank her back, staring into her beautiful fucking face and watching the life shining in those stunning, hazel eyes. I can't speak, just drink her in as tears track down her cheeks.

"Fuck, Princess," I choke out, pulling her in close again and crushing her lips to mine in a desperate kiss. She kisses me back just as fiercely, my fingers digging into her arms as I try to inhale her into me.

She's suddenly torn away from me, and I snarl at whoever thought they could take her, only to come up short when I see that it's Loki, and he has fresh tears falling down his cheeks.

"You're not dead?" he asks, his voice full of wonder as he drinks her in just as I did moments ago.

"No, Loki," she replies with a sob. "I'm not dead."

"Thank fuck," he exhales, pulling her in for a kiss of his own. I watch them, enraptured and unable to take my eyes off her as I assure myself that this is no dream. That we didn't crash on the way over and this is not heaven.

She pulls away when Kai touches her shoulder, his own face full of so much emotion that it's hard to look at.

"I'm so sorry, Kai, my love," she whispers, turning to face him and stepping into his open arms. He brings her in close, wrapping his arms around her and taking in a deep inhale as his eyes close in ecstasy. I know that fucking feeling.

Pulling away just enough so that he can lower his lips to hers, they kiss, more tears falling down her cheeks as they embrace. The sweet kiss comes to an end as Kai places his forehead to hers.

"Shit, sweetheart," he murmurs, still holding her to him.

"I know," she replies, glancing away, and I see the moment she finds Jax, her whole body stiffening.

Stepping away from Kai, who reluctantly lets her go, she steps towards our silent brother who stands glaring with his arms crossed over his huge chest.

"Jax?" she questions, reaching out a hand and laying it on his forearm. "I'm so sorry, I can explain, love."

He grunts, opening his arms so suddenly that even I flinch. I take a step towards him, but stop when he just pulls her to him and encases her in his massive arms.

"It better be a good fucking explanation, Baby Girl," he grumbles. "My soul was broken when I saw that picture," he confesses, and I realise then just how much she's changed us all. Before she came into our lives, we could barely get Jax to talk to us, let alone tell us his darkest feelings.

"It is, I swear," she answers, looking up into his eyes. As if her lips are a magnet and he can't resist, he lowers his own and kisses her roughly, all of the worry and anger for what we have just been through spilling out into her mouth.

As the Queen that she is, she takes it, every last drop. Her kiss is an apology, an assurance that she's still here, and I can see it calm the beast within him until he almost slumps in her arms, his muscles relaxing as their kiss comes to a close.

"Come," she says, taking his hand as she steps out of his arms and looks at each of us, settling on me last. "Ryan is here and can explain everything."

CHAPTER TWENTY-SIX

LILLY

I cast my eyes around the guys that surround me, my own Knights, all within touching distance. We're in Enzo's office, and I'm seated on the worn, leather sofa, sandwiched between Jax, who refuses to let go of my hand, and Ash, who has a possessive grip clamped tightly on my thigh. Loki and Kai are on the floor, refusing the chairs offered in order to sit at my feet, both with warm palms wrapped around my ankles, Loki's massaging and rubbing them, making it very hard to concentrate on what is being said.

"Julian put a hit out on Lilly," Ryan starts, no fucking build-up whatsoever, and I feel each of my guys stiffen.

"How did you find that out?" Ash asks, his voice laced with suspicion, and I cast him an annoyed look. *Surely he doesn't think that Ryan can't be trusted?* Although, I was wondering the same thing myself, and Ryan wanted everyone here before he explained. The man in question gives me what can only be a sheepish look, a blush staining his rugged cheeks.

"Being the bouncer at Grey's isn't my only occupation, just the one I have on paper," he tells me, and it takes a moment, but when it clicks, my eyes go wide and I sit forward suddenly.

"You're a fucking mercenary?!" I all but screech, and he winces but nods. "Jesus. Since when?" He rubs the back of his neck and dips his head, looking away.

"Always, Little One," he says. "It's one of the reasons why your mother and I never got married."

"Well, shit," I huff out, feeling a twinge of guilt for always blaming Mum for not taking that step with him.

"How did you find out about the hit on Lilly?" Kai interjects, and all of their grips tighten on me. My heart thuds, a surge of pain in my chest flaring at the thought of receiving a picture of them lying broken and bleeding, and I grip Jax's hand back tightly.

"I'm one of the best at what I do, so I get the pick of jobs," Ryan tells Kai unabashedly. "As soon as I saw who the mark was I took the job, anonymously of course, and came straight here. The payout was high enough that I knew it would attract attention, so I needed to fulfil the terms as soon as possible."

We all sit in silence for a moment, processing what he's just told us. Julian wanted me dead, offered up a huge amount for someone to come and take my life. And the life of my unborn child, his grand-child for all that he knows. My hand comes up to caress my stomach, feeling my baby move inside me, and my breath hitches at the thought of how close he or she came to never having been born at all. Water fills my eyes, and a huge palm comes to cover my own. I look to the side to see Jax staring at me, his blue eyes full of a fierce fire.

"I will never let anything happen to you or our child," he vows in his gruff voice, and a tear escapes at the way he's claimed my baby as his own. I sniffle, clearing my throat and removing my hand from underneath Jax's to wipe the moisture off my cheek.

"What happens now?" I ask, turning to look at Ryan, then Enzo, and finally Tom. Enzo assured us that Tom will not breathe a word to Julian or any of the others on the board. Tom is loyal to his family, to Enzo, first, and the guys seemed happy with that.

"You stay dead," Ryan tells me, an apology in his eyes but his lips set in a grim line.

"I have a new identity for you, cara mia," Enzo states, stepping forward with a large, manilla envelope that he holds out to me. "Lilly Vanderbilt will be buried and no longer lives."

I take the package, opening it to find all the documents that I will need; passport, birth certificate, driver's licence, medical documents, all in the name of Lilith Taylor.

"But you have to remain hidden for now, Little One," Ryan states, and I look up from the papers into his pleading eyes. "No one can know that you're alive. Not until Julian and the others have been dealt with. I assume you have a plan?" He turns to Ash as he says the last part.

Ash stiffens for a moment, then heaves a sigh.

"Yes."

"Care to share with the room?" Ryan asks, one brow raised and the corner of his lips tilted upwards, as though he finds Ash's distrust amusing. Ash waits for a beat more, eyes narrowed at the three men before us.

"Kai," he says, clearly giving Kai permission to divulge their plan. Kai sits up straighter, though doesn't remove his hand from my ankle.

"Every year we have to go on a late summer hunting trip with the rest of the board," Kai starts, pushing his glasses up the bridge of his nose in a cute as fuck gesture. "Well, with their fathers and my uncle," he clarifies. "It's in a cabin in the mountains, on private land, no neighbours." I lean forward, eager to hear the full plan. "We will drug their drinks on the first evening there, kill my uncle then frame the others, leaving prints on the weapon, shoe marks in the blood, and other forensic evidence that will point to them as murderers."

I sit there, and I'm stunned by my lack of horror at the casual way that Kai talked about murdering his uncle and setting up their fathers to take the fall. A grim sense of satisfaction fills me, and I think that my reaction should worry me, but it doesn't.

"Regardless of the forensic evidence, why would anyone believe that they wanted him dead?" Ryan asks, and my forehead crinkles when I consider his question.

"Kai is due to take over from his uncle, who only held his position until Kai came of age and graduated," Ash states and all eyes turn to him. "We've been laying a trail to show that his uncle is unhappy relinquishing his power and has been syphoning off more than his fair share from company profits."

"Plus leaking important confidential business information to leading competitors," Loki adds, and a small, tentative smile spreads on Ryan's face.

"Very thorough, boys," he praises, and I can see my guys perk up, chests pushing out at his approval. "How will you keep the suspicion off yourselves?"

"Easy, we drug ourselves too, with a smaller dose of course," Loki adds, and I can hear the devious smirk in his voice.

"And how are you going to stop them from hiding the body? Sweeping it all under the carpet?" Enzo asks, his Italian accent lending a beauty to his words that really shouldn't be there when plotting a murder and frame job.

"There's where you come in, coach," Jax rumbles from my side, and I turn to see a dark, wicked grin on his face that should scare me. Of course it doesn't, it just makes Her Vagisty sit up and fucking purr, the horny bitch.

Enzo just nods, so Kai continues.

"An anonymous tip-off from a lost hiker who heard all the screams and called the feds," Kai tells Enzo, who just nods again.

"And where will I be?" I question the room, holding my spine straight when they all swing their eyes to me.

"I have a cabin just over the state lines in Utah. No one knows about it, it's in a false name," Tom speaks for the first time, and I turn to look at him. He looks back at me with softness in his eyes, and not for the first time I wonder who I remind him of to make him look at me like that. "It's about a three-hour drive from here, so far enough away from everything."

My heart sinks, my stomach feeling hollow at the thought of being separated from my guys again.

"I hate having to be apart from you, Princess," Ash says in a low voice, his hand guiding my face to look at him. "But I think that this is the best plan to keep you safe. Julian needs to think that you're dead, otherwise, he'll keep gunning for you."

"I know," I murmur back, moisture filling my eyes once more, and I blink furiously to try and clear them away. "I just... I hate being without you all when I feel like I only just got you back." A hot tear falls then, and I can see the pain in Ash's eyes. The knowledge that just an hour or so ago he thought that he'd never see me again hurts something deep inside me.

"We'll be together soon, my love," he tells me, pulling me close so that our foreheads rest together, and I close my eyes as his warm palm cups my cheek, rubbing my tears away. "I swear it."

I let myself bask in his warmth, breathing in his ginger scent as if trying to memorise it for the time ahead without him.

"I don't want to be all alone," I confess after a few moments, pulling away and looking around the room, my chin wobbling.

"I've already messaged Rowan and Roman," Loki tells me, letting go of my ankle to come up on his knees and grasping my face in both of his hands. "They're coming with Mai. We just need to give them an address, and they'll be there."

More tears fall at that, at the relief that washes over me with his words. I'm glad that it'll be them, the twins keep my spirits up, and Mai was like the older sister I never had.

"We'll wait for nightfall, then head to the cabin," Ryan tells me, and I tear my gaze away from Loki's emerald ones to stare at the man who was like a father to me.

"Tonight?" I ask in a soft voice, and Ryan gives a heavy sigh, his mouth downturned.

"I'm sorry, Little One, but we need to get you out of here," he softly tells me, coming closer. My head moves up and down in a nod in Loki's grip, even as my soul feels like it's being torn into four pieces.

"Why don't you all go upstairs?" Enzo asks us, and I look over to him, frowning.

"Upstairs?" I question, and he gives me a small smile.

"I have a spare apartment above the gym, cara mia," he informs me, stepping towards us and handing Ash a key. "It's yours until you have to leave."

If I didn't feel like my heart was breaking, I'd blush. Enzo, Ryan, and Tom know what's likely to happen between the guys and I in his apartment, but I'm too heartsore to feel anything other than my own pain.

How can I bear to say goodbye after only having just gotten them back?

CHAPTER TWENTY-SEVEN

LILLY

The door shuts quietly behind us, and I gaze around at the clean and neat apartment above the gym. It's a studio with a large bed in one corner, a small kitchen in another, and a living-dining space between. There's a door that I assume leads to a bathroom, and a bank of windows—blinds drawn—along the wall opposite the front door. The apartment can be accessed from the inside of the gym, and there's also a door that leads to a fire escape down the outside of the building.

Soft music starts to play, and I recognise the song as *Lifts* by Lia Marie Johnson. I close my eyes as one of the guys comes up behind me and sweeps my hair away from my neck, his hot breath tickling my skin before his soft lips place a gentle kiss there.

"Kai," I breathe out and sink into his arms that wrap around me, pulling me into his embrace, his fresh, woodsy scent enveloping me.

"When I saw that picture, sweetheart," he murmurs against my skin, and I tense up when I realise what picture he is talking about.

The staged one of my death. "My world ended, and I wanted no part in a new world without you."

I melt back into him, fresh tears springing behind my closed lids as his arms move and he starts to unbutton the front of my shirt-waister maternity dress.

"Kai— I—" I stutter, lost for words at the raw pain of his and the rasp of his voice. A warmth in front of me has my eyes fluttering open to find Loki standing before me.

"I didn't want to believe it," my trickster Knight tells me, his own eyes glistening as he steps closer and helps Kai to push the dress from my shoulders. "I didn't want to believe that I might have to live in a world where you no longer breathed."

"Loki—" My voice catches on a sob, tears running freely down my cheeks as he dips his head, placing his lips above my trembling ones.

"But when I realised that it was really you downstairs, fuck, Pretty Girl. I thought I was gonna pass out," he confesses against my lips, closing the distance and kissing me so sweetly, so rever-ently, it's all I can do to not break down here and now in a sobbing mess.

I hated not being able to tell them, knowing that they would see that picture and assume the worst, but we needed believable reac-tions. We needed Julian to think that I was dead.

"Wait—" I pull back, my heart thudding as I turn to find Ash leaning against the back of the sofa, watching us with dark eyes. "Where does Julian think you are now?"

"He knows that we're here, blowing off some steam," Ash tells me, his arms crossed across his broad chest. He gives a small, devious smirk, his words not a lie, but I'm betting not the whole truth either.

"Doesn't he expect, I don't know, you guys to retaliate?"

Ash's smirk drops, his jaw clenching. "He thinks, because it's what we want him to think, that we are too well trained, too under his thumb and afraid of what he might do to us to seek revenge."

I slump a little, a slow breath leaving me at that confirmation of their safety. I don't even startle when I realise that Kai and Loki have stripped me naked, my clothes in a crumpled heap on the floor. Loki steps to one side, and Ash straightens up, stalking towards me with a predatory gleam in his silver eyes.

Two pairs of hands trace every curve, every dip and hollow of my body, and I'm shuddering under their touch alongside Ash's heated gaze.

"I finally understood why Luc wanted to die," Ash says, continuing the conversation Loki, Kai, and I were having, and I can't help the flinch, knowing that I would have felt the same if it had been one of them. "There's nothing without you, Princess," he confesses softly, stepping right up against me so that I can feel the heat of his body through his shirt against my skin. "I do not exist without you."

My face must crumple then as he reaches out and draws my mouth to his in a bruising kiss. He worships me with his lips and tongue, showing me how desolate he felt, how broken the news of my death made him. I kiss him back, letting him take everything that I have to give, an apology in the way that my tongue soothes his, my lips caressing him.

I jerk away as the door opens and shuts, turning my head to see Jax walking in with something in his hands. His brows are low, his jaw tight as he storms towards me. Ash steps aside to let Jax stand before me in all his vibrating ire. Taking in a sharp breath, I hold my ground as I look up at him, aware that I am the only one naked in the room.

"You know how I felt about that picture," he tells me gruffly, his eyes hard and his muscles corded. "I get why it had to be done that way, but I'm fucking furious at you, Baby Girl."

My eyes widen, and I open my mouth to say something, to argue with the twatwaffle, but he places a finger against my parted lips.

"I'm not going to kiss you now," he tells me, and my pulse picks up speed when he opens his other hand and I see coils of red cotton fabric. "Not until you've been punished for breaking all of our hearts."

My lips drag against his digit as they close, and I look up into his stormy gaze and see the pure, unadulterated need burning there. He can't do anything about what happened, knows it needed to happen that way, but needs to punish someone now to exorcise the rage that's running through his veins. I lick my lips, catching his finger in the process, and a shudder runs over his skin at the contact.

Wordlessly, I bring my hands in front of me, wrists together in offering. He waits a beat, then moves his finger away to grab the fabric and stretch it out until I see what it is.

"These are my wraps, Baby Girl," he tells me as he works to bind my wrists tightly together. "I haven't washed them since I last wore them, the blood from my split knuckles and my opponent is still on them."

My thighs clench, and I gasp as he pulls tight. I give an exploratory tug, but my wrists don't move. Deep chuckles sound around me, and I look up into Jax's eyes first to see the dark gleam of satisfaction there. Turning, I can see a similar expression on Ash and Loki's faces. Kai is still behind me, and I shiver to think of his amber eyes full of heat. He always likes me bound.

I jerk as a tug pulls me forward, and I turn my head to see Jax has the ends of the wraps in his grip and is pulling me towards the bed.

"Loki, on the bed," Jax orders, and my trickster Knight obeys, going ahead and pausing at the side of the bed. He holds my stare as he strips out of his clothes; a printed T-shirt and smart jeans that hug his body and hang criminally low.

My breath stutters out of me when he drops his clothes to the floor, standing there naked and hard, and my tongue darts out to lick my dry lips again at the sight of his pierced member standing to attention.

"Don't worry, Pretty Girl," he teases, reaching down and giving his dick a stroke, the pink tip glistening with precum that I'm desperate to lick up. "You can choke on my dick once Jax is finished with you."

I rub my thighs together once more, trying in vain to soothe the ache that's building in my core, but it's not what I need. I need them inside me to truly satisfy my craving.

Jax tugs the binds again as Loki climbs onto the bed, lying back and watching me with a need to match mine in his emerald eyes.

"Your turn, baby," Jax tells me, keeping hold of the end of the wraps and walking along the side of the bed to the metal-framed headboard. "Thighs either side of Loki, on your knees."

I do as instructed, my heart thudding and flutters filling my belly as I get into position, my bound hands on his chiselled abs.

"I'm liking the view, Pretty Girl," Loki compliments huskily, his hands coming up to frame my hips and his hips flexing slightly so that his hard length rubs against my folds, and we both groan at the zing of pleasure.

"Dick inside our girl, Loki," is Jax's next command, and my eyes widen as a smile tugs my lips upwards. This isn't seeming like a punishment so far.

"Yes, boss," Loki answers, lifting my hips up and then using one hand to line his head up with my already slick entrance.

The song switches to *Call Out My Name* by The Weekend just as Loki thrusts forward, seating himself to the hilt in one sharp move.

"Loki!" I cry out, the slight pain of his sudden invasion quickly overtaken by the pleasurable fullness of having him inside me.

Before Loki can move, Jax gives a tug on my binds and my arms jerk forward, Loki's grip moves up my body quickly so that I don't faceplant into his chest. My head snaps up to glare at Jax, but he just looks at me with a hard, unreadable expression on his handsome face as he keeps pulling, forcing me forward until I'm lying chest to chest with Loki, my breasts and round stomach pressed against him. Seemingly satisfied with the awkward way my arms are pulled above my head, I watch as he ties the ends of the red fabric to the head-board, effectively immobilising me.

I have some movement, my pregnant stomach preventing me from being squashed up against Loki completely, but it's minimal, and I can't help pulling against my bindings, testing them out. The bed dips behind me, and I arch my back when a large, warm palm caresses my arse lovingly.

"For forty-five minutes we believed that you were dead," Jax tells me in his rough voice, still stroking my backside. "But I'm feeling generous, so Ash, Kai, and I will each give you ten spanks." I gasp as his words register and feel the vibration as Loki huffs out a dark laugh beneath me. "And you're going to count them."

"And what about Loki?" I question, raising my head enough to look at the flamed-haired man beneath me. He gives me a devilish smile, his hands caressing my sides, coming around to cup my breasts and brushing his thumbs over my nipples, making my eyes roll.

"Oh, I'm here to make sure that it feels good, baby," he answers, punching his hips upwards and leaving me gasping. "I'm going to make you come again." Thrust. "And again." Thrust. "And again, until you beg me to stop," he informs me, leaning up to nibble at my lower lip. "And then I'm going to make you come some more."

My whole body shudders, goosebumps pebbling my skin as my nipples go rock fucking hard. *Death by orgasms is a fine way to go.* I open my mouth to say something along those lines when a sharp crack lands on my left arsecheek, making me yelp and Loki groan as my inner walls clench around him.

"One," Jax says, voice hard and unforgiving.

"O–one," I repeat, arching my back when Loki nibbles and sucks at my neck, his fingers rolling my peaked nipples and sending shocks of electricity across my body.

Crack.

"Two," I breathe out, moaning when Loki bucks his hips upwards, sinking deeper inside me.

Crack.

"T–three."

"Shit, she clenches around my dick like a fucking vise when you do that, brother," Loki grits out, one hand leaving my nipple to snake between us and find the engorged bundle of nerves between my legs.

Another hit lands at the exact moment that his fingers press down on it, and an orgasm rips through me with such force that I cry and buck, my nails digging into my palms as sparks shoot across my vision.

"What number was that, Baby Girl?" Jax asks, his voice strained and breathless.

"Uh...Four," I stutter out, my climax still zinging through me.

Crack.

"Fuck! F–five," I snarl, the mixture of pleasure that Loki's fingers, mouth, and dick are giving me mixing with the sharp stinging heat that's covering my arse.

My head rests on Loki's chest as smack after smack lands across my lower cheeks, my mouth counting the hits even as my brain becomes a fog of pleasure and pain.

Dimly, I register the bed dipping as Jax must get off and someone else gets on, and I open my bleary eyes to see Jax crouch at the side of the bed, his long arm reaching over and his blue eyes soft.

"Such a good fucking girl, baby," he croons, his hand stroking sweat-slicked hair from my face. "You did so well, Baby Girl."

Crack.

"E–eleven," I croak, twitching when a hand rubs the sore spot.

"That's it, sweetheart," Kai's melodic voice soothes from behind me, telling me that he's taken over my punishment. "Loki, our girl deserves another orgasm, don't you think so, Pet?"

"Yes, sir," Loki replies, his voice deep, and the rumble makes me shiver as Jax keeps stroking my face, his blue eyes boring into mine.

Crack.

Loki begins to rub my clit again, moving his hips so that every time he thrusts upward, Kai lands another blow on my glowing backside in a slightly different place to where Jax landed his hits. My eyes close as the pleasure builds to a crescendo, the tingle all over my body telling me that another climax is fast approaching.

"Open your eyes, Baby Girl," Jax commands, and I instinctually obey, immediately getting caught up in his piercing gaze. "Look at me while they make you come."

Crack.

Another few hits from above and thrusts from below and I'm screaming out my pleasure, tears filling my eyes at the intensity of my climax. Jax grips my hair and forces my eyes to remain on his as I shudder and writhe with Loki still buried deep inside me.

"Fuck, baby," Loki hisses, his fingers digging into my soft flesh as he holds me still. "Your pussy is trying to strangle my dick."

I can't answer him; I just pant, my lids heavy with post-orgasm bliss. The bed dips, and I groan as I realise that my punishment is not over yet.

"You going to scream for me too, Princess, when I bury my cock inside that tight asshole of yours?" Ash's deep voice crawls across my skin from behind. I shiver with the promise his words give, but he doesn't give me a chance to answer, landing a punishing blow to my already pulsing arse.

"T–t–twenty-one," I rasp, my throat dry from all of my cries.

"Here, sweetheart," Kai says from my other side, Jax letting me twist my head to see him holding out a bottle of water with a straw in it. "Drink."

Lifting my head as much as I can, I do as he says, the cold water a balm to my parched throat and mouth.

"Thank you," I say, placing my head back down on Loki's sweaty chest.

Crack.

"T–twenty-two," I say, my words stronger even though they still stutter out of me.

Ash doesn't take his time, landing blow after blow so quickly that I barely have time to count out loud. Loki also renews his efforts, and I'm soon screaming out another release as stars explode behind my closed lids and I strain against my binds as I come and come and come, just like Loki promised me I would.

Panting, I finally call out the final smack, and no sooner do the words leave my lips than a cold pack is being pressed to my throbbing cheeks. The instant relief it gives me has me sighing and crying in relief

I gasp as something cold and wet slicks down my crack, a finger massaging around my puckered hole, then slipping inside.

"Oh, god," I groan as the digit slowly pumps in and out, my hips gyrating with the movement, eliciting a moan from Loki below me.

The finger pulls out only to be replaced with the pierced tip of Ash's cock, and I suck in a sharp breath as he breaches the tight ring of muscle, pushing in until his hips meet my throbbing arsecheeks, the ice pack having been taken away.

"That's it, Princess," he gasps out, voice tight and strained as his fingers dig into my hips. "Take me all the way in that sweet ass of yours."

Incoherent noises leave my lips as he withdraws a little only to push back in, Loki alternating his thrusts from below until they are both pounding into me. I'm jerked upwards, a firm grip in my hair, and I open my eyes to find Jax kneeling, holding his cock to my lips, the tip shiny with precum.

"Open up, baby," he commands, and I do, taking his bulbous head into my mouth as Ash and Loki continue to fuck me.

Jax quickly takes over, thrusting all the way to the back of my throat and holding himself there until I can feel my lungs screaming for air.

"Damn, baby," he says with a grunt, pulling me off, and I gasp in sweet air. "Your mouth feels so fucking good."

"Care to share, big man?" Kai says from my other side, and Jax uses his grip in my hair to turn my head so that Kai's dick is in front of my face, all his piercings glinting in the low lights.

"Open up for him, baby," Jax orders, and once again I obey him, Kai's hand holding his dick as he guides it into my open mouth.

"Jesus, sweetheart," he exclaims as I suck and lather his hard member with my tongue, paying close attention to the piercings that run along the underside of his dick.

The song changes to *Into It* by Chase Atlantic, and Kai holds my throat as he glides his dick in and out of my slick mouth. Heat builds between my legs, Ash and Loki pumping in and out of me and Kai using my mouth is getting me so fucking slick that the wet sounds of our fucking can be heard alongside the sensual rise and fall of the song.

Jax grips my hair, turning me once again as he pulls me off of Kai and thrusts into the back of my throat with a vengeance. I relax into their combined embrace, letting them use me as our bodies move in a dance as old as time, my climax climbing as they build me up. I can feel them getting close too, their movements becoming frenzied and animalistic noises leaving their throats as they don't hold back and fuck me hard.

Loki is the first to break, slamming into me so hard that it pushes me over the edge once more, and a muffled cry sounds around Kai's cock as I come so hard I almost implode. Wetness slicks my inner thighs, the sound of Loki's continued thrusts obscene as my inner muscles clench around him and Ash in a stranglehold.

"Shit, Princess!" Ash yells, thrusting deep as he's dragged under, and I can feel him pulse into my arse as he holds me still and shoots his release deep inside me.

I'm still twitching as Kai pumps once, twice, and then pours his climax deep into my throat, forcing me to swallow every drop as his hands grip my jaw. Pain lances my skull as I'm ripped away, Jax slamming his dick into my mouth seconds before hot, salty cum coats my tongue, and I greedily swallow that too.

When his dick stops pulsing, he pulls out, and I collapse onto Loki, his softening dick still buried in my pussy as we all pant and gasp for air. After a time I feel my wrists being unbound, the ties loosening, and it's all I can do to flex my fingers as I lie in a blissful, exhausted heap on top of Loki.

I hiss as a cool gel is rubbed into my sore arsecheeks, realising that Ash must have withdrawn when I collapsed.

"How the fuck," I say, my voice fifty shades of husky, "am I meant to sit in a car for god knows how many hours it takes to get to Utah after that?"

Masculine guffaws and chuckles fill the room. *Fuckers.*

But, they are my fuckers, quite literally, and I press closer to Loki as my words sink in.

I think a better question is how am I going to survive without them for the next few weeks?

CHAPTER TWENTY-EIGHT

LILLY

All too soon a knock on the door interrupts our post-orgasm bliss, and Ryan's deep voice tells me that we'll be leaving in twenty minutes. As if on cue, *Lost Without You* by Freya Ridings starts to play, and tears spring to my eyes, the words of the song expressing exactly how I'm feeling at the thought of being separated from my Knights once again.

Silently, I get up and have a quick shower, Ash and Loki following me in and washing me so tenderly that the tears fall and mingle with the water that cascades over my skin.

Knowing that we don't have much time left, I step out of the shower to find Jax there with a towel, ready to dry me. Once he's finished, he leads me back into the main room where Kai waits with my clothes.

"We'll send the rest of your things as soon as we can," Kai murmurs softly to me as he helps me to get dressed, his touch lingering as if he, too, is dreading what's to come.

"How will you get them out?" I question in a quiet voice, finding Ash looking at me, eyebrows lowered.

"There'll be a funeral," he tells me, and I wince, freezing as I put my cardigan on.

"A–a funeral?"

"We have to go through with a burial," he tells me, moving closer and helping me into the garment. "I'm sorry, Princess, but we need to keep up with the pretense."

"I–I understand," I reply, and I do. I get that this has to look real, and if the look of sadness on each of my guy's faces is anything to go by, people will believe that I've died.

"It's time, Pretty Girl," Loki mumbles, reaching out and taking my hand in his. I look up to him, willing my face not to crack, and show him how much my heart feels like it's breaking. His pained expression tells me that I've failed, and he pulls me against him, wrapping his arms around me in a fierce hug. "I know, baby. I know." His voice breaks, and I can't stop the sob that rips free from my chest as my pain overwhelms me.

"It's only three weeks until the hunting trip," Kai adds, but his voice is flat like he's trying to convince himself that it won't feel like an eternity. "And here's a burner phone so we can keep in touch."

I lift my head from Loki's chest, my arm unwrapping from his torso as I reach out for the new iPhone that Kai is holding out for me.

"You ready, Lilly?" I hear Ryan ask from the other side of the door, and taking a deep breath, I step out of Loki's arms, wrapping our fingers together as I step towards the doorway.

We head down the stairs inside the gym, following Ryan's broad back as he leads us to a side exit that opens onto a dark alley that runs alongside the gym. It's night out, and the cool air soothes my hot face a little.

"I'll give you a minute to say your goodbyes, Little One," Ryan tells me, squeezing my arm and then going around to the driver's side of the car.

I've still got Loki's hand in a tight grip, and he pulls me into another crushing hug, squeezing me tightly. I don't care though, I need to feel him for the next few weeks so that I know I'm not back at that manor house in England, all alone and doubting the existence of my Knights.

"It's not goodbye," he whispers into my hair. "Just see you later, Pretty Girl."

He pulls back enough to dip his head and capture my lips with his own, and I taste the salt on his lips as he must do on mine, our sadness spilling down our cheeks in the summer moonlight. I cling to him as he tries to step away, but I don't want to be released, not now or ever.

"I fucking love you, Lilly," he says against my lips, giving me one last kiss before prising my arms from around him and stepping away.

"I fucking love you too, Loki," I choke back, a sob stuck in my throat as I watch his angelic features crease with despair.

Jax suddenly blocks my view, taking Loki's place and grabbing me by the back of my neck, pulling me into a soul-searing kiss. I grip his arms tightly, more tears tracing their hot path down my cheeks as I fall into his kiss. It's painful in its softness, in the way he teases my mouth and tongue, the touch of his own at odds with the way he grips me tightly, possessively.

I'm gasping when he pulls back just as suddenly as he grabbed me, looking into my eyes with his piercing blue ones.

"You are my fucking light, Baby Girl. My soul." He places my hand over his thumping heart. "My heart. I'll do whatever it takes to keep you, *both* of you, safe." His other palm caresses my stomach, our baby pushing against it and making him smile in that way that only Jax can.

"I love you, Jax," I tell him, watching that small smile brighten until it outshines the moon above us.

He places a gentle kiss on my forehead and then lets me go for Kai to take his place. My lips wobble, sheer determination the only thing keeping my knees from buckling under me.

Kai steps into me, so close that the heat from his clothed body spreads to mine, and I want nothing more than to bask in it. Both hands come up, palms cupping my cheeks as he brings our foreheads together.

"You are my freedom, sweetheart," he confesses softly, and I love the new nickname, something that only he calls me.

"And you are mine," I say back, closing the distance between our lips this time, desperate for one final taste.

We kiss as though it will release us from the tyranny that still holds us hostage, as though it will kill the monsters that lurk in the dark waiting to spill our blood and devour us.

"I love you," he whispers against my kiss-swollen lips, pulling away but keeping hold of my face for one final moment.

"I love you," I repeat back, swallowing hard when he lets go and steps away to stand back with Jax and Loki.

My darkest Knight, my husband, steps up to me next, and I hate the turmoil churning in his silver eyes.

"We will come for you soon, my love," he tells me, invading my personal space so that I crane my neck to look up at him and his fierce expression. "I swear on my cursed life that we will do what needs to be done, and then we can all finally be free to live."

He doesn't give me time to answer, to say a single damn thing before his lips are on mine and he's kissing the life out of me. It's a kiss that sends warriors into battle, that gives soldiers something to fight for, and I give freely, pouring all of my love and adoration for him into it.

We end the embrace softly, lingering for just another touch, another second more, trying to stave off the inevitable. He heaves a great sigh, like the weight of the world is on his shoulders.

"You are my everything, Lilly Vanderbilt," he says against my lips.

"You mean Lilith Taylor," I try to joke, but it falls a bit flat, and no one laughs, myself included.

"Regardless of your name, you are fucking mine, Lilly, and I am yours," he says vehemently, angling my head with his hand gripped under my chin so that I'm looking into his hypnotic, grey eyes. "We are fused and nothing can tear us apart. Not my father. Not the rest of the board. Not even the devil him-fucking-self."

Fresh tears sting my eyes and fall as I nod my head.

"I love you so much, Ash," I tell him, my own palms coming up to cup his stubbled cheeks.

"I love you too, Lilly."

The engine starts behind us, and the pain in the back of my throat intensifies as I try to swallow but can't. Taking a shuddering breath, I pull the last vestiges of strength I have and take a step away from Ash, then another, my hands falling away from him as his fall from me.

"I'll see you soon," I tell them all, indulging in one final look at my Knights, the moonlight casting them in its glow until they appear like vengeful gods, ready to wage war, all hard lines and corded muscles.

Turning around, I give them my back as I open the car door and get inside, wincing slightly as my sore arsecheeks hit the seat. But I welcome the pain, the reminder of my lovers, of the other parts of my soul that are waiting to be reunited with me.

I just hope that it's not too long before we can once again be in each other's embrace.

The drive to Utah is mostly silent. As much as I want to talk to Ryan, to find out more about his mercenary jobs, I just can't bring myself to make conversation. My soul aches so damn bad, like pieces are missing, and there's a heavy weight on my chest, as if I'll never be able to take a full breath again.

Ryan must sense my reluctance because he just puts some classical music on the radio and drives, leaving me to be lulled into a restless sleep full of broken hearts and dark shadows.

I wake as we pull up in front of a wooden cabin surrounded by forest, the predawn light fading from a deep purple to orange on the horizon behind it.

"Let's get you settled, Little One," Ryan suggests softly, switching the engine off and opening the door.

Taking a deep inhale, I follow, breathing in the fresh, damp air as I exit the vehicle. Looking up at the wooden structure, it reminds me of the hunting cabin that the guys took me to on Halloween, and I pause as I wonder if that's the cabin that they'll be going to in a few weeks. Seems fitting that the place we took revenge on Robert all those months ago will see justice served once more.

This, too, is double-storied, and as I walk inside, I notice that it has a much more homely feel, with cosy sofas covered in blankets facing a huge fireplace. Unlike the guys' cabin, there are no dead animals on the walls, which I am grateful for.

"Lilly, come look at this," Ryan's voice calls from the other end of the room, and I turn, gasping as I see that the entire wall is windows, letting the rising sun filter into the space.

Walking over to where Ryan stands by some open bi-folding doors, I can see there's a deck, and we have an uninterrupted view over the mountains and the valley below, all bathed in the beautiful dawn. Birds are singing, and tears spring to my eyes with the majesty of it all.

"There's always a new day, Little One," Ryan says softly from beside me, his big arm wrapping around my shoulders and pulling me into his side.

"Mum used to say that." I sniffle, breathing in his familiar scent and letting it comfort me, even as my heart fractures at being so far from my soulmates.

"She was a wise woman, your mum," he replies, his own voice a little thicker than usual.

I wrap my arm around his waist in a side hug, and we stay that way, watching the sunrise and letting its rays fill us with light, chasing away the darkness.

CHAPTER TWENTY-NINE

LILLY

I sleep in late, waking up alone and bereft as I remember all that has happened in the last day or so. Ryan faking my death, those wonderful few hours in the apartment, the drive to the cabin.

My stomach growls just as the scent of bacon fills my nose, and I can hear low voices downstairs which confuses me until I remember who is coming to stay with me. With more energy than I thought I possessed, I throw back the covers and clamber out of bed, not stopping to cover my maternity vest and knickers as I rush from the room and down the wooden staircase.

"Mai!" I shout when I see her blonde hair at the dining table.

A huge smile splits her face as she stands up and hurries over to wrap me up in a tight hug.

"Lilly! It's so good to see you, girl," she tells me, laughing when my bump gets in the way. "Look at you!" She steps back and holds me at arm's length to admire my pretty big stomach. "You are positively glowing."

I blush, then shriek when twin blond heads poke around the French doors from the deck, wide grins on their faces.

"Roman! Rowan!"

I launch myself at them, both wrapping their arms around me in a hug.

"Jeez, pixie girl. You need to hold off on all those pies," Roman jokes, earning a poke from Mai.

"Fuck off," I tell him with a smile, all of us laughing when my stomach lets out a huge growl.

"Sounds like someone is hungry," Ryan says from the doorway, carrying two huge platters full of crispy bacon, fried eggs, and toast.

"Fuck, yes," I groan, practically attacking him in my bid to get to the deliciousness.

He chuckles as I pile my plate high, pouring myself a huge glass of tropical juice that was already on the table.

The others join us, filling their own plates, and we each take a seat, catching up on everything that has happened since we last saw each other.

"And I thought our lives were fucked up," Rowan comments, softening his words with a boyish smile.

"Yep, things are pretty messed up at the moment," I say, sighing as I set down my cutlery on my empty plate. I sit up straight, eyes focused on Ryan as I feel the colour drain from my face. "Shit, Ryan, my grandparents! They'll be devastated when they find out."

I'd told Ryan and Lexie about meeting Harold and Petunia last time we had a FaceTime call, and they were unsurprised to learn that Mum was using a fake identity.

"I'll pay them a visit when I get back home, explain the situation and the need for the current pretence," he assures me, reaching over and taking my hand in his, giving it a squeeze.

"Won't that put Lilly in danger?" Rowan asks, and warmth suffuses me at his concern.

"Her grandfather has ties with MI6, he knows how to keep a

secret or two," Ryan explains, and I see both boys' brows raise, a grudging respect in their blue eyes.

"Right, Lilly," Mai says, turning to look at me. "I've bought some bits for you, the guys said you wouldn't have much, and I'd like to do some checks on baby, if that's okay?"

"Thanks," I reply, a lightness filling my soul at the thought that this isolation might not be all bad.

I have friends, am in an amazing location, and my guys are on the end of a phone. It could be worse.

That night I climb into bed, the mattress soft and the room cosy. I leave the curtains open; my room has a view over the valley below, and the sight is breathtaking as the dying rays of the sun kiss the land.

My burner phone buzzes next to me and reaching over, I smile wide as Ash's name appears on a FaceTime call. Swiping my finger across the screen, I answer.

"Ash!" I practically squeal, giggling when he winces slightly, but the smile on his face tells me that he doesn't mind my enthusiastic greeting.

"Hello, Princess," his deep voice cascades over me, and I snuggle deeper into my pillows at the sound. *"How are you settling in?"*

"Mai and the twins are here," I tell him, launching into a description of our day spent unpacking all of the things Mai bought me, including some brightly-coloured fun maternity dresses and dungarees. Ash listens, an indulgent half smile across his lips as I talk. "How was your day?" I finally ask, and he heaves a great sigh.

"We met with the funeral home," he tells me, bringing a glass of amber liquid to his lips and taking a deep swallow. *"Finalised arrangements."*

"Wait, do they have a...body?" I question, no longer quite as relaxed as I was when I answered the call. Another deep exhale passes his lips.

"Yeah, some unknown Jane Doe." He winces as he says it, and my own face scrunches at the thought of some poor girl taking my place.

"Make sure she gets the best," I say after a moment, and he looks up at me, his face full of wonder.

"You really are too good for us, Princess," he says softly, and the need to be wrapped up in his arms is almost overwhelming. Searching for a distraction, I look behind him to see that he's not in the dorms.

"Where are you?"

A small smirk tilts his full lips.

"I'm at my house, in the woods," he answers, moving to the side so that I can see the room he's in. It's dark, the only light from the setting sun filtering through the huge window. It's not a room that I recognise though. *"I wanted to play you something."*

My heart skips a beat, anticipation rushing through me in an electric wave. There's a bit of a wobble on the screen as he props the phone up, I assume on the lid of the piano, as he sits back down in front of it. I have to bite my lips to stop from making an excited noise as he cracks his fingers, looking at the camera with that sexy as fuck half smile that he only gives me.

"Ready?" he asks.

"Ready."

My mouth drops open when he begins to sing, his fingers playing *Love me Like you Do,* the Boyce Avenue acoustic version. I watch, enraptured as he sings for me, his voice husky and with an incredible range. His eyes are closed, his face bathed in the light of the dying sun, and tears fill my eyes at the raw emotion in his voice.

My pulse races, and I'm grateful that I'm lying down, as my knees are weak as fuck. I told him once that I loved this song, and I can't help feeling that he's learnt it just for me, pouring his soul into it and letting me know that he, too, understands the meaning of the lyrics. It's about an all-consuming love, love that defies the ages, and about the fact that you need to grasp it with both hands. It's our love, our journey.

By the time he's softly playing the final notes, hot tears are tracking down my cheeks, and I can't even blame the damn hormones. He pauses with his hands over the keys, then looks up, his own eyes glistening.

"A–Ash," I stutter out, no idea how to follow that up. How to convey to him all that I'm feeling right now.

"I know, Princess. I know," he replies, his voice gruff. He clears his throat. *"Let me play some more while you go to sleep. You need to rest."*

"Yes, sir," I tease, snuggling down and grinning at his arched brow.

I try to keep my eyes open, try to watch him as he plays soothing classical music, but my body is exhausted, and I fall into the darkness with the sound of his sweet music comforting my soul.

CHAPTER THIRTY

KAI

The three weeks since Lilly's 'death' drag and pass by in a blur all at once. The funeral happened a week after she arrived at the cabin in Utah, and we didn't have to fake the anguish at being parted from the love of our lives. We did have to hold back our anger at the fake sadness that Julian and the rest of the board—excluding Mr Black—showed, Jax visibly vibrating with the rage that flowed through his veins. I couldn't blame him, I, too, felt the need to maim and hurt, holding my darkness close. I'll get to unleash it soon. I just need to bide my time until then.

Something comes up at Black Knight Corp, the elders keeping it a secret from us, but the hunting trip gets postponed until late August. I'm not the only one worrying that it's closer to Lilly's due date than we'd like, only two weeks away in fact, but there's nothing we can do but wait, and comb through our plan to ensure that everything is perfect, every possibility accounted for.

Lilly's own disappointment is clear when we tell her, but like the

Queen that she is, she accepts it for what it is and moves on. We are some lucky bastards to have found her.

Finally, the day of reckoning arrives, and we run through the plan one final time at Ash's house.

"Jax, you have the GHB?" Ash asks as we sit around his glass dining table, our packed bags by the door, *99* by Elliot Moss playing quietly in the background.

"Yep," Jax replies. He's withdrawn a little since Lilly went into hiding. Not as much as he was before her arrival, but he's not talking as much anymore, preferring his silence and only answering in single words.

"And you'll get it into their drinks this evening, with enough left over to give us each a mild dose?" Jax just nods this time. Ash sighs, noting Jax's silent affirmation with a head bob of his own. "Kai, are you ready?" He settles his steely gaze on me, and my senses heighten, a slight roiling in my stomach making me aware of my nerves.

"Yes," I answer, not elaborating. They've given me free rein over what I'm going to do to my uncle, the revenge that I'm going to carve into his skin. He gives me a tight nod.

"And I have the playlist," Loki adds, lightening the mood as Ash rolls his eyes, but there's a smile on his lips.

"Excellent," Ash deadpans, adding, "Enzo will come to help with cleaning ourselves up and take our clothes to be burned. But he'll be close the whole time in case we need him."

"Then we're all sorted," I state, each of us looking at the others with steel in our spines, jaws locked tight.

"One for all!" Loki cries, leaping to his feet and thrusting his hand into the centre of the table. I can't help the grin that splits my face, even as Ash gives a long, suffering sigh. Loki wiggles his hand, clearly growing impatient. I get up, placing my hand on top of his.

"All for one," I answer, my smile widening at Loki's beam of delight. He really is a ray of fucking sunshine sometimes. Ash sighs, copying my movement and putting his own palm on top of mine.

"All for one," he repeats in a bored tone, but the tilt of his lips shows his amusement.

"Come on, big guy," Loki cajoles Jax, waggling his eyebrows. "We need our fourth Musketeer."

Jax sits with his arms folded for another beat, then huffing, gets up, and thumps his hand hard on top of ours like a dick.

"Say it," Loki insists, and Jax holds his stare. A lesser man would wither under his intense scrutiny, but Loki holds his ground.

"All for fucking one," Jax rumbles, and Loki fist pumps with his free hand.

All for fucking one.

T he irony of being back at the cabin we meted out justice to that scum, Robert, is not lost on any of us as we pull up in Jax's truck, parking at the end of the row of expensive SUVs.

"Let's get this shitshow started, shall we?" Ash asks, getting out of the passenger side, and we all follow him, grabbing our bags from the trunk and walking towards the front door.

It opens before we reach the bottom step, and my jaw aches as I grit my teeth at seeing Julian standing on the threshold. I did suggest that he is more deserving of death for all that he's put us through, but the guys wouldn't hear of it, saying that his punishment will be to watch as his world crumbles all while he rots in prison. My uncle on the other hand deserves a slow and painful death for what he did to me all those years ago.

It still rankles that we can't just kill them all and bathe in their blood as we watch the life flow from their eyes, but we have to be smarter and play the long game. Anyways, sometimes death is too kind, the lesser of a punishment.

"Boys," Julian beams as if he really doesn't know our hatred for him. He must though. Julian Vanderbilt may be many things, but stupid is not one of them. "Come on in."

He ushers us into the cabin, and I'm once again reminded that it's a place of dead things, the animal heads on the walls from previous kills reinforcing the impression that this is not a place for the living. Just as well given our plans for tonight.

"Son," Rafe addresses Jax, who grunts back. Neither goes to shake the others' hand, they just size each other up like male lions ready to do battle.

"Loki," Chad greets his son, stepping forward to give Loki a man hug, slapping him on the back. "You would have liked the fine piece of ass I had last night, big juicy tits and a tight cunt." Loki visibly shudders, passing it off with a laugh.

"I'm sure I would have, Dad," he replies, and I can see the cringe in his eyes, the skin around them tight.

"Kai," my uncle's voice sounds next to me, and I turn to face him, steeling my spine to face the monster of my childhood.

"Uncle," I respond. Like Jax and Rafe, there are no hugs or back slaps, just a wary recognition of a familial tie.

"Right," Julian's voice booms, taking centre stage as always. "Now that we're all here, let's have a bite to eat, and then we can do a spot of hunting before dinner."

"Let's kill some shit!" Chad cries, his tone excited, and the blood-lust already in his wide eyes.

Let's kill some shit indeed.

CHAPTER THIRTY-ONE

LILLY

I wake up with a groan, a sharp pain tightening like a band across my stomach. It's so intense that all I can do is lie there and breathe, just like Mai has been getting me to practise for the past few weeks.

Once it passes, I get up and head to the bathroom, sitting on the toilet. It's when I wipe myself and notice the jelly-like, pink-tinged substance on the paper that I realise what is happening.

"Mai!" I yell, staring at what can only be my plug, or show as Mai kept calling it. Its presence tells me that the pain I experienced this morning might be my labour starting.

The door is flung open, and I look up with wide eyes as Mai rushes into the room, sleep tousled and still in her cotton PJs. I thrust the stained toilet paper in her direction, and she blinks, then straightens up and looks wide awake when she realises what it is.

"No need to panic, Lilly," she tells me in a soothing tone, stepping closer and around my still-held-out hand. "This doesn't necessarily mean that your labour will start today. Let's get you cleaned up and put some food in you, okay?"

"O–okay," I reply, finally putting the paper down the toilet and flushing whilst Mai starts up the shower.

Getting to my shaky feet, my heart feels like it's trying to fly free.

"Hey..." Mai takes my arm, helping me out of my sleep shirt. "Even if baby does decide to come today, we can handle it, okay?"

"Okay," I repeat once more, stepping under the warm spray and instantly feeling my shoulders relax under the water.

After I get dressed and eat something, we decide to go for a gentle walk, the pains coming fairly regularly but not that often. The twins follow us, both with wrinkled brows and stiff necks.

"Oh, for goodness' sake!" Mai exclaims after Roman hovers so close I almost trip. "Plenty of babies have been born a little early, Lilly is not about to keel over, so give her some bloody space."

I giggle as, chastised, they step back a bit, and a pang of intense sadness hits me when I realise that my guys would be far worse if they were here.

"The guys will be at the cabin by now; they won't be able to come here if things do ramp up," I pause as an intense pain shoots across my stomach, making it go rock-hard.

"That's it, Lilly, just breathe in and out," Mai encourages, rubbing my back in soothing circles until the pain eases and I can straighten up once more. "Let's head back, shall we?"

We turn to walk back, my arm linked in Mai's, and I worry my lip as we walk.

"I think that maybe we shouldn't let them know. I don't want them distracted," I tell them, and although I can see the twins scowling at that, they nod.

"It's shit, but probably for the best," Rowan says grumpily.

He's right, it is shit. I want my guys here with me. Jax was meant to help deliver our baby, but we can't always get what we want; I know that more than most.

Looks like this night may be one to remember in more ways than one.

ASH

We all take our seats on various couches in the main living room after a long day of hunting elk and a meal of freshly caught elk heart. My father likes the idea of eating the heart of our enemies, and it doesn't taste too bad once you get over the idea. The staff that cooked it have gone home as planned, so it's just the eight of us.

Jax hands out glasses of scotch, catching my eye and giving an imperceptible nod to let me know that he's done his part and, at most, we have half an hour before the effects of the GHB kicks in.

The elders talk about business, lots of bullshit back slapping and congratulatory talk about this or that company that has been made bankrupt. I watch, sipping my drink and trying not to sneer at the devil's these men have become. It turns my stomach the amount of lives they've ruined, have forced us to take, all in the name of getting richer.

This isn't how the world is meant to work. Lilly has shown me that with her light and goodness, and her caring for others. We're meant to help people, help to pull them up, and not knock them down for our own gain. How many families have struggled because of us? Because of my father's insatiable greed?

"Asth—" the man in question slurs, grimacing as his eyes try to focus on me. Seconds later his glass slips from his hand, landing with a dull thud on the rug as he slides to the floor, eyes closed and slack-jawed.

Similar noises sound around the room, and I look up to see all four of them lying in a comatose state.

"Stephen won't be out for long," Jax informs us, going over to

Kai's uncle and giving him a vicious kick. A small moan leaves the man's lips, but he stays down. Jax leans down, grabs Stephen under the arms, and hauls him in the direction of the basement.

"You ready?" I ask Kai, pausing him with my hand on his bicep. He turns to face me, and it takes more effort than I'd like to admit not to flinch at the sight of his cold, dead eyes, all the warmth drained away.

"Yes."

I loosen my grip, letting him go, but the stiffness in my shoulders remains as I watch him.

"Let's get this show on the road, brother," Loki says, his usual, teasing tone gone and replaced with the hard Knight that we've all been moulded into.

Taking one final, deep inhale, I draw my own darkness to the front, letting my inner demon take over for this bloody night's work.

One last life to take.

***

LILLY

The pains increase steadily as the day wears on, becoming more intense and frequent as evening draws in. When we returned from our walk, Mai helped me to set up the main living area as my birth space; placing affirmation cards around the room, and plugging in fairy lights that she'd brought with her. The twins helped to set up the bluetooth speaker, and the classical playlist that Loki and I had created specifically for the birth is playing softly in the background. There's a sharp pain in my chest which has nothing to do with my labour and everything to do with my missing Knights.

I keep walking round the space, pausing and breathing every time a contraction hits me. It's full night-time now, the moon shining through the French doors, the curtains left open at my insistence. I'm looking out into the darkness as another pain tightens my abdomen, and I grab hold of the back of a chair in a tight grip as it washes over me.

"That's it, just breathe through them, Lilly," Mai soothes, rubbing my back in circles. "You are doing so well, sweetheart."

Tears sting my eyes at the endearment. It's Kai's new nickname for me, and I would give anything to have him here. To have all of them here.

"They're getting stronger," I pant out, straightening up once it passes and resuming my pacing, Mai giving me the space to walk.

"And closer together," she says with a smile. "Baby is growing impatient to meet its mama."

"Here," Rowan says, holding out a bottle of some kind of sports drink. "You need to keep your energy levels up, especially as you haven't eaten much."

I take a sip, my heart aching when mango fills my mouth and I remember Jax taking care of me in his truck after Julian had said those awful things at the paintballing centre.

I gasp as another searing pain hits me, and Rowan quickly grabs the bottle before I can accidentally drop it. I grasp his arm, digging my nails in as I pant, this pain stronger than the last and much sooner.

A cool cloth smelling of lavender is pressed to my forehead as the contraction subsides, and I sigh, breathing in the relaxing scent. It reminds me of all the bubble baths the guys ran for me.

"Sorry." I wince when I see the crescents in Rowan's forearms left from my nails digging in.

"No worries, pixie," he assures me with a grin.

The next hour or so is more of the same, walking and panting through the pains, time slipping away as I get lost in my own body and the war that is raging inside me.

I come to realise that's what birth is, a war with only one outcome. Your body is literally being ripped apart, and all you can do is ride the waves of agony, praying that you both come out of the other side.

JAX

Agony contorts Stephen's face as the cat-o-nine tail lands on his torn-up back, blood spraying over Kai holding the whip. *Can You Hear Me Now* by The Score plays loudly in the background, Loki dancing around like a fucking insane person as the lyrics ramp us all up to a state of fury.

I lift my gaze to Kai, watching as he observes his handiwork with a cold detachment that's fucking scary. His chest is bare and glistening with crimson drops and splatter covering his face as he brings the whip down again.

Stephen struggles against his binds, crying out around his gag, but Ash tied him up good, hanging from the basement ceiling as Kai requested, so the fucking paedo isn't going anywhere. The beast inside me purrs in approval at the bastard finally getting what he deserves. Kai meting out the punishment that his uncle gave him all those years ago is the icing on the cake.

Tears track down the man's face, fucking pathetic sack of shit. He's saying something, and Ash steps forward, removing his gag.

"What was that, Stephen?" he asks, and a dark bark of laughter bursts out of me at Ash's tone. It's like we're in one of those shitty board meetings at Black Knight HQ, his tone bored and unemotional.

"P—p—please," Stephen rasps out, the whites of his eyes showing as he looks at Ash.

"Did you listen to a small boy's pleas, Stephen?" Ash questions and his voice is fucking arctic, his hand fisting in Stephen's hair. He holds his grip as another hit lands on the man's back, and we all relish in his loud scream, the sound unhindered by the gag.

Roughly, Ash lets go, stepping away and leaving bloody shoe

prints on the concrete floor. Luckily, he's wearing his father's shoes, we all are except Kai who has plastic shoe covers over the top of his. Gotta keep up appearances and all that, footwear marks are evidence after all.

There's a loud sound of wet leather and metal hitting the floor as Kai drops the whip out of his gloved grasp. Casually, he strolls over to the workbench, and I watch, my arms folded as he picks up a pair of bolt croppers, a small blowtorch, and pliers. Turning, he catches my gaze, and there's no warmth there. A demon stares back at me, calling to my own, and when he holds out the blowtorch in a gloved hand, I don't hesitate.

I walk up to my brother, and with my own double-gloved hand, take it from him, knowing what he wants. Giving the pliers to Loki as he walks past, Kai strides to face his uncle, the man broken and bleeding, sagging in his chains before him. Stephen lifts his head, his wide eyes taking in his nephew and the bolt croppers he's holding.

"You forced your disgusting dick inside me when I was a child, when I thought that you were my savior, but soon discovered you were nothing but a monster," Kai tells him, his voice deep and rough, and my hand tightens around the blowtorch at his words. "So I thought that I'd cut it off."

Stephen struggles, and I wrinkle my nose as piss springs out from the appendage, the smell adding to that of blood in the room. Fucking disgusting.

"Y–you won't get away with t–this!" he cries, his voice hoarse and cracked.

"Yes, we will," Kai answers. "Loki."

Loki steps forward, grabbing the end of Stephen's dick with the pliers, and Stephen lets out a cry of pain as Loki pulls it out. It doesn't go far, small dicked motherfucker. Although, I guess if someone had my cock in pliers, I might not be showing them all I have to offer.

"Doubt you'll miss this much, Stephen," Loki comments, clearly thinking the same as me.

I light the blowtorch, Stephen's eyes darting to me as I step up close.

"You didn't think we were going to let you die that easily, did you?" I ask him, my voice low and dark. I laugh.

Rest in Peace by Dorothy starts to play, and I arch a brow at Loki.

"It's the perfect song for revenge torture!" he argues, his head bobbing with the rock music.

"Fucking madman." I chuckle, turning my stare to Kai.

"This," Kai tells Stephen, opening the cutters and placing them around the base of Stephen's dick, "is going to hurt."

LILLY

"Aaarrrggghhh!"

My scream echoes around the room as wave after wave of agony rips through my body, barely letting me breathe.

The pads that Mai placed on the floor cushion my knees as I kneel, my upper torso resting on the seat of the sofa as I grip Roman and Rowan's hands so tightly I'm surprised I've not broken them.

"That's it, Lilly!" Mai encourages me from behind. "I can see baby's head, breathe deeply and let your body do its thing."

I manage to follow her instructions, breathing through gritted teeth as I feel my vagina being stretched to an impossible size. Fuck, I thought Jax and Ash together down there was a lot, but it has nothing on this. This burns like nothing I've ever felt before.

"Good girl, that's exactly it," Mai praises, and it's all I can do to focus on just breathing.

Shit, I wanted to be all zen earth mother, and here I am screaming like a fucking banshee. Some things never change, a brief flash of meeting Loki for the first time flits through my mind before the overwhelming urge to push fills me.

"I—I need to push," I gasp out, sweat dripping down the side of my face.

"Then push, my lovely," Mai encourages, and I take a huge inhale, pushing as I breathe it out through another loud scream.

A rush of liquid and something else expels from between my legs, and my muscles feel suddenly weak as all tension leaves them. Seconds later the most wonderful, unexpected sound of a baby's cry sounds behind me, and I straighten my back as Mai passes a wriggling slick bundle between my legs.

Oh shit.

Instinctively, I grab my baby and bring it in close, marvelling at the miracle that I'm holding.

"Congratulations, Lilly," Mai says, her voice thick, and I sit back on my heels twisting to look at her.

"Is it a boy or girl?" one of the twins asks, and I look down at the bundle in my arms, the cord still attached and pulsing slightly.

"A girl," I whisper. "She's a girl."

I look up at them with tear-filled eyes, my forehead creasing as another slight pain hits me followed by more slickness between my thighs.

"That's the afterbirth," Mai informs me, and I do an awkward shuffle to see a large blob of red on the sheets we put down, the cord flowing from the placenta to my baby. My baby girl.

My eyes trace her tiny body, taking in every detail, and a choked laugh falls from my lips when I get to her head.

"She's ginger!" I exclaim, delight filling me as I look at her mop of red hair, just like her dad. "And has so much hair."

"She's beautiful," Mai tells me, coming beside me and wrapping her arm around my shoulders. "The cord has stopped pulsing, so let's cut it and you can have a lie down with her."

Mai orders the twins to get me something to drink and eat then helps me onto the sofa that's been pulled out to create a sofa bed. She helps me clean up after she's checked me over to make sure there were no tears, all the while I hold my baby girl to my chest and just fucking marvel at her existence.

"Does she have a name?" Roman asks, and I look up to find him and Rowan waiting with snacks and a drink.

I look back down at my baby, who's happily taking her first feed, and I can feel my lips lift up in a soft smile, warmth suffusing my entire body.

"Violet," I reply, not taking my eyes off her, my hand gently stroking her soft head. "Her name is Violet."

CHAPTER THIRTY-TWO

KAI

I watch as the life drains from my uncle's eyes, leaving them dull and lifeless, and what was left of his blood drips down the slit in his neck. Lowering my arm, I still clutch the knife in my hand and look down briefly to see blood dripping on the already crimson-splattered floor.

I'd expected to feel something, relief maybe, but I'm still lost to my darkness and all I feel is numbness. I feel nothing for this man that was meant to take care of me but instead abused me for years. There's nothing but an emptiness inside of me as I look over his dead body.

"Come, brother," Jax says, placing a hand on my shoulder. "Time to get cleaned up."

Slowly blinking, I turn to face him, and the darkness recedes enough that my hands begin to tremble and a slight lightness infuses my limbs. Without saying anything, I hand the knife to Ash.

Walking over to the door that leads to a bathroom, I step inside and then strip my gloves and remaining clothes off, bagging them up to be taken away and burned by Enzo before the Feds arrive.

Footsteps sound on the basement stairs, and my heart ricochets in my chest until I hear the Italian trainer's voice. I turn the shower up high, stepping under the almost blistering spray and watching the pink water running down the drain, my head bowed.

A blast of cool air hits my back, then a warm body steps into the shower with me a moment later, muscled arms wrap around me from behind in a comforting embrace.

"Let me show you that you're alive, and not the monster he tried to make you into," Loki's husky voice whispers into my ear, his hard dick pressed into my ass.

A breath stutters out of me as I watch one of his arms reaching beyond me to grab the shower gel. I look down as he squeezes a dollop into his palm and then coats my thick length, the breath hissing out of me as he moves up and down in firm strokes.

"See how good that feels, sir," he rasps in my ear, his hips moving in time to his hand. A few weeks ago I would have freaked the fuck out at his dick near my asshole, but now it just feels incredible and I want more.

"I want you to fuck me, Pet," I say, my voice thick with lust, and his hand stills.

"Are you sure?" he asks, his voice breathless.

I twist my head, my hand coming to the back of his neck, and I pull him to me, slamming my lips against his. Wasting no time, I thrust my tongue into his mouth, and with a groan, he kisses me back just as fiercely.

Red hot lust pours through me, coating my insides and making me rock-fucking-solid in Loki's grip. His deep moan matches my own and reaching behind me, I wrap my hand around his own cock, nipping his lip as I grip him hard. Pulling away from his lush, kiss-swollen lips, I look him dead in the eye.

"I want your fucking cock in my ass, Pet," I tell him, my voice hard and full of command. "And I won't ask again."

"Yes, sir," he replies, placing his hand around my hip and tugging me back. One hand goes between my shoulder blades and pushes ever so slightly so that my ass is sticking out, ready for him as my chest is pressed against the cool tiles. A shiver races over my skin at the mix of cold from the tiles and hot from the water and Loki's hand caressing my ass.

I hear him spit in his hand, then feel the prod of a digit entering my back hole. A deep groan leaves my throat as he pumps in and out a few times, then the head of his cock replaces his finger when he pulls it out, the metal of his piercing cool against my fevered skin. I hear him spit again, feeling the wet glide of it between my cheeks as he pulls them further apart.

My heart races as he slowly pushes against the tight bud, and my fingers claw at the tiles that they are resting against when the burn of him entering me becomes almost too much. Before he thrusts in any more, he drapes his body over mine and reaches around to grab my dick in his palm, resuming his firm stroking.

"Fuck, Kai, you feel— Godamn," he gasps as he pushes in more, and my eyes roll at feeling him inside me, his hand pumping my dick.

Tired of waiting, needing him to be inside me all the way, I snap my hips back until his pelvis is pressed against my ass, and we both cry out at the feel of it.

"Fuuuuck," I hiss, and we pause there, just absorbing the intense sensation of being connected like this.

I needed him to fuck me like this not just to feel alive again and chase the darkness away, but to finally rid myself of the ghost of my uncle's abuse. The memories of his depravity don't try to take over because all I feel is Loki, his lips on my shoulder as he kisses me softly, telling me how good it feels to be inside of me.

Tears sting my eyes at the sheer relief which courses through me, knowing that I can embrace this side of myself with Loki without fear of my trauma rearing its ugly head.

I quickly get lost in sublime pleasure when Loki starts to move his own hips in a sensual dance. The push and pull of his hard dick inside me, his hand jerking me off at the same time, it builds me to a new kind of high.

"I want to fuck you harder, sir," he growls in my ear, waiting for my permission.

"Do it," I snarl, and he takes one of my hands, wrapping it around my own dick, both of his hands grabbing my hips in a bruising grip.

He starts fucking me hard and fast, and Jesus, it feels so damn good it's all I can do to stroke my dick as waves of ecstasy flow over me. The sound of our wet bodies slapping together is loud in the room, our breathing and grunts adding to the cacophony of sound.

"Fuck, Kai, I'm going to come in your ass—" Loki cries out, his words cut off with a deep groan as he slams himself deep inside me and pours his release.

He drags me with him, my balls drawing up and lightning shooting up my spine as I come all over the tiled wall. Lights dance in front of my eyes, my whole body alight with tingles as my climax races through me with a spine bowing effect.

Panting, I release my spent cock, and gasp when Loki pulls out. He grabs my shoulders and spins me around, cupping my face in both palms and lowering his lips onto mine. He kisses me with such tenderness that tears once again sting my eyes, and a sob stutters from my lips. He keeps kissing me, even as I cry into his mouth, my own hands tangling in his hair and pulling him closer.

The kiss comes to an end, Loki placing his forehead against mine, and we stand under the spray as my heartbeat returns to normal.

"Lilly's gonna be pissed she missed watching that," Loki jokes in a rough voice, and I huff a laugh.

"We'll have to do it again for her then," I reply, moving to place a soft kiss on his lips. "Thank you."

He steps back so that we can look in each other's eyes, his hand still clutching the back of my neck.

"Always."

"Let's get cleaned up," I say with a sigh, feeling lighter than I have in years.

One step closer to our new lives.

LOKI

Once we're all cleaned up and dressed in clothes that we'd placed there before the fun began, Kai and I exit the bathroom to find Ash and Jax carrying Julian down the stairs, Rafe and my sperm donor already situated, slumped in chairs. Sweat drips down the side of my temple, the heat on full blast to confuse the time of death.

It seems so strange to have shared such an intimate moment with Kai, our relationship moving up to the next level, one moment, then being faced with the remnants of our revenge plan. My fingers tingle in Kai's grip, his hand in mine as we approach the others, careful to avoid the blood on the floor, plastic covering our shoes.

After heaving Julian in the final remaining chair, Jax goes about putting their shoes back on their feet while Ash carefully carries the various tools that we used on Stephen to each of them, wrapping their hands around the handles of different ones so that it'll be their fingerprints that the Feds find.

Fingerprints on a murder weapon is a surefire way to earn a conviction, plus with the other evidence we've planted; footwear marks in the blood and the digital trail of my uncle betraying the company, there's no way they'll be able to avoid rotting in jail for a very long time.

We watch as Jax takes the blood that we collected from Stephen's slit throat, and using the knife, dips it into the container and flicks it over the three comatose men, before wrapping his own father's hand around the murder weapon.

"We'll get cleaned up, then join you guys upstairs," Ash informs us, stripping where he stands and dropping his clothes in the open bag that Enzo will take to be incinerated.

We'd brought clean sweats and shirts down before the torture party got started, leaving them in the bathroom, ready for this phase of the plan.

"Sure, I'll take these up," I reply, snapping another pair of gloves on and grabbing the bag.

Kai remains silent as we make our way upstairs, but it's a relaxed quietness, and a light-hearted feeling fills me up to think that, just maybe, he exorcised his demons tonight.

"It is done?" Enzo asks as we step into the living room from the basement, and I nod.

"Yep," I answer, for once no jokey comeback on my tongue.

"Good," he replies, glancing over at Kai with a shrewd look before taking two big steps and pulling him into a hug. "You did well, caro mio."

I watch as Kai takes a shuddering breath, wrapping his own arms around the older man and hugging him right back. A sense of calm washes over me at the sight of Kai not only accepting an embrace but returning it. He'll be alright.

"Right, boys," Ash states, jogging up the stairs with damp hair. "We're on the home stretch. Enzo, you take that final bag, burn it with the others. Give us thirty minutes, then call the cops."

"Si," Enzo agrees, taking the bag from me and then heading out of the door. He pauses when he reaches the threshold, turning and looking back at us. "I'm proud of you, boys, and honoured to watch you become the men you were always meant to be."

My throat tightens at his declaration, and I notice the others shift and stand a little taller at his words. With that, the older man walks out, leaving us to implement the final part of the plan. The part that I'm dreading if I'm being honest.

"Come on, let's get this over with," Ash says with a sigh, clearly feeling the same reluctance as the rest of us.

We enter the living room once more, collecting the glasses that our elders dropped, and Kai takes them to the kitchen to rinse them out. Jax sorts us new drinks, this time with enough GHB to knock us out for an hour or so, just enough time that if all goes to plan, we'll wake up in hospital after the cops have found us all. If it doesn't go to plan...well, who the fuck knows what happens then.

Jax hands us our glasses, giving Kai his when he returns.

"Bottoms up," I toast, raising the glass and slugging the measure back in one go. Best to just rip that band-aid off, I always think. I grimace with the burn of good quality scotch, wincing slightly at not taking the time to appreciate it fully.

"See you on the other side," Ash comments, drinking his next, not even making a face as he swallows. He's used to drinking this shit more than any of us, his father practically bottle-fed him on it.

Jax doesn't say anything, just throws his back like a badass before setting his glass down on the side table. Kai is the final one to bring his glass to his lips.

"Here's to a new life," he says, drinking it down.

The drug doesn't take long to take effect, and I feel a pleasant buzz start to loosen my limbs just as we hear a door crash open.

"Whath the fuckth?" Ash slurs, all of us unsteadily rising to our feet as the door to the basement flies open and Jax's dad is just fucking standing there, blinking and weaving around, gun in hand.

Everything happens too fast then, his unfocused eyes catching my gaze as I'm the closest to the door. The gun raises, and all I can do is watch as he levels it at my chest. My ears register the loud bang, my body jerking, and I watch as Rafe topples back down the stairs.

My ears are ringing, and I sluggishly shake my head, catching the red that's spreading across my left pec.

"Wellth, f–fuck," I stutter, looking back up to see horrified looks on the faces of my brothers before their eyes roll and they fall to the floor. I follow them down, darkness taking me in its embrace before my head hits the floor.

CHAPTER THIRTY-THREE

LILLY

I wake up with a jolt, my heart pounding and a feeling that something isn't right making the hair stand up on my arms. A snuffling sound next to me brings my head down to see my baby, Violet, snuggled next to me, my body curled around hers protectively. Taking a deep inhale of her addictive baby scent, my panic subsides somewhat, but I can't shake that feeling of unease.

Needing the toilet and something to drink, I decide to get out of bed, but can't bear to leave Violet behind, so I pick her up and take her with me. She stirs a little but soon settles into my embrace, and it feels as natural as breathing to carry her in my arms, but also weirdly alien. I can't believe that she's here.

Padding quietly downstairs, I'm surprised to hear the murmur of voices, and even more so when I round the staircase and find the twins and Mai in the living room, all with concern written across their faces.

"What's wrong?" I ask, my voice lowered but my mouth really

dry with all the possible scenarios running through my head.
"Tell me."

"Loki's been shot," Roman states and my body goes ice-cold and
numb, instinct alone making sure that I don't drop Violet, pulling her
small body closer as if to protect her from the news.

"W–what?" I rasp, sinking down on the same sofa that I leaned
on a few hours ago to give birth.

"We don't know all the details, just that something went wrong
and Loki got caught with a bullet," Rowan elaborates, his knee
bouncing.

"W–where is he?" I ask, pulling Violet closer to me, breathing in
her scent which is the only thing helping me to stay calm right now.

"The private hospital, back in Brompton Lakes."

"We have to go there then," I say, standing back up and turning
to head towards the stairs to get ready.

"Lilly, you only gave birth a few hours ago," Mai interjects, a note
of concern in her tone. "It's a three-hour drive."

"Plus," Rowan interjects, "you're meant to be dead."

"He's Violet's father, and my soulmate," I say, needing them to
understand that any discomfort I feel is secondary to my need to
make sure that he's okay. Mai sighs, then gets up too.

"Luckily, we bought a car seat for Violet, just in case you had her
whilst we were here," she tells me, giving me a small smile. "Let me
take her while you get ready."

"Thank you," I reply, handing over Violet, careful not to
jostle her.

I rush up the stairs, well, as much as my aching body will allow,
and say a prayer to anyone who's listening that my baby gets to meet
her father.

JAX

Ash, Kai, and I sit around Loki's bedside, watching his still form lying there, and all I feel is sick with the thought that our freedom may have cost him his life. The doctor said that it was a clean entry and exit wound, the bullet passing through his shoulder, and although he may have limited use of the limb for a few weeks or months, with physical therapy he should make a full recovery.

But fuck, that was too close for my liking.

A groan pulls my worried gaze back up to my brother's face, finding his eyes blinking as he struggles to open them.

"Fuuucck," he rasps out, his voice cracked and painful sounding, and I leap to my feet, grabbing him a cup of water that the doc left for him.

"Shit, it's good to have you back," I say, holding the cup to his lips when his gaze finds mine. He drinks deeply, finishing the whole thing before resting his head back on the pillow with a long exhale.

"I feel like I've been hit by a fucking truck," he comments dryly, closing his eyes and wincing, then opening them and looking around the room. Ash and Kai are on the other side of the bed, both with grins on their faces, their previously tight shoulders slumped.

"You were shot," Ash tells him, and Loki's forehead creases, then his eyes widen as he remembers.

"By Rafe!" he exclaims, though his voice is no more than a cracked mumble.

"Yeah," I reply, then give a smile that I know is pure evil as I recall what the cops told us when we woke up a couple of hours ago. "Turns out he fell back down the basement stairs, cracked his head open like Humpty fucking Dumpty, and died in a pool of blood and piss at the bottom."

I mean, I wish I'd been the one to put a bullet in his brain after I beat the shit out of him, but I guess, this way at least, he's no longer walking the earth. Perhaps it's not the way a son should feel about his father's death, but I'm glad the bastard is dead.

"Talk about silver linings," Loki jokes, and we all chuckle, the tension dropping away from my limbs.

My shoulders tense once again when I hear a commotion outside, a harried woman's voice sounding in the hall.

"You can't go in there, miss!"

"Fuck off!"

"Is that Lilly?" Kai asks in a confused tone, but before we can answer, the door to the room bursts open, and in strides the woman herself, looking exhausted but beautiful in her wildness.

"Loki!" she exclaims, rushing across the room and practically pushing me out of the way as she flings herself on top of him.

He lets out a pained groan, but what makes me really pause is what sounds like the cry of a baby.

"Oh, poppet, I'm so sorry, shhhh," Lilly coos, pulling back and rocking the bundle in her arms that I'd somehow missed when she came in.

"Lilly?" Loki asks, his eyes wide as he, too, takes in the squirming bundle she's holding.

"Loki, guys," she says, her eyes swimming with tears as she looks around at our stunned faces. "This is Violet, our daughter."

She pulls the blanket away to reveal a beautiful baby with a shock of red hair on her head. I stare, stunned at the perfection of this infant, a wave of such intense love almost bringing me to my knees.

"Here," Lilly says, placing the baby in Loki's good arm, and a moment of panicked terror flashes across his face before he looks down at his daughter and he just fucking melts.

"S—she's perfect," he whispers, bringing her in close and nuzzling her hair. "Look at her hair!"

"I know," Lilly beams, and I wrap my arms around her from behind, taking her weight as she sags into me.

"Fuck, Baby Girl, you should be resting," I scold, trying to direct her to my chair, but she resists.

"Jax, I just spent the past few hours sitting in a car, feeling like my fanny was going to fall out every time we hit a bump, I really don't want to sit down right now."

I wince at her description, my respect for this woman increasing tenfold when I think about her having to give birth without us, or without full medical attention.

"But you're okay? Nothing went wrong?" I can't help but ask, pulling her closer as my heart beats wildly at the thought of her pain.

"I'm fine, fucking exhausted, but fine," she tells me, her arms wrapping along the length of mine. "More to the point, Loki, how are you and why the fuck did you get yourself shot?"

"It wasn't a choice, Pretty Girl," Loki murmurs back, not taking his eyes off Violet. "But I think I'm okay."

"He'll be fully recovered in a few weeks with some physical therapy," Ash answers softly, coming round the bed to draw Lilly into his arms and out of mine.

As much as I don't want to, I let her go and watch with a warm feeling in my chest when she nuzzles into him and he kisses the top of her head.

"I'm so fucking proud of you, Princess," he says, pulling away slightly to look into her eyes. "You are incredible."

Violet makes a little squeak then, and Lilly steps away from Ash, taking her from Loki, planting a quick kiss on his cheek, and then turning around to face us. She steps close to me, holding her arms out, and automatically, I take Violet from her, feeling a little awkward with this tiny bundle in my huge arms. She looks so small and breakable, but Lilly helps me to support her head, then steps back to give Kai a hug.

I look down, Violet's eyes closed, yet when I bring my finger up to her hand, her fingers grasp onto mine with a tight grip.

"She's strong, just like her mother," I marvel, my throat tight as I look up into Lilly's tired gaze, her lashes damp with tears but her smile wide. "Perfect like her too."

"I'm sorry you weren't there, to help with her birth I mean," Lilly says, her mouth downturned, Kai's arms wrapped around her from behind like mine were moments before.

"I'm sorry too," I say, and fuck, I hate that we weren't there when she needed us. One look at my brothers and I know they're feeling the same.

"D–did it all go to plan?" she questions, looking at each of us, settling on Loki last. "Well, apart from Loki getting shot."

"Yeah," Ash answers, taking a step towards me and brushing Violet's hair back, placing a soft kiss on her tiny head. "Everything else went to plan, and Chad and my father are in police custody."

Reluctantly, I hold Violet out for him to take, and he reaches for her with a gentleness that surprises me. None of us are soft men. We are hard and full of scars, our bodies built to hurt and take life, not to nurture it, but maybe we could be something more than what we were raised to be.

Ash kisses Violet's head again before turning and handing her back to Lilly when she starts to fuss, Kai's arms coming round both of them as we all stare at the miracle of new life before us.

Yeah, we are definitely more than what our fathers trained us to be. Life is not black or white, but a mixture of greys, and looking down at my brothers and our woman and newborn daughter, I know that they will help us to become what we were always meant to be.

CHAPTER THIRTY-FOUR

LILLY

The next few weeks pass by in what can only be described as a hazy bubble of life with a newborn. The lack of sleep would be crippling if it weren't for my guys taking turns rocking and holding Violet so that I can get some much-needed rest.

Violet takes to the breast in a big way, Mai exclaiming how well she's doing when she comes to check us both over, assuring me that Violet spending hours at a time feeding is normal to start with as she encourages my milk to come in. When I'm still not convinced, she points out the full nappy bin—Kai had organised getting cloth nappies, citing that not only is it better for the environment, but also for Violet. When my milk does come in, my boobs become what Mai calls 'porn star breasts,' aka huge as fuck.

The guys, obviously, think that they're great, Loki lamenting that Violet is the only one currently enjoying them, perving on my feeding sessions until Jax smacks him upside the head for sexualising something which is completely natural and beautiful. Loki sheepishly apologies, telling me it was only my breasts he'd ever accost, making me laugh, then cry because, well, hormones are still a thing.

We recover in Ash's woodland house as I like to call it, and being surrounded by the forest in the late summer is perfect, the trees providing coolness to what might be oppressive heat. Kai takes Violet and I on walks in the late afternoon, carrying Violet in a stretchy baby wrap that he watched many YouTube videos to learn how to tie correctly. There's something about him carrying her that makes me all hot and bothered, and I look forward to our daily walks more because of it.

The date of Julian's and Chad's trials fast approaches, and the night before I find myself waking up, Jax asleep on one side and Violet on the other. We put a wooden bedside guard on the bed, making sure that whichever side Violet is on, she can't fall out. Sleeping with her in the bed, and feeding her lying down has saved my sanity because I often fall asleep with her happily sucking away, and sleep is precious at the moment.

Carefully getting out of the bed, I pop to the bathroom down the hall, not wanting to use the en-suite in case it wakes Violet up. As I leave the room, I hear the faint sound of a piano being played, a smile tilting my lips upward. I make my way down the corridor, pushing open the door to Ash's music room to find Ash shirtless at the piano, Loki sitting not far away with his guitar on his lap. He's also in a state of undress, wearing just sweatpants, his sling having been discarded even though he should still be wearing it. Men.

Jesus H Roosevelt Christ, how is a girl meant to function when they walk around topless?

Ash finishes up the song he was playing, an instrumental version of *7 Years*, just as Loki looks up and catches my eye, giving me a panty-melting grin.

"My turn to play for you, Pretty Girl," he tells me, and I remember back to the first night in the cabin when Ash called me from this very room and sang to me for the first time. "Why don't you hop up onto the piano there, let Ash take care of you for a bit."

I glance at Ash to find he's turned to face me, his heated stare on me, taking in my sleep vest and knickers.

"Come here, Princess."

Slowly, I walk further into the room, coming to a stop in between his splayed thighs, and his hands skim up mine, grabbing my arse and pulling me closer.

"I—" I start, biting my lower lip, unsure how to tell them what's swirling around in my mind. I want them, I am desperate for them; we haven't had sex of any kind since Violet's birth, all the guys allowing me to heal. But, although my body has now healed, it's not the same as before. It's soft and well, wobbly in places that were toned, and I've stretch marks all over my breasts from how big they've gotten. Not to mention the fissure of worry that it'll hurt, or be painful. I did push a baby out of Her Vagisty, and I'm not sure she's forgiven me yet.

"What is it, baby?" Loki asks, and I look over my shoulder at him, before looking back at Ash, then over his shoulder, not able to keep eye contact with either of them as I voice my worries.

"I'm not the same as I was before," I haltingly tell them, and tears sting my eyes, fucking hormones. "I'm soft and wobbly and marked, and I'm scared that you won't find me sexy." I say the last part in a whisper, but I know by the way that Ash stiffens, he heard it.

"Look at me, Princess," he demands, his voice unyielding as his hands tighten on my hips. I look down, swallowing hard and chewing my lip again. "You are more gorgeous now than you have ever been. This stunning body brought Violet into our lives, and continues to nourish her every fucking day." He skims his palms up my sides, cupping my breasts and sending delicious tingles across my skin. "I will never not find you sexy as fuck, marks and all."

Tears spill over onto my cheeks as a small laugh leaves my lips, and Ash stands up, his hand cupping my jaw to guide my lips to his.

"You will always be beautiful to us," he whispers the words over my lips before closing the distance in a kiss that reaffirms everything that he's just told me. He kisses me as though I am something to be savoured, something that he can't believe he is allowed to touch.

He manoeuvres us so that my arse hits the side of the baby grand, his hands coming to the hem of my vest and tugging it upwards, breaking our kiss so that he can pull it over my head. Lowering his head, he kisses each new mark that covers my tits, and I gasp as his lips worship my new body.

Loki begins to strum his guitar, singing *Thinking Out Loud* by Boyce Avenue, and fresh tears fall as he holds my gaze. My attention is stolen again by Ash when he hooks his fingers in the side of my knickers and pulls them down my legs, encouraging me to step out of them.

I squeak as he lifts me under my thighs, hissing when my bum hits the cold surface of the piano lid as he sets me down on top of it. Placing a hand on my sternum, he gently pushes me down so that I'm lying back on the lid, my legs hanging over.

"I'm scared it's going to hurt," I blurt out, and he gives me a soft look, his long, inked-up fingers trailing down the centre of my breasts, over my soft stomach, to the apex of my thighs.

"I'll make sure you're too wet for it to hurt, Princess."

Ash drops to his knees, and a low moan falls from my lips as his tongue licks my damp core.

"Still fucking delicious," he murmurs, his hot breath over my lower lips making me shiver and my nipples peak.

He doesn't say anything, just returns to my core, slinging my legs over his shoulders as he proceeds to eat my pussy like a man starved. His tongue explores every inch of my cunt, from my swollen clit to my opening, thrusting it inside my channel and licking me as if I'm a well that he's desperate for a drink from. Lightning trails up and down my body, my breath coming out in quick pants and gasps as my orgasm approaches embarrassingly quickly.

"Ash–shit–Ash—" I moan, glancing over at Loki who's still playing, his eyes burning into my skin as he watches us.

"That's it, baby, come all over my face like the good girl I know you can be," Ash commands, resuming his tongue fucking, and I can feel my body succumbing to his order, my legs shaking as my climax rips through me with a force that should shatter all the glass in the room.

I lose myself to it, to the pleasure that rolls me over and under until I'm floating, and Ash doesn't stop, his tongue licking, his mouth sucking, and his teeth nipping until I'm begging him to stop, my hands clawing at the surface of his precious instrument.

Finally, he relents, and I crack my eyelids to watch him stand up, his erection pressed against the front of his sweats as he looks at me with a predatory gleam. His chin glistens with my release, and I watch, shivering as he swipes the back of his hand over it, just to lick my cum off like he can't get enough. Loki has finished playing, the room quiet apart from my panted breaths.

"Perfect, Princess," he praises, pushing his sweats down and palming his thick cock. "Loki, do you have a condom?"

"I got an IUD last week," I say, my flushed cheeks heating. "Mai fitted it. I couldn't stand the idea of anything being between us."

Ash gives me a Loki-worthy smirk, stepping closer as he spits into his palm, Her Vagisty fluttering as he rubs it all over his cock to lubricate it.

"Are you ready for me, Princess?" he asks, his voice deep and husky.

"Yes," I answer without hesitation.

"Good girl," he replies, lining himself up to my slick opening and slowly pushing in. I wince at the slight sting, and he pauses. "Are you still good?"

"It's a bit sore, I guess," I murmur, and his brow wrinkles.

"Loki."

I turn my head to watch Loki come swaggering up, *Dusk Till Dawn* by ZYAN and Sia playing softly over the room's speakers.

"Yes, boss?" Loki gives Ash a shit-eating grin, and it makes me smile.

"Play with those tits you've been lusting after," Ash orders, and my smile drops as Loki's grows wider.

"Yes, sir."

Loki's eyes ravish my body, focusing on my huge tits that are leaking milk all down my sides. I can feel it pooling underneath me on the lid of the piano, and I flush, grimacing.

"You can blame this next part on my lack of being breastfed as a child," Loki tells me, dipping his head and lapping up the spilled milk, his hot, wet tongue making my heated skin pebble and small moans escape from my lips.

"Fucking yum," he says between groans, bending over me to give the other side attention. The more he sucks and licks at my breasts, the more milk leaks out, and I'm soon writhing and squirming.

"Fuck, that's making her wet," Ash growls out, and I gasp as he begins to push inside my heat, Loki distracting me from the slight discomfort. "Shit, Princess, that feels so fucking incredible."

His fingers grip my hip hard, and then I feel his touch on my clit, my cry loud as he starts to play it as skillfully as he does the instrument we're fucking on.

"Ash–oh god–Loki—" I gasp the words, my fingers tangling in Loki's hair as his tongue swirls around my sensitive nipple, drinking the milk that's flowing from me.

I get lost in a myriad of sensations; Ash's thick cock thrusting in and out of my now drenched cunt, his fingers toying with my tight bud, and Loki lavishing his affection onto my breasts. A maelstrom begins swirling inside me, heating me up from the inside out and incoherent noises fall from my lips as they build me higher, bringing me closer to what is promising to be a mind-blowing climax.

"You're so close, aren't you, baby?" Loki asks, and I crack my lids to see him hovering over my nipple, his mouth wet and his pupils blown with lust.

"So fucking close," I whimper, my whole body tingling with my impending release.

"Don't worry, we got you," he tells me, and I watch as he opens his mouth, lowers it over my stiff peak, and sucks. Hard.

I explode and implode all at once, my body going impossibly rigid as my climax takes me in its thrall, electricity zinging out to all my limbs. Milk shoots out from my breasts, and I feel Loki drinking all that I give him, the thought prolonging my pleasure. My pussy clenches around Ash, dragging him down with me as he orgasms with a snarl, burying himself so deep inside me that it triggers a second wave of flutters in my core.

Suddenly Loki's lips leave my nipple, and I open my closed lids to watch him gripping his dick, stripping it in a punishing rhythm. Seconds later, hot cum hits my body as he covers me in his seed, and that triggers a third orgasm, Ash groaning as my cunt grips him again, more wetness leaking out of me.

Loki raises his hand, his own cum glistening on his fingers, and brings them to my lips. Instinctively, I suck them into my mouth, licking his salty release off with a moan.

"Good girl," he says in a breathy voice, withdrawing his fingers and leaning down and kissing me, his tongue invading my mouth.

My hands stay limp at my sides as I kiss him back, my whole body sated and relaxed. He pulls away, and I glance down my body to see Ash giving me one of his beautiful smiles that used to be so rare.

"You are everything we could ever want or need, Princess," he tells me in a gruff voice, his own body loose. "Don't ever fucking forget it."

"I love you, all of you," I tell them, gasping as Ash finally pulls out, and Loki helps me to sit up.

Ash wraps his arms around me, kissing my forehead and pulling me in close so that our sweaty bodies are pressed together.

"I love you too, Princess."

Loki trails his fingers down my side, kissing my neck and cheek.

"I fucking love you, Lilly."

"Should you guys still call me that, you know, given my new

name?" I ask, and they pull back to look at me, considering looks on their faces.

"You'll always be Lilly to us," Ash states, running his palm down the side of my face. "And we can always say it's your nickname."

"Although," Loki starts, and when I look at him he has a shit-stirring grin on his lips so I know that whatever will come next may earn him a black eye or two. "Technically, she is now free to marry whoever she wants, given that your wife died."

Ash growls, and it's only my arms still wrapped around his waist that stops him from lunging at the trickster.

"Only if I get to marry all of you," I blurt, realising how right that feels as the words leave my mouth.

Both pause, barely even breathing as they look at me, a mixture of consideration and hunger on their faces. Before anyone can say another word, the sound of Violet crying, then Jax's deep, soothing voice can be heard down the hall.

"She probably wants feeding," I tell them, the sound of her cries hitting me hard in the chest. Ash steps away immediately, he knows how a sense of panic washes over me when she's upset, and he helps me down off the piano and Loki pulls up his sweats and grabs my PJs.

"Go get cleaned up, Jax can soothe her for a minute," Ash tells me gently, pulling his own sweats up and intertwining our fingers, leading me from the room as Loki follows.

We walk into the big bedroom to find Jax rocking Violet in his huge arms, wearing only boxer briefs, and the sight stuns me for a moment before Ash gives a chuckle and pushes me into the bathroom.

"Clean up first, fuck him later," Loki says with a quiet laugh, and Jax looks up with a smirk, his blue eyes heating as he takes in my nudity and freshly fucked appearance.

Kai walks in then, carrying a tray of freshly baked cookies and a thermos of mint tea that I know will be the exact right temperature to drink straight away. I place a kiss on his cheek, his own eyes growing warm.

"You look stunning, sweetheart," he murmurs in my ear, and I shake my head with a giggle.

Reluctantly, I head to the bathroom, turning around as I reach the door to see all four of them cooing over the small baby in Jax's arms, and my heart feels so full it might just burst out of my chest.

CHAPTER THIRTY-FIVE

ASH

Guilty.

That one word holds such weight. A word that signals our freedom.

Both my father and Loki's are charged with first-degree murder, life in prison with no parole as their punishment, and we've made sure that they won't be able to bribe their way out by getting there first.

We drive the new mini bus that Jax picked up yesterday back to my place in the woods, Violet asleep in the back with Lilly at her side and Loki next to Lilly. *Lost My Mind* by Alice Kristiansen plays quietly over the speakers, and I can't help feeling that this is our song. All five of us lost in each other.

"I can't quite believe it," Lilly whispers, resting her head on Loki's shoulder as we drive through the fall afternoon. "Is it really over?"

"It's really over, Princess," I say from the front, craning my neck to look back at her.

"And what happens now?" she asks, a small smile playing on her lush lips.

"Anything we want, sweetheart," Kai tells her, and her smile grows, rivaling the sunlight filtering through the trees alongside the road.

"I'd like to invite my grandparents over, and Ryan and Lexie," she replies.

"I'll message them now for you," I say, pulling out my phone and sending an email to them all asking if they'd like to visit, an idea forming in my mind of what we could all do while they are here.

We sit in comfortable silence for the rest of the journey, letting the fall sun wash over us as we drive home, unencumbered for the first time by the shackles that our parents put on us.

We're finally free to live, and I intend on doing just that with my brothers and our woman and child.

CHAPTER THIRTY-SIX

LILLY

TWO MONTHS LATER

"Motherfucker!" Ash roars as he storms into the living room, the morning sunlight casting his inked-up body in a soft glow. I wince, glaring at him as Violet starts wailing at the noise.

I rock her in my arms, shushing her and trying to settle her as he looks devastated at upsetting her.

"I'm sorry, darling one," he tells her gently, coming up next to us and stroking her head in the way that always calms her down.

Once she's fallen back asleep, I pass her over to a waiting Jax, who continues to rock her in his huge arms because she has him wrapped around her tiny finger and he adores her sleeping on him.

"What happened?" I ask Ash quietly, Loki and Kai having come into the room, Kai handing me a hot chocolate with a kiss on my cheek.

"Somehow, my father has managed to change his sentence to some bullshit and is getting out on parole later today," Ash seethes, his whole body vibrating with anger. "Apparently, he has proven that he was coerced or some shit."

"What the fuck?" Loki exclaims, his voice lowered as he glances over at a sleeping Violet. "How the ever-loving fuck did he manage that?"

"He's Julian fucking Vanderbilt," Kai responds in a tired voice. "We should have known that something like this would happen."

"We did," Ash argues, running his hands through his hair and leaving it messy. "That's why we spent a small fortune bribing every goddamn official we knew."

"Do you know what time he's being released?" I ask, and they all look at me then, even Jax, blinking.

"Uh, midday I think," Ash answers. "Why, Princess?"

"We best be there to greet him, don't you think?" I answer, not saying anything more as I stride from the room and up the stairs to get changed.

"Why do I feel like there's something she's not telling us?" I hear Loki ask the others, and a smirk curves my lips as I make my way upstairs.

A lady never divulges all her secrets now, does she?

LOKI

I can see the others watching our girl as we make our way to the prison that Ash's cunt of a father is due to be released from, even Jax is casting suspicious glances her way in the rearview mirror. She won't spill her secrets, no matter how much we press her, just telling us that we'll see with a sexy fucking smirk on those kissable lips.

Violet is making cooing noises as we pull up outside the prison gates, and just as Jax turns the engine off, the devil himself comes striding out of the gates, shaking the hand of the officer in charge, a big, stupid-ass smile on his lips.

My blood boils at the sight of him, at his smug fucking grin as he spots us getting out of the car.

"Boys!" he beams, strolling over to us looking pristine in a tailored suit, and it just pisses me the fuck off. Ash's fists clench at the sight, his back ramrod straight.

"How did you convince them to let you go?" Ash grits out, asking the question that has been plaguing us since we discovered the news. Julian's smile widens, and I'm reminded of the Cheshire Cat, teeth gleaming and ready to pounce.

"It always pays to have friends in high places, you know that, son," he tells Ash, holding his gaze, and I can see the sick enjoyment he gets from ruffling Ash's feathers.

The noise of the van door opening sounds in the quiet standoff, and Julian's gaze flickers over Ash, his eyes widening as he takes in what's behind us. I turn to see Lilly holding Violet, standing to the side of us.

"I–it c–can't be—" Julian mutters, his face pale as he looks at her smiling face. "–you're dead."

"Am I?" she asks, taking a step closer, that serene smile still on her lips. "I don't feel dead." She laughs then, like this is all a big joke, and the beautiful sound is so at odds with the conversation that tingles race up my spine.

Jax comes around the other side of her, his forehead creased, standing close enough to jump in if Julian tries anything. But as I look back at the man in front of us, he just stands there, slack-jawed, and his eyes dart all over her, clearly trying to work out what the fuck is going on.

"H–how?" he questions, narrowing his eyes in a way that makes me take a step closer to her, standing on her other side.

"How does anything happen, Julian?" she volleys back, and I watch her with wide eyes as she takes on our biggest adversary with an ease that fucking astounds me and makes my dick hard. "Ah, just in time."

I look beyond Julian to see more cars have pulled up, official-looking ones, and my mouth drops as federal officers step out of the vehicles, all heading our way. They have 'FBI' emblazoned in yellow letters on their vests and jackets.

"Julian Vanderbilt?" an older officer asks as Julian finally turns around to see what is happening. Lilly takes a few steps to the side too, and Jax and I follow her so that we all have a perfect view of Julian's face.

"Yes, who are you?" the man in question demands, still an arrogant prick.

"I'm Special Agent Sawers, and you are under arrest for the murder of Lilly Vanderbilt. Anything you say can and will be used against you in a court of law."

Another officer grabs Julian's wrists and cuffs them behind his back before Julian can even formulate a sentence.

Fuck. I did not see that coming.

I glance over at Lilly who looks smug as fuck, kissing the top of Violet's soft hair as she looks over the scene before us.

"She's right there!" Julian screams, struggling against his cuffs as he's led away. They don't even pause, dragging him to one of the cars and roughly shoving him inside.

"Care to share what the fuck that was all about, Princess?" Ash asks, arms crossed and a scowl on his face as we watch the cars drive away. Though, even I can see a small tilt of his lips, and respect shining in his eyes.

"Fingerprints on the murder weapon will really screw a guy over, don't you think?" she sasses Ash, stepping towards him after handing Violet to Jax, and placing a soft kiss on Ash's cheek.

"You had this planned all along, didn't you, Pretty Girl?" I question, stepping behind her so that she's sandwiched between Ash and I. I grin as her body shivers.

"Ryan suggested it," she tells us, her voice breathy and hitching when I push her hair aside and begin to nuzzle her neck. "When we faked my, well, you know. Better to be prepared and all that."

"What happens when he tries to pay them off again?" Kai asks from the side, and I glance over at him, his forehead creased as he tries to think all of the options through. *Sometimes he's cute as fuck.*

"He's not the only one with friends in high places," Lilly murmurs, and I look down to see Ash kneading her waist.

"Harold," Ash guesses, saying Lilly's grandfather's name as a statement more than a question.

"Yes, Harold," she answers, tipping her neck to the side so that I can access it more. I oblige by sucking a mark into her peachy skin, and she moans, the sound going straight to my dick.

"We best get back, Violet will be hungry soon," Jax interrupts, and just like that we all sigh. I love our baby, fiercely, but damn if my dick doesn't miss the opportunity to just bury itself inside our girl anytime we want.

"I'll feed her before we set off again," Lilly says, stepping from between Ash and I and taking Violet off Jax to go and give her a feed in the bus.

I look at my brothers and see matching looks of sheer fucking awe on their faces that I know is reflected in mine.

She's a Queen alright, and we best not forget it.

CHAPTER THIRTY-SEVEN

LILLY

"I don't see why I'm coming to Enzo's with you. I can hardly do a proper workout so soon after birth, and as far as I know, Enzo doesn't offer any kind of post-natal program," I grumble, Violet snoozing in the back while I ride up front, Jax in the driver's seat of his minivan.

I like to call it the sunshine bus, and much to Jax's annoyance but to my delight, Loki paid some kid—Jude Taylor I think his name was —to cover the outside with suns, rainbows, and unicorns one night. Jax was so pissed when he saw it in the morning I thought he was going to strangle Loki until I begged him not to as I loved it. I also may have burst into tears at the idea of it being painted over, so here we are, driving in the sunshine bus, complete with motherfucking unicorns.

"Trust us, Sweetheart, it's a surprise," Kai tells me from behind, and I look to see Loki and him holding hands and snuggling in the middle seats. It makes my heart warm to see them openly sharing affection. Plus you know, they always let me join in, and fucking hell, watching them fuck each other, feeling them fuck me at the same time as each other, is something I am here for always.

"Fine," I relent, folding my arms across my chest, or at least trying but failing because porn star boobs are still a thing. *Codswallop!*

Soon we're pulling up outside the gym, Ash taking Violet who woke up as we arrived. We walk in to find it empty and quiet, with only Enzo and his wife, Rosa, standing there. She's stunning, tall and slender, with tumbling blonde hair falling in a waterfall down her back.

Rosa rushes forward, enveloping me in a tight hug, and the breath rushes out of me at the way she pulls me close. My arms automatically go around her, and my brows lower when I feel her whole body shaking. Shit. She's crying.

"My beautiful, beautiful girl," she says, pulling away and gripping my face in both her hands. Then, after a lingering look, she apologises, letting go to take a step back whilst I look on in utter bewilderment.

What the ever-loving fuck is going on?

"Principessa," Enzo says roughly, his own eyes wet.

"What's going on?" I finally ask, looking around at the guys who've come to stand in a loose semicircle around me. Everyone seems happy, smiles on their faces, but there's definitely an edge of sadness, and an air of melancholy, like something has been missing, or time wasted.

"Princess," Ash starts, handing Violet to Kai and taking my hands in his, turning me to face him. "Enzo helped your mom escape Ace. He gave her a new identity, just like he did for you, and got her out of the States. He's also your uncle by marriage."

My head whips back to Enzo, then Rosa.

"Rosa is your aunt," Ash continues gently, his grip on my suddenly cold hands a warm comfort. Rosa nods, her face wet but split into a big grin. "And Tom, he's Rosa's brother. He's your father, Lilly."

My world freezes as Tom, the Black Knight driver steps forward. His image wavers as my own eyes fill, and I can see the glistening of tears swimming in his blue gaze.

It all suddenly makes sense. The way he said that I reminded him of someone, the way he always looked at me as if he recognised me. I look so much like her after all. Like my mother.

We stand there for a moment, staring at each other, drinking the other in. He's handsome, with dirty blond hair that's getting a little grey at the temple, bright blue eyes, and scruff on his jaw.

"Lilly, I..." he begins in a rough voice, but before he can say another word, I'm throwing myself into his arms, wrapping my own around him tightly.

He's my fucking dad.

He catches me with a gruff sob, returning my embrace tenfold, and we just cling to each other for what feels like forever. There are so many years we've missed out on, so many hugs to catch up on.

"H–how?" I ask, pulling back to look at him, then around at the rest of them. "How did you find out?"

"Ryan, Principessa," Enzo says, stepping closer. "I thought that I recognised your last name, the one that I gave to your mamma, and so I asked Ryan what her name was." He wraps his massive arms around Tom and I, Rosa coming to do the same, all of us weeping happy tears as we cling to each other.

Violet gives a cry, and I disentangle myself to rush over and take her from Kai with a quick kiss to his cheek. I walk over to the little group, my dad, uncle, and aunt.

"Violet, meet your grandpa, and great-uncle Enzo, and great-aunt Rosa," I tell her, giving her a kiss, then holding her out for Tom.

Eyes wide and glistening, he takes her from me, immediately

starting to rock her in his arms and kissing her soft head. She quietens in his embrace, and my cheeks hurt with how wide my smile is as I watch Enzo and Rosa reach out and stroke her on opposite sides of her face, both taking turns to kiss her lightly on top of her head.

Large arms wrap around me, lemon filling my nostrils as I lean into Jax's body behind me.

"Happy?" he asks, his voice low and gruff as usual.

"So fucking happy," I reply, hugging his forearms to me.

We stand like that for a moment, soaking in each other's embrace, and as I look at my daughter, father, aunt, and uncle, then around at my Knights, I feel like I'm about to burst with sheer happiness. My family is finally all together. Both my biological and chosen family.

We're all together now, and my heart has never felt so full.

EPILOGUE

LILLY

A sense of déjà vu hits me as I glide my hands down the silk of my dress, only this time, instead of a white dress with an ombre that reflects the sunset at my hem, my whole dress is a rainbow. It's in a Grecian style, gathered at my shoulders and waist, flowing in soft silk to pool on the ground. A golden, jewelled belt glints around my waist, a gift from the guys, and I'm praying that it's not real gold or stones, but knowing them it just might be.

And the best bit? It starts as a lilac strip on my right side, moving through pastel rainbow colours all the way round, and when I twirl, I feel like I'm the pot of gold at the end of a rainbow. The gold sequin heels probably help with that too.

"You look so beautiful," Willow tells me, voice soft, and I look up into the mirror to see her elfin face beaming back at me. It took time, but she forgave me for the whole faking my own death and having to attend my pretend funeral thing. "Again."

We both crack up until I scold her for almost making me cry, and we end up wrapped up in a tight hug.

"You are the best bitch a girl could ever have," I whisper, my voice a little thick as I fight to hold back happy tears.

"You too, babe."

"Come on, Lilly Bear," Lexi calls, striding into the room and looking fucking stunning in a form-fitting, gold dress. "You don't want to keep them waiting, otherwise they'll come up here and you'll never get to the ceremony with you looking so gorgeous."

We're in the main bedroom at Ash's—I guess our—house in the woods. We've made it into a home, somewhere away from the hustle and bustle of a town or city. Somewhere peaceful, and full of fresh air for Violet. Plus, the crazy security that the guys have installed means that we all feel safe here.

"You're right, bloody cavemen," I answer with a chuckle, picking up my skirts because I always wanted a dress that I had to do that with, and what better day than now? "Is Violet okay?"

"She's with Ryan and Enzo. I swear those men are wrapped around her little finger," Lexi chuckles as we make our way downstairs, and I pause when I see who's waiting for me at the bottom.

"You look beautiful, Lilly," Tom states, his eyes glistening as he gazes at me in wonder. I'm sure I look back at him with the same expression. I still can't believe that after all this time, I know who my biological father is, and he's here to give me away to my soulmates.

"Thank you for today," I tell him when I reach the bottom step, a lightness suffusing my limbs as I take his hands in both of mine. "It means...a lot."

"I am honoured to walk my daughter down the aisle," he answers, his voice thick with emotion and laugh lines etched into his face. "I never thought that I'd experience it."

I squeeze his hands, once again fighting those damn tears, otherwise, Willow will scold me for ruining my makeup.

"Ready?" I ask him, and he chuckles.

"Isn't that my line?"

Laughing, we walk out of the front door into the late afternoon sunshine, and the feel of it caressing my skin has me sighing in bliss. Butterflies start flying around in my stomach as we walk down the floral-decorated path to the clearing, and the sound of a piano being played reaches my ears. My breath catches when we arrive and I see Ash sitting at the instrument dressed in a beautiful, light grey linen suit that showcases all his glorious ink.

He looks up, and just like that first night at the cabin, he starts to sing. I recognise the song as *Infinity* by Jaymes Young, and the world stops spinning as he holds my gaze, telling everyone in the clearing how he feels. My breath catches, and I just watch enraptured as he serenades me with his beautiful, husky voice.

I don't know how we arrive at the end of the aisle, only blinking when the song comes to a close as I realise that the others are all there too. Loki in a floral shirt covered in lilies, suit trousers, and a waistcoat, the shirt and waistcoat unbuttoned to reveal his delicious, inked chest, his nipple bar twinkling in the sun. Jax is next to him, looking positively delicious in his signature black; black shirtsleeves rolled to the elbow, black trousers, and black boots, laces undone. Kai is on my other side, gorgeous in mustard chinos and a green, chequered shirt with a forest green waistcoat. Ash comes up next to him, his gaze intense as he takes me in. I do the same to them all, drinking them in as if for the first time, my heart thudding in my chest as I realise that this is really happening.

"Take care of her," Tom tells them, pressing a kiss to my cheek and stepping away.

"Always," they reply together, and I would giggle if they didn't look so serious. Kai takes one hand, Loki the other, and we turn to face Oleta, our celebrant, the sounds of the woods tickling our ears.

"Gentlemen, Lilly, shall we begin?" Oleta asks, and my cheeks ache with my wide smile. We all nod. We decided that we'd use my real name, I just couldn't stand the idea of doing this under a false name, and we trust everyone present, they all know who I am after all.

"I'd like to start with a poem by Rev. Daniel L. Harris. It's one that Asher suggested as it encapsulates what he, Loki, Jax, and Kai feel for Lilly and what this ceremony means to them. It's called The Blessing of the Hands.

'These are the hands of your best friend, young and strong and full of love for you, that are holding yours on your wedding day, as you promise to love each other today, tomorrow, and forever.
These are the hands that will work alongside yours, as together you build your future.
These are the hands that will passionately love you and cherish you through the years, and with the slightest touch, will comfort you like no other.
These are the hands that will hold you when fear or grief fills your mind.
These are the hands that will countless times wipe the tears from your eyes; tears of sorrow, and tears of joy.
These are the hands that will tenderly hold your children.
These are the hands that will help you to hold your family as one.
These are the hands that will give you strength when you need it.
And lastly, these are the hands that even when wrinkled and aged, will still be reaching for yours, still giving you the same unspoken tenderness with just a touch.'

Tears fill my eyes at the words, and I have to swallow hard to stop them from falling, my grip on Loki and Kai's hands tight. My whole body feels alight with feeling, my heart so full that it's a wonder it's not exploded.

"And now, your vows and the handfasting," she continues, smiling broadly at us.

Loki lets go of my hand, Kai using his grip to turn me to face him. We place our hands between us, and Oleta brings out a beautiful woven rainbow cord, made up of ribbon, the colours matching my dress perfectly.

"You were my light when there was only darkness, Sweetheart," Kai begins, and my eyes stare into his honey brown ones, the image wavering at the edges with my unshed tears. "You showed me that there was something to hope for, that I could be loved. You are my soul, my heart, and my light."

As he speaks, Oleta wraps the cord around our hands binding us together. The tears fall by the end of his speech, tracing a hot path down my cheeks, and he reaches up with his spare hand to wipe them away, his smile beatific.

Loki steps up next to us, placing his hand over the top of ours.

"I knew that you would change my life, our lives, from the first moment that you stepped out of that shower," he tells me, his emerald eyes glowing in the sun. "I just never knew how much you would become a part of me. You are buried so deep inside, Pretty Girl, that if they were to cut me in half you would be there too, in every part of me."

I bite my lip, my breath hitching as he speaks, the cord wrapping around his hand and binding him to us. Jax is next, the massive bastard stepping up behind me and reaching around to lay his huge palm on top. He's so close I can feel every ridge, every outline of him, and it sends a heat searing to my core when he leans down to rumble in my ear, letting only me hear his declaration.

"You are mine, Baby Girl, and I am yours until we draw our last breaths on this cursed earth. And even then I'll fucking hold your soul to ransom and I dare anyone to take it away from me."

Gods, this man. When he makes a love confession, he doesn't do it by halves. My body aches for him, my heart soaring, and I don't know if I'm more emotional or turned on right now. Grey eyes capture mine, as Jax's hand is bound to mine, Loki's, and Kai's. Ash steps to the side of Kai who shifts a little so that my dark Knight can stand in front of me.

"You are the best part of me, Princess. You taught me how to love again, how to live again, how to breathe again. You arrived like a shooting star, burning all the bad that came your way and leaving only good. We were destined, it was written in the stars that we would be together, and I will never stop worshipping you, never stop thanking whatever god decided that I was worthy of you."

Ash always had a way with words, and he's just proven it to all our friends and family. I stare into his intense eyes, full of swirling emotions, and feel a completeness deep in my soul. His hand, too, is wrapped in the cord.

And then it's my turn. Taking a deep shaking inhale, I look at each of them in turn, my lashes dotted with tears.

"You all gave me love at a time when I'd lost everything. You gave me hope when I felt hopeless. You gave me back the parts of myself that I never knew were missing. You captured my heart, we are all bound together for eternity, and I never want to be released from your love."

I pour all that I have, all that I am into my words, and know that they affect my Knights as much as they do me when I look into jewelled eyes, all glistening. Jax pulls me closer, and I feel the shudder of his shaky breath.

The final knot is tied, and Loki pulls our clasped hands upwards to a cheer of the crowd behind us. Laughter falls from my own lips as tears drip down my cheeks, my body feeling weightless with happiness. I glance over and see all of our loved ones here; my grandparents, Ryan and Lexie, Enzo and Rosa, plus Tom who's holding our daughter, who seems delighted by the whole thing and is beaming a huge, gummy grin.

Jax's mum is here too, standing with Loki's sisters who whoop and cheer. Ash's mum is in rehab, undergoing a withdrawal from years of being drugged by his dad. Loki's mum has fled the country, having emptied the family bank account upon hearing of her husband's arrest. I'm glad, I never did like her, so we're looking after the twins too, our woodland home full of life and laughter.

"Well, I believe you have rings you'd all like to exchange?" Oleta asks, her own smile wide, and we all laugh again as we almost forgot that part.

I manage to place simple bands of platinum on each of the guys' left ring fingers, Willow holding them out for us. Kai then takes the puzzle ring that they had made for me; four intertwining bands of rose gold, platinum, gold, and white gold. One band for each of my men. He places it on my left ring finger, Loki taking over to push it down a little, then Ash follows, and Jax pushes it the rest of the way. The cool metal warms quickly to my skin and having taken off my wedding ring and engagement ring when I 'died,' a sigh of relief leaves me at having the familiar weight back on my finger.

"And that concludes our celebration," Oleta says. "All that's left for me to say is—"

She's cut off by Loki grabbing the back of my head and slamming his lips to mine. I laugh into his kiss, soon having to hold back a moan as his tongue caresses the seam of my lips, begging me to open to him. He kisses me soundly, my toes curling in my shoes when Jax's free hand wraps around the front of my throat, clearly not giving two fucks about our audience.

Loki pulls away with reddened lips pulled up into a shit-eating grin, and gives me a roguish wink. I just shake my head, my movement stopped by Ash grabbing my jaw and pulling my lips to hover millimetres from his.

"My turn," he says in a low voice, the words caressing my skin before his lips close the distance and he destroys me with his kiss. It's all Ash; hard, controlling, demanding yet full of tender worship, and I give in to him completely, my free hand resting on his chest, feeling his heart beating underneath my fingertips.

He pulls away with a lingering peck, and my eyelids flutter open to find Kai waiting. His free hand cups my cheek in a gentle gesture, and I nuzzle into the touch, my eyes briefly closing at the comfort. Achingly slow, he brings our mouths together, peppering light kisses over my lips, a small whine leaving mine. I can feel the smirk just before he finally deepens the kiss, plunging his tongue into my mouth and stealing my breath. His kiss reinforces his vows, tells me how much he loves me, and I return it, confessing my truth into his own mouth until we part, both gasping and needy.

Jax moves his grip from my throat to my jaw, turning my head to an almost uncomfortable angle before he lowers his lips and presses a soft, chaste kiss to my own. He pulls away just enough to stare into my eyes, his own filled blue fire.

"I'll get a proper kiss between those sweet thighs later, Baby Girl," he murmurs, stroking my lower lip with his thumb.

Fuck.

Me.

Boom, there goes my knickers. Grinning with a look that tells me he knows exactly what state he's left me in, he lets go of my jaw, but moves his palm to the top of my collarbone, holding me in such a possessive way that I can feel how ruined my panties really are. *Fannymuncher.*

"Time to party!" Loki shouts, and another cheer goes up as *Dancing in the Moonlight* by Jubël and NEIMY starts to play over speakers placed around the clearing.

"I love this song!" I cry, quickly untangling myself from our binding, the guys chuckling at my enthusiasm.

Once free, I then drag them all to the dance floor that's been set up to one side of the clearing behind us, a buffet table and bar on the other, beautifully decorated tables dotted around, glass jars of fairy lights twinkling on their surfaces.

We dance together, wide smiles splitting our faces, and as I look around to see all the people we love here with us, Jax holding our daughter who squeals with delight as he twirls around.

I can't help but think that maybe, just maybe, it was all worth it. All the pain, all the uncertainty, all the heartache and trauma.

Because all of that led me to them. To my Knights. To the other parts of my soul.

And I wouldn't be without them for any-fucking-thing.

LILLY

I'm still laughing as Loki drags me into the woods, the sounds of the party dying down the deeper into the trees we go. Moonlight surrounds us, lanterns lighting our way down a narrow path.

"Where are we going?" I giggle, clasping his forearm which feels fucking delicious as it flexes under my grip.

"Can't ruin the surprise, Pretty Girl," he chides me, his own teeth gleaming in the moonlight as he grins back at me.

Suddenly, I can see more lights between the trees, and we come out into another small clearing, a huge yurt covered in fairy lights sitting in the middle.

"Loki—" I gasp, pulling him to a stop. "What about Violet? She hasn't spent a night away from me yet and I—" He cuts me off with a finger to my lips.

"She's with Lexi at ours, and we won't be sleeping here so we'll be back with her before she wakes up. They have some expressed milk just in case," he assures me, stepping closer until his body is flush with mine and I can feel his heat through my thin dress. "Just for an hour...or three, maybe four." He gives me a wink and a cheeky grin that I just can't resist. *Cockwomble.*

"Okay," I agree, excitement making my fingers tingle, and my heart rate picking up. I love our daughter more than life, but having some time to be me again, to be us again, feels right and important. So that I remember that I'm still Lilly, as well as a mum.

"Good girl," he praises, and I shiver, but not with cold as he drags me the rest of the way.

He pushes open the flap, and I step inside, taking a sharp inhale at the beautiful sight before me. Colour is everywhere; bright rugs and cushions dotted around, plus an enormous bed in the middle of the floor, and it's all lit up with soft candlelight coming from count-less tea lights in jars as well as more fairy lights in the roof space.

"Do you like it, Princess?" Ash asks, stepping from the shadows, and I swallow as I take in his naked, tattooed chest, his linen trousers slung low on his hips, and his feet bare as he stalks towards me.

"It's breathtaking," I tell him, not taking my eyes off his stunning body, tilting my head upwards as he gets nearer so that I can look into his beautiful, swirling grey eyes.

"I'm glad that you approve," he replies, one side of his lips tilted up in a half grin that he knows drives me crazy. His long fingers reach out to hook under the shoulder of my dress.

The belt falls to the ground with a soft thud, the sound of the zipper at the back being undone fills the quiet as Loki undoes my dress, Ash pulling first one shoulder down, then the other. The dress pools at my feet in a rainbow puddle on the floor, and I watch as Ash's face goes slack when he takes in my white corset, matching lace thong, and white suspenders and stockings.

"Do you like it?" I ask, parroting his own words back at him, my voice low and husky at the hunger in his eyes.

"You're breathtaking," he repeats my words back to me, reaching out again to run his musician's fingers across the top of my breasts. My skin pebbles as I shiver under his touch. "I believe that Jax owes you a kiss."

My breath stutters, heat flooding my core as Jax's words from earlier fill my mind.

"I'll get a proper kiss between those sweet thighs later, Baby Girl."

The man himself emerges from the shadows, and Ash steps aside to allow Jax to stand before me, also shirt and shoeless. His body practically thrums with power, and something in me preens at the sheer masculinity that rolls off him in intoxicating waves. The soft sounds of music fill the air as he sinks to his knees, *365* by Mother's Daughter, and I know it's Loki's doing as I've been obsessed with this artist recently.

I squeak when Jax grabs my arse, his huge hands squeezing my cheeks to the point of pain, and he yanks me closer. He buries his nose in my lace-clad cunt, taking a massive inhale, and heat floods my core, ruining my knickers further as he rubs his face in my scent like a cat. A big, fucking gorgeous cat.

"You always smell so fucking good," he growls the words, his hot breath brushing over the dampness and leaving me trembling.

"Yes, you fucking do," Loki murmurs, nuzzling into my neck and sending sweet vibrations straight to my nipples which peak under my corset. His hands come around, dipping into the top of my corset, and pull first one breast out and then the other. The heat from his now bare chest sizzles up my back where our skin touches.

Kneading my breasts in his palms and rubbing my sensitive nipples between his thumb and forefinger, he distracts me until the sharp sting of ripping fabric tells me that another pair of knickers has joined the many others that Jax has ripped off my body. I can't even be cross anymore, he replaces them all anyway, and as his mouth descends on my aching pussy, all thoughts of calling him out for it vanish.

"Fuuuck—" I groan out low and long as Jax's hand leaves my arse to grab my leg and place it over his shoulder so he can go deeper.

What he then does with his tongue should be fucking illegal, making low appreciative noises in his throat as he licks, sucks, and nibbles my dripping cunt. Fire begins to burn under my skin as Loki starts sucking my neck, mimicking Jax's movements until it feels like I'm in a tug of war with one man on either end, pulling me closer towards release.

"You look so fucking perfect like that, Princess," Ash's low drawl has my closed eyelids opening to see him standing behind and to one side of Jax. I follow the movement of his arm, sucking in a sharp breath when I see his inked-up hand wrapped around his dick, the magic cross piercing glinting in the low light. "Doesn't she, Kai?"

"Beautiful," Kai answers, stepping from the darkness at the edges of the yurt, shirtless and shoeless like the others. His own hand strokes his hard length, and my breath stutters as my eyes flit between him and Ash, watching as they pump their fists.

I yelp as a sharp slap lands on my pussy, wetness immediately following the sting.

"Stop getting distracted, Baby Girl," Jax admonishes in a low voice full of threat. "Or I won't let you come." I make a keen noise at the threat.

"Maybe she needs to be punished," Loki suggests, and I whimper, a full body shudder making me tremble in his arms.

"You have something in mind?" Jax asks him, and I feel Loki grin against my neck.

"Let go of her," he says, and when Jax does, Loki twists us around, my back still to his front, and pulls me backwards, towards where the bed was. He drops down, dragging me with him and scooting us back until his back hits the headboard.

"Loki!" I protest, gasping when he arranges me on his lap with my legs over his forearms, my bare pussy completely exposed.

"Now take out that monster cock of yours and whip her with it," Loki tells Jax, ignoring me completely.

Lightning races up my spine at his suggestion of my punishment, and my core clenches so hard I'm almost coming from the thought alone.

"Oh, she liked that," Kai comments darkly, his gaze fixed on my slick opening, his lips pulled up into a grin.

"You want me to whip that dripping cunt of yours with my big dick, baby?" Jax asks as he stalks towards me, unzipping his trousers when he reaches the end of the bed and stepping out of them. His dick is thick and full, so big that I always have a flutter of fear when it's near me. I nod. "Use your words."

"Yes, please."

He gives me a full, masculine smirk, kneeling on the bed and grasping his cock as he gets into position, his knees spread so that his dick is hovering over my pussy.

"Count for me, Baby Girl," he commands, then brings his hard length down. Hard. I cry out, my back arching as wetness seeps out of my lower lips.

"O–one," I gasp, my core contracting with the force of his hit. Fuck, that felt incredible.

"She really likes that," Ash comments and I twist my head to see him to the side of us, on the bed, his stare fixated between my legs. "Again."

"Yes, boss," Jax teases, bringing his cock down again, harder this time, and the wet sound of his flesh hitting mine is obscene, louder than the music playing in the background.

"T–two," I rasp out, my whole body shaking in Loki's grip.

"Again," Ash orders and Jax obeys, giving me three slaps in quick succession leaving me writhing in Loki's arms.

"What number are we on, Baby Girl?" Jax pants, and I crack my eyelids to look at him. His face is flushed, his chest slick with sweat. His dick is covered in my cream, precum leaking from the tip as he grips it hard at the base.

"U–uhum.." I stutter, my mind a fucking mess, just like my body is.

"Five, Pretty Girl," Loki whispers in my ear, flexing his hips, and I can feel how hard he is beneath me.

"Five."

"Good girl," Jax praises, trailing his fingers up my thigh. "Five more I think, or until you come. You're so close aren't you, baby?"

"Yes," I moan, feeling my climax fluttering at the edges, leaving the world hyper-focused.

"Then come for me quickly, and I'll fuck you hard with my monster cock," Jax tells me, and Jesus fucking Christ his dirty talk is something else that needs to be a crime.

The hand not gripping his cock skates up my body, gripping the front of my throat tightly until I can barely get any air into my lungs.

"Eyes stay on me," he orders, and I look into his blue orbs as I feel another hard slap of his hard dick against my sensitive folds.

Shit.

My body jerks with the movement, more wetness seeping out of me and splashing my thighs as he does it again.

And again.

And again.

The next hit has me screaming his name as my fingernails claw Loki's arms to shreds when my orgasm slams into me, stealing my fucking breath and soul as I soar into the stars.

Wave upon wave of hot pleasure smashes into me as my whole body feels like it goes rigid and liquid all at once. Loki holds me still, telling me what a good fucking girl I am as Jax starts to fight against my pulsing cunt and pushes inside my fluttering channel.

"Fucking hell," he growls out, sinking deeper into me and prolonging my climax as I writhe and buck beneath him.

He gives me no time to adjust, my wet body accepting his intrusion easily as he bottoms out, then immediately starts to pound into me with such force that I hear Loki grunt behind me.

"Shit, bro, I'm glad that's not my asshole you're fucking right now," Loki exclaims as his grip tightens on my legs, holding me open for Jax to fuck even harder.

"You wish," Jax teases, his hand still gripping my throat as he destroys me with his dick, and I am fucking here for it, my tits bouncing painfully with each surge of his hips.

"Jax–fuck–shit—" I mumble, unable to say much when his grip around my throat tightens and only lets a trickle of air into my lungs.

I can feel a second release fast approaching, Jax building me up again every time he slams inside me and his pubic bone hits my clit. Pleasure zings up from my core, making my entire body tingle with the impending explosion.

"That's it, baby," Loki murmurs in my ear, licking up sweat that drips down my temple. "Come for him, cover him with your release."

Jax picks up the pace, then suddenly pulls out, and I squirt all over him as I come with a scream. His own release covers my corset and breasts, the hot cum dripping between them as ropes of it shoot out of his tip.

"Shit, Baby Girl," he rasps, falling to the side only for Ash to take his place.

"As much as I like this," he indicates my heaving chest that's covered in lace and Jax's climax. "I want to feel those breasts more as I fuck you and fill you with my cum."

Reaching forward he undoes the clasps at the front of the garment, undoing the suspenders that hold my stockings up.

"You can leave these and the shoes on," he tells me, pulling the corset off and tossing it behind me. I can feel some of Jax's cum slide down between my breasts, and Ash's eyes trace its journey down my body. "Fucking perfect."

Loki keeps hold of my legs, bringing them up more as Ash lines up his pierced cock with my opening then starts to push inside. My eyes roll, my thighs already quivering as he thrusts further inside me until he's all the way in.

"Ash," I say with a gasp, his hand cupping my cheek as he presses our foreheads together, my own gripping the back of his neck.

"I know, Princess," he whispers, his hips moving in an undulating rhythm that has me seeing stars at the edge of my vision. "It feels so fucking good, so fucking right when I'm inside you."

He keeps our foreheads pressed together while he fucks me slowly and deeply, a contrast to Jax's frantic fucking. *Call Out My Name*, also by Mother's Daughter, begins to play as Ash whispers sweet, love declarations in my ear all the while bringing me closer to the edge.

"'When in disgrace with fortune and men's eyes,
I all alone beweep my outcast state,: And trouble deaf heaven with
my bootless cries,
And look upon myself and curse my fate,
wishing me like to one more rich in hope,
Featured like him, like him with friends possessed,
Desiring this man's art, and that man's scope,

With what I most enjoy contented least;: Yet in these thoughts myself almost despising,
Haply I think on thee—and then my state,
Like to the lark at break of day arising
From sullen earth sings hymns at heaven's gate;
For thy sweet love remembered such wealth brings,
That then I scorn to change my state with kings.'"

Tears fill my eyes and track down my cheeks at his recitation of one of Shakespeare's sonnets, and I remember all the other times that he quoted my favourite poet's words at me, using them as our own love language.

"Come for me, beautiful," he demands, his voice raspy and deep with how close to his climax he is. "Show me that you are mine."

One hand keeps cupping my cheek as the other comes between us and starts playing with my swollen clit, rubbing it in a rhythm that has the stars at the edges of my vision exploding and covering my body with stardust as I cry out his name. My limbs feel as though they are heavy and weightless all at once, like the stars really have come to earth and are filling me up with their light.

"Lilly—" he grunts out as he thrusts deeply a final time, filling me with his climax, his whole body rigid.

Panting, he stays buried inside me, our breaths intermingled as we share each other's air, unwilling to part just yet.

"I love you, Ash. So much," I whisper against his lips.

"I love you, my Lilly," he replies, placing a kiss against my lips before pulling away and out of me. I hiss as he leaves my body, but Kai gives me no time to mourn the loss as he moves up between my thighs.

"Kai—I—I can't," I whimper, my whole body aching as Loki finally lowers my legs, which tremble and shake.

"Yes, you can, Pet," he tells me, his voice a hard command. "And you will take Loki and I beautifully, because you're our very special girl, aren't you?"

I shudder as I feel Loki taking off his trousers beneath me, watching as he kicks them off his feet and Kai throws them off the bed. Someone hands Kai some lube, and he squirts some into his palm, reaching between my legs. Loki groans underneath me, dropping his head to my neck and biting me as Kai lubes his dick up.

"Shit," Loki curses, his palms squeezing my thighs. Contrary to what I believe, my body reacts as my pussy pulses with the harsh touch.

"We're both going to fuck this sweet pussy, aren't we, Pet?" Kai asks, and I'm not sure which of us he's talking to, but we both moan. "Lift up a little, Sweetheart." And I know that command is for me, so I place my feet on the bed and lift my hips, gasping when I feel the metal of Loki's piercing against my swollen channel. "Good girl, now sink down."

Again, I do as commanded, and a small whimper sounds in my throat as Loki's dick goes all the way in, impaling me on his hard length.

"Fuck, you feel epic," Loki rasps out, his hand hooking around my thighs and opening me further as he scoots us down a little.

I watch as Kai slicks up his own cock, the metal of his piercings sparkling in the candlelight. Loki groans as I clench around him, his hips making small movements that make me gasp and groan in turn. Kai leans over us, positioning himself at my opening which is full of Loki.

"Deep breaths, Pet," he instructs, surging forward and slowly pushing himself alongside Loki.

Fucking hell.

There's pain, but Loki quickly overrides that with his fingers playing my clit like he plays his guitar, and wetness that I didn't think was possible given how much I've already come, seeps out of me.

"That's it, baby. Take us both like the good fucking girl you are," Loki moans in my ear, and I pant as Kai pushes in further, all of us groaning when he finally bottoms out.

"That's so fucking hot," Jax comments, and I glance over to see his solid dick in his hand which is pumping up and down at the sight of us before him.

"Eyes my way, Pet," Kai orders, and my gaze snaps back to him as he slowly starts to withdraw, only to thrust back in hard, making Loki and I cry out.

"Fuck, your piercings—" Loki exclaims, and I can imagine how good they feel rubbed up against him inside me.

After that, I'm lost to the push and pull of Loki and Kai as they find a rhythm that leaves me breathless and shaking all over, sweat covering my skin as I ride out the pleasure that they are giving me. It takes surprisingly little time for another orgasm to sneak up on me, and I'm crying by the time the wave crests and drags me under in sheer bliss.

My whole body goes limp between them as they continue to use me, finding their release inside me together and filling me up with their seed. I hear Jax grunt, and then Ash as their release hits my torso and breasts, marking me as theirs.

"We are your Knights," Ash states, and I open my closed lids to look at him above me.

"But you are our fucking Queen," Jax adds, his fingers caressing my cheek until my head turns to him.

"And we will always love you," Loki whispers beneath me, placing a kiss on my neck, my cheek, and my temple.

"And we will always be yours to command," Kai adds, and I gasp as he pulls out of me, Loki slipping out at the same time.

"And I will love you for all eternity," I tell them in a breathless whisper, gazing around at the three Knights above me, Loki pulling me closer to him beneath me.

We stay in our tent, making love and dozing until the sun kisses the horizon and it's time to go back to the last piece of us; our daughter.

After cleaning up, we walk through the forest, the sound of the dawn chorus serenading us as we make our way home. I look at my soulmates, my lovers and husbands, and am filled with a sense of peace as I walk, seeing a similar expression on their faces.

Somehow, we found each other, and amongst all of the terrible things that have happened to each of us, we found ourselves too. We discovered a love that defies all the monsters of the world, that dares them to try and rip us apart, to break our bond. We brought new life into a world that was full of darkness, and now as the sun rises I can't help but think of all the light that is to follow, chasing away the dark, until it is all that is left.

We have been released from our shackles and bound ourselves together, our hearts captured in a love so strong that it can never be broken.

The Motherfucking End!
Are you intrigued by Hunter and the twins? Well, don't you worry because I have their story right HERE for you.
Not ready to let Lilly and her Knights go yet? Click HERE for a little steamy bonus scene.
If you enjoyed my Highgate Preparatory series, you might like Addicted to the Pain, book 1 in my Dead Soldiers vs Tailors Duet. But be warned, it's much darker than these books, and just like Lark and her Tailor boys, you may end up ruined...

AUTHOR NOTE

If you enjoyed Released, please consider leaving a review. They help our books get in front of new readers as they teach the algorithm that we're bloody awesome. You have that power, so use it wisely my fellow smut slut.

How are you feeling after that? I can't quite believe that it's the last instalment of Lilly and her Knight's story. Talk about all the emotions!

Released was actually pretty hard to get finished. I think the last book in a series is always more pressured as you've got to tie everything off in a way that won't disappoint readers! Jeeze!

But here it is, all done and I'm so fucking pleased and proud of myself for getting it done and finishing my debut series!

And now onto the next project...be on the lookout for what's coming (*snort) next, but I can promise you it's dark and oh so fucking delicious!

ACKNOWLEDGMENTS

I wouldn't be here, writing all the extra bits for my THIRD FUCKING BOOK (I'm still a bit disbelieveing that I have an entire series out!), without the help of many simply wonderful people.

My gorgeous alphas and betas who give me incredible feedback, help the story to grow and tell me there is never too much sex. You are all so appreciated and your comments are more precious than gold.

My wonderful editor Polly who literally gives me life with her comments! She makes these books shine and I honestly would be lost without her.

I'd also be totally lost without Julia, my wonderful PA who does so much more than she gets paid for!

And my lovely Rosebuds and Darlings, my Arc readers and Street Team. You guys don't know how much you do giving me awesome reviews and recommending my books. I love you all!

And of course, my amazing husband who supports me in all that I do, and enjoys the benefits of being married to a steamy romance author (you all know what I'm talking about!). I genuinely wouldn't be where I am today, as a person, craftsperson or author without him.

ABOUT THE AUTHOR

About Rosa

Rosa Lee lives in a sleepy Wiltshire village, surrounded by the beautiful English countryside and the sound of British Army tanks firing in the background (it's worth the noise for the uniformed dads in the local supermarket and doing the school run!).

Rosa loves writing dark and delicious whychoose romance, and has so many ideas trying to burst out that she can often be found making a note of them as soon as one of her three womb monsters wakes her up. She believes in silver linings and fairytale endings...you know, where the villains claim the Princess for their own, tying her up and destroying the world for her.

If you'd like to know more, please check out Rosa's socials or visit www.rosaleeauthor.com

Rosa's Captivating Roses

Linktree

ALSO BY ROSA LEE

Also by Rosa

HIGHGATE PREPARATORY ACADEMY

A dark whychoose romance

Hunted: A Highgate Preparatory Academy Prequel

Captured: Highgate Preparatory Academy, Book 1

Bound: Highgate Preparatory Academy, Book 2

Released: Highgate Preparatory Academy, Book 3

DEAD SOLDIERS VS TAILORS DUET

A dark whychoose enemies to lovers romance

Addicted to the Pain

Addicted to the Ruin

THE SHADOWMEN

A dark gang & mafia whychoose romance

Kissed by Shadows

Claimed by Shadows

Owned by Shadows

STANDALONES

A dark whychoose Lady and the Tramp(s) retelling

Tainted Saints

A dark whychoose stepbrother Cinderella retelling

Tarnished Embers

A dark whychoose mafia romance Co-written with Mallory Fox

Printed in Great Britain
by Amazon

44719294R10215